The Mind's Evil Toy

The life and death

of Amy Dudley

A Historical Fantasy

By G. Lawrence

Copyright © Gemma Lawrence 2023
All Rights Reserved.
No part of this manuscript may be reproduced without
Gemma Lawrence's express consent.

This book is dedicated to all seeking answers

to questions never resolved, and

to all seeking peace,

in chaos.

Prologue

Cumnor House
Oxfordshire
September 1560

"This is a story with an end I think you will not like," says Death.

He stands, arms folded behind his back. That face I should find fearsome lies mostly in shadow, yet the eyes are shadows deeper than the rest, a deeper darkness than ever I have seen. His darkness, intent and boring, gouges deep into my own eyes, seeking and seeing the darkness within me. I should be scared, of him, of this moment, but I am not. There is something familiar, comforting, about this dark shadow with whom I converse.

I glance down at my body, at the bottom of the stairs, then I look back at Death.

I wonder, fleetingly, if this darkness I see in him is how Death finds us, each of us, as the light falls from our eyes, as we tumble from life to death? The darkness in him, the tug of that same element within us, perhaps they call to one another, touch in the shadows of the soul, kindred parted now meeting once again. Does Death know the cool of the long hush of night within our spirits? Does the dying of the light of life bring forth a new babe's cry, born of the darkness finally free, finally no more hidden? There is no hiding in death.

"Why will I not like the end?" I ask, looking down at the body on the stairs again. She does not look peaceful, this young woman who once was me. I was told people looked at peace when they died. One arm draped over the last step the body lies, this body who not long ago held my spirit within its flesh and bone. The eyes are vacant now, the mouth hangs open like an imbecilic fool, which I do not like. Her eyes stare, blank and empty, at the ceiling. Although it cannot be seen for she lies on her back, there is a damp stain at the rear of the gown where the body pissed itself in the last moments of life. There is, as I have found most recently, small dignity in death, but to be found looking like a slack-jawed, damp-dressed dolt when I was such a pretty, clever thing in life seems like another insult. There are so many to count in life, and death it seems is the last insult to endure.

I do not like to look on the body, but I do not find pure horror in seeing myself dead, either. Curious, truth be told, for you would think I would. As I am detached from my body now, I appear to be detached from fear of that body dying. I am dead, it is done, but there is one thing I would know and that is why. Why did I die?

"You will not like the answer as to who is responsible," he says.

"I will not like the name of my murderer?" For this is what I asked after all, to know the name of the man who took life from me, or indeed the woman.

"You know who killed you."

"I saw the face of a stranger, nothing more. I saw the face of the one who killed me, but I know not the hand nor will of who was behind it."

I look down at the body again, and note her hood. The one who killed me rearranged it. It will seem odd that it is there, in place, after a tumble down the stairs. The body has been posed so it looks like an accident. Is it supposed to appear that I died after a slip of slipper on the stairs? There are curious things here if that is the case.

The stairs are shallow and not long, but the cuts on my head are deep. My hood is in place. I have been alone most of the day, by my own foolish request, but there are people in the house who would have surely heard my cry as I fell, if fall I did, down the stairs. The edges of the stairs are not sharp, so will not account for the wounds on my head. It looks like an accident at first glance, my death, yet if eyes look closer there are things wrong with this scene, as if someone is trying to *make* it look like an accident, which means it was something more sinister.

Someone took my life, that I know, yet that person was a stranger. That stranger had no cause to kill me, so someone sent the stranger to take my life. Pains have been taken to make it appear at first glance as if I fell down these stairs and died. Yet these things have been done to my body, the arrangement, the wounds, the hood, either on purpose or because of clumsy thought. I am not sure which.

Either those responsible for my death have tried to make it look like an accident, or they wanted it to look odd.

I cannot decide who has sent the man who hit me, several times, on the head. Was it my husband or his love who sent this murderer to me, and they are trying, badly, to make it look like an accident? Is it someone else, someone who wants people to suppose murder was done, and the killer *tried* to make it look accidental in a way clumsy enough to cause suspicion? Was someone trying to get me out of the way, or were they trying to frame my husband or his mistress the Queen for murder?

"Are you sure you want to know?" Death asks, moving to stand at the window so the light of the sun, a sun of this world or the next, I know not, shines on the white bones of his face. It is a pretty light, gentle and sweet. "The answer may not be one that grants you peace, and I am here to bring you peace."

"Death is peace?" I ask, almost with a laugh, for never have I thought the end of life could be such a thing. Staring down at my own body, at the expression of frozen horror in my eyes, that last moment of fear suspended in my pupils like a pond set still by winter's hand, I do not think there is peace in the body I have just left.

A flash. I see the stairs again as I fell down them, the aching slowness of it. It seemed impossible I could be hurt so badly. Slow did time feel as I fell. I even remember the moment of seeing the step my eyes were heading towards, and thinking if I should hit it with my head it would hurt very much, I might break my neck. Odd how one's last thoughts may become a prophesy. How quick Fate is to take advantage of our imaginings. The blows to my head would have killed me eventually, but the step took my neck too, a mercy in the end.

"Death is the great peace," he says, interrupting my memories. "I am the guide to bring you to it, if you can let go of the life, here, that you have had. If you wish, you can forget this life. Some choose to, to leave it all behind and enter death, an existence much longer than life, with clean minds, a fresh start." He turns that head to look at me, orbs of darkness so pure, burning almost, staring into my blue eyes. "Tell me," he goes on. "Was your life one of peace?"

I hesitate. Normally, in life, at gatherings of country nobles, at court on the rare times I was there with family, when people asked how I was, I lied. It came so easy and so swift in life, a reaction, nothing more, like breathing. I suppose I did not want to explain all the sorrow in my life, and another part of me thought it would make the ones who asked after me uncomfortable, and no one, or only very few people really care how you are. Asking after you is just a formality.

I feared exposing too much of myself. But now, standing before Death himself I find I am tired of lies, of pretence. Perhaps it is freeing to be dead, after all.

"I do not think I have ever known peace," I say. "Either my life was excitement or it was torture, I think. The times I felt clement are few, so few I can remember every one of them." I shake my head. "I have not known peace, lasting."

"That is because you have never been dead before," he says.

I imagine, perhaps only imagine, there is a smile in what he says. None shows on that face, there is no flesh on it so lips cannot lift to indicate humour, but there is a hint of a smile in his tone. Strange how a face may be impassive yet a voice may betray amusement.

"Well, I do hear you may only do it once," I say, smiling.

"And yet once here, it is a longer state than that of life," he says.

"And a longer state of peace?"

"A state of peace unlike any you have known, as you admit," he says.

"Then I must know how life ended before I can be in this state of death forever," I say. "I will know no peace unless I do know."

"Some say ignorance is bliss."

"Yet more value is set by the pursuit of wisdom."

"Yet more of your kind pursue ignorance than wisdom," he says, "and those who do so would say they are happy."

"I am not one of those."

Death sighs. "Very well," he says. "As I am here to guide you into death, I must know that you can rest in eternity, and if you cannot rest unless you know, then know you will."

He looks up at me. "But I do warn you one last time, you will not like the answer."

I look away from the figure on the floor. I feel too sorry for her, for those last moments of terror still stuck on her face. "Like it or not, if I know the answer, I can leave behind this life. But only if I understand the end can I leave it behind."

Death inclines his head of bone, and agrees to show me who it was who murdered me.

Chapter One

Stanfield Hall
Norfolk
August 1549

Whirling white smoke rose from many campfires in the fields beyond the house of my father. Smoke, meat and fretful anticipation rode the air, a feeling that although summer was on the wane something was coming, some wind of great change, something to fear and possibly to admire. Excitement and dread drifted in the air, joining white curling smoke to dance in the skies above my head.

We were walking, Death and I, through the camps of the soldiers. A moment before and we had been at Cumnor Hall, standing over my body, and now we were somewhere else entirely. For a moment I did not know where I was, did not recognise the hillsides, the broad, rough moors beyond, even the wide-open skies of Norfolk, where I was born. It seemed familiar, the place, the smells, but as I found myself in step with Death, walking at his side, suddenly I knew I was home.

And not just the home of the present but home of the memory, home of the past. The perfect home of childhood. Home where I was not returning as an adult, when all is changed and yet the same, and there is sadness in that, but the home I lived in as a girl, unchanged, always unchanged for it had, until that moment, only ever been a place of the past.

I was walking in the past. My past.

"They cannot see or hear us?" I asked, nodding to soldiers sitting beside fires, chattering, cleaning boots and wrapping their swollen and bloody feet. They had walked far in bad boots to reach this place. I watched one man patch a young lad's feet with mint leaves and comfrey, a balm to soothe blisters.

"They are memories," Death said, and that hint of amusement rose in his voice again. "We are ghosts to them, as they to us."

"People see ghosts, that is why the legends exist."

"Many more walk abroad each day and night than ever are seen or heard or sensed," said Death. "Your kind, truly, are blind."

I sniffed the wind, woodsmoke and herbs, sage I thought. There was meat roasting somewhere, rabbit I suspected. Grain was bubbling in a pot along with oats, making a thick pottage. "You judge us harshly."

"It is an observation, not a judgement. It would not be a good thing for you to see all the ghosts that surround you. Humans are, too, a panicky kind."

I chuckled a little at that.

We stood by a fire, and though he said they were ghosts I could smell the sweat on their bodies, a little rank after they had marched many miles to reach this place. I could feel the warmth of the fire on which they cooked meat, mutton on this fire by the scent of it. My father had provided what he could. The King's armies had to be fed when they turned up at your door. In truth, if you did not offer willingly, the stores would just be taken. It was better to at least choose which goods you wanted to give away.

"The rebellion," I said, glancing at my companion. "I remember it so well, so fresh in my mind. It is odd, for I remember yesterday less well than this day, and that was not so long ago."

"Times when humans think they may die tend to stick in the mind," said Death. "You feel more alive, the closer you are to death."

I smiled a little, for walking beside him I indeed felt alive. I had been unwell for some time, and low of spirits for longer than that. There had been aches and pains, and I had woken often with sadness in the bed beside me, a dull and depressing companion to wake with, for she will stay with you all that day, poking your heart and your mind and sitting on your chest so you cannot breathe. But now, I did not feel like that. There were no aches in my body. Although I supposed I had bones no more, I could feel energy in them and vim in what was my flesh. My mind was clear, not fogged with pain or dull with lack of sleep. I was closer to Death than all these soldiers, many of them sure they were on their way to die, and yet I felt more alive than I had for years.

This time I remembered so well. It was strange being here again as the army of King Edward, but more accurately of John Dudley, who soon after would become Earl of Warwick, came to rest at my father's house on their way to battle the rebels who had risen in the north. The rebellion of Kett, it was often called, though he was but one man and in truth many thousands rose with him. We like to think there is but one person to blame for a time of terror. Sometimes that may be true, but oftentimes the truth is more complex than we chose to imagine, or remember. It is far easier to rid the world of the threat of one man than it is to rid the world of thousands. Vanquish the one man, the leader, the name of the rebellion, and the rebellion falls. It has worked for many kings. Yet the idea behind the rebellion is harder to kill. That is why they rise, time and time again. The men die, but ideas survive. Kings cannot kill ideas, they try but it does not work, but men they can kill. Kett's rebellion would die with Kett, it was supposed or perhaps just hoped by men in power. In truth, it would live on, quiet and hidden, in the hearts of all who had risen, all who followed, and some who did not.

All around the fields there were tents, makeshift and temporary, and carrying that air of impermanence that lends itself to messiness. They were not too out of order, of course, officers in the army made sure of that, but many of the men here present were not soldiers trained. They were farmers and field workers, many having marched from fields much like the one Death and I walked through at that moment. At home, if they had not been called by their young King, these men would be tending the last crops of summer, storing many more, taking in the last of the hay perhaps, but now had been called by the King, by John Dudley and by Edward Seymour, Earl of Somerset to reap the lives of men instead.

They looked pale, fearful, many of them. Many were little more than children, young faces hollow with fear, while others were older, some too old to be marching, their bodies already broken from years of hard work.

Others still told jests at the fires as they cooked, brushed boots, sewed on buttons, told stories of conquests with women. Many rang false, fake boasts made to calm hearts full of terror for what would come, but men laughed anyway, congratulating braggarts on sexual victories over women, all of whom were apparently reluctant until their maiden eyes spied a man's member, the bulge of it, then awash with lust those maidens were.

I rolled my eyes. Men might not doubt this part of the tales of other men, but men are often far more impressed with their loins than women are. For my part, I never met a woman who told me in confidence or otherwise that her favourite part of a man was what was between his legs. For all the caprice and changeability women are supposed to own, I found it was more often men who noted the body, and the body is a changeable thing. Women told me how they loved a man's kindness, his heart, or his humour, sometimes eyes and hands. We are so often accused of being material beings, we women, yet it is men who speak of the flesh of their women, and not the soul.

"Why did you bring me here?" I asked as we walked past a party who broke into loud laughter at one of these tall tales. "I asked to know who killed me, how my life ended."

"This was where the end began," said Death. "In the beginning."

"This is not the beginning of my life," I said.

"It was the beginning of your death," he answered, and extended an arm.

I looked around, and there he was. A gasp of breath tried to invade my body and was stopped by a barrier in my throat. I choked, for I had forgotten he was ever so young. A boy he was, perhaps I had forgotten I was a girl once, too. "Robin," I breathed.

He looked up, my way, just for a moment and I thought he had heard me, but then his eyes dropped and he moved along. I almost smiled, for why would he see me now in death, when he had ignored me so long in life?

I wanted to dislike him again, but he looked so much like the boy I had fallen in love with rather than the man I had come to hate. Tall and strong he was, with a kind of wiry grace. Later he would grow into his body more, become muscular, but that day he was not eighteen, and he had grown tall long before his muscles had plumped out to fit his frame. Walking amongst his troops, stopping to charm, and he always was so good at charming, to jest and to ask after men he knew, their wives and children, he was an elegant, friendly figure, noble yet approachable. Robin was always good at getting people to love him. He knew the paths into hearts as other men know them into palaces, into chambers, as if he had been a map to find the heart of people when he was born unto this world. Some people are born with a talent for the bow or the pen, but Robin's greatest talent was seeing to the centre of people.

He was handsome, with those dark eyes and that strong jaw. Young, too, to be in command. Both those things had impressed me, I remembered. At the edge of my hearing I seemed to hear a noise and I looked around, to the house. And there she was, watching him. Eyes peeking from a window, she was on the long wooden window seat, concealed by a heavy curtain of green leaves and flowers embroidered in silk on a hanging of yellow. I could just see her face, next to the gillyflower on the curtain. I smiled, feeling the excitement in her breast even from here. She was not supposed to be looking, was not supposed to be seen by the soldiers, these rough men on their way to do rough deeds. But she watched. She always was a little of a rebel herself.

"You were supposed to be sewing in the great hall, by the window," said Death, gazing the same way as me. Or I supposed he was, by the turn of his head. It can be hard to tell where a skull looks.

I nodded, still looking at the girl sitting behind a curtain, staring out. I could remember the smell of that curtain, a little dusky with smoke and the scent of candles from the night before. There was a maid not far away, begging me at regular intervals to come back, come away. When I heard the creak of a step on the wooden floor, covered in rushes and meadowsweet above or below, the girl I had been, sitting at that window froze, held her breath for a moment and then carried on watching. I had not wanted to miss a moment.

A strike of pain flashed in me. I knew who her eyes were upon. She had seen him at court, moved in the same circles, she had teased him and played him, ignored him and flirted with him, and now here he was, and now he was on his way to war. All the games they had played, ones most enjoyable and light, now had faded to the horizon of her thoughts, and instead she was struck with thoughts more serious, more intense.

When she had heard he was coming with the army of the King, she had wanted to see him again, to trade quips as they often had at court, but now, seeing the army, the reality of it all, she was in fear for him that day. What if the rebels should hurt him? What if he should die? Her heart I could feel even now, even through all the years of pain and disappointment and hurt there still was an echo of that heart so innocent and clear inside me. Inside her, it was bleeding for him. I remembered that pain. All she wanted was to reach out, to touch his face as a lover might, and yet they had never been such to one another. She had never told him she admired him, thought him handsome. Now that girl feared that she might never get the chance.

Inside me, that heart had ceased to bleed. There is only so much blood that can be spilt for one man, by one woman. I was dead. It was enough. In my eyes I saw a flash again, the stairs as I tumbled down. Had he sent the man who pushed me down them?

"I was always doing something I should not be doing," I said, watching the curtain flicker as the girl tried to see more of the field. "My father despaired of me, but also he was proud, I think. He liked that his one legitimate child had spirit, even if I was a girl."

"He was proud," Death said in an offhand way, as if it was not something of great importance. "He said it oftentimes, when you were not there."

"That is a good thing to know," I said. It made my heart ache to hear that. I wished he could have said so himself, but my father was never a demonstrative man. He had tried in his own ways to show affection, but a hand on the shoulder was as much as could be expected rather than an outpouring of love.

I wondered, fleetingly, if that was why I had loved Robin so. He too had become to me someone I wanted to be close to, and never felt close enough. His was at times a fierce love, and at others distant. There was an echo of all I had felt for my father, in the love I later knew.

"You feared to lose him," Death went on, stopping to peer over the shoulder of a pikeman who was greasing the metal of his weapon.

I turned. "My father?"

Death looked up at Robin Dudley, walking through the lines of men. "The boy who would become your husband," he said.

I sighed. "I did," I admitted. I felt shame to admit to it now, to having loved him. "I feared I would lose him before I had found him, before he had found his way to me. I could not help but admire him. He was the same age as I was, yet he was off to subdue rebellion, in command of his own men! I thought him more wonderful than I had before, when we met at court, and even then I was awash with admiration though I tried not to show it for he was vain and proud enough already, so I thought. Robin was one of those men who do not like it when women gush over them, though they do like it too in a way for it feeds their inflated self-opinion. But men such as he do not *respect* women who show open admiration, so at court I teased and I played the game, but when he came here on his way to battle I felt I could pretend no more. He seemed to me then as Achilles or Hector. At court I had admired him as a fine lad, a witty courtier, a skilled jouster, but here, walking this field before battle, it was as if he became suddenly real to me.

I saw him as a man, and a man I not only thought attractive, but a man I loved."

"Yet you had exchanged few words," Death pointed out, coming to stand beside me.

"Girls often fall for the possibility inherent in a man, rather than the man actually there. We are taught to, you understand? We are told that we will find love in matches arranged, taught that we should see the best in people, taught to think well of people. We are trained to see what a person might become, with time and perhaps with the right help, and we are taught it is our place to aid others always, our families, our children, our husbands, so girls often fall for the potential in a man, for the possibility they see in him. It is fantasy, I agree, and so often we are disappointed, unless the man strives to live up to the person we see he can be. So often, however, we are left with the fantasy, and the men become a lazier reality. Once they have their wives, they do not have to do any work for them. It is women who do the work, in truth. We support them, bear children, bear their infidelities. We labour to be loyal, as they disappoint us with disloyalty and indifference."

"You sound bitter."

"All fruit sours, given time."

Death gazed up at the peeking girl. "You were not bitter then."

"No," I agreed. "I could not be, for I was filled with anticipation, and fantasy. I was sweet with it."

We walked on.

"Tell me of the rebellion," said Death.

"Surely you know."

"I like the stories of people," he said. "No two people experience something and tell the same tale of it. There are as many ways of looking at the world as there are eyes to see it, and most humans possess two eyes, so always have at least two ways to tell a tale."

I chuckled, but was silent a moment as I thought. It was not that I had forgotten the times he asked of, but it took a moment to settle them into place in my mind.

"Kett and his rebels rose up," I said as if in a trance as we turned the corner of the field. The scent of yarrow and cow parsley rose in my nose, a tickly scent of pollen. "Enclosure began it, people said, and then quickly the rebels had religious demands to add to political ones. Through London this army came to face the sixteen thousand or so rebels said to have gathered at a great oak named the Tree of Reformation. Led by this Robert Kett, a tanner, rebels calling for religious freedom had taken Norwich. Dudley had been sent to stop them, and he had brought his sons along as some of his commanders.

"King Edward had only been on the throne two years. People said he was our saviour but there had been no evidence of that. There was a brief period of exultation as the old King died, and who was to miss him? His court had been formed of hungry wolves pretending to be fluttering butterflies. There had been a new Queen every two years, or so it felt. In place of the old, corrupt King, the new King was an innocent boy, dedicated to the new faith and to learning, and people said he would be good and kind, wise and fair when he came to his majority, but he was too young to rule alone, and the men who ruled him were not good or kind.

"Seymour was the main one, at least at first. Brother to the third Queen of the old King, uncle to the new King, he was clever, ambitious, but people did not like him. He was cold, they said. Dudley, the father of Robin, seemed the opposite. He was warm and charming, but in truth his ambition burned no less bright."

We stopped by a blackthorn hedge, the sloes budding on the bushes. People told me when I was a girl that witches lived in blackthorn, and some people feared such plants in their gardens or lands because of that, but my father liked the fruits, stewed with honey and apples to make a jam, or mixed with the cider made by his men for a tart, crisp drink.

"The rebels who rose at this time wanted more freedom," I said, putting a finger to one of the thorns. I pressed my finger to it, but there was no pain or blood. I suppose it should not have surprised me. "They desired freedom to speak of their beliefs, the freedom to worship as they wished, publicly and in open sight. Seymour, our hard Lord Protector, was too lenient at first with such men, or so said my father, and therefore men rose thinking they could make demands upon our boy-King where they had failed to be heard by his father."

Death shrugged.

"You do not think faith important?" I asked.

"It has sent plenty of your kind my way," he replied. "Discussions of faith seemed to me to start always with talk of freedom and liberty and end with one group of people taking those same things from another and proclaiming it is because the other were wrong, were foolish, and so need to be saved from their own selves. Faith, to humans, is not so much about the worship of any god as it is about being right, and to humans only one person can be right, so all other people are fools, and all other people are wrong." Death sighed, his breath louder than his silent steps upon the ground. "You are an arrogant race."

"You don't like us?" I asked.

"I like you very much," he said. "That is why your flaws, and the very worst of your flaws, sadden me so. You can do so much better."

"Some of us do, do better," I said.

"Some," he agreed.

We walked on in silence. "You still are watching from that window," said Death eventually.

"I was a curious one, in many ways," I said. "I always was where I was not supposed to be. My father warned me so severely, yet his eyes were so much more worried when anger was strong in him. He knew how to be angry, my father, but he understood so little of other emotions." I smiled. "But he was not a bad man, he was in many ways one of the best I knew.

"I was to stay away from the soldiers' camps upon our fields. Women could be ravaged in times of war, Father told me, and my meagre status as the daughter of a *Sir* would not keep me safe. He commanded me to sit by my fire with my maid, with not even flames to look at since it was summer and the hearth was full of flowers, and he told me I was to sew and ignore the troops in our fields, but all I wanted was to look, and how could any girl or boy resist looking at something so exciting, so fearful come to camp in our very backyard?"

"Not all," said Death.

"Not all?" I asked.

"To look was not all you wanted," said Death.

I smiled. "No, you are right. I wanted to shave my hair and bind my breasts, set boy's clothes upon my flesh and go off to war, hidden within the troops so I could fight, so I could do something with my life. Especially when I saw…"

I looked again, backwards now at the young man moving between his troops. How could I have forgotten he was ever this young? It is hard to recall a face of such fragile youth when we have look at that same face so many hours and days afterwards as it changed. Perhaps it was because it had changed gradually, so one person could come to look like so many others, a thousand lives and every moment played of life, a story etched in skin.

He was seventeen, only just turned, yet he walked with the confidence of a man. He had a swagger to his gait, not only of one who has lived at court, but one who knows themselves to be handsome. He was clever, shared lessons with our young King and some had said he was quick with the blade. He had arrived with all the others on the 22nd of August, the army led by John Dudley, his own father.

Robin's brother Ambrose was there too, so was John, I think. At Warwick Castle they had gathered. At only six thousand foot soldiers and one thousand, five hundred horse, the King's army was not a good match for the rebels, even if the rebels were not trained to fight. Robert, my Robin, as I thought him even then, was in charge of his own company of foot soldiers, often the first to be sent into any battle.

And it was feared the rebels would not deal nobly with men of noble blood, for Father had told us over dinner one night of Lord Sheffield, who had faced the rebels in another incursion. Sheffield had been clubbed to death by Kett's men after he fell from his horse. There was low confidence in Somerset, Lord Protector Edward Seymour. Northampton had been sent against the rebels too, but he had fled. Now Dudley was sent, and he was determined not only to beat the rebels, but to prove he could succeed where other men had failed.

So they had come here, to the fields outside Wymondham, the hometown of Robert Kett himself, and the home of my father and my family.

"This cannot be all of the army?" asked Death.

"Indeed no, the camps went on for miles, but the officers and their men were closest to our house," I said.

"You look excited," said Death, glancing back at the peeking girl again.

"I was," I said and smiled. "It was odd perhaps, for everyone was talking of doom, saying we should be afraid of what would come. Men were spinning tales of rebellions old, and of the civil wars of York and Lancaster, saying here there was nothing but chaos and horror, yet I was excited, for I got to see him again. I was alive with fear and elation. Those days when the men came marching to our house, I never felt more alive than I did then. I cannot remember ever being so happy, and yet I was afraid too, for him, not for me."

I looked at these men, some of whom would never march home again, some who would.

"Joy was in me, though the world was burning and bleeding. I was joyful and fearful in equal measure, all because of him, every emotion I had became tied to Robin at this time. I was excited to see him here, see him as such a man as I had dreamed he was, and it seemed my dreams were true for here he was, a soldier, a commander, about to head into battle and face rebellion and death. I was a girl, though I thought myself a woman, and to me then it seemed as if I had been in darkness all my life, and then someone had lit a candle under the obscurity of the new moon, and I could see, could see for the first time."

I gazed over at Robin. He moved between groups of men, he always had a way about him of grace. Like a young cat he moved, not a stumbling kitten or broken, aged moggy, but a cat in full possession of all its muscles.

"Everyone said we should fear, and I did, for Robin, for my family, and yet I also felt free, wild even. There was something feral about that time, as if anything could happen and perhaps would. Everyone said everything would fall apart, and yet I knew then that all parts of me could shatter, all of the world under my feet could be torn asunder, and it would be all right, for if we, the world and I, could find our way to him then we still would have a steady point to fix ourselves to, a light to guide us. Everyone said we should fear, and yet I never had, and never had since, more fire in my heart than I did then. I had become one of the girls in the stories I was not supposed to read, giddy and joyful. All the poets spoke of love, so could it be so wrong to feel it?

"The air smelt cleaner, the sun shone brighter. I felt seen in a world where so many fail to notice another. And it was not moon-calf love, or so I thought, for he had fire in his wits which matched my own, a flame which encouraged the fire in me to burn brighter. My family had always said I was possessed of a sharp tongue, but often it had seemed a bad thing to them, but such things as sharp wits he liked as much as my looks, my waist, my breasts, my eyes, and so I thought this a different love, a deeper one."

I sighed, gazing at the girl I had been, at the man I had loved.

"What a fool I was," I said.

Death touched my hand, and time slipped.

Chapter Two

Hampton Court Palace

The Court of King Edward VI

Summer 1548

I would say it was like falling, but it was not. That idea may come close to explaining what the sensation was, but when I think on it more it was like water. Once, when I was a child, I fell from a boat into a pond. I was leaning too far over the edge, trying to see the fish winging through the water as if it was air, and I fell. The sharp cold shock of the pond, one of the ponds of my father where the fish were kept until they were hauled out to be made into pottage and pies for our table, stole my breath. The servants, fearful I would drown for I could not swim and they should not have let me come with them, but I had insisted, threw me a rope. Through the water I was pulled, feeling that strange resistance water has where, by our touch, by hands and feet meeting it, what is liquid feels solid just for a moment. That is how it felt to fly with Death through time, through events, through the past. A strange sensation of resistance and yielding, of solid and liquid, and a rushing sound passed my ears, like birds in flight over a marsh, all breaking into the sky at once, startled by some wandering creature of jaws and teeth and pounce. And then we were not where we had been, but somewhere else.

It was a corridor of court, Hampton Court in fact. I knew it well for the view from the window. Diamond-panes letting in glimmering light displayed a garden of knots and flowers and heraldic symbols etched in sand. It was raining, a steady light rain, like so many that have and will fall upon England in time. Inside, there was laughter and conversation.

"You look fair this day, Mistress Robsart."

I turned in shock, but the compliment was directed at the girl I once was, not the ghost I was then.

"Fair as what am I? As the sun or as the wind?" I heard my own voice quip, and I looked full into my own face, young and bold as I was when I was first at court. This younger me was surrounded by men and women, half of whom now I could not tell you their names, and yet back then they had been all the world to me. "Fair as the pale moon or as the justice of the land? There is much that is fair in this world, therefore to be but one of those things is a compliment most common."

"I take it back," the one who had delivered the compliment laughed. "You deal unfairly with a man trying to pay an accolade to a woman."

"A man must understand the tribute he delivers, or all is chaos."

Men around this little vixen laughed, their eyes bright on the deliverer of the compliment to see what he would retort. Light reflected from the painted cloth on the walls of the corridor shone on young faces. The scent of vinegar from the walls being so recently scrubbed, and of musk mingling with sweat in the crevices of skin filled the air.

"You knew each other from court," said Death, standing at my side as we watched this younger me trounce a younger Robin.

I nodded, watching these shadows of my life who could see us not. "That was why I thought I knew him," I said. "Why I thought my love was deeper. So many girls fall in love in a day. It took me longer, so I thought it real."

"Perhaps it was."

"Perhaps, although I believe it only can be real when both feel the same. Like a mirror reflection, there is a person on each side."

"But one of those people does not exist," Death pointed out.

"Perhaps love never really exists, and we all are watching reflections of the people we wished existed." I smiled at the girl. "I was so pretty then," I said. "I did not think so at the time, but I was."

There I stood, a young lass, my hands on my hips as I taunted Robin Dudley who was trying to play the young gallant and woo me. His friends had told my friends that he aimed to seduce me, had boasted I would be a fine conquest, but I would have none of it. He was entirely too arrogant, although in truth I glowed to see his confidence. But I was not about to let him know that. I was a fine young woman of court, one many men flocked to, one many admired, even though I was not of the higher nobility. My looks were sharp and pretty and my tongue was witty. I was everything a woman of court should be, and I was only just at the start of what I thought would be a long career. I was not about to be seduced by fine words and compliments only for a young man to leave me and go on to another, promises of love fading with the sound of his footsteps down the corridor. I was no fool, not in that way at least.

I was a fool in some ways though. I liked the fact that Robin had boasted he would have me, liked that he had admitted this attraction to friends. I should have been more insulted by it, in truth, for he thought me a diversion for an hour or two, some creature to be disarmed with a fine word here and a posey of flowers there, and then he could lift my skirts and take what he wanted and go on with his life never caring that mine had been ruined by him, for I would not make a good marriage having surrendered my virginity to the likes of him. He thought I was foolish enough to be easily caught. Oh yes, I should have been more insulted, but I wanted him to want me. I just wanted him to want me forever, not just for an hour or so.

I thought I knew what I was doing. Part of the game of court was to be available and unobtainable at the same time. It was a thin line to walk, but I knew the steps. I was spirited, unlike so many dull women who had taken the standard advice to be meek and mild to heart. Men might proclaim that was what women should be, but it was not what they wanted, not most of them in any case. Only a weak man wants a dull woman. I was not dull, and for good reason. I had pride in myself, I would be mistress to no man.

When I took a husband it would be a man of fire and ambition, a man whose soul matched mine, a man who would challenge me and would not shy from me challenging him. I was so confident, then. I thought I knew what I wanted and how I was to get it. I thought I knew everything, and would always be the one in charge, the one who would win.

"I was adored at my home, and so naturally thought it was so everywhere," I said. "My father had a bastard son, and stepchildren from my mother, Elizabeth, after he married her but I was their only child, the only one they made together. I grew up with half-brothers and sisters who loved me, the Appleyards. I was their pet, they said, and I had too a father and mother who might have wanted a son, but were content that I was their child. I was accustomed to being thought important, you see, so I thought it was what I would find at court."

"You did," said Death.

"Of a kind," I replied, lacing a hand on the tapestry, the bright silks twinkling against the pale luminosity of my fingers. "I came to court when I was sixteen, serving the Duchess of Richmond, for my father was close enough to the Howards to arrange such a position. My father had some influence in the north, and the Howards were as kings there, so our families had ties of loyalty. I was not high, for I was a chamberer, but I was not low either. When men came to me, as they would for I was pretty, I was wise enough to be not flattered by their attentions but to bat them away with words and wit. Low at court I might be, but I had been Queen of our household in Norfolk. I knew I was worth more than men would offer if I merely blushed and came willingly, a fool for love as some women were. Some believed the men who swore love and lay with them, and then found that love once so ardent had cooled the moment the men had what they wanted. My mother had always taught me that I could do well if I was aloof with men, if I teased and played with them as they did with us. A girl could be so much more interesting than others, and if she played the game well she could end up with a higher station than she was born to."

"And so you met him there, at court."

"So I did, and I did not fall before him as so many did. I held myself apart, I parried with words and fought with wit. And he liked me, I knew it as did he. He did not love me yet, not then, but I think I loved him more than I wanted to admit, in case I could not have him."

"And then he came to your house, on his way to war."

"Yes," I said. "And then, like a fool, I told him how I felt."

Chapter Three

Whitehall Palace

Autumn 1545

"I thought you were to show me the night we pledged," I said, looking around as my vision cleared and the world ceased to slip and spin. "Yet this is not that night."

We were in a garden. Looking back, I could see the place was Whitehall, once York Place when Wolsey lived here, and then the King's when Wolsey handed it over to him, along with his life and all else he had. The gardens were falling to the colours of autumn, reds and copper and gold burned in the trees. The grass was fresh with dew. There was a chill in the air, the scent of the river too not far away.

"There are others in this tale than you and him," said Death. "Regard."

He pointed to two children. One, a girl, had hair red as fire. I touched my own; my blonde hair had always had a hint of fire in it, but not like this girl. She had the touch of a dragon's heart upon her head. There were women with her, guarding her. They were much older, more drably dressed than the girl. She was on a path, walking with her dark eyes lost in the prettiness of the day, and there she came upon the other child, a boy.

"Robin," I said, my voice barely a whisper.

A child indeed, but in that face I could see the man he would become. I knew how the lines would come to rest at the edges of his eyes, how lines of a frown would settle between his eyebrows where that day his skin was smooth and clear. I knew how his temples would grey, just a little, after the war. I knew how those eyes would gleam with excitement and anger, with joy and expectation. I could see the years that would come to him and all they would bring, and though I never had met him at this time, never had known him as a child, I was glad I had been brought by Death to see this time, to see him now, long before the world started to bite into him, started to rend flesh.

The lad sitting on that bench, a book in his hands and a crease of frustration on his brow, was so familiar. Was this what our son would have looked like? Those dark eyes I would know anywhere. The girl had ones to match, and outmatch his. She was not as she should be, being a redhead. They are supposed to have green eyes, perhaps blue, but she did not. She had eyes as deep and dark as his, almost black. People said her mother had had the same eyes, ones that could peer into your soul without ever betraying a whit of the owner's thoughts.

"Elizabeth," I said. "She has eyes like yours," I said to Death. He was standing back a little. I realised I had crept towards the children, like some kind of slinking ghoul. I had not realised I had moved, but each of them had the potential to draw people to them, and I was not immune to that.

"Often enough she has stared into my eyes, and will again in her future," Death said. "It is not surprising hers should hold a fragment of mine, so often they have reflected each other."

"You admire her." It was not a question, I could hear it in his voice.

"It is hard not to admire one who has danced so often near my hands, and yet slipped away each time," he replied.

"So you do not admire me?" I was, after all, dead, so had not slipped by him.

"I have admiration for many people, for many different reasons."

I stared at them, the children, for a while. "I knew they were young when first they met," I said. "I did not think they were so young."

"They were not, then. They were that day the oldest they had been."

I laughed a little as we listened to their chatter. "He must have just joined court," I said.

Boys were sent from every wealthy and noble house in the hope they would serve Prince Edward, as he was then, become his companions and one day therefore the close friends of the future King. Much the same had been done when Henry VIII was young; the companions he had played with as a boy were those honoured when he came to his throne. Each family given a chance to place a child within Edward's house tried to select the most promising of their children, so Edward grew up a precocious boy surrounded by precocious boys. Some were strong and fast, and Edward admired their skills at archery and running at the rings practising the skills required for jousting. The old King, Henry VIII, would not let Edward do this himself. It was too dangerous and Edward was the only precious male heir, but it was said Edward had the utmost admiration, in a slightly jealous fashion, for any other boy skilled at this sport.

Some of the boys were hardy young warriors and others were intelligent and ready to argue Thomas Aquinas from the break of dawn. With those boys Edward was entirely the King already, ready and able to exert his formidable intellect over them and prove his worth. Some of the boys were blessed enough to be both talented in the field and at the book. Theirs was a lively household, full of young boys as eager to impress each other as they were to impress the young Prince. Robin had been one of them. I would guess this day he was around eight years old, Elizabeth the same.

As Elizabeth walked the gardens with Kat, they came across this young Dudley sitting in a grove and sighing in frustration over a book. His hands were pressed to the sides of his head next to his eyes. Clearly he was not enjoying the book he was reading.

"What causes you to sigh so, Master Dudley?" Elizabeth asked as she approached. I peeked over Robin's shoulder to see one of my favourite versions of Cicero in his lap. I smiled.

"Robin never got along with Cicero," I said, smiling at Death, and then I remembered I was watching the first meeting of Robin and the woman everyone would later claim he loved instead of me, and I scowled.

Robin rose and bowed to the Princess, a fluid, graceful motion. Robin always looked as though he were dancing, even in the mundane actions of everyday life. He held out the book to her and she took the volume in her hands. "You do not find interest in the works of the masters?" Princess Elizabeth said, a faint reproof in her voice. I could tell that she, like me, loved this book. Even then she was protective of the things she loved.

He smiled, charming even when in trouble. "My masters say I must read it in order to advance my mind," he said. "But I must admit that I have little love for the work. There are other books I do love, but this is not one."

"And what other books do you love, Master Dudley, that could best Cicero in his knowledge and wisdom?" Elizabeth stared at him imperiously.

"She was not to be trifled with, even as a child," I said. Unwittingly, something of admiration rose in me.

Robin's black eyes twinkled at her merrily. He seemed to take delight in Elizabeth's riled temper; something he had also enjoyed doing to me, much later in life. "I love the study of mathematics," he said. "Navigation, charts and geography. I would love to know the world, my lady. I love to see maps and see the different kingdoms and oceans of this world."

Elizabeth smiled, and I knew why, for tutors of this time had been rather divided on the value of mathematics and preferred their students to understand the worth of the classics. But as a child I too liked to see charts and images of distant lands that bold men were discovering; strange and far-off kingdoms, brave new worlds, captivating creatures never before seen, and treasures from far away territories. Robin always wanted to travel, to take to a ship and see the wonders of these new worlds being found.

"I too would love to know the world," Elizabeth said, handing his book back. "There is much to be said for the discovery of new lands, new riches and the expansion of the Christendom."

He bowed. "You are a wise princess, my lady," he said. "Perhaps if your father marries you to a foreign prince, you will get to see many of the worlds that I dream of being allowed to see."

Her face fell, and he noted it. Of course she would look sad. Elizabeth would have supposed it her fate, then, to be sent to another land to wed a man she had never met before, to have him sire children on her whether she wanted it or not. She was a precocious child, Elizabeth, and although every princess was made aware of her destiny, she would have been more aware than other young women of the horrors that might lie in her future, for she had more imagination, and more intelligence. She had no wish to leave England, I could see that plain. It was written with sorrow on her face.

His expression turned gentle as he saw her sadness. He had wished to pay her a compliment and express that her fortunes were on the rise; being used as a pawn in the international game of royal marriages was after all an indication that Elizabeth was again valuable as a recognised and legal heir to her father's throne. If I remembered rightly she must just have been restored around this time after years of being left out of the succession. But Robin knew as he looked at the Princess that she would not wish to leave her England.

"Do not be sad, my lady," he said. "Perhaps if we ever get the chance, I shall discover such lands for you. One day I will bring you the golden crown of the kings of the Indias, and rubies from the Emperor of the New World. I will bring you new lands to name after yourself and emeralds from the lair of the dragon at the end of the world."

Elizabeth laughed and Kat Ashley, her companion, laughed too. I could not help but smile. He was a gallant boy.

"Such a bold adventurer!" said Kat admiringly. The Princess nodded and smiled wider at him. Robin looked pleased to have the rapt attention of them both.

"I should like that, Master Dudley," Elizabeth said, smoothing her gown of green and white, Tudor colours which went well against her pale skin and red hair. "But perhaps you should stay closer to home. Your father may have many plans for you in mind, as my father has for me."

"And we should all do as our fathers wish," he said dutifully but with mischief riding over his handsome features. "I have the advantage however, my lady, of being subordinate also to *your* wishes as well as to my father's. So if, one day, you should wish to travel the seas and see what treasures there are out there, I should be willing to be your captain. I would have no choice but to place your wishes above that of my father. You are after all, a princess of England."

"Should we be pirates together then?" she chuckled. "I had never heard a woman might be a pirate as well as a man."

He grinned. "A gracious princess such as yourself should be able to be and do anything she wishes. That is the gift that God gave you when He bore you into the royal family."

Elizabeth smiled, but her lips were tight, thin. "Sometimes, God moves us in ways that we do not expect," she said. "But I do not think He placed me here to indulge in piracy."

Robin shook his head. "No, of course," he said. "I jest, but I do believe there is more in store for the Princess Elizabeth than simply marrying and leaving our fair country. Your father in his wisdom would not marry off such a prize and lose you."

It was flattery; the way things were at court where men advanced through pretty words and less noble deeds. But I felt as though he meant it in truth.

"Why do you show me this?" I asked, rounding on Death, feeling my heart pained. "So I might see that she always had a claim to him that was older, better than mine? Do you tell me that they were bonded here and now, and all else which followed never could compare? Should I hate her more than I did before for stealing my husband, or hate myself for I was not there as she was at the start of all this? Do you tell me she stole nothing from me, for he was always hers?"

"I told you that you might not like the answers you seek," said Death. "But all of this is required to be seen, to be known, if you truly wish to find the truth. She was an influence upon your life, as she was upon your death."

There was silence a moment.

"So it was him, then?" I asked. "Do you need to show me more if it was him and he killed me so he could be with her?"

"There are others in this tale, than just three," he said, and reached out to take my hand.

Chapter Four

Stanfield Hall

Norfolk

August 1549

It was dark, and the air smelt of smoke. I looked at my companion, and he nodded to me, indicating with his bone-white head, hazy in the moonlight, to a figure creeping from a chamber into the dark corridor, and along it. Even in the dark I knew who it was.

"It is that night," I whispered, even though no one could hear me. "The night we swore to marry."

Outside in the darkness there was the scream of an owl, and the creeping figure stopped short, catching a breath sudden and sharp into his throat. In the distance a clock ticked, a mouse scuttled. Outside the window cloud stole across the blue-black heavens, and the stars shone brilliant, white lights in the dark veil of night.

We followed Robin as he snuck from a chamber in the guests' quarter, along the corridor, down a flight of stairs and into the garden. "It is the night before the morning they marched away," I whispered to Death, although he knew where and when we were of course, he had brought us here. "It is the night we swore we were of one heart, he and I."

The door squeaked as Robin pushed it open, and under his breath he cursed it, using many parts of God to do so. Out into the night he padded, leaving the door ajar for his return. A blast of the warm air of a summer's night came fluttering into our faces, along with a hint of dampness. It had rained a little that night, I remembered, for I had been forced into an arbour as the squall fell and as it had lifted. I had thought he would not come. I had not known until I saw him that he had.

With Robin I skulked into the gardens, along long, winding paths snaking black and damp through avenues of cherry trees and apple too. How I had loved my father's gardens! They had been one of my favourite places in all the world. Even as it was dark and damp, I could imagine all the spring and summer and autumn days I had sat out here with a book or my sewing. How I had lain under the trees and watched the blossom and the bees who danced before the flowers, worshipping them. I remembered being stung by a hornet here, up a tree where I was of course not supposed to be. Girls did not climb trees. But I had, and when the hornet found me and I accidentally pressed him to a branch with my leg, not seeing he was there, I had thought the sting had been sent as punishment from God for doing something I had been told not to.

A thousand, thousand moments of summer I could remember here, and the same of every other season. Even in winter I had wrapped up warm and walked the frozen paths, the ice cracking underfoot. I had dreamed of much here, and I had been at peace. Looking at Death, walking calmly at my side, I wondered if I should tell him this was one of the times I had felt at peace with myself, as he had asked, but in my heart I was sure he knew already.

The lingering scent of all the bonfires of all the soldiers hung heavy in the late summer air, captured by wispy clouds of night roaming over the pale moon. There too was the scent of blackberries rising from the hedges nearby, the dark black berries ripe and heavy on their thorns. Through the gardens Robin came, a shadow of a cat, so lithe and certain of his steps, and then there was a whistle. I looked up to see myself, so young and full of trepidation and excitement, emerge from a bower in the gardens of my father. There was an apple leaf on my hood, from where I had ducked through the orchard, thinking to take a strange path from my rooms in case I was followed. I was followed, but only by my one maid, standing back in the shadows, twitching like a nervous sparrow. Poor Martha, she had not wanted me to come. I had convinced her with pleas and threats, then with bribery. She would lose her post if we were found. God forgive me, I cared not a whit for that then. All I cared for was that the boy who had my heart was marching out with the dawn and I might never see him again.

"I thought you would not come," the girl I was whispered to him, and Robin was at her side so fast it was as though he was light itself, moving without seeming to move.

"I would never fail you," he said, kissing her hands. "I will always come."

"Yet tomorrow you leave me," the girl said, a tremor in her voice.

"To march to war, on the orders of the King and my father, otherwise you know I would not." He paused, holding her hands. I could remember the warmth of his hands that night against my cold ones. "You never gave me hope to think that you cared so, before now."

"I never thought I would lose you, until now."

There were tears in her voice. How well I remembered the pain of them. It was true that until that day, that night when the sons of Dudley had eaten in the great hall with me and my family, I had given Robin no hope that I thought of him with affection, and yet as he and I had parted a short conversation whispered in a hallway had told him that I did care, that I cared greatly, that I feared for him, and we had agreed to meet in secret, so we might talk freely.

"It was the rebellion that forced my heart," I said to Death, watching the two young people converse, passion in their voices. "I thought I would lose him and suddenly he became more to me than I had thought, more precious. I felt more than I had believed I did before, at court. I knew I admired him, thought him handsome, but that night something changed in me. My heart, once closed, once unbelieving of all that men would say to get a maid to abandon her virtue, my heart opened. Like water in he poured, poured so well there was no space for anything or anyone else."

"Proximity to death brings on many feelings, and exaggerates others," said Death.

"You think that all it was, that we feared death so fooled ourselves into believing in love?"

Death shrugged. "I do not say what you felt was untrue. I simply say that being close to death may enhance what humans feel and think. There is a sharpening of emotion, a clarity of vision. Humans need death, in order to feel alive."

"Perhaps that is so. What if he had not come that day, that night, would I have felt the same? If his father had stopped at another house would my life have been different?"

"Of a surety, but this is the way it happened."

I watched as Robin gathered the young me in his arms, and kissed her. I had never been kissed before, or only by family. I remember that one well, for finally I understood what it was to want a man with all my body, the tingling excitement of pressing lips to lips, to feel hands that desire you upon your body, wishing they could take more, take all they wanted, and yet holding back, and in that holding back there was respect for me, and that too felt like love. They whispered, I remembered not all the words but I remembered the sentiment, and it all was love, a love that had become only more vivid and bright since it had burst in each of their hearts, and since they knew it might soon be lost.

He kissed her and they slipped apart, breathless, their eyes shining in the darkness. They parted with a promise, and one I remembered well, a promise of love, a promise of marriage.

"Will you show me the day?" I asked, watching both figures slip away into the darkness.

"If you wish."

The world lightened, flowers changed, skies raced from darkness to sunlight, and we were no more at my father's house, but in London. It was high summer, the 4th of June, in the year after the rebellion.

"They stood not a chance, the rebels," I said, looking around at the gathering at Sheen Palace. We were in the gardens there, many of the guests looking pale and ill, for they had celebrated a wedding only the day before, that of Robin's older brother John Dudley, Lord Lisle, who had wed Anne, daughter of Edward Seymour. Our marriage, held the day after that of Warwick's heir was a smaller affair, with many of the same guests. Robin and me, we were not as important as John and Anne, but I cared not that day, nor for many after. I did not care how important we were to others, only how we were to each other. At that time, that day, had you asked me, I would have said he was all I needed, and I was all he needed. I might have been right, that day.

"The royal armies fell upon the rebels and crushed them," I went on as we wandered through the crowds, men and woman laughing and chattering, all the court gossip there was flittering over our heads. Words and talk that at the time had seemed so important, yet those scandals were now long forgotten. "Kett fled and was found hiding in a barn. They hung him in chains from the walls of Norwich Castle, and eventually his flesh fell from his bleached bones, slipping to the ground, trying to bury itself."

Death nodded, but of course he would know that.

"Somerset, Edward Seymour, he was damaged in the eyes of the people by that rebellion. Warwick, as Dudley became not long after, had been the one to defeat the rebels, and people looked up to him, the King looked up to him. Somerset was seen as ineffectual and cowardly and, hearing a plot he was to be arrested, he fled to Windsor Castle, taking the young King with him. For a week he holed up in there, the protesting King with him, and for a while we all thought there would be war, yet then Somerset was tricked into surrendering his person to the men of Warwick, the King was released and Somerset found himself arrested."

I gazed over at Anne Seymour, standing with her new husband. "But Warwick was a clever man," I went on. "He knew that no matter the crimes of Somerset, the King was reluctant to execute yet another Seymour uncle. Thomas Seymour had already died for much the same thing; kidnap or attempted kidnap of the King. I often think what secured that Seymour's fate was shooting the King's spaniel, for Edward was often more at home with animals than he was with people. Thomas had died, but Edward Seymour did not, not yet. Warwick had what he wanted, for now and made himself Lord President of the Council." I nodded to the man who that day had become my father-in-law. He had his hand on some other man's shoulder, was roaring with laughter with them. People had told me the old King could lay his hand on a man's shoulder and that man would feel as if he was the King's best friend. Dudley had the same magic in his touch.

"He knew the King's affection was the key to how he was to remain in power. He managed to defeat a Catholic faction striving at that time to set Lady Mary on the throne as regent, he had brought down the rebels and saved the King from his own uncle, and for that he had Edward's gratitude. The spring that followed the rebellion saw Somerset walk free of the Tower when all had thought he would lose his head upon its green, and that June, the day before Robin and I married, Warwick married his heir to the daughter of Somerset, and all said peace had come upon England."

I looked around. There were people milling everywhere, expressions of happiness on their faces, even those who were clearly suffering after wallowing deep in their cups the night before. "It was a good time to be married," I said. "There was an air of anticipation upon England then. The King was merry, closer to his majority and full power than ever before. Everyone was talking of who he would wed, there were wagers placed. Somerset and Warwick were united, but of all the happy people, I was happiest. I could barely believe in truth that I, daughter of a *Sir*, certainly, but not a great prize in marriage, had been allowed to marry Robin *Dudley*. His father was the most powerful man in the country after the King, his other sons were making great matches with women of families almost as powerful, and yet here I was, little Amy Robsart, being wed to a Dudley. I could not believe my good fortune." I paused; "and I loved him, loved him so much that I thought my heart would burst with all the happiness it was trying to contain." I shook my head. "I thought it was as Robin told me, that our match had come about because Warwick had listened to and been moved by his son's pleas about true love. I was a fool to think a man like Robin's father cared for such."

I stared at Robin and me, on our chairs at the head of the wedding feast. Robin was feeding me little dainties from his plate. Warwick had been charming, welcoming me to the family, and his sons were gallant, every one of them a talented apprentice to the charm of their father. Their mother too was sweet, evidently devoted to her family. She had told me what beautiful children we would have, and I had agreed, never once thinking it would not come to be. People married and had children, that was all life was made of, was it not?

Robin had done little more than stare at me all day, as if he could not believe his luck. This struck me for I thought I was the fortunate one, thought I was the one who had done better than any would imagine. Yet to look at him that day, it was he who was the most fortunate of men, for he had me.

"It was enough to turn a girl's head," I said. "Enough to spin my thoughts, make me so giddy and grateful to have what I wanted, the only thing I thought I wanted so I did not consider the truth: that Warwick had not allowed the match simply because Robin loved me. Love was only one reason it was permitted. Power, money, land, they were the true reasons."

I paused. "I did not find that out until much later."

I was silent a moment, feeling pain in my heart again. It is always painful to find that something we have believed in so faithfully was nothing but a lie. Yet it was not all a lie. Robin had desired me, had loved me, then. He had asked his father for permission to marry me, it was just that after declarations of love and romance, there had been other things spoken of, things that to me cheapened the higher reasons. Perhaps it did not soil our love to these men, but men are ever wont to think of their pocket books as well as their hearts. I should not have expected it to be different, although I had hoped it was so.

"Why do the thoughts of others matter so to humans?" Death asked, peering into one of the bowls where a few capon were left, covered in saffron and honey, as the servants cleared them so the wedding party could dance. "If you yourself were happy, feeling love and knowing that then you were loved by the one you loved, why does it matter what motives others had? Your intentions were pure."

"But later I wondered why Robin married me," I said. "I suppose it may not have mattered what Warwick wanted or thought, why he agreed we might wed, but it mattered to me what Robin wanted and thought. It mattered to me that he loved me. I had thought it a certainty, and then I was made unsure."

"Even so," said Death, trailing a finger of bone about the green-glazed dish. "If that robs some of the joy of the experience, it cannot steal it all. The reason he chose you was love, even if there were other considerations that counted more to his father." Death nodded to the happy couple, now rising to dance before the guests. "Even if it faded, even if it changed, he loved you on this day. You were, to him, the most beautiful and wonderful of women. Some people are never looked upon like this once, no matter how long they live, but this day you were the sun and the moon to him. He was proud to be your husband. He wanted no other but you."

"And yet not forever did it last."

"Forever is a long time, and in it there are many moments. Just because a moment is fleeting does not mean it has no meaning. Many things of the most meaning happen in a short time. You were loved this day, and many after. However it ended, this day was one of meaning to you."

I nodded. "Yes," I said. "That is true."

"And this day there were others present who one day would be a part of your story," he said.

I looked to where he pointed. The King was in conversation with a young man; they both looked serious, but then the man laughed. Young, plain but in an interesting way he was, and I knew his face as well I as remembered the King.

"The King," I said. "I wonder often what might have happened if Edward had lived. Robin was growing to be a favourite of his, you know. We might have risen high, I might have served his wife when he took one. People said he wanted to marry his cousin, Jane Grey, and how different life might have been for all of us if that had happened. Robin and I would have always been at court, together, then." I looked at his companion. "And Cecil," I said. "Elizabeth already knew him, I think Robin said once that her stepmother Katherine Parr introduced them. What would she have done, if she had had another advisor other than Cecil? He was her right hand, and her right foot. She took not a step without him."

I watched as Cecil walked to us, watching us dance. To Warwick he spoke, and I knew the two knew one another for it would not be long after this that Warwick would make Cecil Principal Secretary to the Privy Council. Cecil was one who, like many of us, rose in the ranks with Warwick tugging him along.

"They seem most young to be married, my lord," Cecil said to Warwick.

"Perhaps, but sometimes the best matches are made young," he said. "They are in love, too, which will aid them. There will be a new Dudley lad in our Norfolk lass's belly before the year is out, I'd wager."

I saw Cecil steal a swift glance to his master, or mentor, I was not sure which. Cecil saw the plan Warwick had, I was sure, the plan I was in ignorance of then, to subdue the north by covert means, to infiltrate by marriage, by children.

"Her family are well respected in Norfolk, I understand," Cecil mentioned.

"Aye, her father is little more than a squire, but a good man, solid, dedicated to the new learning and to the right of the monarch to be Head of the Church. He is to settle all he has on Amy, and therefore now on my son."

"It can be hard to provide for sons, when one is blessed with as many as you, my lord," said Cecil. "Her father's money will be of use to your son, for he would have had a much smaller share from your estates."

"Indeed, although Robsart will not part with much before death, and he will give up Amy's lands only when his wife, too, is with God, so I will give them enough to live on. It will be worth it, when the Robsart lands become part of my family, and the girl comes of a fertile line, though she is the only legitimate heir. Her mother had four other children, and her father a bastard son, so there will be fruit enough. Soon, Cecil, you will see my grandchildren north, south, east and west." He smiled and sighed. "And as I said, it is a love match."

"A lust match, more like as not," Cecil muttered as he walked away from the Earl as Warwick became distracted by something else.

"He may have had a point," I said to Death. "Perhaps ours was more a match of desire than durability."

"You think so?" Death asked.

Chapter Five

Camberwell, town house of the Appleyard family, and

The Tower of London

Summer 1553

I watched the girl, still so young, weeping. Her maid at her side, whispering words of condolence which meant nothing to the bride weeping for her husband. The King was dead, and my husband was in the Tower. Men of his family had tried to place another Queen on the throne rather than Mary, the King's sister, and they had failed. Rob had tried to proclaim Jane Grey Queen in King's Lynn, but the people had supported Lady Mary, had captured Robin and sent him to Framlingham Castle to face the new Queen. After that, he was sent to the Tower to await trial and death, with the rest of his family.

"You mean to show me it was more than lust, our marriage," I said, watching the poor girl weep. "That there were emotions other than desire in our match." I turned to Death. "I did not mean it was lust for me, but for Robin perhaps."

"Yet there were elements durable and resilient in your marriage," Death said. "This time was one that tested that."

"I thought the world at its end," I said to Death, "and all had been so well, so well until the King became ill. We were at court often, as often as I could be with Robin I was there, and although it was not as often as I would like, as Edward was unmarried and so there were few female posts at court, and wives could only visit, I was in London with my husband. I liked London, and that time. It felt as if we were rising, becoming important, as if we were on the cusp of some greatness. When there were court events I was there, and we danced before the King. Edward complimented me once, I thought it odd perhaps for he noted my gown and never did Edward think much about women. I think he wanted to please Robin, and that was why he complimented me."

I looked away from the crying girl. "Robert was doing well in the household of King Edward, he had been offered and accepted posts and the King seemed to like him. Who would not? Robert was athletic and charming, good at so many things, a jouster most promising, and Edward liked that, for he was a serious, studious boy still. The lessons of his father, trying to keep him safe, had pushed him to study more and attempt feats of strength less, but he was just starting to break free of the lessons of his youth, just starting to become a man, and then he died and all the work done seemed for nothing."

I moved to stand near the weeping girl, as if I could offer her strength somehow, tell her this was not the end, not even close. "Warwick, by then Duke of Northumberland, knew Edward was dying long before anyone else," I continued. "He was the one who helped Edward draw up his 'devise', that foolish statement for the future. Mary was excluded from the succession, in opposition to the will of Henry VIII, on the basis that she was a Catholic and the dying King would not return England to live under the boot of Rome. Everyone supposed he would pick Elizabeth, but it was not so. She was excluded too. People said it was because Edward believed her mother truly was a whore, and perhaps he had to believe that since his own mother supplanted Anne Boleyn, but I think not. I think it was more Warwick's doing than Edward's, that part of it at least. Jane Grey was named heir, and her sons after her. Warwick married his youngest son Guildford to her, and so it was done. Warwick, the power behind the throne, would set a grandson upon the throne, and a son there as King Consort before that. It was a risky gamble, but he thought he could do it. He was popular until that time, until Edward died and he tried to steal the throne from Lady Mary. He thought the people would be with him, would support him. Arrogance had made him blind."

I nodded to the weeping woman, candlelight falling soft and amber about the chamber. Martha, surrendering her task to try to stop me crying, had decided to at least allow something bright into the chamber by lighting the candles, one by one. "And Robert, his son, was to bring about this wish along with the rest of the family. All of Dudley's sons were brought to their father and given tasks, and all of their wives were told only after, and we were all told we had to obey, help the family. The Dudleys all thought the people would follow Warwick, but they did not, they flocked to Mary. Robert tried to name Jane Grey Queen in Norfolk, and he failed and was arrested. This is the day they told me he, along with his father and his brothers, had been taken to the Tower." I paused before I said again, "I thought the world had ended."

"Humans often think such, and then another dawn rises and they are still alive, as is the world," said Death, walking by one of the candles so it guttered. Martha frowned at it, shivered a little. I wondered if she could feel Death strolling past her. "What is odd is that they never seem to note that all these ends of the world come to nothing, another day begins and the world is as it was. Often what seems like a disaster that none may recover from is not so dire, but you humans never seem to remember that."

"We are, often, creatures of the moment," I agreed.

"You often are forgetful," said Death.

"To live in the moment one must be forgetful, or the past would take up more room than we could spare."

"But this was not the end, not of the world, or life, even of love," said Death.

I glanced up and we were at the Tower. I knew it even without looking from a window to see the circling, sloping walls, the white tower, the many other towers in which so many people had been held over the years. I knew it from the scent of cold stone and fear on the air. The Tower never lost that scent, damp, cold stone and terror. It was seeped into the bricks and the floor, it crept, a thing living and skulking, along the dark corridors, up the winding stairs to all the towers and their many chambers, along the windy battlements where the scent of the river washed. It stood beside you as you stood at a window, looking out onto the green where so many people had died, up the hill to Tower Hill, where even more had. Even the river seemed to sing soft and low and mournful there. Once the Tower had just been another palace, but too many ghosts lived within those walls by that time for me to see it as anything but a tomb. There are some places where too much ill has been felt and done, so even the living feel the dread of all those who passed before them. Sometimes, when I came to the Tower to visit Robin, I thought I could hear people mumbling, speeches made before death all melding into one, mingling in the breeze bustling through the winding streets of the ward and inner ward, along all the bricks and the stones and the cobbles, a touch of the past and every sadness it contained floating on the wind, trying to touch me, touch my heart. Robin had been a prisoner for a few weeks before I was allowed to see him. Each time after that as I came to the Tower, I thought it would be the last. I thought the order would come and he would die, and I would lose him.

"I hated it here," I whispered, looking about the short corridor we were in. The Beauchamp Tower, I knew every brick in this wall, for I had looked at it often enough. There were scratch marks on the bricks, from prisoners past, or bored guards watching them, I knew not which. I was not sure it mattered, each mark whether of someone bored or someone desperate to make one last mark on life was a mark of hopelessness, was it not? Time and life wasted.

"Even were it not for Robin being a prisoner here, even were it not for every time I came here thinking the next time I saw him he would be dead, I would have hated it. I was scared to come here every time, and every time I left I had to bathe and scrub the scent of the Tower from my skin, and weep, and I barely knew what I cried for. I would have told people, I did tell people it was for Robin, for I was so scared for him, and yet it was something deeper, more primal than fear of losing him." I looked up at Death. "When I left here, I felt as if I had gone into a graveyard and sunk into the earth and walked through all the bones and rotting bodies, so flesh and bone was stuck in threads and shards to my skin. All the water of the world could not wash away the corruption I felt here, the corpses I smelt. I walked with ghosts when I came here." I shuddered. "And the guards helped not a whit. They made my skin crawl too."

I was standing outside the chamber in which my husband was kept. Queen Mary, in her mercy, had allowed the wives of the prisoners to visit. It was odd, perhaps, for she showed little mercy to others, and yet to the remaining sons of dead Warwick; was he dead at this time? I knew not, but to his sons she showed pity.

The guard made a lewd remark about me to his friend, barely bothering to drop his voice, and I saw the girl I had been set her jaw. I smiled a little. I had hated it so then, the words of the guards, their leering, the crude and hurtful remarks about what I could do once my husband was dead, who else I could service if not him, I had hated it then, but I smiled now because of the girl's resolve, her grace. There was no point in talking back to men like that. I was alone but for a manservant waiting for me outside, and answering back the Queen's guard could put me in a potentially dangerous situation, so I could not retort, but I could ignore them, my head high and figure graceful. I remembered the fire and anger in me. Had I had the strength or the protection to do so, I would have struck them, but as it was I but stoked that fire inside me and kept it safe, as I went to see my husband, the only reason I was there.

I watched as the girl gripped her basket tighter, treats for Robin, bread and some fruits, a blanket and a book. One of the guards had already stolen an apple from it, eaten it in front of me as if daring me to say something. I had looked ahead and not met his taunting eyes. "I feared the Tower, feared to enter it, to walk its halls, to stand near those guards, and yet time after time I did it. It got no easier. I could hear the wailing of people long since dead, or so I thought, feel the ghosts of all who had died there as they passed me in the hallways. At one point there was still blood upon the ground where they had taken the heads of Warwick, and then later of Guildford and Jane Grey, poor girl."

She was not much younger than I was then. Such a child, and a pawn as all knew. She had had no wish, no desire at all, to become Queen. They had taken her head all the same. Queen Mary was to marry Phillip of Spain and we had all heard that one of the terms of their agreement to marry was that Jane Grey be executed, it was too dangerous otherwise to send the new King to England to meet his new wife. He might be attacked by one the rebels of England wanting to put Jane Grey, Protestant Queen, upon the throne. Mary was desperate to wed, to have children, and Phillip was quite the catch of Europe, so Mary had taken the life of her cousin, so she might marry the man of her dreams. There were times I could sympathise, and times I could not. It seemed an ill way to begin a marriage, with blood. Perhaps she did things opposite to her father, for his had often ended with blood, as hers began.

"Jane Grey was a sacrifice, the last Mary perhaps thought she would have to make, to gain her perfect life. There had been so many dead along the way." A fingertip I trailed down one of the pictures etched into the wall. Was it a boar, or a bird? I could not tell. Possibly the person who had carved it had not had much time, or perhaps not much energy. This mark, made as some effort to leave a memory lasting in stone, could not even be recognised. Another attempt at immortality that would fade. "Why do we try so hard not to be forgotten, when that is the fate of most of us?" I whispered.

"It was her father who condemned her in truth," said Death, apparently not having heard my whisper. He stood staring out of the thin, tall window which looked out onto the White Tower. "Henry Grey could have chosen not to rise up in yet another failed rebellion whilst his daughter was the Queen's captive. Had he stayed at home, the Queen might have set Jane free. Mary knew well enough the girl was a pawn, as you said."

Yet perhaps the deaths of her cousin and Jane's unwanted husband, Guildford, as well as the death of Warwick, had been enough, for Robert and his brothers lingered long in the Tower, too dangerous to be freed, but not dangerous enough, apparently, for the Queen to kill.

And there I came, time after time, as I had come that day. Time after time I faced the fear I possessed, or that possessed me, my revulsion at the place, my panic as I walked, quick as I could, through dark, winding corridors and then the open green leading to the Beauchamp Tower and his cell. I faced that place for him, so I could see him and so he could see me. "I would have done anything for him."

It was comfortable enough inside the cell, Robin had a desk and a stool, a bed in which we could both fit and I was allowed to stay sometimes for hours, that we might comfort one another in the ways men and women can. He had some books and I was allowed to bring food and wine. There were straw mats on the floor and walls and they were changed often, so the room did not smell. Robin could look from the window to the green and sit in sunlight when it came in at the right angle, and he was taken to the chapel to pray. I wondered if that brought comfort, for there were people enough buried under the altar there, Anne and George Boleyn, Catherine Howard, the Countess of Salisbury, and they had displeased their monarch, just as he had displeased his. Did Robert think of them, of their fates and that of his father and brother, as he prayed? I did not know.

"He little wanted to talk of such things," I told Death as we walked into the cell behind the other Amy. "He wanted tales of the outside, of what we would do when he was free, just little things. After a while, you see, he came to hope that he would be pardoned. Warwick died and then Jane Grey and Guildford, and then there was nothing for a time, and we wives could visit. Some days the brothers met sometimes for a walk in the gardens of the Tower. Robin hoped he might be set free, and then sometimes he had no hope and when I came to him it was as if I had wandered into a cell not with a living man, but with a dark storm of winter encroaching on the last days of autumn, like a warning of hardship to come. He said at such times that I was his sanity, come visiting him from the outside, for in there, alone, he was not sane. But I came whenever I could, when I was allowed, and then I brought sanity to him, and that was enough, he said." I swallowed, watching the young Amy kiss her husband, watching him smile to see her. It was a genuine smile. "I was enough, I was all he had and all he needed, besides his freedom. He was grateful for me, then."

Time slipped, just a little, so Amy as I was, was sitting on a stool beside him at his desk. Robin was talking of the future, of a future he had in his mind, one we never would live.

"When I am free, we should live in the country, together," he said, those dark eyes agleam with a strange fire, one of fantasy. "The court is no more the place for us. Once, when Edward was alive it could have been. I could have been his man and you would have served his wife, Amy, but there is no place for us with Queen Mary. There would not be even if she was not of the old religion. I think she will not keep the peace in that way for long."

"You think she will return the country to Rome?" There was fear in my young mouth, salty and bitter on my tongue, for all my family were Protestants, as was Robin and as was I. We had been the ones who were safe, the ones in charge, and now Mary had come and the faiths had flipped. It was whispered it soon would not be safe to be Protestant in England. People already were leaving.

"I think marrying Phillip of Spain could be no clearer sign," Robin said. "So, it will be dangerous at court, and I am the son of a traitor and a traitor myself! We must leave London, but no matter. There can be another life for us, a better one! We can be as we were supposed to be, Amy, just a country man and his wife. In Norfolk we can be together, and we can be respected as we once were. Let England have Mary and her court! It will be no place for us. We will have each other, and that will be enough."

"And children," Amy said almost shyly.

I knew why she was shy with him. Sometimes it felt as though I barely knew this man I had married. When he was free he had often been with his father, doing whatever he was told to do for the family, and then he was arrested and we saw each other for only hours here and there. We were married, we were intimate and I loved him, but often I felt like a stranger with him.

"And children," Robin said and smiled. He kissed his wife. "And the making of them will be easier when we are away from this awful place, and you are happy."

I looked at Death and smiled. "I believed him," I said. "What easy lies we may tell to ourselves and to each other and they may be believed. I thought he was in earnest about living quietly, just us and our children in the country, yet I should have known that any son of Warwick could not live without ambition in his heart. It pumped as blood in them. I should have known that Robert could not be a mere country squire as my father had been. I could have done it, you see, so I thought he could. I loved court, I loved the excitement of London, the foods that could be got with ease there and nowhere else, the parties and the entertainments, the busy streets and all the sights and smells, but I would have traded it all to be with him, to live a life where he was with me each day, a life where he was safe. Then, all I wanted was Robert to be free of the threat of death, that was more important to me than anything… but not to him, not once he was free."

"I would love to live in the country again," said the younger me.

I stared out of the window for a moment. "I think that was why, when later I had need of him in a dark time and he was not there, it hurt so. It was not just vows sworn to love one another, to be there in sickness and health, but it was that I had aided him when he needed someone the most and he would not aid me when that time came for me. There was not even the most basic instinct of reciprocation, of repayment for all I had done for him. There was not the idea that even if he did not love me anymore he could be there for a friend who had been there for him when his dark times fell. He took, and gave nothing back. And it was the notion that I was only and ever supposed to be there for him without expecting anything in return that made me believe less in his love and then eventually, in the evidence to prove it was dead."

We watched as the days started to fly. For eighteen months he was a prisoner, for more than a year I was his visitor. He walked the flat roofs of the Beauchamp and Bell Towers as I kept our money in order. We had no estates of lands for a while, they had all been captured and taken by the Crown, when Warwick died. "I was often hard up for money," I said as we watched the days and nights turn and come about again. "My family sent me an allowance, they had to or I would have had nothing."

We watched as Robin carved his symbol of the oak spray into his prison walls as I bargained with men to keep us in coin. We had been married three years, and I was twenty-one years old, so young to have faced so much. I had no home, since Somerset House belonged to Robert's family no more, and we still had not inherited our estates of my father. It was my family who took care of me, since my husband could not. I lived at a town house in Camberwell, owned by the Appleyards, my mother's family of her first husband. My mother called on me to come home, but I wanted to stay as close to Robert as I could, so when Queen Mary allowed I could visit.

"He was the last of his family to be charged formally," I went on as time settled on one day, and I watched Robin listen to men who had come to see him, then he sat down, heavy and dull upon his stool. His face was blank with shock. "Not having proclaimed Jane Queen in the capital may have delayed his hearing, for his proclamation was not taken as seriously, it seemed. Yet eventually it came and he was found guilty of taking King's Lynn in a warlike manner, and of traitorously proclaiming Jane Grey Queen. On the 22nd of January 1554, he was marched through London to the Guildhall, and a formal sentence of execution for treason was made upon his name."

Chapter Six

Camberwell, town house of the Appleyard family

London

January 1554

Time flowed, like light it streamed past us. There were sounds, sights, amongst the myriad of colours and shapes that drifted past my open eyes. This time, as we came from it, it was like stepping through a waterfall so all is distorted, fragmented, then through the water comes the head and the world is there again. We were on a street. There was snow swept into banks on either side, dirty with mud and blood and piss and horse dung. The streets were cobbled, I knew it was London, and they were wet and dirty too. I sniffed and wrinkled my nose. Had I forgotten how ill the world could smell?

I watched my younger self come from a horse, jump down with ease from her saddle lined with brown velvet, and walk into a house I knew well, for I had stayed there much as I waited to see if Robin would die or live. Daintily I stepped over a puddle thick with floating hay and lingering ice, and into the house I went. "The world is a dirty place," I said with distaste as Death and I followed Amy into the house.

"I was much distracted at that time," I said, stepping through the dark doorway with Death before the servant closed it. Dark oak it was, heavy with iron bars over the front. It groaned, a sound my heart recognised, as it closed. Up the stairs went Amy, taking off her gloves, her wet riding cloak, as she climbed.

"I knew little of what was going on at court at this time," I said to Death as up the dim stairs we followed. The windows let in but little light. "I was taken up with fear for my husband, but there was much to hear of in between the times of terror. My cousins came to me for dinner some nights, and told me how Queen Mary was restoring the country to the Catholic faith, which many supported, and also to Rome, which fewer did. Many wanted the old ways of faith returned, but they did not want to lose their new lands, or other privileges, and few wanted to send English money out of the country into the hands of Rome. And then there was Elizabeth. Mary did not like that her sister, born of the body of Anne Boleyn and a known Protestant, was her successor. Elizabeth tried to slip through the cracks often enough, but eventually she had to hear Mass of a Catholic fashion, had to attempt to pretend she was of that faith, for it was rumoured Mary would have her head otherwise."

We went into the house with the younger me, followed her through the gloomy hallways to the upstairs rooms. "Watch that board," I said to Death. "It always creaked and there was woodworm in it, so I thought I might go through it." I smiled as polite Death actually walked around it. As I had said it I realised there was nothing he could do to that board to make a foot go through it, we were shades passing through memories, and he was Death, a being of the lightest foot.

"Mary wanted a child, but we all thought it was too late for her, and when that failed she tried to dilute the threat of her sister by marriage, and how many names we heard for whom Elizabeth would wed! The list was dazzling, and there were many rumours she would be sent out of the country, but somehow she evaded each plot and proposal. People said Phillip, the King of Spain and King Consort of England was sweet on his younger sister-in-law, and hoped if Mary passed sooner rather than later, he might get to wed one sister after another. That was what people said, but I knew not if it was true. Elizabeth had once sworn to Robin that she would never marry, and although if any other woman said it, it would seem impossible, it did not with her."

I watched the younger Amy stand at the window and sigh. She threw her wet gloves on the wooden window seat, and her maid snatched them up; there was a cushion there she did not want tarnished with a water stain. There was an expression in Amy's eyes I knew well, for I remembered seeing it each morning in my polished mirror of copper. It was both a willingness to accept Robin's death if it came, and an unwillingness to allow it to happen. I was so trapped then, so bound to his fate. Robin was an anchor holding me fast to the bottom of the sea.

I looked around from the window, and I was in the Tower again.

"She will not accept this man. Princess Elizabeth said to me she had no wish to ever wed," Robin told another me in the Tower. "We were eight, and her stepmother Catherine Howard, her own kinswoman, had just died on the block. I think that was what led her tongue, but unless she plans to become a nun I do not see how she will avoid the married state."

"It is not so bad a one to be in," young Amy said.

"That you say this, even now as all things are so dark, is a wonder to me," he told me. "You always know how to find the brightness in life, Amy, even when there is none to be had."

"There is always some to be had. I am here, with you, and you are here too. That is a good thing."

"Where we are is not a good thing."

"We are alive, and as long as we are alive there is hope," young Amy said. "So I rejoice in the knowledge of life, and of both of us living, and as for the situation, all things change."

"Let us hope they do not change this situation for one more public and with more blood to be seen," said Rob, wryly.

"All I could see then were his troubles," I said to Death. "Yet others were having more, some worse and some less. It is always the way. We look at the lives of others and think them so controlled, so tranquil, so much more advanced or better than ours, and we do not see the truth, that there are struggles everywhere."

"Or you see the opposite," said Death, standing before Robin's fire so he was silhouetted in red, a shadow standing before the light. "You watch the struggles of beggars and poor people and think yourselves better than they, for they are worse off, yet it takes only one slip and any man may fall so low as they."

"That is probably why many turn their eyes from the poor," I said. "For fear that they may look into their eyes and see a fate so easily granted to them. What does it take, after all? A year of poor luck? The decision to support one powerful faction over another? The loss of a harvest? We fear such people, for we could become them."

"Disgust often has a bare and fruitful root in the soul of the one who expresses it," agreed Death.

"No one liked Mary marrying Phillip, all of England was disgusted about that," I went on. "His envoy was pelted with snowballs as he rode through London. Jane Grey and Guildford had gone to their deaths, and after that Elizabeth was arrested and was too sent to the Tower. People said Queen Mary would kill her sister as her father had killed Elizabeth's mother, for Mary thought her sister involved in yet another rebellion, that of Wyatt and his men. Wyatt had wanted Edward Courtenay and Elizabeth to be wed and placed on the throne instead of Mary, and people said Elizabeth had agreed to the terms of the rebellion, had agreed to be a figurehead and that was why Mary arrested her, yet others doubted it. It was clear quite swiftly that there was little evidence when Elizabeth was questioned, and her being sent to the Tower was a poor move on Mary's part. The people loved Elizabeth, and I was starting to think my husband did too."

Another whirl of time, but only time, for we were still in the Tower when I looked, still in the same chamber. The bed was rumpled. We must have been together some time before this conversation.

"I have sent her a message of support," said Robin to the younger version of me sitting on a stool beside him.

"That is dangerous." I did not like it, the message or the tone of reverence he had for the Princess Elizabeth, for it was she to whom he had sent a message of support.

"I sent it via some children of the servants who clean my chambers, they will not betray me," he said, and smiled. He was holding my hand and I pulled it from his.

"That is even more dangerous," I said. He thought my anger was because of the message and means by which it was sent, but I was jealous, in truth. "Children might betray without meaning to, if an adult asks them they might tell!" I glared at him. "Promise me you will send no more messages to her! You are under threat of death and if found conspiring with another prisoner, who is also accused of treason, you will be judged guilty and they will kill you!"

"I cannot leave her so alone here, knowing myself what it is like," he said.

"You are alone, when I am here?"

He looked away, his brow showing anger. "You cannot know. You think this now is an insult to you that I say this, when I say I am alone and you cannot understand it, but you think of yourself, Amy. I am the one in prison, the one under arrest."

He was right, so I thought, and I watched myself rush to console him, hiding my jealousy of this Princess, this friend he spoke of with such a tone in his voice he might be thinking of an angel. Once his voice had rung like that for me, but now I was his wife, and wife is an ordinary state to be in.

"I hated her then," I confessed to Death. "Elizabeth even then was the untouchable woman, a princess, highly educated and beautiful and a virgin, as long as what she and her servants had protested after the Thomas Seymour affair was true. More than anything I *had* to hate her, for I could not hate my husband for admiring her, if I did that then I would have to blame him for something and I could not blame him for anything, not when he needed me so much, not when he was under threat of death. I thought it would make me a bad person to think ill of him then. No, it had to be she who became the object of my hatred, for she was all I wanted to be to him, and was not."

"Yet it was him you were in anger with."

"At times I could be angry with myself, that I was not enough. I, who had been here in all weathers and ridden all storms with him. I, who kept what money we had together, who came to the Tower I hated just to cheer him, who lived in the house of another person, so I never had a place of my own, just so I could be near him. I could have abandoned him when he was arrested, and no one would have thought too badly of me for it. He was a traitor after all. But I had not. People praised my wifely loyalty, but in truth it was for my heart as well as for him I stayed. I could not bear to think of a world without him."

Death took me to another day. Elizabeth was being freed, or freed from the Tower at least. This was when she was sent into house arrest at Woodstock. Mary sent her into the country, locked her away. I think she was trying to decide what to do with a sister so dangerous to her, one who supported the new faith, one who would return England to the rule of the monarch over faith if she inherited the throne.

Upstairs in the Beauchamp Tower, Rob watched Elizabeth walk out of her prison, her head high, and his hand was pressed to the window. When she looked up, he blew her a kiss.

"People said that was where their bond started," I told Death. "In the Tower, you hovering close to them, but it was not so. It began when they were children, their fates linked even then. I could never compete, you see? She was there first, and she was there after. I was just something that came along in between, and got in the way."

"She was not in your way, unless put there by your husband," said Death. "She had her own troubles."

"And five months after she was free, so was he," I said.

Chapter Seven

London

October 1554

We stood in a hallway, all of the Dudleys and their wives, black bands on our arms. "John," I said, watching the grim faces, the eyes that filled so easily with tears. The family, awkward in grief, stood near one another not knowing what to say. I, who never seemed to know what to say to the Dudleys, gazed at the floor.

It was out of compassion they were set free, all of the sons of Dudley left in the Tower. John was sick, and so as their mother and as we, their wives petitioned, Mary let them from the Tower to walk amongst the free again, but it was too late for John. He died four days after they walked free, but at least he died in his home and not in a cell in the Tower.

"My father died too that summer," I said. "He was far away from me, I never got to say goodbye. I was waiting for Robin to be released. At first Rob thought we would get the money and estates that were promised to me, but my father's will did not give that to me until my mother had too left life, and she was still with us." I shook my head in sadness. "Robin seemed more annoyed about that, than concerned I too had lost someone I had loved. He understood love for his own family, but he did not seem to understand it in others. He should be my first care, he thought, and in truth he was, but he never saw how losing my father hurt me. I tried so hard to be a rock at his side, to comfort him when his brother died, that he never saw my sorrow, my mourning." I looked away from him. "But I think he could have seen it, had he tried. He could have stood for me in strength as I did for him, but he did not seem to think that way. I was to give up all I had and was and felt, putting him first. There was never a time I came first. Perhaps that was the beginning of the rot that came to destroy us. I was never first, to him."

Time whirled as water blown in a pool and we came to Robin and me standing facing each other, our cheeks red but not with happiness of any kind.

"We have been fighting," I said. "We did that much more than I had thought we ever would, once he was free."

"You are being unreasonable!" Robin shouted at the younger me.

I shook my head. "I thought after he was free it would be different, that we would do as he said and go to the country and live, but all he wanted was a place at court. There was some sickness in him, to do as well as his father had, to rise as high. The more I mentioned living in peace elsewhere, in Norfolk, the more he became angry at me for it."

"But you said, you said we could go and live just as we should in the country!" the younger me was shouting as Death and I stood quietly at the edge of the chambers Robin and I had shared in London. Ambrose had offered him the rooms. It was not much, but we had so little it seemed like a lot to me then. "You said it would be so, that all we needed was each other!"

"We have nothing, how would we live?" Robin shouted back. "Your father put in his will that he will give us nothing until his wife dies, so we would live always dependent on others? Everything my father could have given is gone, and you brought precious little to me when we married."

I watched the girl I had been step back, stung by the viciousness in his voice. "You wanted to marry me for love," I said.

He laughed. Such a cruel sound, such a cruel thing to do at such a time. To laugh at my pain. That was the first time I saw contempt in his face when he looked at me.

We watched, Death and I, as Robin told the younger me why Warwick had allowed the match between us.

"Robin was a younger son," I said quietly to Death, watching him shout at me in the past, "the fifth son of the Dudleys, and so there were fewer lands for him than for his brothers. Men did not like to break up estates, so the lion's share always went to the eldest male heir. My father owned much property in Norfolk and further north, and it would all be left to me, therefore I was a good match in terms of awarding the son of Warwick estates in the future. I was beautiful and his son wanted me then, but Warwick was always a man with an eye on the end game. I could be advantageous in the future. He wanted to be great in the north, and Norfolk was its key. In truth a man who was secure in the north could command great power at court in the south. He wanted to rival and unseat the Howards, and this move, marrying his son to me, was a way to begin that. Robin would start to hold sway in Norfolk, then the north, through marriage to me, and in time the Dudleys would unseat the Howards there, and then no one would ever be able to contest their power. I did not know that when I married, did not know it until Robin shouted it in my face on this day. I thought love had been the thing to persuade Warwick, for Robin told me he had said he would accept no other but me as his bride, so if his father did not want him to become a monk, I would have to marry him."

We watched Robin storm from the chamber, leaving the me of the past to sit down, stunned and broken by his words, on a cushion by the fire.

"A few months after they walked free of the Tower, the remaining brothers were pardoned," I went on, "and their mother died the very next day. I think she lived just long enough to know they were as safe as she could make them, and then she surrendered the last of her strength.

"That winter they were back at court, and I was visiting too. Ambrose and Robert were in the jousting, heading the defenders against the Spanish lords who came with Phillip. The year after we were cast out, as Mary did not trust the sons of Warwick to be near her when she was in confinement, waiting for her first child. Then there was no child and it was safe to return.

"Rob was sent to join Phillip on the Continent, to serve him. It was a surprise, but it was a welcome one for him. I did not want to be separated, but…"

"You had an argument," said Death.

I nodded. "Yet another. He said it was a mistake to have married me. He could have done better, had it not been for his infatuation with me."

"And no sons!" Robin shouted at the Amy of the past in their London chambers again. "All this time and no children!"

"We have been together but rarely since you came from the Tower!"

I shook my head. "I think I knew then there was a problem."

We watched her shout that he was unfair, cruel to have mentioned their lack of children. Robin retorted she was unfair to him, for not providing him with heirs.

"After that he left," I said. "He carried messages for Phillip, delivered letters. Sometimes he was sent back to England to give them to Mary and we would meet, but the rot had begun. We had little that was our own. The sons of Warwick were still under attainder, and so we could not inherit the property of the family. I had to rely on my own family to aid me.

"Rob had small choice but to accept the post with Phillip. We had nothing to live on, and he had to farm his wife out like a sheep to a green pasture to feed me. In 1555 Ambrose made a deal that gave Rob land and money, it was something, but we had to settle the debts of his mother and make payments for the house, Hales Owen, to his uncle and Ambrose. We never lived there, I do not think we even visited the house, but it was enough property to borrow money against. We could have lived fairly happily, but it was not enough for Robin. He wanted more of life than the life he had told me we would have."

I looked at Death. "He said he wanted children, but he was rarely in England then. When he came home sometimes he had the time to see me, but it was little more than a night here or there, and then he was gone again and I was staying at the house of another relative, or friend. I never had a base that was mine. I became used to telling people he was away, working for his Queen and her husband, and I missed him. I did, but in truth I came to feel lonelier when he returned."

Chapter Eight

Somerset House

London

March 1557

"We have moved some years," I said as we wandered into a chamber in a grand house I knew well. Once it had been the house of my father-in-law. Somehow I knew it was not anymore.

Something caught my eye, something that had been encroaching little by little each time we travelled. When we stepped to a new place, a new time, it was as though I could look back and see a glimpse of another place. Gossamer and glistening, there was a film to its surface, like water glimmering in a pond, so I could not see fully inside, but it seemed like a chamber crafted of the most delicate of spider web, not fearsome but soft and silver, a dim light shining inside. Shadows moved within, grey and graceful, and something in me wanted to reach out a hand and touch that silver skin of a place just beyond my reach. I turned from it, and felt it tug upon my soul, not insistent but urging, tempting me to come to it, as I wanted to. I stepped away, and I felt a jolt of sadness as the world of spider web and soft pearly light slipped away from me.

"You did as you said in those years between Robin being set free, and these years," said Death, seeming to note nothing of my distraction with the other place. "You were sad and you missed him, you told lies for him and you carried on."

"I learned to draw in those years, I may claim that as something I did," I said. "I went to talks and listened to worthy men argue about faith and politics, I went to gatherings in London and I danced. Sometimes I would go to a house of a cousin or friend for dinner, and come home late at night, my head full of wine. Sometimes I wept and sometimes I laughed. Often, I felt alone, but sometimes I was with people I would call friends. But you are right, I do not want to see those years again. They were sad ones."

"But much started to occur, as the end of Mary's reign approached."

"None of us knew it was the end then," I said.

We walked past people talking. On a visit to England that year, Phillip brought with him two female cousins, the Duchesses of Parma and Lorraine, and although it was not necessarily unusual for an entourage to come with a king or prince when travelling, their presence was much commented on, and wondered at. Royal men usually travelled with noble men, and aside from wives or mistresses, women had little place in the upper ranks of male royal households. Phillip's mixed party was unusual.

"The arrival in England of the Duchess of Lorraine was commented on much behind the velvet sleeves of court, for she had once been Christina, Princess of Denmark and then by marriage Duchess of Milan, widowed at the age of only thirteen." I smiled. "When Henry VIII was seeking a wife after the death of Edward's mother, Jane Seymour, he had seen a portrait of fair Christina, and had become much enamoured of her pale beauty. He had sent Ambassadors to woo the Princess for her hand in marriage, but Christina, then a young widow of sixteen years, made clear that she was much opposed to the match; in the courts of Christendom it was already widely whispered that the English King had a habit of mistreating his wives."

I chuckled. "Christina was obviously not given much to subtlety in her youth as she refused the King, saying that if she had two heads, then *one* would surely be at the disposal of His Majesty of England. This rude refusal of his hand greatly embarrassed old Copper-Nose Harry, but this did not stop him continuing to pursue the match for over a year."

We wandered from the house and into the street. "I remember it being said that Phillip tried often to bring the Duchesses into Princess Elizabeth's company, as if wanting the women to be seen together. It was odd, and many wondered what it was he was up to."

"He wants the Princess to wed his stooge, Emmanuel Philibert," I heard a woman say in the market as Death and I stood, listening to the living of the past as they gossiped. Maids bustled about with trays held to their fronts, supported by rope about the back of their necks, selling hot pies and cool ale. Merchants were hawking their goods and silk rustled in the breeze on stalls where faded, patched gowns, worn many times by a first owner, were sold to another. The light of the outside burst upon my eyes, and my eyes seemed fragile suddenly. The light pained them. I remembered the cool quiet of the soft silver world I had seen, and knew it would be easier on my eyes than this place. I stepped back into the shadow of a house overhanging the road, to listen.

"He wants her out of England," said a man, "and the Queen too wants the same. They fear her."

"Bless little Elizabeth!"

"I often wondered how she escaped," I said to Death. "It seemed so sure she would be sent away, married off, and I was a little relieved, thinking Robin's obsession with her would end, but then the match fizzled."

Death pointed. We were at court, and two figures were sitting opposite each other, playing cards. Phillip and Elizabeth. He was asking her if she had had a chance to consider the match with Philibert.

"I have thought on it, Your Majesty," said the Princess.

Fascinated, I walked to her. She was young then, twenty-three perhaps, and her red hair was so bright. Even under a hood it shone. She was dressed in green and white, her Tudor colours again. Every time Phillip looked up, his eyes became a little unfocussed. I wondered if he was thinking what she would look like without those clothes upon her. There was attraction in his eyes, and he did little to conceal it.

"He was handsome," I said, regarding his strong, if slightly long, jaw, his dark eyes and hair.

"Have you reached a conclusion?" Phillip asked his sister-in-law.

She looked at him, and I was surprised to see how soft his face became as their eyes met. "There were always rumours," I said. "But I never believed them."

"Rumours of?" asked Death, coming to my side.

"That they were lovers, and he hoped to marry her after Mary, to gain the throne again."

"As ever with humans, part of that belief may be true," he said, and pointed.

"I still feel, Your Majesty," the Princess ventured, "as though I am too young to marry."

"Therefore," he said quickly, "you should be advised by those who want the best for you. The Queen and I have more worldly experience than you; perhaps you should allow yourself to be guided by us."

"I have not even seen a portrait of this prince you propose for me," she faltered. "I know not what he may be like in person or in character. Although others give good report, how am I to know what manner of man I pledge my life to?"

"Royal marriages are often made so, my lady," Phillip shrugged. "But I can arrange for a portrait to be brought to you so you might look on his face. I am surprised Her Majesty did not offer to show you one herself. Philibert is a most handsome prince and a fine general; you would be married to a strong and worthy man."

"There are other men, who could also be worthy… *more* worthy," she said quickly, then, dropped her eyes suddenly to her cards. He looked sharply at her, but Elizabeth was rearranging the cards in her hand as though fascinated by the game.

"She always was the cleverest person in any room," I said, watching her eyes, then looking to Phillip's. "Look how she has him captivated now!"

"There are?" Phillip asked, his voice harsh with a tinge of jealousy. He thought she wanted another. "Know you of any such, my lady?"

Elizabeth's dark eyes met his and I saw him take in a little breath. Her eyes were vastly pretty, one of her best features and she never had been a conventional beauty. But her eyes, they had magic in them.

"Although I have been kept much from the company of men, much in seclusion, I feel as though there may well be a man that is worthy of my hand." She cast her eyes downwards. "But I fear…"

"What do you fear?" His voice had become gruff, and he leaned forwards, eyes intent on her face.

"He is starting to understand what she is suggesting and is interested by it," I said. "He desires her, an attractive and intelligent princess was not so easy to find no matter what the poets said, and she offers him another chance at the throne. Power, position and desire." I shook my head. "Robin was right to admire her. There was no one like her."

"You do not think badly of her, playing him?"

I shrugged. "He was playing her too. Men resent when women play the game, only more so when they play it better, yet they made all the rules. If they are beaten they protest, but the game was of their making. I see that only clearer now. She did not want to leave England, did not want to be married off to a man she loved not who would control her. If I was her, I might have done as she did." I paused. "In truth, I was played into marriage. She tries to play to avoid it. If she did better than me, I can only admire it. I think she saw the world with more clarity than the rest of us."

"I fear," Elizabeth was saying in a faltering voice, "...I fear that I may have already seen the man I should wish to marry, and yet he does not see me."

"How could anyone not see you, my Lady Elizabeth?" Phillip asked, leaning forwards intently and for once, past the courtier's appearance, there shone the heart of a man who was truly infatuated with the woman in front of him.

"Your answer brings me hope." She smiled warily. "But if that hope is yet to remain, then any talk of marriage, such as this proposal to Prince Philibert, would have to be abandoned. I would hope, I would wait given only very little faith to survive on, if there was a chance for something... *greater* for me, in the future."

He looked at her carefully. I could hear his mind clicking like a clock. If she was kept unmarried, doors would be open to him back into England upon the death of her sister. But could he trust that she meant what she said? It was a gamble, but Phillip was a man who enjoyed a fine bet.

Elizabeth took a ring, a little diamond set in gold, from her finger and slipped it into his hand. "For friendship," she whispered, "and to remind you of the promise that the future might bring, for both of us."

He took the little ring. It fitted on none of his fingers, so he slipped it into a link on one of the many golden chains that hung from his neck, and kissed it. Then he unhooked a brooch from his chest, a crest of his house made in gold over the polished sphere of a sapphire. It was a thing of beauty, and high value. Quietly he handed it to her. "For friendship," he replied warmly, "and for the *fulfilment* of promises."

I laughed, I could not help it. Phillip did not entirely trust her, and nor should he, but she had won. Death looked at me a while, and I thought I could see him smiling too.

Chapter Nine

Whitehall Palace

June 1557

"By that summer, the true purpose of those elegant ladies who accompanied Phillip to England that year became clear," I said to Death as we walked in the Whitehall gardens. "Elizabeth found out through the network of informers of the French Ambassador Noailles, who was happy to keep her informed, and we knew of what was going on because Elizabeth had ways to let such secrets slip to the public, when it was to her advantage."

"You are right," said Death. "It was Elizabeth's lady Bess Brooke who brought his warnings to her. One day as she walked in these gardens the Ambassador came upon Bess as though by accident." He extended a hand and I gazed across the knot gardens to see the Ambassador loitering. Clearly he was waiting for someone, although he made a good play of examining each and every flower in the gardens. He settled by the roses, glancing occasionally at the grey skies with the foreboding of one who senses the dampness of rain soon to fall.

"The years of Queen Mary's reign were unusually wet and grey," I said as we stood, watching the Ambassador. "Rain fell through the summer and the people whispered that God caused rain to fall so often on England to quench the fires that burned the flesh of Protestants caught and executed by Mary, her Bishop Bonner, her Cardinal Pole and her Council. God wept, the people said, spoiling the harvests to demonstrate His displeasure at the Queen's fires of faith. Elizabeth had many people looking to her for some hope for the future, for it felt then that we had none in the present."

As Bess wandered in the gardens, the Ambassador finally left his roses and crossed her path. Noailles suggested she show him the rose gardens for which Whitehall was famed, the very ones he had just lingered at and therefore knew were clear of other ears which might hear what he had to tell her. Stopping to admire the beauty of the early budding flowers and their subtle fragrance, the Ambassador passed on a grave warning about the actual purpose that those two Hapsburg cousins of Phillip's had been brought to undertake. We watched as Bess's face turned to horror and she all but ran to her mistress through the gardens, through the long halls of court. Quicker than the breeze, we followed her as she flew to Elizabeth.

"They are here to offer a disguise, of a kind," Bess whispered to Elizabeth breathlessly, within the confines of the Princess's chambers. Another of Elizabeth's women was there too, Anne Calthorp, Duchess of Sussex. "A front of respectability for a plot that Phillip hatched before he came."

"The Duchess of Sussex was an interesting woman," I mentioned to Death. "As unconventional a woman as she was unconventional a noble; once part of the inner *salon* of Queen Katherine Parr, Anne, to the horror of her husband, a pious Catholic, turned to the Protestant religion during the reign of Henry VIII. There were rumours that she also dabbled in the arts of magic and sorcery, although so often when women are but outspoken and self-assured, rumours spread about them having demonic powers. It is more often than not a way to discredit them in the eyes of the world." Death nodded. "If I remember right, Anne's husband had at this time managed, with great difficulty, to divorce her on the grounds that she was '*unnatural*'." I shrugged. "Which I suppose would mean anything men want, since they are allowed to decide what makes a woman natural."

"And the plot itself?" Elizabeth was asking, her tone measured and slow.

"If you were not amenable to the marriage with Prince Philibert, my lady, Phillip would take you prisoner, abduct you, ship you abroad secretly to some stronghold of the Hapsburgs and therein have you married to his lapdog by force."

Elizabeth paled. Phillip had come to these lands determined to take her as a vassal for Spain in one way or another. He was truly a ruthless man at heart. "I would rather die!" she cried loudly. Bess and Anne looked about, fearing the Princess should be heard. "And *that* you can return word for word to the Ambassador," Elizabeth spat.

"She was justified only more so to play Phillip," I said to Death. "He would abduct her, have her raped by a forced husband? That man deserved to be duped in all ways."

"The English people would never stand for such, my lady," said Bess. "There would be open war against the Queen, if not with Spain, too."

Elizabeth nodded, but her face was pale. With courage she lifted her chin.

Anne shook her head, looking concerned. "I doubt that the truth of any abduction would be discovered, before they had forced Your Highness to marry their man," whispered Anne carefully. "We should take this warning with all due consideration and seriousness. You must never be put in a position where it could come to fruition, my lady."

"I believe the risk to be small," Elizabeth said, taking care to control her fear. "But we will also keep in mind your warnings, Anne. Send secret word to Cecil and to Parry of this plot that they may keep watch on it, and mention too that if I am suddenly gone or they hear naught from me, then this is what may have happened. Get them to keep a close eye on

Spanish vessels or merchant ships at the ports. Should it come to be that I am abducted, I will be expecting a rescue before I have left the sands of the English shore." She nodded to her women. "Thank God for all your work for me, ladies. I am well served in my house."

"We want nothing more than to serve you, my lady," said Anne fervently. "You are our greatest care in this world. When we were most in need you took us into your house and gave us the protection of your grace; these are not things one easily forgets."

"Indeed not," said Bess. "You opened your home and family to us, my lady. We are ever in your debt."

Elizabeth reached out and took a hand from each of them. Tears stood in her eyes.

"She always knew how to make people love her," I observed. "I suppose I never had the chance to see it until now, for Robin kept me away from court so much. She made people love her, because she loved them."

"And as she showed love, her sister entered war," said Death.

I nodded. "It was around then that the French brought England into a war that Mary's Council had previously declared our country would never fight."

The war between France and Spain had begun, as most wars do, over lands and territories. In 1551, France had declared war upon Spain for control and possession of Italy, since whoever controlled that territory would also dominate the affairs of Europe. Both France and Spain had hereditary claims to Italy, and both had fought over her in the past. Until this time, the terms of Mary's marriage had kept England a neutral party in the wars on the continent, but then, in 1557, the French struck at England and drew her into war.

"I always thought it a clumsy thing, the reason we entered war," I said as we wandered around Mary's Council chamber, the members there arguing about the conflict they had reluctantly entered. I watched a man slam his hand on the table in frustration, but oddly I felt most disconnected to his anger. "Perhaps thinking they should rattle England before she entered the war as Spain's ally, the French sent Sir Thomas Stafford, an English traitor to the Crown, with a volley of men to ruffle the feathers of the English Queen. Stafford's mother had been Lady Ursula Pole, so he was therefore a cousin of the odious Cardinal Pole, Mary's most beloved papal legate. Stafford had been involved with the rebellion of Wyatt, and had been much opposed to Mary's match with Spain. When the Wyatt rebellion failed, Stafford had been captured and imprisoned in the Fleet prison, but he bribed his guards to grant him freedom and escaped to France. A known intriguer with other English exiles of Mary's reign, Stafford was a prime candidate for bringing unrest to England once more."

About the table we walked, watching men turn quiet and some turn red and purple of face as the fighting went on.

"Stafford and his men reached English shores under cover of darkness and they took Scarborough Castle with but a small force. Stafford marched most bravely into the largely unprotected castle and declared himself 'Protector of the Realm', calling on honest Englishmen to join him in rebellion against Mary to return the power of the Crown 'to the true English blood of our own natural country'." I shrugged. "I suppose he meant Elizabeth? Perhaps even the Poles since they had royal blood in their line. People had started to see Mary as Spanish, especially since she wed Phillip. They had once spoken of her as a daughter of England, but the moment she started doing things they liked not, she was born of another country."

"Your kind are prone to do such things," said Death. "You like the faults of your race to be amongst those of other countries, and the virtues to belong to your own kingdom." He ran a hand over the table about which the men still argued. "It is an interesting fiction, made only more fantastic by your ideas that countries exist."

"Countries do not exist?" I asked.

"Land exists, there is land and there is water, but countries are created by men who drew lines on paper. They are a fiction, a means to divide your one race into many. How often have thousands have been killed, just so a man can erase one line and draw another? A meandering line of ink is, I have often thought, a poor reason to sacrifice so many."

I frowned at that notion. "Stafford and his men were quickly overcome," I went on, needing more time to make sense of what Death had told me. "It took the Earl of Westmorland and his men only three days to take back the castle and place Stafford and his men under arrest for treason. The men of England had not risen to the call of Stafford to arms and to rebellion; they had seen what happened to the last rebels against Mary's reign. The English were becoming inactive with fear for what their Queen would do to those who opposed her. The burnings of Protestants and hideous torment and executions of rebels to the Crown were, it seemed, a constant sight during Mary's reign, and although the people of England had ever seen a trip to public executions as a fine day out in the last reign, they were becoming sickened by the constant and unrelenting stream of deaths which seemed to emanate from Queen Mary's skeletal hands.

"Stafford and thirty-two of his followers were executed for treason that May. Stafford went to the block and lost his head for his failed invasion of England, his men were not so lucky. Base-born and lacking noble blood, they hung from the neck until their eyes bulged from their heads, their legs kicking in desperation, then they were freed from the rope only to endure the extraction of their entrails before them, and finally the sweep of the axe which brought blessed death."

At that, I again had the impression Death smiled.

"The Queen had had enough of mercy to those who opposed her," I said as I looked up to see we were amongst a crowd. We watched Stafford's head fall and the crowd let out a low cheer. It sounded more like a grumble. "Even though this 'invasion' of England was quashed quickly, the threat was such that Mary and her Council spat defiance in the face of the King of France, and declared war on his country, joining their forces to those of Spain. It was foolish of France to have acted so rashly."

I paused as we watched them haul Stafford's body away. There was that silver-soft light again, a lustrous white blaze glimmering near the scaffold where he had died. For a moment it was there, like a haze of heat shimmering over a cobbled street in summer, and then it was gone.

"I could not help but wonder if somewhere, somehow, Phillip had been at the back of some plot to encourage this reckless act of Stafford's," I mentioned to Death as we watched the crowds at Stafford's execution file away. "I thought it at the time, and mentioned it to Rob when he came to see me on one of his trips home. He said Phillip would not have acted so, there was too much risk, but it was of much advantage for Phillip to have another ally in the war, and France must have known that sending such a small invading force was at best a gamble. Was it too much to think that perhaps Phillip's own men, working covertly in France, might have engineered this platform from which England was launched into war?"

"I do not think it unreasonable," said Death. "Men have done more for less gain."

"I thought so too. Although the marriage contract between Phillip and Mary stipulated that England would not be encumbered to take part in any Spanish war, England went to war. Having achieved at least one of the objectives he set himself when he came to England, Phillip announced he was once again leaving for Spain, and then for his armies, to lead them in battle against the French."

"And your husband was to join him."

I nodded. "Rob thought it the fastest way to recapture the complete trust of the Crown, and his fortunes," I said. "I begged him not to go. All that time in the Tower, all I had wanted was for him to be safe, and now he was to use his freedom to go to war?" I shook my head. "His brothers, too, wanted to go. They all had ideas of glory in their heads, and rich rewards afterwards. There was no telling them no, even if I had had that power. No woman may command her husband."

I put my fingers to the bridge of my nose. Even thinking about Rob's resolution now made my head hurt. "Less than a month after Phillip's ship sailed for his homeland, Mary announced once more that she was pregnant," I went on. "It was another of those times when people said the end had come, and I thought it might be so, for Robin was set on going to war."

Chapter Ten

Whitehall Palace and

Hatfield House

July 1557

"If I can prove myself in war, our fortunes may be restored," Robin said to another Amy.

I watched a younger me try to point out that he could die, leaving no fortune and no future for us, but to no avail. He had brought me to the palace, a rare occurrence since I had no position there, to say goodbye to me.

"Protesting more would not have done any good anyway," I mentioned to Death. "Queen Mary ordered us to war, so the men were to war. There was nothing I could say that would avert a royal command, even if any of my words had succeeded in stopping my husband charging into the fray."

As the forces of England followed the armies of Spain out to France, we watched my husband ride out to meet another woman. "He told me he was going to her," I said as we appeared at Hatfield. "But he said it was just to bid the heir to the throne a goodbye, a formality, he said, nothing more. I did not know it was a significant moment."

"You never knew, for he did not tell you," said Death. "But your lack of knowledge does not mean this was not an important moment in your story." He was standing near a crop of lavender, and as his cape brushed close to the rough stalks the purple flowers bloomed brighter. I gazed at the plant with shock and I had the impression he was smiling again. "It is not only humans who feel more alive, the closer they are to Death," he said.

To the doorway we walked, and stood under the arch. It was a normal enough July day for England during the time of Mary's reign; heavy rain pelted the earth, the world was wet and heavy, grey and brown and drab.

"The gentle summers of England deserted us in Mary's sovereignty," I said, "and all there was about us was the constant pounding of rain on the roof above our head, a lather of seas of mud on the roads. Riding had become more and more difficult, the roads through and about London more and more impassable, even for the fine horses of the royal stables. It was hard to gain messages that summer, easy to feel cut off."

There was no one outside the house Robin rode up to. The Princess and her women were inside. I saw a face at the window, a woman peeking. It was Elizabeth herself, peeking at Robin just as I had when he had come to my father's house. "Were any of us not fools for him?" I asked Death, feeling weary rather than angry.

He did not answer, but we followed Robin in, through the halls to where Anne, Elizabeth's woman, greeted him at the door. There was a cheeky grin on her face as she told her mistress who had come to see her that wet day. "What is it, Anne?" Elizabeth asked. "Why do you look like the child who found the cakes hid for Christmas night?"

Anne's smirk broke into a smile and she curtseyed. "How well you read me, Your Highness!" She beamed. "You have a visitor."

"Who calls?"

"A gentleman who says I am to convey all greetings of grace to you, my lady," she said, grinning. "And who asks also if you have ever had cause to wonder if the life of a pirate would have been preferable to that of a princess?"

For a moment the Princess stared blankly, and then she smiled. It was all an act. She knew who had come. "What does he look like now?" the Princess asked, her voice low. A little smile played on her lips. It hurt, that smile, her enjoyment of knowing she was important to men, in one way or another, her pleasure that he had come specially to visit her.

"A *fine* man," Anne replied warmly. There was admiration in her voice.

"A fine man, indeed? Well it is for certain that he has made an impression on my ladies. Let not your head be turned by a handsome face, Anne." There was a little edge to her voice of reprimand. "I need you looking in the right direction at all times, not distracted by a pretty visage."

"No, of course, my lady." Anne bobbed eagerly on her heels. "Will you receive him?"

"He was released from the Tower, then?" Elizabeth asked. "I had not heard such."

"Another lie," I said. "She must have known. She would have heard."

"She always preferred not to divulge all that was in her mind," said Death.

"Many have been released on whom the suspicion of treason was growing old, my lady," Anne was busily gushing. "They have been given the chance to fight for England, against France in the coming wars and redeem their honour in that manner."

Elizabeth looked sad a moment, probably at the thought of Robin going to war along with all the other men. One thing I knew of this woman was that she loved her countrymen deeply. "I will receive him," she commanded. "I am interested to know what the years have done to him. Bring him in."

As Anne bustled out to collect my husband, Elizabeth stood up and straightened her gown, pinched some blood into her cheeks. She looked excited. How well I remembered feeling that way for him.

After a few minutes, in walked Robert.

He bowed to Elizabeth, a deep and long bow that spoke volumes of his respect for her. When he straightened, she nodded to him, and took a long look at the man before her.

He had outgrown his boyhood for certain in the Tower. Twenty-four years old or so he was, and a handsome man. Gone were the dangling limbs and clumsiness of youth, gone even was the boyish plumpness that had still been on his cheeks on the day we married. I had fallen in love with a boy, but it was a man who presented himself to Elizabeth Tudor that day.

He was more handsome now, with those dark and sparkling eyes, cheeks flushed from riding, and he possessed a powerful figure that stood a fair shoulder and head above the Princess. In the first two years out of the Tower he had often looked pale, wan, but by this time he had regained his strength. The dark hair on his head was thick and curled a little near his neck. His beard was short and fashionable, trimmed to accentuate a strong jaw. His face was just simply the most handsome I had ever seen, on any man. And I knew I was not the only one to think so.

Elizabeth was talented at hiding her emotions, but I could see how deeply she was attracted to him. I doubt he realised. Men always think that women they desire must be playing them, they never really believe they adore them. "As for women who do care for them, they do not care for those women," I said aloud. "What is the challenge in winning something already won?"

"Not all men, even in your time, think so."

"But enough did, and the only man who mattered for me did," I said. "And once wed to him, what was I to do? I could not leave him, though he was leaving me, a little every day. I could not divorce, for I would never marry again, and it was a rare thing if women could find a reason to separate from a husband. Men could lock wives away or beat them, they could take a thousand lovers and sire as many bastards, but women could not even talk to other men alone without it being suspect, and then have their names cast down for all time." I shook my head. "I was wed to the man I loved, and he would have been enough for me, but once wed there was nothing I could do to replace him without risking everything I had. Believe me, had the option been open, I would have looked elsewhere for a man who could have been satisfied with me and I with him, but I had not that option. Marriage tied me and it chained me. There was no escape for me." I turned to watch Robin and Elizabeth.

"My Lady Elizabeth," he said, bowing again.

"My Lord Dudley," she said eventually. "Seeing you has brought all manner of memories to my mind. I find myself quite lost in the past."

He smiled, a charming, easy, warm smile, and a faintly mischievous one. Elizabeth could not help but smile back at him. "I hope they were pleasant memories, Your Highness?" he asked.

Her smile clouded. "Some were, my lord. Some… were less so."

"I believe I may guess which were less so." He tucked his lips together in sympathy. "You have faced much hardship since we talked as children together in the gardens of your brother, my lady."

"And do you still hate Cicero as once you did?" She was smiling.

"You remember." He seemed so pleased that he quite forgot his formal addresses to her, but she did not mind. "So much time has passed since then that I wondered if you would remember such a slight conversation from so long ago."

She laughed. "It was a memorable conversation, my lord. Did you not swear that you would make me a pirate queen some day?"

Robert laughed. His was a good laugh, deep and rich; it bounced from the walls. "I hope you will forgive that boyish comment now, Your Highness," he pleaded. "One feels that such a path is not necessarily the one either of us would take now."

"No?" She smiled impishly.

He raised his eyebrows. "Perhaps we can always keep it as an option, my lady," he said, "for the future."

"He speaks to her as though they had long and ever been good friends," I said in a whisper. "They had not seen each other for years."

"There are some who are like that," said Death. "People who may be parted long, yet come together as if only a day had passed."

"With me, he was awkward when we had been separated."

"As you were with him."

I sighed impatiently, looking away. Death was all too reasoned and reasonable for my liking.

"For the future," Elizabeth repeated, nodding, "but what now of the present? My ladies tell me that you are shortly to depart for France to fight in the war?"

"Her Majesty's Grace has allowed me to prove my worth, and my loyalty, by joining the war," he said earnestly. "I long for the honour to fight for her, and for my country."

"And your purse," I added with scorn. Death let out a noise that made me look up. It sounded like a cough, but I believed it was a chuckle.

"You are not worried that you may not return?" Elizabeth asked. "Many do not return from wars, however loyal they may be to their queen and country."

He smiled again. I could see in his eyes there was a thirst for battle, for action. After all, he was a young man, and most young men dream of such foolish things. "After so long spent in a prison, my lady," he said, "I relish the feel of the free air on my face, whatever Fate may hold in store for me."

"I understand that well enough, my lord," she muttered quietly, no doubt thinking of the day she herself was released from the Tower of London.

He bowed, his face suddenly concerned. "I would not have wished to bring memories to you that would cause sadness, my lady. All England must praise the day that the Lady Elizabeth, by the grace of God, walked free from suspicion of treason and returned to the favour of Her Majesty."

"Most carefully said," I said.

"I remember such a time, however," the Princess said, "when I was much without friends, and yet another prisoner, shut away from the world as I was, importuned me to remember that *many in this country love her.*"

I shook my head. "*That* was his message?" I demanded of Death. "Did you bring me here to make me angrier?"

"You asked to know the truth," said Death.

I turned from his dark gaze and glared at my husband.

"It is still true, my lady, that many love you," Robert was murmuring softly to his Elizabeth.

She nodded. "I remember well my friends, Robin Dudley. And a friend of but fair weather is not one I value. Luckily, God has granted me much foul weather in this life, so that I might see who are my friends in truth. I do not forget my friends, if they do not forget me."

Robin smiled and bowed again. He was bobbing up and down like an apple in a pond. "I too have known much of the storm. But I had a flame on which to fix my eyes, and her light was what saw me through."

I wanted to look away, to look away for I knew that I, who had been there through all of that time, was not the light he spoke of. But I could not look away. He stopped his mouth and locked his dark eyes to those of the Princess. Elizabeth almost blushed, so intense was the meeting of their eyes. "My eyes are still locked on this light," he said. "So you see, I cannot fail, nor fall, for soon she will become a light for all, to lead us from the darkness."

For a moment they did little but stare at each other.

"I wish you good fortune in the battles which are to come, my lord," the Princess murmured eventually. "And with the grace of God, will pray for your safe return."

He bowed. "There is no man in France, Spain or England who could prevent my eventual return to these shores, my lady," he said boldly. "And when I do, I would like to petition for a place in the household of Your Highness. Whilst now, treason still clouds the name of Dudley, I hope to prove my loyalty to Her Majesty the Queen, and come home to take a position in the house of her loyal royal sister."

I smiled bitterly. "So that was the purpose of this meeting, was it? He was there to secure his career? Another man full of promises for the future. If Mary would never promote him far, her sister might. I suddenly wonder how truthful all this flirting was."

Elizabeth did not seem to care, however, for she laughed suddenly. "Done!" the Princess exclaimed gaily. "Done, my Lord Dudley! Go and array yourself with honours on the battlefields of France, and when you are returned, should my sister allow such, I will have a place waiting for you in my household."

He dropped to one knee before her. Elizabeth held out her elegant, long-fingered hand for him to kiss. "Your position will see us evened, my lord. A position in my household as payment for the comfort of a message, sent to a princess in the Tower, long ago," she said as he rose.

"Nay, my lady." He shook his head. "That message was my payment to *you* for the comfort you brought to me as a prisoner, given when I looked from my window each day in the very depths of despair and misery, watching a beautiful woman light up the darkness of hell." He kissed her hand again. "You gave me hope then, where there had been none."

"It would seem then, that you are further in my debt, Robin Dudley," she teased. "You will have to work hard to see these lines of credit balance."

He smiled. "One day I will repay all that Your Highness has bestowed on me, that I swear."

"Did you bring me here to hate him more, and so make leaving life easier?" I asked, rounding on Death.

"You asked for truth, and I offer it. I told you that you would not like it."

"All that time I was going to him, thinking of him, worrying for him, trying to bring him hope and love, lying with him in his rotten bed in the Tower and he was thinking of her?!"

I stared into the distance, not wanting to look at Elizabeth and my husband, still rapt in each other's conversation. "Later that week, he went out to France to join the armies of England," I said in a numb voice. "The fight had begun. England lifted her head, and roared into war."

I looked at Death. "And that roar swift became a whimper."

Chapter Eleven

Whitehall Palace

London

Late Winter 1558

We stood outside the door to the chambers of the Queen, that much I knew by the wall hangings, but it was dark, quiet, gloomy in a way. "1558," Death said, answering my silent question. "Whitehall."

I looked from a window to see winter, late and white, on the ground. "Early 1558," I said, glancing at Death for confirmation and he nodded.

"Almost we have our Elizabeth," I said. "That is what everyone called her, as though she belonged to each of us."

"Then, you did not know that time was close."

"We all knew Mary was not well." I nodded at the figure of Elizabeth who entered through a door and there stood, apparently composed, with her hands behind her back. The door to the Queen's inner chambers was closed, and so she waited. The room was dim, with few candles or lamps and it was outrageously warm, even for winter when the palaces were well kept with fires in every hearth. Yet sweat that was not entirely of the room's heat created crept on Elizabeth's brow. I saw a line of perspiration snake down the side of her neck, from behind her ear.

Elizabeth was waiting to enter. Although her face was calm, her eyes were not. Her thumb rubbed her index finger, a little sign of being ill at ease. I was not surprised she was nervous.

Mary was unhinged at this time, all said it. The Queen thought she was with child again, but she was the only one.

"Was it the second or third time the Queen thought she carried a child?" I asked no one in particular. "We all knew it was not so. Doubt had started with the first pregnancy that just faded away as if it had not been announced, and then there was another. We all thought it would be a miracle if she could get with child the first time, she was old to conceive and since her father's abandonment of her mother she had not been hale, and after that first time we all knew every pregnancy was a lie, a fantasy of desperation the Queen was lingering in. Some condemned her for it. In truth, I felt sorry for her."

Fantasy moved within Mary during this time as freely as the air roams the skies: fantasy that a child would be granted to her by the grace of God, fantasy that our lost territories in France would be restored by her hero Phillip, and fantasy that her husband would come home to her at last, and he would love her. It was as desperate as it was sorrowful. All her subjects had to humour the Queen during this, her latest awful daydream of pregnancy.

Jane Dormer took Elizabeth in, and we followed on silent feet. Mary's chambers were darkened, and they were so warm. The heat would have been enough to choke me, but I gasped a little to see Mary. In the darkness, in her bed, she could barely be seen, but her eyes glowed, bright and unnatural, with fever. It was like seeing a cat hunting in the darkness. I felt like the mouse.

Elizabeth bowed before Mary as the Queen sat up in her bed, supported by masses of cushions and pillows. She was too unwell, too "weighted down" by "the child within" her, she explained, to receive Elizabeth sitting in her usual chair. A smell hung, a sickly blanket, over the fug of heat that shimmered in the darkened rooms, a cloying smell, heavy and sultry, too strange, too repulsive and far too persistent to ignore. The Queen was not with child, she was dying, rotting slow from within.

"We are pleased to see you, sister," rasped Mary as Elizabeth rose before her, "and joyous that you have come to see us before we enter the time of our most blessed state."

She paused and those dark, febrile eyes glinted in dim candlelight as she looked on her sister in triumph. "Finally," she said, her voice growing stronger and louder. "Finally, God has listened to our prayers and has advanced a child unto us for the preservation of our realm and our faith."

Those dangerous eyes shone, glassy and strange. Her words sounded confident. The force of her conviction told me all that I needed to know. Mary was indeed unhinged, her fantasies made real to her through the force of her own desires and the tricks the fever played on her. I liked not the way in which she stared, with her too-bright eyes. She was alarming, for all doubt had been removed as her sickened body plunged her into a state that teetered on the clifftops of madness. Elizabeth knew it too, knew how dangerous her sister was. "People said the Queen had an evil toy in her mind," I whispered, even though they could not hear me. "There was something in her, making her think wild and perilous things, making her turn on people."

"I am grateful that Your Majesty chose to call for me to witness the miraculous event of your pregnancy," Elizabeth said carefully. "Truly, you are blessed by God, and He will ensure your safe delivery, and that of your child."

Mary's skeletal face loomed bright and pale as she shifted forwards. Her face was a deathly grey, skin as pallid as the moon.

"I would that I could hope as you do, sister." Mary stared at Elizabeth, fixing her sister with her stare. "But I believe I may not live to see the child that God has blessed me with. Such is the trial of the task He has granted me." She dropped back on her bed; her breathing laboured, wheezing painfully from her. "But if I should not live to see the face of my beloved child, I will know that he is left in the best of care."

"Please, Your Majesty." Elizabeth bowed again, skirts rustling against rushes on the floor. "Please speak not of leaving us. Your child, my own nephew the Prince, will need his mother as well as his father as he grows."

I heard a little snort of laughter from the shadows. It held no mirth.

"I am *sure* that is what you want, sister," Mary muttered. "But the wants of men are not always aligned with the will of God. That much I have learnt in my long life; that much *you* still have to learn. It is our duty to submit to the Lord's will and if He has decided to take me into His Kingdom, then I should never stand against those wishes. I have such dreams, sister…" She trailed off and sat up again, eyes locked on her sister's face as she struggled to hold herself up with hands like claws on the bedsheets.

"The Holy Spirit comes to me again, at night, in my sleep," she said. "As he did when I was brought low with the choice of whom to marry. The Holy Spirit whispers to me of the child I will have; a fine boy he is, sister, a strong boy, who looks much like my own father but I see in his eyes the wisdom of my beloved mother. This child will be the one to carry this realm into the light, after so long hidden in the darkness of revolt and heresy. I am but the *vessel* to bring forth such a child. Although I could never think myself as worthy a vessel as the beloved Virgin, I know I have been *chosen* to give life to the child who will be the Saviour of England. My son will lead first the English, and then all the peoples of the world to a true understanding of God. All heretics will fall to the wayside as he approaches, and God's angels will fight at his side to reclaim the world for the true faith of Christ."

Mary smiled at Elizabeth, her grey face so dry and hard that it looked like stone. "My child *is* the Saviour," she proclaimed. "And although I may never live to see him perform the task that God has given him, I know I will have given my own life to ensure his and thusly, to save the world from all evils." She fell back on her bed again and panted. The effort of talking had exhausted her. "In that end," she whispered. "I can take comfort and die a woman who has achieved all she could for her country and for God."

"All England will praise the day that Your Majesty gives us your son," Elizabeth said carefully, and curtseyed.

"Go now," Mary rasped. "The time of my lying-in approaches and I have women, ample and able to the task of caring for me. You will return to your country estates and pray for me. Perhaps, sister, this will be the last time you and I see each other in this world."

Elizabeth went to contradict her, but Mary stopped her. "Should that be the case…" Her voice was faint and weak, "… I would urge you, not only as your sister and your sovereign, but as one *soul* to another, to put aside these heretic beliefs that I know well enough you still harbour in private. I have protected you in this world well enough, but when you come to face the Lord God in truth, there will be none who can protect you from the force of His vision. God will see the truth of your heart. When you come to face the Lord of Heaven, Elizabeth, do so as a disciple of His True Faith, or face the burning fires of hell and the removal of true grace from your eternal soul forever."

She paused and coughed. "You and I may not always have honoured the same ideals in life, but I would be sorrowful if you were not taken to the arms of God when you face death as I do. I would like, sister, to see you again when this life is over."

Elizabeth looked for once in her life lost for words.

"Go now, please." Mary croaked and rolled over, spluttering out a hacking cough which turned to dry retching over the side of her luxurious bed. Her ladies ran forwards to aid her in her struggle to breathe. They waved Elizabeth away as she took an involuntary step towards her sister.

"By God, Mary was a pitiable creature, even as she was a dangerous one," I said.

"She knew she was dying," said Death. "She just did not want to die without having fulfilled the destiny she thought was hers."

"A son, a child for the Tudor line," I said and sighed. "How many died for that, in the reign of her father, and in her reign? Even in Edward's, or with his passing, people who could have been heirs died, and the ones who tried to place them upon this so coveted throne. It seems to me more people died for this destiny, as you say, than lived, and life was the point."

"Indeed," said Death.

Elizabeth was led from the room by the candle of Jane Dormer.

"I hear you have lately become promised in marriage," Elizabeth said to Jane, trying not to show that she was gulping in the fresh air like a fish put back to water. "I congratulate you, although I am sad to hear your marriage will take you from England. The Duke of Feria is a good man, so I understand, a clever man, and his titles and lands are vast. You will become a woman of great standing."

"Thank you, my lady." Jane nodded and glanced back at the door towards Mary's rooms. "Although I have promised Her Majesty that I shall not leave her until… after the birth of her child." Her face puckered and her eyes filled with tears.

Elizabeth squeezed her shoulder. They both knew that Mary was dying.

"It is a hard time," the Princess counselled. "But I take comfort from knowing that my sister is surrounded by those who truly love her." She paused. "That is indeed all that she has ever wanted in life, to be loved."

Jane nodded. "*Many* love Her Majesty," she said defensively. "She is a great Queen, and a good woman."

"I hope that she will continue to reign over us for a long time yet," Elizabeth agreed, but her words were hollow. As long as Mary lived, Elizabeth would be in constant danger and turmoil. Mary spoke of protecting Elizabeth from her enemies, but more often Elizabeth had been in danger from her own sister than from other people.

Elizabeth left, saying to her maid that they were to go to Hatfield as soon as possible.

"Should we follow?" I asked.

"Unless you wish to stay here?"

I shuddered, thinking of the Queen's eyes. "I do not," I said.

Chapter Twelve

Brocket Hall

Hatfield, Hertfordshire

Spring 1558

I looked around; it was spring, the flowers told me so, light yellows and blues wavering in the breeze in the gardens and by the edges of the road. We stood at a house I little knew, but by description. Brocket Hall. I knew it as the place Elizabeth had retired to as she waited for her Queen and sister to die. It was two miles north of Hatfield, the River Lea to one side of the mansion. She had chosen it for this time as it was a good base from which to communicate with her followers, and a handy place to hide a little away from her official residence in case of trouble, such as her sister trying to arrest her for some trifle before she died.

"Robin was away at war," I said. "I was alone at the house of my family in London once more, and we heard of Elizabeth then, heard through others, heard she was up to much."

"The throne was in her sights," said Death.

"Cecil and Parry were busy," I agreed.

"There they are," he replied.

I looked to the gardens, two men wandering those paths together, deep in conversation. We walked close enough to hear. "Her supporters on the Council grow day by day," said Cecil, his boots crunching the stones on the path. "But we must make sure she has not only the right to claim her throne, but the power to take it and to hold it."

"Men are tired of the present rule," Parry replied, "yet no matter how poor this rule has been it has demonstrated that a woman may take the throne. There is a precedent, and now our Princess can allow that to grow, show there is not only a place for a woman on the throne, but that she may do well." He chuckled in a grim fashion. "In truth, Master Cecil, it is good for us that Mary has done so poorly, for now we can put Elizabeth forth and she can never do as badly as her sister."

"I have more hope in her than just that she may do better than a poor ruler," said Cecil, a white feather in his dark velvet hat dancing in the breeze. "That girl is the most promising person I have seen come close to the throne for years. Her brother might have become something, but he was uncaring of others where she is fiercely loyal. Edward thought England owed him much, whereas Elizabeth believes she is the servant of her country as well as its ruler. She has the mind to bring England to a state of peace and glory, if she but has the chance."

I lifted my ears to something in the wind, voices murmuring. It sounded as if they were saying my name.

"To many of us, she is our best and only hope," said Parry.

There was silence between them a moment. It was as if both had expressed love for the same woman and now knew not what to say.

"Sir John Thynne, once a servant of the ill-fated Duke of Somerset, Edward Seymour, has declared in private for us," said Parry eventually, plucking some rosemary, rather straggly still after winter's cold caress, from a stalk and rubbing it into his hands. "He has waited long years to return to a seat of power in the government. Thynne is powerful and has promised us his whole standing army should the acquisition of the Princess's throne require force."

Cecil nodded thoughtfully, but said nothing.

Parry sighed, crumbling up the rosemary and scattering it on the path. "Another ten thousand troops are promised from the garrison of Berwick-upon-Tweed, the largest battalion on English soil. Thomas Markham, a captain in the garrison, came the other day with papers cleverly written to assure Lady Elizabeth that these troops will be provided, if needed, *'for the maintenance of her royal state, title and dignity."* He gave a short laugh. "That is good, and ambiguous, since none may say what maintenance of such might mean."

"I had the same thought." Cecil sniffed. "Lord Clinton, the Lord Admiral and commander of Her Majesty's forces in the Fleet, is our friend now, through his wife's admiration for the Princess."

"Elizabeth Fitzgerald, Lady Clinton, was she a friend and companion of Elizabeth's in childhood?" asked Parry.

Cecil nodded. "When Mary and our lady lived together at Hunsdon, Lady Clinton went to live with them and eventually became one of Mary's ladies, but she always admired our Princess."

"Lady Clinton is a woman I admire as much for her spirit as for her beauty. When she was a young woman, I hear, the Earl of Surrey, that reckless son of Norfolk, wrote poetry for her, immortalizing her as the "*Fair Geraldine*"."

"That is what our Princess calls her." Cecil nodded, smoothing his dark doublet. "In truth, she is closer to Elizabeth than Mary in religion, and when Mary noted this Lady Clinton left court. Her husband, the Admiral, is one of few men the Princess can stand upon the present Council, and that is a good thing, for we need some continuation of men there, although it must be made smaller. Mary tried too hard to appease all people and there are so many men on the Council that I wonder at anything getting done, it is so unwieldy, full of confused voices."

Parry's lips twitched with a smile, and I could almost hear his thoughts. "Cecil wants to be the one voice Elizabeth listens to," I said.

Instead of voicing what he had been thinking, Parry chose other words. "The Princess's lady, Bessie Brooke, has secured her husband William Parr for our side too. He is her husband who is not her husband, their union not being officially recognised by Queen Mary who refused to acknowledge his divorce from his first wife on grounds of her adultery. Elizabeth swears to uphold their marriage."

"I heard when he came here the Princess called him uncle," said Cecil.

Parry smiled. "She knows how to disarm people, just as her father did."

"More men came," said Death as we watched them turn a corner. Days flickered by.

"Robin," I said, watching the hours turn and darken, turn and grow light. "He went to her when he came home before he came to me, that is what you are going to tell me?"

Death nodded.

I looked up to see him riding to her. There were many soldiers there that day, many men come home disillusioned from the war, but his eyes and hers sought only each other. How I wanted to hate her in place of him! Yet it was his choice to go to her. His choice to put her first. "He would have said to me, had I known, that it was for his career and therefore for both of us that he did this," I said. "He would have said there was no other choice, but there was. There always is. People complain about there being no time to do things, but we make time for the things we want to do, for the people we want to see. We make time for what matters to us. It is, always, a choice. He chose her. She was the first one he came to. I was the second best."

"His ambition could be satisfied in her, and not in you," said Death.

"I suppose I can understand his never wanting to be in the position he was, when he was in the Tower, when we had nothing," I said. "But there are other ambitions, others I could have fulfilled. Ambitions for family, children, a life together. Once he spoke of it just being us, a country man and his wife and how happy we would be." I sighed. "I wonder if he believed that once, or ever," I finished.

We shifted inside, a room in the house where many had gathered. Others were there to support Elizabeth, pledge themselves to her, but she only wanted to speak to one of them. He looked different in some ways, not in others. The war had been hard on many men. Robin had seen his brother Henry die in front of him, his head blown clean off by a flying cannonball. He spoke of it only once, and I never saw a man look more hollow. His eyes were blank as he spoke of Henry, and then he never mentioned him again.

The war had been hard, too, because the English had not done well. We would lose Calais too, soon enough, and gain nothing, not even glory and fame. The young men who came home from that war came home disenchanted, and they were the fortunate ones.

"It is good to see you, Lord Robin," Elizabeth said. "It seems I was wrong to fear that you would not keep your promise to return."

"My lady." He bowed. "The idea of seeing you once more was all I needed to keep me from death in France. What could compare to the want in my heart to see you again?"

She laughed. "A pike or dagger might, should they have had a chance."

"Many struck close, my lady, but none could dent the *armour* of your promise to me."

She smiled. Others in the room were looking a little amused at his overly embellished phrases, but Elizabeth did not mind, and I knew why. Under all that praise there was a spark of truth in all he said. I could feel it.

"Well now you are returned, Robin," she said. "And have you come to claim my promise of a place in my household?"

His dark eyes sparkled at her with mischief. "No, my lady. At least, not at this moment."

She looked astonished. It must have been an unusual moment for her, after all. What did he mean by turning down a place in her household when it was offered? It was impudence at its highest, to refuse a royal offer. Others in the company looked equally shocked, and there was a muttering of disgruntled voices. It was a public slight on the Princess's name and titles to be refused so, and by a man of lesser standing. Anger began to rise in her, I could see it. Part of me wished she might strike him.

"If I may, my lady?" he entreated.

She nodded curtly.

"I come on this day, my lady, to make an offer of my own wealth, such as it is. I place it at your disposal for your own needs, which must be many. I do not seek a place in your house at this time, but I seek to offer my wealth and my own men to you, knowing that you will make good use of them." He smiled; a knowing and a most charming smile. "And I hope that you will remember your friends in the future; remember those who served you to the best of their ability when *you* had need of *them*."

The anger in her face receded, and Elizabeth glanced at Parry, at her elbow as always. His face was unreadable to me, but the Princess saw something in it. He gave the slightest nod.

"Her resources were under strain," I said, understanding. "The growth in her supporters as Mary edged ever closer to death led to a bleed on her resources. There must have been so much at that time to be planned and bought, paid for and promised in return for the support of her smooth ascension. She was fighting to keep good her accounts." I looked at my husband. "Robin saw this," I said. "Clever Robin. He refused a place in her household then, and instead offered her his own wealth and men, because he knew the rewards would be greater if he but waited a little longer. And his offer would encourage others to do the same, would it not? He might just have gained her more money than she could have raised alone." I shook my head. "But we had so little, and all of it he gave to her? Just after his return he took the accounts back from me, saying I had done enough. I thought it sweet at the time, that he was trying to help me as I had him. But it was done to cover this up, was it not?"

Death inclined his head.

"I once said, my lord," Elizabeth said, "that I was glad God had sent much of foul weather my way, for a friend in times that are foul is of much more weight to me than friends who come only in times of clement skies. It is pleasing to me that you would offer me both men and money for the preservation of my honour and titles. I will accept, but I make to you this promise. Such service as you do me now shall not be forgotten and shall be returned to you *threefold* when the time comes."

Robin bowed, a swift, graceful movement.

As the day's visitors filed out, Elizabeth turned to Parry. "What think you, Parry? It turned out to be an interesting and profitable day did it not?"

"Indeed, my lady," he replied. "The acquisition of income is all the more enjoyable when it comes as a surprise."

"Does he have much, then? My Lord Robert?" Her eyes followed Rob through the window. He was outside, waiting for his horse, chatting to a groom.

Parry nodded cautiously. "Much of his own property was returned when he was released I would think, although many of his father's and brother's lands have not been returned. They are still property of the Crown, I believe. But his wife came from a family of some means and lands in Norfolk." He paused. "I do not think that Lord Robert has as much as he would like others to believe. There is much of the clever courtier about him, to cover the dignity and honour lost as a consequence of those charges of treason and his family's fall from grace. But what he has will certainly help us." Parry looked rueful. "The demands on the coffers have been great of late," he said.

"I had almost forgot that he was married." She looked sad a moment, then laughed. "So much the better, for I prefer a man to keep a wife at home. It leads much less to those proposals of marriage that so mar a friendship, do you not think, Parry?"

Parry smiled at his mistress. "As you say so, Your Highness."

"I thought perhaps, Master of Horse?" she said quietly to Parry, "for the Lord Robert?"

Parry nodded. "He is an interesting man, my lady." His great brow furrowed as he thought. "He understood well enough, and better than others, what our cause needed and how to offer it, and that shows a greater understanding than most of these lords who come now to offer their support. But he also comes from a long line of traitors, my lady. His grandfather, his father and at least one of his brothers were executed for treason to the Crown. Every branch of your tree has had to deal with a Dudley working treason. Do you wish to have one of such a family so close to your person? Could you ever trust one who has so lately been kept in the Tower for scheming against the Crown?"

Elizabeth smiled. "Do you forget, Parry? Who else was lately kept in the Tower?" She laughed a little. "It was not so long ago that Robert sent messages to me as *I* was held for treason, not so long since *you yourself* were held there too. There are many past traitors amongst those who serve me, but I do not care for what they were accused of once, only what they may do for me in the future. I do not deny that the ancestors of the Lord Robert have been tried and found traitors to the Crown, but whilst they lived and worked with the Crown, they were valuable servants. A traitor in one reign can become the chief advisor in the next."

Elizabeth reached out to take his hand. "Parry," she said. "I am in truth surrounded by liars and schemers. The only thing that I want to have assured is that they are *my* liars and schemers and no one else's. I want Robin as my Master of Horse. If he is equal to the task then he shall keep it, if he betrays me then he shall lose both his position, and that handsome head."

Parry nodded and she laughed at his serious face. "Come, Parry," she sang. "There is still much of this business of housework yet to be completed before our day is done."

We watched her flounce out of the room, and I turned to Death. "She never wanted him," I said. "She never wanted to marry him."

"He did not know that," said Death, standing at the window, watching Robin ride away.

Chapter Thirteen

Hatfield House

17th November 1558

Beneath an old oak, in the grounds at Hatfield, Elizabeth stood. The gloaming was coming swift and true, but there was a bright sun of a dying day glimmering at her back.

"Her day of glory," I said.

I knew what day this was. Death needed to say not a word for me to fix the time and place. The image of Elizabeth waiting for her Council on the day she was proclaimed Queen was one we all knew. It was told to children now, a little fable of many different lessons made. I would have known what day it was almost without looking, for there was a scent on the air, a perfume of expectation, trepidation, of excitement. It floated with the fragrance of damp grass and autumn leaves, with bonfire smoke and the scent of fallen apples. Autumn, the last breath before the death of the year. Perhaps Death was right to say many things are more alive when close to death. Autumn, the burning fire of the year, certainly was.

I did not resent Elizabeth it, this moment of triumph, for all I had seen and all I knew before, I knew she deserved to have this day, this moment. There should be, for all of us, something of this day in our own lives. A moment where we may stop, hold our hands out in the wind and lift our faces to the sky, to God, and say this, this is my day and it is deserved.

"She worked hard to get to this place so peacefully," I said.

"As did her men, and women," added Death. "This was no feat done by but one person alone, but by many who believed in her."

The day of Elizabeth's ascension was growing old, I could see it in the skies. Her name had been proclaimed as Queen and none had moved to stop it. There had been none of the fiasco of when Jane Grey was called Queen, and Mary at the same time, and all thought there would be war. I remembered that day, for I had heard Elizabeth proclaimed Queen in London, outside the house of my family, and all about me had cheered and agreed. There was no other serious candidate and it would not have mattered if there had been. England wanted Elizabeth. England wanted peace. England wanted a Tudor on the throne. This young woman filled them with hope for the future, but she was, too, a continuation of the past. The red hair on her head, the pale skin, she was a Tudor more than enough to please them. They would forget who her mother was, aside from those who wanted to insult her, or those who never had believed Anne Boleyn was a traitor. Most people would only see Elizabeth's father in her, and see the best of him, when he was young and he seemed to bring hope, as this young woman did now.

The Council were on their way to inform Elizabeth of her new title, as if she did not already know, and to pledge themselves to her. "Parry did not need the extra men he was offered to secure the throne by force," said Death.

"I'd wager Elizabeth did not let them stand down yet, though," I said.

"You are correct," he said. "How did you know?"

I shrugged. "It is what I would have done, and she always was quicker than most." I looked at her, so fresh. I had to remind myself I was around this same age on this same day, perhaps a year older I was. Would I have been ready for this, as she looked?

I could see her little ruse already. Elizabeth wanted the Council to find her in the gardens, as if she was wandering, not expecting them, as if she was unprepared. I smiled despite myself. She was ever good at setting a scene, showing people an image they wanted to see. She wanted them to think she was unprepared for the honour she was given, that she had not been waiting all day, indeed all her life for it. She would catch them off guard, them thinking she was but a girl, when in that girl's form there was a vixen hidden.

"And an oak," I said and snorted. "Of course she would be under an English oak on the day she was named Queen." I shook my head, for it was, too, Robin's symbol, and mine a little. I had married him, so his symbols were mine, but my family too had links to the oak, *robur*, Robsart. At our wedding I had been painted, a portrait where I wore gillyflowers to show I had just been married, and a spray of oak to shown whom I had wed. Now here was Elizabeth, under her own oak.

But watching her there, I no more wanted to snort with contempt. I did not feel it, but felt its opposite. Admiration. I could not help it stealing into my heart, however much I did not want to like this woman my husband loved in place of me. There was something at once fragile and strong about her, a sense of great courage and a heart true, but one who had learned to hide such a heart. It would take a great deal for a woman such as this to entirely trust anyone. She knew how dangerous people were. Elizabeth stood alone in more ways than one, but she was not afraid to stand alone. I, who always had feared to be alone, admired this.

She stood under that oak, dappled light flicking through the few remaining leaves and branches to dance upon her pale skin, her hair of fire. She looked calm. Her ladies and the rest of her household were far beyond her, back at the house. She stood alone, as she must, as a Queen should.

Red-gold leaves danced in a gentle breeze above her. The sun twinkled between them. There were no jewels in the entire world more perfect and beautiful than that image. Across the path, I saw the delegation of the Council arrive and Elizabeth stepped out into the sun, letting the light touch on her red-gold hair. She folded her hands before her; the perfect image of humility, youth, and sanctity. Her men would remember this day always. No wonder so many spoke of it as if they were there.

The men of the Council jumped from their horses and walked to bow before her. Nicolas Heath, the Archbishop of York and Lord Chancellor, spoke of Queen Mary's death, and of Elizabeth's proclamation as Queen.

"We are much sorrowed to hear of the death of our royal sister," Elizabeth said in a strong voice.

Behind her were Cecil and Parry, Kat, Bess, Blanche, Anne, Geraldine, William Parr, and John Astley. Beside them were all the servants of her house, coming out in little streams at first, then becoming like the great flow of a river. All standing behind the new Queen. The Councillors looked at the gathering crowd behind her, and I saw nervousness in their eyes. But those people were not gathered to harm them; they gathered thus only to honour Elizabeth.

"I am amazed at the burden that hath fallen to me," she continued. "But I am God's creature. He has granted to me the grace of this crown. This office is His design. I will do all in my power to uphold His will, and protect His people."

She paused. The Council delegates were still on their knees and she made no sign to allow them to rise. Elizabeth wanted their full attention. "In this great task ahead of us, I ask for the great care and assistance of all our subjects, so that I with my ruling, and you with your service, may make a good account to Almighty God. I mean to direct all my actions by good advice and counsel, for the preservation and protection of my people."

She paused, and glanced back up at the leaves of the oak behind her. The fading light of the day lit her gold-red hair so it shone like flames against her pale skin. Her dark eyes sparkled as she looked onto the faces of men who had once sought to imprison and trap her, those who had once sought to take her life. Now, she was their master.

Elizabeth unfolded her hands and spread them before her as though praying. "*A Domino factum est; mirabile est in oculis nostris.*" Her voice was powerful. *"This is the Lord's doing; it is marvellous in our eyes."*

As Mary's former Councillors dropped their heads in prayer, I noted something on the horizon. In the distance, a rider on a snow-white horse came plunging towards Hatfield.

Elizabeth smiled as she too recognized the rider. Bitterness rose in my throat. No one else would ride as boldly as the Queen's new Master of Horse. Robin Dudley was riding to her side, his sense of occasion as dramatic as her own, riding on a great white horse to his princess, to his Queen.

In the light of the fading sun, under the strong branches of the oak of England, Elizabeth stood, their Queen. As she stood with her arms outstretched, Councillors bowed before her, and her household bowed behind; she was surrounded by both those who had made her Queen, and those who had sought to destroy her, all bathed in the last light of the day.

"That was her day of glory," I said. "And it was that day, in truth, that I lost my husband to another woman."

Chapter Fourteen

Throcking House

Herefordshire

Winter 1558

We stood in a garden watching a lonely figure walking, collecting what flowers were left after winter's storms, with her maids. "Every day was much the same," I said, looking at myself. "Elizabeth came to the throne, and Robin was at court. There was no place for me. I tried to ignore how alone I felt. I tried to believe my husband when he told me that he would try and try harder to gain me a place at court, but the Queen was so jealous of me that she did not want me there. At first it was said the Queen wanted no additional women at court, or men, for England was a pauper when she came to the throne. Mary had used up all our money on fruitless war with France, and Elizabeth had to become as miserly as her grandfather to make amends."

I paused, watching myself. "But Robin said I was not to come to court, to the coronation. His ability to rise at court depended on his own talents, he said, and when he came back he told me the Queen loved him as her closest friend, and despised the idea of him being married, so if I went to court I would make him fall from favour. It would be different in time, he said. When she married, she might not mind so much that he was."

We followed the sad figure. "We had no house of our own, so I was still with relatives, or supporters of Robin and his family. I tried to ignore the thoughts that came, that it was he who did not want me there, tried to ignore the thought that it was him who did not want me close, not her." I looked at Death. "And what was I supposed to do? He was my husband, I could not leave him! He was what I depended on in the world, in terms of my heart and my purse. I had small society without him, and I could barely stand the pitying glances of those who asked me to dinner or to hunt. He swore himself to me, and then one day I found how hollow his vows were."

We walked on, and I could feel a grief long contained rise in me, a sorrow mingled with confusion and anger. Why had I been so abandoned when once he had sworn he wanted me and no other?

"He came so rarely, saying he was busy all the time, and when he did come it was brief. When he left, the feeling was like grief. The silence of the house, the hushed tones of the servants, it was as though someone had died, and yet no one had. I went about my day, trying to find things to occupy myself with so I would not think of how alone I felt. We had been two, always two, through all the joy and the troubles we had experienced, and now, though he said we were still two, I felt like one. I had not known until I was left alone in the country just how much I had relied upon him. Even when he was away at war it had not felt this lonely, for now he was in the same country, but chose not to be with me."

Death said nothing, but simply listened.

"Robin was the light of my day, and the soft hush of the moonlight at night. He was the one I stored up stories of the day to tell to, just little things of people's moods and words, of flowers I had seen or amusing things I had thought of, but they had been stored so I could tell him when we ate together, or in bed after we had coupled. Now I had no one to tell those tales to but myself, and I already knew them. I could not surprise myself with a jest, light and free, that had been spoken in the day. I could not amaze myself with a description of a perfect flower spotted in the gardens or the woods. Without him in my life I felt alone as I never had before. Before, even before him I had had my family to tell such tales to, and now I had only my maid, Mrs Picto or my companion lady, Mrs Odingsells. They did not understand me as my family or Robin had, did not comprehend the same jests, did not understand all the little code words we had for amusing times or tales. They did not know me as he and they had."

I looked up at the skies, the clouds turning grey. "Sometimes I think all people want is for there to be someone who remembers our days of importance, or even those not important, without explanation because they were there with you, and can remember those days too. I had that not anymore, but he did, with another woman. Together, they owned days that I knew nothing of."

"But he had been away before, at war?" Death asked.

I nodded. "But then I wrote to him, and he to me. Once he came back word from him at court was scarce, and more often about our financial affairs, or what he was doing at court. I had small room to share my day with him. He was not interested, and made that plain, so all wish to share left me. In the end I felt shamed when I tried, as if I was a person most dull and drab in his eyes."

We stopped near the house. Throcking Mansion was the house of William Hyde, a good friend to Robin. Part way between the Robsart estates of the north and London, it was a good base for me then. I could see family, and Robin when he wanted to could see me. I was far enough from London that the Queen should not have to see me, and not so far that the occasional conjugal visit could not be made. Sometimes it felt that was all he came to me for, a tumble in the bed and then he was away again.

"It was a sweet enough place, though I felt alone here," I said. "There were woodland and fields enough to wander. I set myself every day to a certain walk and would complete it along with some reading, some making of clothes for the next time I saw Robin, or, in a fantasy of mine, for when I went to court. I prayed and I slept and I walked and I sewed, all the time trying to pretend I was not alone. Rob sent me gifts of cloth and food for my table, and I sent him items I had made. I tried to believe Robin's lies, that one day there might be a place for me at court. I dreamed of those times."

We wandered about the front of the house, and I pointed out features. "The house was pleasant, surrounded by a moat through which water flowed, keeping it mercifully free of biting bugs, and the Church of Holy Trinity was next door, a good place to go when a cool air and a prayer were needed. The walls were whitewashed, for they used to hold pictures painted of holy scenes, but such frippery was thought unholy by that time, and the churches were painted over. There was one place, though, that I liked to go, one corner where the tiniest edge of a foot could be seen, bare and turned a little, and it looked as if it was dancing. I liked to go and see that edge of that foot, for it made me feel as if there was someone dancing in a place where it was not allowed, and that made me feel naughty too."

I sighed, watching myself. "Robin was at court most of the time. His uncle had a house near Westminster, and other family had houses too, but the Queen was swift giving him his own rooms at court and so often he stayed there. He did not tell me that many of his rooms were near hers." I looked at Death. "It did not take long for the gossip to start, and once it had, all heard it."

"They say you are the Queen's lover!" a voice shrieked from the rooms above us. My voice. The days had changed. I wandered the gardens no more, it was raining that day and I was inside the house, screaming at my husband. Robin had come to me and I remembered that later I cursed myself for the way I spoke to him, but I also could not help it. It was winter, and I was far from everyone, from all I loved and knew, and everywhere there was rumour that the Queen's Master of Horse was also master of her heart. I was humiliated. My husband was serving the Queen in many ways, said all tongues.

"Parry was made Treasurer, Kat Ashley chief Gentlewoman, Cecil of course was Secretary of State and Robin got Master of Horse," I said to Death. "It would seem to some a much lesser post and in many ways it was, but what it did allow him was access to the Queen. He was at her side at the hunt and during progress. He was the one to share her free time, and enjoy that time with her. Robin was the man at court who often arranged entertainments. He had her ear at a time when, theoretically at least, she was off her guard, although I do not think Elizabeth was ever such a thing as that. Her guard was always up, and when it seemed down she was pretending.

"Cecil tried to send him away that November, I remember him coming to tell me and so proud he was that Elizabeth had not wanted him to go. Cobham was sent to Spain in his place, for Elizabeth did not want to do without Robin. He said to me then that this would be the making of him, therefore of us both. He was doing this for us, he said, but as the months passed I little believed him. Then he came home to me here, just before Christmas. He was not to spend Christmas with me, he told me, and I had been looking forward to it so much that all I had tried to hold in came out. Every filthy rumour I had heard came from my mouth. Oh, how I regretted saying what I did for he stayed away even longer, until I was quite desperate to see him and willing then to accept any moment he had to spare and never rebuke him again, and probably that was the reason he did it. But right then, oh I was never so mad as I was that day."

"You are the Queen's lover!" that voice cried again and a wicked laugh, so unlike me, came from the mouth to follow it, like a dog on the insult's heels. "You are the Queen's mistress," I jeered. "You are her little whore!"

"Silence!" Robin screamed. "You are delusional and know not what you say. I attend the Queen and we are friends, that is a good thing for us, madam! Who else is going to further our wealth or estates if not me? All you are good for is spending my money!"

"I see you have not scrimped there yourself, dear husband," I sneered. "Is anything you wear now old, or was it all made a day ago? And think not that I am the spendthrift here! I have clothes as a lady must, but I do not spend as you do! I see our accounts, all of them! I am the one who goes over them today, as I was the one who kept us in some coin when you were a prisoner, a time you appear to have forgotten!"

"I forget nothing. You were not the one in that jail."

"I was in there as much as you were, for my heart was tied to you, and yet the moment you are out you are also out of England, and then when you come back all your time is for the Queen and none for your lawful wife, who stood loyal and loving beside you when you were low and cast off by everyone! You swore once that you loved me and you swore to be my husband, but now you go off and play the gillyflower to another woman, and even if she be the Queen it is still a sin!"

"I wish I had never come here."

"I too wish the same, for I have no wish to stand in company with a man of no morals and no honour!"

We watched as Robin stormed from the house, anger high on his forehead, and I stood at a window, my back to him. My back was turned not in anger, but so Robin would not see I was weeping. I did not want to give him my tears, only my fury.

Death and I stood near the other Amy, watching her cry silently.

"He had been away for most of 1556 and 7," I said, "and I thought when he returned I would see him all the time, but I did not. He was gone more than he was with me. And now I was far from family, *and* far from Robin. When we made up he said if he wanted to advance our fortunes he had to play the romantic suitor to the Queen, had to do as she wished. All rulers are capricious, he told me, but she was more so than the men he had served before her. 'I would rather be here with you, or have you at my side at court than go alone,' he told me after this argument and for a while I believed him, yet in time I came to think he liked this arrangement. We had married so young, out of love as I had thought, but now he had the chance to have the best of all worlds. He had a wife he could come to in the country, always waiting, seemingly I was to do little else than wait for him, and when he wanted to be a grand man about court, single and free, he could be that too."

I watched the younger me shudder, trying to control weeping. Two years had gone by with but spare visits and letters, and I had sustained myself on dreams alone, then he had come home and I had been shown how false my dreams were. He did not care about this wife wed seven years ago, but about the Queen just made months ago. He did not care about trying to start a family, but about making sure his career was given fruit. I was not his first concern. I was an afterthought. It would have hurt less, had he been my afterthought, rather than my first thought.

Robin climbed on his horse and was away from the house in a fierce rain of hooves, mud flying behind him. We walked to the window, watched him vanish into a mist at the end of the road.

"He stayed away a long time. I thought he was punishing me, as I said. By the time he came back I was desperate. I had been alone so long, I was willing to forgive anything, anything. I told myself I should not have listened to the rumours, that it was beneath me to have done so and if he would return I would show him I was loyal, I was loving, I only wanted him with me and did not want to be alone. I thought I could explain to him and he would understand and it would be as it was."

I smiled ruefully. "I think even then I knew it was a fool's hope I had. The bond between us had stretched and now it was loose, sagging between us and neither could gather it in, him because he had no wish for more of that bond in his arms, and me because I could hold no more of it. I could not hold all that he was failing to. On my own, I was not enough to save us."

Chapter Fifteen

Throcking House and

The Tower of London

Winter's End 1559

We stood near a welcome fire. Outside the hall I could hear the wind wailing. "1559," I said. "I remember. It felt like the longest winter, as if the storms never would end."

Days swirled by us. Windows froze and unfroze, patterns of frost as ferns wending up the glass. The wind howled and snow fell. I watched myself leave the fire for bed, and then come back as daylight rose in reluctant skies of grey and blue and black. Outside the roads were impassable and more snow fell. Great walls of snow and ice had blocked many of the roads, trapping us, delaying news. All there was to do was to rise, go to the fire and sew or read, and then go to bed once more, and listen to the storm. "My host was away that winter, his lady too, so we had small company. We played cards sometimes, Mrs Odingsells, Mrs Picto and me, but it was so cold. Most of the time, especially as the winter wore on, we just wanted to sleep. I felt I could sleep forever then, I was so tired. I did not know I was already not as I should have been."

The Amy I had been looked wan, as if even her bones were exhausted. There was something in me that had crept in, an enemy seeking my life. I did not know it, but it was there already. The end was on its way.

"At court, though," I said. "They were merry."

From the cold room we vanished, to the warm halls of court. Fires blazed in every hearth and candles on each table. Twelfth Night, I knew it by the games people played. There was a masque in which performers appeared in habits of the clergy, but on their faces were masks that told of the inner dissatisfaction that the Queen felt with the present English Church. Robin, as Master of Horse, had arranged it. He knew how to make Elizabeth laugh, and how to make a point most political at the same time. On the faces of those playing bishops were masks of asses, the cardinals wore visages of carrion crows and on the faces of the abbots were masks of wolves. The Queen laughed heartily to watch the masque, and then she danced long into the night, her partner my husband.

"And I just sat there, waiting for news, sleeping through my days because I was so sad," I said. "I wasted a lot of time being low because I was cast off."

I glanced down at my gown and saw there, clinging to the damask of the skirt I wore, strands of silver. Something of the soft world of webbing and silver light was clinging to my dress. I shook it, and the strands dropped and fell, vanishing as they reached the ground and as they disappeared, I felt a sense of slight sorrow, and regret, as if I missed those strands of silver web.

Trying to shake the feeling off, I looked up again. We were back to my fire at Throcking, and I was telling my maid Mrs Picto about the Queen's troubles.

After the Queen's demonstration at the Christmas Mass, where Elizabeth had left the ceremony for it being entirely too Catholic a ritual, it had become clear she was trying to show she did not wish Catholicism to remain where Mary had left it in England. As a consequence, there had been a rebellion of sorts amongst the bishops. All of them still in office were Catholics, remnants of Mary's reign, during the time when Christianity and cruelty had walked hand in hand in our country. The problem was the new Queen required an English bishop to perform the ceremony of coronation, but after Christmas, it seemed there were few bishops willing to do so. She had not yet appointed an Archbishop of Canterbury, and

Archbishop Nicholas Heath of York had flatly denied the honour of crowning her, saying that if the Queen denied the transubstantiation of the host then she was little more than a heretic and he would not crown a heretic. A few others, bold but not as brazen as Heath, had refused on the grounds that they feared what Elizabeth's stance on religion should bring to the country. Still more had refused on questionable grounds of ill-health or infirmity, and everyone knew those excuses were just excuses, but the Queen was not overly perturbed. The bishops of England who held their titles presently were mainly old men. The Queen was young. It was not inconceivable that there would come a time when the old would pass, taking their ways and objections with them, and the new would rise.

"But she still needs one to crown her!" said Mrs Picto.

"I read here," said the younger me, turning a paper in my hand, "that the Welsh Bishop Oglethorpe has agreed to take the honour; the self-same bishop whom the Queen enraged and confused by leaving in the middle of his service on Christmas Day."

"When she walked out?"

I nodded.

"Well, better him than no one!" Mrs Picto was watching me, I could feel it. "Has my lord sent instructions on what you are to wear and where to stay for the coronation?"

The younger me put the paper down and stared into the fire. "I am not to attend," I said. "My lord cannot afford it, and the Queen wants to pay for no one who is not vital."

"Surely, my lady, we could go and watch from a house in the city?"

"My lord does not want me there, let that be enough for you," I said.

I looked away, and as I did, Death took me to the Tower.

Elizabeth was standing before a mirror. Given the clothes she was wearing, I knew what day it was. "14th of January, 1559," I said. "It must be for her to be dressed like this. The day before her coronation, when she processed through London."

I walked about her. Twenty-three yards of cloth of gold and of silver, I remembered from reports, were sewn into the magnificent dress the Queen wore; tight against her slim waist, it curved and cupped her small breasts. Bright white ermine lined the collars and cuffs; gold lace, delicate and intricate, was laid over the whole dress. Tiny pearls, their drop-like ends encased in brilliant gold, dangled from Elizabeth's ears, mingling their creamy lights with the larger pearls that hung at her neck and diamonds that were sewn into the folds of her dress. Every slight movement she made caused her to shimmer with brilliance, light and colour reflected from the universe of gemstones that covered her lithe body.

"She is beautiful," I said.

On her head was a cap made of the same delicate gold lace that covered her gown. Over this was placed a dainty golden crown, so light and so elaborate in its metalwork that it seemed as though it could never have been made by the fingers of man, but only by those of angels. It crested her head like a halo. Elizabeth's face was dusted with powder of alabaster, so that even her skin sparkled.

"They were her sister's robes," said Death. "She could not afford new, so she had them altered."

"The eve of coronation procession," I said. "I wished I could have seen it." I walked around her. "She looks calm, but I think she is anxious, inside."

"Why?"

"I would be."

Kat Ashley, standing to one side of the Queen and dressed in crimson and gold, wiped a tear from her eye as she gazed at Elizabeth, her charge since the Queen's childhood. The Queen smiled. "You are sad today, Kat?" Elizabeth asked gently and Kat shook her head fervently.

"Happier than I have ever known, my lady. These are tears of joy!" She laughed and gulped at the same time. "For finally I have seen you become the Queen I always knew you would be."

"Ah, Kat." The Queen reached out for her, but Kat hung back.

"I would not mess your gown, Majesty," she said, scandalised, but Elizabeth brushed aside her arguments and pulled her into her arms.

"There is so much metal sewn into this dress, Kat," she said, holding her, "that I doubt any mortal could cause it to fold or to crinkle."

"You look beautiful." Kat pulled back to reach out and touch the Queen's face as though in benediction. "The most beautiful woman I have ever seen."

"Gold and silver, pearls and diamonds may make any woman look like a queen."

"There was never another who looked more a queen than you, Majesty," breathed Kat with passion. "Nor any with as good a heart as yours, with more pure intentions toward her subjects. Gold and silver may make any woman look like a queen, but it is what you carry within you that sets you apart from any who have walked this path before you, or any who will come after you. England will never have a ruler who loved her people more, nor who wanted so much for them. They love you for it, Majesty, and all of them can see it in you. That is what shines from you today. Not gold and silver, but the pure heart of a queen who loves her people."

Elizabeth looked thoughtful. "Today is the day my people show me what they expect of me, Kat. The pageants on the eve of coronation demonstrate to a monarch what his people wish for his reign." Elizabeth turned back to Kat, grave of face, "I hope I can be all they wish of me."

"You will be, my lady." Kat reached out to straighten the gems at the Queen's throat. "Since you were a girl, it was all I could do not to lose you to the pages of a book. Your head was always working out the moral, the end, the story and the lessons held therein. You never missed the slightest aspect of any story, always understood the meanings better than anyone else. If you put yourself as diligently to the cause of your people, you will do more than any other in the God-given grace granted to you." She smiled gently. "They need you to be a *reader*, Majesty, and you were ever a diligent and dedicated pupil."

"Since times long forgotten," I said to Death, "the procession on the eve of the coronation was filled with much cheering and celebrating, but it was also a chance for the people of the realm to perform pageants for their sovereign; plays, songs and skits. Through costume and allegory, the people of England would show what they expected of their Queen: wisdom; excellence; strength; courage; love. All these things that we hold as noble and virtuous in any person would now be demanded of her in everything she did, in every decision made." I looked at Elizabeth. "She feared to let them down. I hardly had a thought that she feared anything."

"All people fear something," said Death.

I looked to the window. Outside, the skies were grey. Light, delicate flecks of snow danced in the air, whirling prettily around the heads of nobles, bishops, groomsmen, lords, ladies and servants as they gathered together outside for the procession. Although the skies were like lead, and the air around them freezing, a joyous sound came from those below. They, like the common people who lined the streets of London, were waiting for Elizabeth.

A knock came to the door, and Kat went to open it.

Robin stopped at the threshold to bow. "Your Majesty," he said, rising, "the procession is read…" He stopped, mid-word, as his eyes met the flaming, glimmering sight of Elizabeth Tudor. His dark eyes roamed over the skin-tight gown, the soft ermine at her throat, the tiny pearls that gleamed from her ears; across the curve of her breasts, the lines of her slim waist, over the shimmering cream of her skin. And then he blushed. I could have choked on the jealousy and misery that rose in me then. I turned away, walked to the window.

"Are you well, Lord Dudley?" I heard the Queen ask from behind me. "You seem to have lost your words."

I turned back.

Robin swallowed and smiled cagily at the Queen, his handsome face still flushed, making his eyes sparkle even more than usual. He looked fine; his crimson tunic tight against the hard muscles of his chest, his legs showing their goodly shape through close-fitting dark silk. His clothes spoke in whispers of the fine figure that was beneath their folds, and Elizabeth was admiring all that he had to show.

"I am more than well, Your Majesty." He recovered himself. "This is a glorious day for all of England."

"I am glad to hear you are well," Elizabeth teased, almost shyly. "We have a long day ahead of us. I thought for a moment that you might faint as you came in."

The blush upon his cheek burned deeper. "I was struck by the vision of Your Majesty," he said softly, and I heard a gruffness of desire in his tone that I knew well. Once, I had heard it arise from him, for me.

The Queen turned to Kat. "Check if all is ready in the hall to start the procession." Elizabeth motioned to her other ladies to follow Kat too. Robin looked at the ladies as they left the room, a flock of pretty birds in crimson and gold plumage, all eyeing him with undisguised admiration.

"You cut a fine figure, Rob," Elizabeth noted as they closed the door. "You look wonderful." Robin walked towards her slowly. When he reached the space before her he stopped and she extended her hand. The air between them seemed to crackle as one by one, he kissed her fingers.

"You are the most beautiful creature I ever saw…" he lifted his dark eyes to her "… Your Majesty," he added swiftly.

"More beautiful than your own wife?"

Robin looked sad for a moment. He shook his head. "My wife is like every other woman in this world, my lady; a mortal woman. Your beauty is above all others, for you are a supreme being… The Queen."

"Each time I think I can hate him no more, you show me something else," I said.

"There are many conversations we never get to hear between others, about ourselves, that we would not like," said Death. "I would beg you to remember you will have had some about others too."

"I never said aught behind his back I did not say to his face," I said. "And of that, at least, I am proud. I was not the one who did wrong here."

"Perhaps something to remember," said Death. "If he gave his heart to another woman, it was because of him, because of her, not because of you."

I looked away, to the Queen. Perhaps Death was right, but still it felt like an insult.

"Some parts of even Queens are mortal, Rob," Elizabeth was saying. "We have the same blood, the same flesh, the same hearts as all those below us."

"I would give anything to know my Queen's heart." He looked at her earnestly, still holding her hand.

"As I would give anything to trust to show my heart to another," she whispered, reaching out and touching her hand to his chest. "For so long I have had to hide the woman inside me in order to protect the Queen to come."

"I would that you would never hide from me." His voice was gruff. "I will always work to protect you and to honour you, as the Queen of my country, but also as the woman I…" He broke off as a sound at the door startled them both.

"A moment," the Queen cried loudly at the closed door, and looked back at Rob.

"… As the woman I love!" His voice was rushed; his words tripped over themselves.

I stared at him, eyes wide with shock.

The Queen, too, looked astonished he had said it aloud. "You are… special to me too, Robin." I felt a stab of joy as I watched his face fall at her hesitant words. "But I am not made like other women." Elizabeth touched his face with a gentle hand. "The love of a normal woman may be bought with a pretty flower, a gem cast in gold, a promise of security. But to my heart, the efforts of loyalty and friendship are the most important offices. Do not think for a moment that your words fall on empty ears, or an uncaring heart. Your words mean more to me than I can tell you."

He kissed her hand. "I give you my heart, such as it is, my lady," he said. "And whilst I know I could never be yours in truth, for I have a wife already, and you are too great a possession to ever be mine, I will serve you loyally all the days of my life. In the very darkest of my days, when we were imprisoned together in this Tower, you were the light that kept me alive with hope. You are my heart, the very thing that keeps the life beating within me. You are everything to me and to England, *Elizabeth*." He spoke her name like a caress.

She stood on her tiptoes and kissed his cheek. For a moment I thought he would embrace her, but his hands dropped to his sides.

"He talks as if she is God," I mentioned.

"And perhaps that is what she fears," said Death. "That he puts her more on a pedestal than she already is."

"She would fear that?"

"Where is there to go from the greatest height, other than down?"

I nodded, seeing the sense in that thought. Her mother, after all, had been raised up only to be cast down, and all for love.

Robin stood back. "I am your servant, Your Majesty," he said and bowed.

"As I am your Queen and master." She looked a little sad, but I wondered if it was true sadness.

"Come, Robin," she said. "It is time I found out what my people want of me."

He smiled. "They want only you," he said. "As I do."

"If only, my lord, that were all they wanted! Myself, I can give to them as freely and as readily as my parents gave life to me. The Queen they want me to be may take some more work and toil to achieve."

The door opened and Kat strolled back in at the head of the Queen's ladies, looking at Robin and her mistress, standing so close together, with barely disguised curiosity. Kat's face was not the best pleased.

"Come, then," said the Queen, stepping away from my husband. "It is time we discovered what my people desire of me."

A day swirled as we walked through London. We saw the procession in parts and I smiled at Death as he went to slow time and show me the pageants. "It does not matter now," I said. "Then, it mattered much to me, but there are other things I would rather see now."

Death inclined his head, and took me on, to the day of the Queen's coronation.

It was dry and bright; a light touch of snow still covered the ground. London's streets were slushy with ice and mud mingled together to form brown, soggy drifts. Tree branches and stone walls outside the palace sparkled with crystals of frost, and the air was delicious. Elizabeth shivered as ladies dressed her in her coronation robes once again, as she stepped delicately into expensive, imported silk stockings with gold lacings.

"They were from Robin," I said. "I know because all of London spoke of it, what an intimate gift it was."

There was a knock at the door. Kat opened it, and in walked Cecil.

"Is all prepared?" the Queen asked.

"Yes, Majesty." Cecil bowed, frowning with a grim expression. "Although Oglethorpe is being most resistant about the coronation ceremony and the following Mass."

She sighed. "I have agreed that they adorn me with the title *'Defender of the Catholic Faith,'* however incongruous that is going to sound later on. The bishop must allow some room for compromise in the service itself. I have not asked for a great deal to be changed."

"He is objecting to the use of the vernacular, Majesty, in both the coronation ceremony and the Mass, *and* he wants to elevate the host." Cecil poured himself some wine and looked at the Queen suddenly, as though he had only just noticed her. "You do really look quite stunning, Your Majesty!" he exclaimed, gazing at her with veneration. "How proud your father would be to see you thus! You are the image of him." He smiled, lifting his goblet to her. "Although with a great deal more womanly beauty, and far less beard."

She smiled, but lifted her eyebrows. "Would my father be pleased, *Spirit*? He never intended for a *daughter* to reign. It was supposed to be my poor brother who would take up his mantle into glory, and his sons after him. For all the time my father spent seeking a male heir, I do not think he intended for a daughter to rule instead."

"God took King Edward, rest his soul, and so this is as it was supposed to be," Cecil said. "And perhaps our Lord had another purpose for the daughter of King Harry that even your father, in his wisdom, could not see. All men, even kings, are fallible, but the plans of God are always right and to a purpose."

The Queen grimaced. "Many are saying that I come to the throne not by the will of God, but by that of the Devil. I hear that my cousin, the Queen of Scots and Dauphine of France, has already quite decided that *she* should be the Queen of England in my place, and her husband, François, is having his clothing embroidered with *my* rightful badges. Mary's Guise uncles and Henri, King of France, believe the throne belongs to their Scots strumpet, rather than to me. And that is before we even start on what the Spanish think of me!"

"The French and Scots have ever been uneasy neighbours, Majesty, and it is natural for them to try to irritate you. That is, after all, what neighbours do to one another," said Cecil, taking a gulp of his wine. "Rest assured that we will keep a close eye on them. No true Englishman wishes for any other Queen but you."

"Good, for they will *have* no other Queen but me, of that I am determined. Now, what said you of flabby Oglethorpe? He dislikes that the coronation and Mass should be said in English? Well, he will just have to learn a little compromise, won't he? I am having both said also in Latin for the consciences of my Catholic subjects, so I too am compromising."

"I believe that is what is confusing him," chuckled Cecil. "He believes that since you have asked for him to read the service in both languages, you are merely repeating what has already been said, and of course he likes not the use of English, as it smacks of Protestantism."

"Entirely the point," Elizabeth laughed. "I will have my people know of the changes which are coming in religion, but such will be done in a gentle fashion, which does not threaten them with suddenness and surprise. Besides which, I want *all* my people to be able to understand the words of the ceremony when it is reported to them. Whilst you and I may have an understanding of the languages of the ancients, not every soul in that Abbey will, still less all those waiting outside. And more than that, by including both sides of the Christian faiths within my coronation Mass they will all see, Cecil, how I mean to rule; by compromise between the faiths."

"Compromise cannot always be achieved, Majesty," cautioned Cecil. "Many on either side of the divide would rather die than dilute their faith in any way."

"Then let them die," she said coldly. "Mistake me not, Cecil, I will not fail to punish dissenters, traitors, fanatics, and troublemakers within my realm with all the hearty strength of my father, but I will give all ample chance to compromise and live in peace together. If any choose not to do so, then by all means *let* them die. And when each of us comes to explain our worldly actions to the Almighty Father in Heaven, I am sure that He will look on my path with favour over the paths chosen by those who would breed intolerance and suffering in order to satisfy their own cowardly, uncertain souls."

"Majesty," Cecil concurred, bowing.

"So tell Oglethorpe that he *will* read both the Latin and the English versions that are laid out before him. I *will* have the modifications we talked about and if he raises the host during the Mass, then I *will* leave the service. I *will* swear on the English version of the Bible, but he can crown me *Defender of the Catholic Faith* as well as Queen, if he so wishes."

"Certainly, Majesty," Cecil agreed, and his usually serious face beamed at her again, the whiskers of his moustache bunching up around his nose.

"What are we grinning for, Master Secretary?"

"Your father would have been proud to call such a prince as you his child, Majesty," said Cecil softly. "Of that I have no doubt."

"Thank you, my friend." She turned to her ladies. "Well?" she asked. "Will I do?"

"You are breath-taking, Majesty," Lettice Knollys gushed.

"She was," I said, almost to myself. "In so many ways, remarkable."

Chapter Sixteen

Greenwich Palace

Winter's End 1559

Another swirl, soft and silver, and we were in the gardens at Greenwich. I dusted my skirts again, more of the strands of silver clinging to me each time we travelled in time and space. One strand curled about my finger, as if begging to stay with me and I smiled with affection as I blew it away.

It was that winter, I was sure, the winter after her coronation. We walked behind Elizabeth and Robin, falling into step just behind them. "You shone in the tournaments, Robin," the Queen praised as their feet crackled down paths crisp with ice. "Many noted how brave and well you rode. How many matches did you win in the end?"

Robert grinned. "Seven, in all, Your Majesty." He shrugged carelessly. "And several with the sword."

Elizabeth laughed. "Do not tell me that you cannot remember the exact number, my lord! I don't believe there is one victory in your life you do not remember with ease." She stretched her arms into the cold air and breathed in the frosty wind.

Robin snorted. "Your Majesty sees through me, as always."

"Perhaps, but do not alter that trait in you; you should have pride in your accomplishments." She stopped on the path; her ladies were following some way behind, and the gardens of Greenwich surrounded them in a magical landscape of ice and light. Diamonds seemed to twinkle from every twig and bare branch. The frost of the winter was sweet with freshness and newness. Yet when I looked, I could see that glimmering place, silver light and spider web, just on the edge of my vision. It was temperate there and gentle, so much so that even the beauty of the winter's day here where we walked seemed harsh and brittle by comparison. Voices flowed, as wind, from that place and it seemed they were calling to me.

"There are so many people in the court," Elizabeth had continued, "who would seek to hide their true souls beneath manners and riches. Too many dissemble and evade me. Do not become one of them." She coughed a little. The Queen had suffered a cold after the coronation, I remembered. People said it was because she prayed most of the night on the cold stone floor of the chapel, asking God for guidance.

"I would never hide anything from you, Majesty," Robin said quietly. "Your friendship is the most important in my life."

"I feel the same way, Robin."

As they walked on, she spoke without looking at him. "I am informed that the Council and Parliament are to beg me to marry, and marry soon," Elizabeth mentioned. "Have you heard aught of this?"

He blushed a little. "She knows that he knows," I said.

"Do not make yourself uneasy, my lord," the Queen said, and smiled. "You have known me since I was a child and you know well enough my thoughts on the matter and state of marriage."

"I do, Majesty," he agreed, "and I would urge caution, rather than speed, in this decision. Your sister's mistakes in the matter of marriage are a fine example to avoid. The English will not welcome a foreign match."

"Nor will my Councillors welcome a domestic one. If I were to marry at all, then it would be for the sake of England alone. I do not wish for it for myself."

"Is there no one who can claim your heart, my Queen?"

"None who are free to marry," Elizabeth laughed, and then looked as if she wished she had not said such words.

Robert stared. "If they *were* free," his words came from his mouth awkwardly, and his eyes widened, "would you have them?"

"How to be free of your wife, Robin?" I said, almost shouting. "I was alive! I was waiting for you! Yet you talk here as if I might be cast aside with such ease!"

Even the Queen snorted derisively. "And how can I tell you that? I cannot make judgements on things that are not, or cannot be. A queen is not a free woman, able and hopeful to marry for love or for her own satisfaction. As Queen, my marriage, should it ever come, would be a matter of policy and government. Love is a freedom I have not."

"Your father married for love," Robert insisted.

"Aye, and killed for it often, also," she said sadly. "None of the rulers of my house have found the happiness they sought in the love they desired. There is too much to interfere in the natural feelings between a man and a woman when one is King."

"She knows he would try to command her, if they were married," I said, and Death nodded.

"I do not believe that," Robert disagreed. "A queen or a king should have the same rights as any mortal."

The Queen smiled, but it looked sorrowful. "You have the heart of a poet, Rob. But poets weave words to make the world a prettier place than it is. My marriage is not a thing of poetry, only of politics."

"Is that the way you would have it?"

"No, but in all times and places I must be the emblem of my country. I will do my duty to her and serve in the position I have been given as well as I am able for the good of my people." Elizabeth paused. "But there is enough woman within me to wish that I could be wooed rather than bartered, to be courted not for the crown of the Queen, but for the soul of the woman within. But men cannot see me, Rob; the light of the crown blinds them and so I am beautiful and desirable to many who will never know or understand me. I am a rich prize for marriage, but I fear that every man or prince who desires that pact with me will court me for the throne alone. Neither part of me can be satisfied, for if I were ever to marry for love, then my country would surely suffer, and if I were to marry for my country, then the woman behind the throne would never have the love she desires."

"She is warning him," I said.

"It does not hold that if you married for love then your country would suffer, my lady," Robin said.

"All that has passed before this time tells me that that is indeed the case."

"You see the past clearly." Robin shook his head. "But the future and the present are filled with new possibilities and outcomes."

"Think you such?" she asked, her tone light. "When I see the works of man in history, I am reminded constantly that the same mistakes are made over and over, each new person thinking that they can succeed where others failed. Am I so different to all the others, who let their façade of knowledge blind them to the realization that they but tread the footsteps of others deeper into the earth, on the same path?"

"You, you are different." Robin's eyes searched her face. For a moment I thought he would reach out to her, but his hands stopped.

"How so?" she asked, turning from him. "The sufferings and trials of any one person always seem more important to them than to others. The accomplishments I have made are no more than many others, wiser men and women who have passed before me. We go through life believing ourselves to be so different to others, so individual, and yet in essence, we are as similar and everyday as the rising sun."

"And yet the sun is glorious and different *every* day," Robin grinned. "In the winter it rises in pale and liquid light, and in the summer it is a hazy dawn of orange, pink and yellow. Perhaps it is because you do not see yourself that you do not realize how you seem to the rest of us."

"And how do I seem, then, Robin?"

"You are dazzling," he said. The low flush across his high cheekbones gathered more colour and grew.

"I am not as beautiful as many ladies at court," she said.

"You are more beautiful than any woman alive."

"Because I am the *Queen*…" she said ruefully.

Robin shook his head. "No," he said earnestly. "Because you are *Elizabeth*."

He had moved her, I could see it. He sounded earnest enough. She touched his face. "*Robin,*" she whispered, warm affection spilling from her voice. He caught the hand that stroked his cheek and held it there.

"If I were free and unmarried," he whispered sharp, "if I could dare to hope that I was worthy to win your heart, then there would be nothing on this earth that would stop me from seeking it."

"But you are not free," the Queen muttered. "And neither am I. We are both trapped, Robin; you because you are married and I because I must marry to please my country." She took her hand from his face and put it against his chest.

"If I were worthy enough to win you, then there is nothing I would fail to do, for you or for England."

Her hand rested on his chest still, and Robin reached out and touched her hair with his fingertips. "I love the colour of your hair…" his voice was husky, "… and your eyes. It is as though you can see to the centre of my soul when you look on me. There is no one like you, Elizabeth."

"*Stop,* Rob," she breathed, looking about, but she did not pull away. "You are married."

He released his hold on her hand and hair, and stepped backwards. "I am," he conceded.

"Finally, my lord remembers," I said scathingly.

"Sometimes," the Queen said, "we have need to remember what we are blessed with, when we regret what we may have had." He looked away. His face was fighting to hold back words. "I will always cherish your friendship," Elizabeth said.

He looked at her. "I am your servant, Your Majesty." His voice sounded bruised. "And I am your friend, Elizabeth, for as long and as ever you want me. I am yours. However you need or may want of me, I am yours."

"If there ever was a man worthy to win my heart," she muttered, falteringly, "then I believe it could have been you."

His eyes jumped to hers once more. "Sometimes," he said, with a lighter and jesting tone to his voice, "we have need to remember what we are blessed with, when we regret what we may have had."

The Queen smiled a wry, tight smile.

"But sometimes," he continued gently, "we should also remember that whilst we cannot change the past, the future is as yet unknown to us."

"What do you mean?" There was a sharp look on her face.

He shrugged, his gaze unflinching. "Just to remember, my lady, that our situations may alter and change. For what man can know what the future may hold, after all?"

"The future is never certain, Robin," the Queen agreed, taking his arm and walking on. "But always, be assured of my affection for you."

His hand clasped over hers on his arm. "It is the most precious of all that I possess."

"It will always be yours, Rob."

We watched them walk away. I turned to Death. "People said he was poisoning me, to make me weak, to get rid of me. Was that what he meant when he said much might change in the future? Do you tell me that he was thinking of killing me, here and now? That as he spoke words of love to one woman he plotted to murder another?"

"I do not believe I have said anything."

Days passed. We watched Elizabeth argue with her lords and Council, trying to make a middle path in the faith for England. Suitors seemed to be popping up everywhere at court; the lord of this, the duke of that, a missive from a king, a prince, a viscount, an earl.

"She was the most eligible match in Europe," I said. "And she was young and comely, if in an unusual way."

We watched many arrive, and many more eyes watch them. Count von Helfenstein came to court that winter, seeking our Queen as a bride for either of the two sons of Ferdinand I of Austria, the Holy Roman Emperor. He did not seem to mind which, though he thoughtfully informed the Queen that there was a greater chance of harmony with the younger of the two, since the elder was a zealous Catholic.

Prince Erik of Sweden, though he did not get one, had tried to demand an answer to his suit even before the Queen's coronation, and then showered her with furs and tapestry afterwards. The Duke of Saxony sent ambassadors, weighed down with messages of their master's undying adoration for her. The Earl of Arundel, a distinctly foolish Englishman, seemed to think that his vast wealth would buy Elizabeth where his manners failed to charm her into marriage. Sir William Pickering, a most handsome young gallant, thought that the Queen's admiration for him as a courtier was enough to warrant a spot for his pert bottom upon her throne, and lastly Phillip II of Spain sent Duke Feria to attempt to convince Elizabeth to hand her power and country over to him, as her sister had done.

This bewildering array of suitors inspired not only a spate of wild and salacious gossip in the halls of court about whom the Queen would choose to marry, but also bizarre rumours of elopement or kidnap, vast wagers made on the strength of but a kind word, gifts and bribes made to Elizabeth's ladies for their information, and the rise of many young men at court, all who fancied *they* must be the man for our Queen.

"They all think I must marry," the Queen said to Kat one morning as Kat rubbed oil into the Queen's legs. "No one questions *if* I will marry." She shook her head. "This is all most amusing, but I have larger problems at hand than which cockscomb will prance before me today."

"Your Acts of Supremacy and Uniformity," said Kat, nodding, her hands moving up and down. A scent of rosemary rose from the oil, warmed by her palms.

"Indeed, so much of moment is going on and yet all people think I should think of is whom to wed. As if a woman can only ever have love in her brain and that should fill all her thoughts as well as her ambitions." Elizabeth looked down into Kat's eyes. "There are more important things than marriage or men."

"Men will never believe you on the second point, Majesty," Kat said, a smile on her face.

Chapter Seventeen

Throcking

Winter's End 1559

It was the end of winter, and Elizabeth had been ours for some months by then. Everyone was saying she should marry, and it should be done, and everyone was saying she could not choose for all of the princes and dukes and lords and kings of Europe and beyond wanted our Elizabeth, and she was dizzily dancing about the lot of them. But the only one she wanted to dance with was Robert.

"I had letters, many dictated and that felt worse somehow, as if he could not even be bothered to spare ink for me," I said, watching myself draw. I was in a window seat, charcoal in my fingertips as I sketched. I drew many things then, the rooms I was in most of all, it distracted me. "Everyone was talking of them. There were ugly rumours too, that he was going to kill me. I did not know what to believe, for if I thought of the man I had loved and married, the one who had met me in that garden and kissed me, even the one in the Tower, I could not think he was capable, and yet when I thought of the stranger who came to whatever house I was at that day, when I thought of his cold eyes and all our arguments, I realised I did not know the stranger. He just looked like someone I knew once, resembled someone I trusted."

I gazed at myself, sketching in my little book. "And it felt like, as the years went on, we had less and less in common."

Once, men of Robin's family had had such a position as he had now, so it could be said that Master of Horse was a restoration of his fortunes. When Edward was King, John Dudley, Rob's elder brother, had held the same post, and his father had been Master of Horse to Anne of Cleves and Catherine Howard. Horses were important to the Dudley family, and at that time Rob was obsessed with them. When he came home to me, all he spoke of was horses, a conversation I found endlessly dull, truth be told, but I was so desperate for a moment of time from my husband, almost from anyone, that I listened and stuck a mask of rapture upon my face as if everything he said was fascinating.

But to Elizabeth he really was fascinating. They shared private jests, and he could always make her laugh. They understood each other in a way no one else did. Everyone said it. They hardly needed to speak or to listen, for they understood each other well simply by spirit.

I nodded to myself, at the window. My hands were moving on the drawing book I held. "I was listening that day," I said. "I often was, and I never heard anything I wanted to hear."

Below me were two old men, weaving baskets of the willow cut that autumn. There was a fire out the back to keep them warm, and one made baskets and the other a fish trap of some kind. There was a basin of water soaking the rest of the willow between them. The kitchen maids brought to them ale and warmed pies, and their breath steamed from their mouths as they worked, and talked.

"They say the Queen has said she is certain he would die for her, and that is why she never wants to be parted from him," said one, twisting his length of willow up and about, winding in between other sticks. He had a pretty pattern of red and green and yellow willow on his basket. I wondered if it was a present for his wife, or he was making it fine enough to sell.

"They say no one else can make her troubles lessen," said the other, "for he knows her, as he was a prisoner as she was, as he lost people to the block as she did." The man sucked what teeth he had left. "Yet for all that, I think it a bad thing for our Queen. The man is married, and yet he acts as though he has not a wife here…" he waved behind him with his willow stick

"... and she a sweet lady, right enough. The Queen should find herself a prince or a duke and keep friends with women, for there will be no scandal in that."

"Aye," said the other. "Many is a time in life a man might be tempted from his wife, but a good man will know he has a good woman."

"Mayhap he thinks they are both good women, and one is richer with fairer prospects than the other."

"What can that mean to a man married?"

"The Queen's father was married, and then he was not and then he was again, perhaps she means to do the same as he, or have a man who might do so for her."

I turned to Death. "He wrote to her when they were apart, but not to me. To me there were scrappy notes, to her letters full of all the doings of his day. She called him her eyes, and I think to him she was his heart."

I never knew why I had stopped being enough for him. I never had an explanation. It was as though one day he had woken, the gritty dawn in his eyes, and there was another woman in his heart. I had been there and then I was not. He had said he loved me and then he had fallen out of that love.

*

By the spring of 1560 my husband and his new love were at Whitehall, and we followed them there.

In March, the early spring lambs were born, and the woodlands came alive with the sound of animals rustling in the undergrowth. "It was then Queen Elizabeth's Acts of Supremacy and Uniformity were put before the House of Lords," I told Death as we walked along a corridor where the scent of musk perfume lingered. "They had become merged into one bill within the Commons, and passed through there in a bare fortnight, aided by the intervention of Cecil, who held a seat for Lincolnshire in the House. When it came to the Lords, however, it was received rather differently. I was interested. I followed the case, what the Queen was doing. Many women did not care to, mainly because they were told it was beyond them, but I never believed anything was beyond me. I was born with a good mind and I used it." I shrugged. "Besides, it was something to do, to care about other than my own troubles.

We wandered the hall, past portraits of queens and kings of old, their eyes following us as we walked unseen amongst the living. "The merged bill for a religious settlement was thrown into vigorous debate. The Lords had postponed the reading of it, no doubt allowing those who opposed it ample time to gather their arguments. They all seemed to oppose it, Catholics and Protestants alike, and so the Queen's simple idea for a moderate path for her people was thrown into danger as the Lords erupted into endless debate and attack. Catholic bishops and lords were a majority in the House and they went at the bill like wolves to a hog's corpse. They attacked it on grounds of political danger, clashing with the papacy, possible sentences of excommunication from the Pope, threat of invasion by other countries, revolution, heresy and schism. The final blow was to question how Parliament could give authority over spiritual matters to a woman, who, according to the writings of St Paul, was forbidden even to *speak* in a Church, let alone become its spiritual leader."

We wandered up towards the chambers of the Queen. "The Queen's moderate ideas for our country were torn apart on one side by the fearful Catholics, and on the other Protestants, who wanted more dramatic reform and change than she had offered. The Lords sent the bill back to the Commons; it now contained the provision that the Queen would be *allowed* to assume the position of Head of the Church, if she wanted, but that it was a title that conferred no power. The clauses of uniformity were struck out entirely."

"A mess," observed Death.

"Indeed. The Commons were stuck. Mainly made up of Protestants, they did not want to accept the bill as it was, but they also did not want to reject it, leaving England to remain a Catholic country, complete with the unpopular laws against heresy. They accepted it. The bill was set to return to the House of Lords once again."

We turned into a doorway, to find Cecil there, looking annoyed.

"This is a mess, Cecil," Elizabeth stormed to her most trusted man as she marched into that same chamber in Whitehall. "They have *mutilated* what was to be the defining act of my reign. They have pulled it apart and left us with so little."

"The Lords were underestimated," agreed Cecil. "I will admit, Majesty, that I did not expect such a violent reaction to the idea of your resumption of the title of Supreme Head of the Church. I thought that, seeing as your great father and brother had held the title, then the Lords would see no issue in your use of it."

"People fear what is new to them," said Parry from the corner of the chamber. "They cannot see what might help them for all their dread of what they have never seen before."

Elizabeth nodded. "I think you are right, Parry. We have grown too confident in ourselves here, and now the unification of our country is in peril." She frowned. "I will not allow this to end here. I will not allow this slip of our judgement to become the death knell of my country's peace."

"She indeed had other things to think on rather than just men and marriage," I said quietly. "We had more in common than I knew, for they told her too to keep out of certain matters, not trouble herself with them, and she would not."

"Give me this night to think on the matter," she went on, "before this proclamation is made public. In the morning you shall have either my approval, or another answer."

Cecil and Parry nodded, bowed, and left.

I stood beside Elizabeth, a ghost she could not see, as she stood staring from the window. "Such things as she had to do and has to think on, I never had anything so important," I said with a sigh. "I tried merely to keep up with such news, not to make it happen. I envy her and I do not at the same moment. That my life could have been as important as hers, it is a wish for most women."

"All lives are important," said Death. "Some are more significant to others, it is true, but none is less important than another. The lives of all people affect others, change the world. Most people do not see what impact they have, but you will."

"She prolonged Parliament, I remember this time. Everyone said it was no good for a woman, no matter who that woman was, to fight men in politics. The Queen had been beaten back, but she would come out fighting. I remember that, too."

We shifted to another moment; it was London in the spring.

We followed the Queen to the Chapel Royal where she went to an Easter Mass celebrated in English, with a Protestant wooden Communion table, during which Communion was offered to all. Her face set hard, Elizabeth led the procession to the table to receive Communion, and professed her faith in the redemptive nature of the body and blood of Christ, leaving it open to interpretation whether she considered the body and blood to actually *be* Christ or not. "She would have her way," I said, smiling with affection now. "Like her father she was. She wanted both sides to make peace, make a middle way, much as her father had forged. It was one of the few good things he ever did."

In the days that followed, during a recess in the Houses, the Queen set up a public debate in Westminster Abbey. Delegates, eight Protestant and eight Catholic in number, were brought forth to publicly submit their conflicting thoughts on questions set by the Queen, to be weighed up by a panel of judges made up of her own Privy Council.

We watched as days passed and debate turned into bickering, yet all the while there was a light glowing in the eyes of the Queen. The debate was weighted in favour of the Protestant argument, so she was likely to win, but she did not exclude Catholics. She wanted it to appear fair.

One by one, the Catholic bishops refused to read their prepared statements. As each of them defied the Queen, and Council, she ended the day with ominous words. "And since you will not that we should hear from you, my lords, you may perchance shortly hear from *us*..." Elizabeth glared at the rebel bishops.

That night, she had two of the Catholic leaders, Bishops White and Watson, taken to the Tower and locked up in cells charged with contempt for the authority of the Crown. Since White had been the man who compared Elizabeth to a living *dog* at Queen Mary's funeral, his arrest was particularly unsurprising. The rest of them, the Queen left free.

"They just blundered straight into an open declaration of defiance, Your Majesty," said Bacon, one of her new men, chuckling, on the evening the bishops were arrested. "They were so annoyed by the debate, and they all argued so much over the tiny details of who should go first and who should speak in what language, I don't know if they even noticed that what they were doing was an act of contempt for the Crown until it was too late."

"They knew," Elizabeth said ruefully. "They knew well enough. They want to test us, to see if they cannot have the Catholic

Queen they so desire if they could have a Protestant one whom they can control and manipulate. They wanted to see whether I would fall if they pushed me, but they will come to understand that I am the bough that does not bend nor break. I am the cliff they cannot chip away. I am the eternal they cannot outlive. I will have order in my realm, and they will not take it from me."

"They certainly seemed surprised when we arrested them, Majesty," grinned Parry.

"I'm sure they did." The Queen winked at her old friend. "But it was their own fault. They acted in outright defiance of the will of their Queen; such an act cannot go unpunished. They have ruled the roost for too long. Under my sister they were strong and felt they could bully the Crown. They will find that I am made of a different mettle. I will not keep them locked away for good of course, but I think we will delay any hearing of their pleas for release for a while, to teach them a lesson."

"Perhaps until the end of the next session of Parliament, Majesty?" asked Cecil slyly.

"Yes," she said to Cecil, as though she had thought about it long and hard. "Until the end of the next session of Parliament indeed. That should give White and Watson ample time to think of the consequences of defying their sovereign."

I laughed, seeing what she had done. She would win the vote by keeping those men under arrest. "It was not fair, was it? Those men would oppose her bills and she was making sure they could not, but when has this world ever been fair? And since men so often make the rules and yet fail to follow them, why should women not do the same?" I smiled. "She won, by a handful of votes if I remember rightly. Probably just the number of the men locked away, and only released once Elizabeth of England had her way."

"You seem pleased for her."

I glanced at him. "Not all she did was bad," I said. "She played bad with me, for she stole away my husband, but she did much that was good for England. Her moderate settlement, it was a good thing."

"You admire her."

"Perhaps."

Chapter Eighteen

Richmond Palace

Spring 1559

I watched Elizabeth sashay from her chamber after roundly besting the Spanish ambassador, sent to explain why, after his master had proclaimed everlasting, undeniable, painful love for the English Queen, Phillip had then gone on with unseemly haste to become betrothed to the eldest daughter of the French royal house, Princess Elisabeth de Valois, daughter of the French King Henri II and his Medici Queen. Peace was made between Spain and France, and sealed with the pact of marriage, but Elizabeth looked more pleased than any of the parties actually involved. She had avoided marriage yet again, and made the King of Spain look like a fool into the bargain.

"Did she want to marry anyone?" I asked Death.

"A question only she can answer, or time will tell."

"I remember that time too," I said, gazing about the hallway full of people who had been waiting to see the Queen now milling about, starting to disperse. "I was at Camberwell, another house of another supporter of Robin's. The news came to us, and we all talked of it. It was not long after that her bill was passed and the new English Mass was celebrated in her personal chapel. Where leaders lead, others will follow, and soon churches all over London had adopted the service, earlier than was legally required. Overnight, it became most stylish to worship in the new *English* fashion."

"It was a time of change."

"And promotion. Rob was granted the Order of the Garter on the feast of St George, along with Norfolk, Northampton and Rutland. There was much muttering about it, as whilst Norfolk, Northampton and Rutland were premier peers of England, Robin was the son and grandson of traitors to the Crown. The fact that those traitors had also once been the most trusted and loyal servants of the house of Tudor was ignored in the face of court gossip. To Robin's new titles the Queen added mansions, such as Knole Park in Kent, and lands in Leicestershire and Yorkshire. We were rich, and I was sent many presents. He was one of the stars of her court, and although he had no official political role in government, as the Queen's Master of Horse he was a trusted friend and advisor. She promised she would reward him three-fold, and she did. Elizabeth was not one to forget a debt owed."

"Norfolk did not like it."

I looked sharply at Death. "No," I said. "He did not."

People do not like to see others rise over them, even when such rivals warrant their promotions because of loyalty and trust. Norfolk, especially, saw Robin as an upstart and was resentful of the Queen's obvious preference for his company. Was Death suggesting that Norfolk took revenge on Robin, using me? But surely if he was the one to blame, he had done what Robin wanted, had he not? He had removed me, and Robin could now wed the Queen.

Not knowing what to make of Death's intervention here, I went on. "Everyone was talking of the Queen and her Master of Horse," I said. "It was hard. People, even my own maids, would stop talking when I came into a room. It was hard to pretend that I heard nothing, saw nothing, imagined nothing. People must have thought me a doll during that time, blank-eyed and unaware of the world or anything in it. And yet I was aware. I had to hide a shamed soul and a broken heart all that time, and then I came to think that he had indeed broken my heart, for there was something wrong with me."

We were at Camberwell then, in my chamber, Mrs Picto hovering like a bag of nerves over me.

A doctor was hovering over me too, the younger me although now not so much younger. Only a year or so there was between us now. "A canker," he said, removing his cold hand from my gown. I remember thinking at the time that he could have warmed his hand a little before cupping my breast.

I remembered that moment too well and not enough. There were words said, visions that came to my mind. I remember the tears in my eyes and the dreadful hope when he said there were potions to be tried and medicines to rub into the skin, but I knew what a canker was. There was something hard in my breast; was it a heart broken and rotting within me? I knew not, but it felt like it.

"You should write to Lord Dudley, call him home to you," said the man.

"Yes, I will," I said. "Thank you, doctor."

He left, and I saw him shake his head on the way out. I was young and we always pity the young when we know they are to die before their time. A canker in the breast, and it was growing fast. It had been such a small mark before, and then it grew, and pits appeared in the tissue about my nipple. There was a hardness there. I had been so tired each year when winter came, as if I had no strength, and now there was a reason. Something of evil was inside me. My heart was broken and festering inside my chest, and it would kill me. I wrote to Robin, and he did not come.

"He was busy with the Queen, and could not get away," I said in a numb voice. "That is what he told me. When he did come, eventually, he said he was sure I would be fine, and then he told me of court. I sat there listening to him, and I heard not a word. I could barely speak I was so astonished. A doctor had written to him too, told him I was sick and yet it appeared that either he had not read it, or did not want to talk of it. I was dying, and I was scared."

I looked away from that stunned girl sitting at that table as her husband tried to tell her of court. Perhaps he was trying to distract or cheer me, but it did neither. He left the next morn. I had not wanted to lie with him, because I was ill. He seemed annoyed when I said that to him.

"I was sick, and he had sworn vows to be with me if I was, and yet my husband was nowhere to be seen. I think that hurt the most. When he had been in danger of his life, something brought about by his own actions, I had been there for him. I had come to the Tower and comforted him, did all I could to make him feel better, and yet when I needed someone, when I was ill and it was not my fault I was, he was nowhere to be seen.

"How may I describe the sense of abandonment?" I asked Death. "To face death alone, and not in an immediate sense but due to a creeping sickness each day making one sicker and sicker, it is an awful fate. One moment I wanted to laugh and do all things I never had done and make the best of what time I had left, and at others I wanted nothing more than to crawl into my bed and pull the covers over my head, so I might retreat into something like the womb which gave me life. And like a fool I had thought he might care, that this, this trouble in my life might make him remember that he had loved me once, or even, simply out of human decency, might urge him to come to me, to spend time with me. But no. He came less. I was alone more. In the time I needed someone the most, needed love the most, I was more alone than ever I had been."

I walked to the girl, sitting on the edge of her bed, staring at the wall. "It was then I knew he did not care for me, for even if one has but a passing affection for another person, they would be there. He knew not what to do to help me, and did not care to ask. He abandoned me more fully than before, once he knew I was ill. I was left to face death alone.

"I do not think I have ever thought so badly of a person as I thought of him then. If an enemy had told me they were dying I would have sympathised, and he could not, even with his own wife. There was no support, nothing for me, as a gillyflower uprooted and thrown into the wind I was tossed by the hand of fate, and so, wilted and dying, I was flung into a tempest of the soul. There was a darkness upon me then, that of illness and that of hatred. I never felt so let down by anyone, and I had been let down by the person who was supposed to be the one I thought highest of. I knew then what I was to him, nothing more than an inconvenience. I was a thing in the way of his dreams, a toy he had loved once in childhood and now he was grown I was embarrassing, a memento of a time he wished to forget. I was the doll stuffed in the chest, left to rot. I was the toy once beloved, now despised, and yet I was more than all these things for I was a person, alive for the moment at least. I was a wife, a legal partner, unless he could rid himself of me. But he was busy with his Queen.

"Perhaps he thought of her as his future, and if I was dying I was of his past," I said bitterly as we watched Elizabeth and Robin ride across open fields and through woods together. They were laughing. He looked as if he had not a care in the world. "People said they were lovers but she seemed not to care if that damaged her reputation and he did not care either, not about his wife sick in the country. Perhaps he hoped I might die and leave him free to wed again. It would be less scandal than an annulment."

"They were not lovers," Death said, leaning against a tree.

"I know. Anyone who took the time could see that. It was not just that she was guarded so well by women and by her own careful caution, it was how they were *like* lovers. No one is more in love than those who have found affection but not acted upon it. The act itself, so often it is comical, disappointing even, a bumbling joining of bodies, but those who have not yet done the deed are full of expectation and purity of love's fantasy. Any who looked on them could see it, that they were not lovers in anything but mind, but the connection between them, the desire, it was strong."

We were in the Queen's chambers then. I could feel a strand of that welcome silver on my wrist, winding about my fingers as if seeking to hold hands with me. I squeezed my hand about it, as if returning its gesture, and the silver strands turned to smoke in my fingertips, drifting away.

"Send for Lord Robin," Elizabeth was calling to her ladies, raising her eyebrows and pursing her lips tartly. She looked as if her temper was roused. "Or are you all so dull of wit this morning that the Queen must become her own messenger?" They scurried from her displeasure. I shook my head. I had never been so rude to my servants, and what was amusing, perhaps, was they respected me less for it.

In short time, Rob arrived. He looked fresh and lively as he bowed to his Queen. A new blue doublet covered his fine chest. He had taken care to sweeten his breath with mint and to wash carefully so that he gave no offence to the Queen's famously delicate nose. "Horses," she said to him brusquely as he rose from his bow upon entering the room.

"An unusual name to give me, Majesty," he replied with a naughty smile. "But I suppose it is fitting in a way."

She laughed. "Silly colt." Elizabeth rose from where she sat on the pile of cushions on the floor to cuff him playfully on the shoulder.

"I think I preferred being called *Horse*, Majesty," he jested, following the path of her steps as she walked to the window.

"I wish to expand the stables, Rob, and I want to talk to you of horses." His eyes sparkled. Robin loved fine horses, loved the freedom and the excitement of riding them, and he loved to have new things to play with.

"She could always offer him that," I muttered.

"My sister had no interest in the breeding of her mounts," Elizabeth continued. "And I wish to change that. My father had an avid interest in good horseflesh, and his royal stables were known for it. From now on, I want the stables of England to be talked of with deference in the courts of the world. I want our horses to be the best there are." She turned to him. The light from the bright morning bathed their faces. "What would you advise to add to the stables?"

Robin's face turned introspective. A slight frown touched that handsome face and he stroked his short beard, something he often did as thoughts raced through his head. "Some would say Arab, Majesty," he mused. "But I have often thought that they are unsuited to our climate, and do not perform as well on the green hills of England as they do in the dust of the desert."

"I did not ask what '*some*' might say, my lord. I asked what *you* might suggest."

He grinned wide. "I should always know never to repeat thoughts that are not my own within your hearing, Majesty. You are never kind to thoughts lacking in originality."

The Queen sniffed. "The wisdom of others should never be ignored, but it should also never be followed with such slavish abandon that we forget to use the matter of our own minds."

Robin stroked that beard once more. "I have long liked the horses of the Irish, Majesty. You will not find it a popular suggestion amongst the general riders of court, but amongst those of us who have actually mounted a good strong horse of Ireland you will find many who would agree with me."

"I would take *your* opinion, Rob," she assured him. "You do not have to bring others into the conversation."

His eyes were soft with pleasure at her trust in him. "Then take some good Irish horseflesh into the royal stables, Majesty, and some Barbary. You will find their stamina outmatches our present breeds, and their strength is such to match that of our Queen."

"It will be done, and you, Robin, will be the one to choose the horses personally. Send no servant to this task, for I wish for the best only, and you understand my wishes better than any other."

Robin bowed. "It is the greatest pleasure you have given me today, my lady," he said, looking most pleased. "Not only to spend long hours considering and buying the best horses in the country, but to buy them for your pleasure? What man could ask for more?"

"Then add one thing to that consideration, and buy them also for *your* pleasure," she commanded, grinning at his surprised face. "For I have an idea that the horses you would have for your own, my lord, would be the ones I would want for my stables."

Robin laughed. It was a great booming laugh, readily infectious. It hurt a little to hear it, for long ago I had been the one to make him laugh like that, but now it was her.

"Prepare my horse for this afternoon, Lord Robin," the Queen ordered, smoothing her gown of crimson and gold. "And we will talk more about improving my stables as we ride out. All expenses for this will come from my own Privy Purse."

"Would your ministers not grant money to the Crown for its betterment, Majesty?" Robin asked, and she laughed.

"What do you imagine the Privy Purse is, my lord? My personal allowance from the country is for those expenses required to ensure the glory and honour of my station as Queen. For that, I can see that I require not only dresses and stockings, but good horse beneath me. The requirements of my people and our country will be paid from the budget allowed by our means. My own requirements will come from my own purse alone." She pursed her lips. "Would you think that £12,000 would be enough to make a start on purchasing our new horses, Rob? That is all I can offer at present, although I will add more in the future."

His slight intake of breath made her laugh again. "I will take that as a yes, then. And you will, in this matter, be as you are in many others for me and be my eyes where I cannot see."

He kissed her hand, and his eyes lifted to hers, soft and as warm as a shaded glen on a summer's afternoon. "I will be all you want of me, Majesty."

"What did she want of him?" I asked my companion.

"I think she did not know, yet," was his answer.

Chapter Nineteen

Greenwich Palace

Summer 1559

It was early July, and the court was at Greenwich. "I heard the Queen liked this palace because she was born here," I said as Death and I wandered the paths. It was busy there that day, people bustling past us on pathways in fine clothes, barrels of drink and baskets of food being brought up from the water steps where boat after boat was pulling up to deliver wares to the waiting hands of impatient servants. Two pages ran past us, sending my phantom skirts billowing out a little, no doubt racing each other to see who could do their lord's bidding the fastest, and thereby earn a coin as a reward. There was a joust that day, and people were talking of the feasting and dancing that was to go on at night. "All the ideas of her Majesty's *horse lord*!" tittered one lady as she walked arm in arm with another.

"Whore lord more like," said the other, laughing.

"Plenty must have spoken of him so," I said, watching them go. "He was rising fast in favour, and people always are jealous. Perhaps that was hard for him, feeling censured simply for being himself." I felt bad for Rob, even though I had reason to hate him enough. He had worked hard to get where he was, had sacrificed much, including our marriage. No matter how unfairly he had dealt with me, I did not relish hearing other people slander him.

We wandered on, watching the events. Robin had obviously thrown himself into an excess of activity, arranging processions, jousts and entertainments for Elizabeth and her court every day and night. The array of sights and sounds was impressive. Since he had a great talent for this kind of pleasure, the Queen had been happy to hand him the strings of the Privy Purse to allow him to fund these celebrations. "She was showing how different she was from her siblings, that there would be joy in England as her father had brought, that we all would play again." I looked up at the skies. "But the weather did not want to comply with her."

It had been wet that summer, almost the last I was to see. From early morning rain would pour on already sodden fields, making travel hard and work dangerous for the people. But despite this, and fears about the productivity of the harvest without much sunshine, it seemed that there was a song in the air, and a joyous lilt to the step of all those at court. At this time I had spent days on end indoors, worrying about my health, praying on my knees, and all this had been going on at court. I shook my head, wondering at how different the same time might be for different people. I had been desperate, as they had been dancing.

I wished then that I had been dancing, no matter how tired and ill I had felt, no matter if I had danced alone. I wished I had spent my time in pursuits I had enjoyed, while I had the time to do so.

In times of good weather, when soft skies provided sun and balmy winds brought delightful fresh scents, we watched the Queen and her people take afternoon meals in the arbours and pleasure gardens of the great parks, sheltered by the shade of simple trees or by coverings of velvet held aloft by sweating servants.

We watched Robin surprise the Queen by having a whole pavilion constructed in the grounds at Greenwich; fine, tall, white and green painted poles held aloft a canopy of birch branches, decorated with wildflowers. White and red roses, scented gillyflowers, purple lavender and bright marigolds hung over the party of court in great garlands as they feasted on salty cheese, roasted meats, and pies stuffed full of syrupy strawberries and sour-sweet cherries. The scented herbs that covered the floor released fresh and perfumed scents as courtiers walked or sat on them as they talked and listened to musicians play their flutes and lutes.

"Did he remember me, when he ordered those gillyflowers hung?" I asked, trailing a hand over one of the garlands by Elizabeth's head. "They were the flower of our wedding. I wonder now if I even crossed his mind, it was so full of her."

The nights were given over to masked dances where the court moved as one dressed as animals or creatures of myth. Every night we watched Elizabeth dance with many of her courtiers, but Robin was her clear favourite. When they moved together it was as though they were two parts of the same dancer. Their feet tapped in time to the rhythms of the drum and the pipe, and the flowing swish of her arms flew like the wings of a bird in the sky.

Almost every day Robin and the Queen rode out together with her ladies. In the chill, wet dawn of the dark early morning, horses' hooves thundered across the parks. Sometimes the court hunted and sometimes Elizabeth and my husband just relished the feeling of freedom that was granted by riding out.

"Glorious!" Elizabeth cried, as she pulled her horse up on the crest of a hill, the sun still wending its way to the skies, pockets of woodland glittering in the dull light. The lush green of the grass was moist with dew and there was a sparkling blueness of the rivers flowing and burbling down the rivulets of the hills.

"Glorious," agreed Robin. She looked around at him, cheeks pink and bonny from the speed of her ride. He was not looking at the landscape, but at her. The Queen blushed and tossed her head, turning her eyes from his gaze. "Shall we ride on?" he asked, eyes sparkling with eagerness to continue.

"I must return to meet with my Council." Elizabeth pulled a despondent face.

"Another hour would not hurt, surely, Majesty?" suggested Robin, a sneaky look on his face, his hand stroking the sweating side of his chestnut horse.

"My Council would not say as you do." She gazed longingly out at the woods.

"Perhaps you will listen to the *counsel* of a friend then?" Robin requested. "One who understands that his Queen may find that she thinks more clearly when she has taken good exercise for her body?"

"You seek to instruct us, Lord Robin?" She was teasing.

Rob shook his head. "Instruct?" he laughed, releasing his grip on his reins and holding his hands up in mock defence as his strong thighs gripped his horse. "I should never dare to try to *instruct,* Majesty. *Advise* only, offer my humble opinion that a good Queen must also be allowed to have her own pleasures as she so diligently cares for the good of all her people. Life cannot only be made up of papers and signing!" He pulled his lips downwards in a most dramatically dejected manner, which made him look like a toad. "Of words and arguments and parchment and law and petitions and missives and seals and pardons and sanctions and…"

"Stop!" she laughed, waving a hand at him. "You have said quite enough to put me off for good, my lord."

"I do not wish for that," he promised, "but one morning, may a Queen not take just one more hour for her own pleasure that she might return to her tasks as a ruler sated in her own needs?"

"One more hour, Robin," she agreed and laughed, kicking her horse and yanking on the reins as she turned him to the woods below. "And I wager I can beat you through the wood and to the other side!" she screamed back to Rob as her horse plunged over the edge of the hill. Robin gave a shout, and turned his horse, leaping after Elizabeth as hooves raced across the dark earth and into the woods beneath. Behind them, guards raced to keep pace, as the Queen's powerful horse charged into the darkness of the woodlands, leaping his way over a fallen trunk, thundering through the shadows of the trees.

But later, it seemed things were not so well. Time turned, silver swirled, and we were in the gardens of the palace with Elizabeth, a scent of herbs wafting from the far away kitchens came floating towards us. I closed my eyes and inhaled the welcome perfume, and then the peace of the day shattered. There was a shout and a furious looking Robin came storming towards the Queen.

"What do you mean by sending that message to me?" Robin demanded, thunderous with rage, staring at Elizabeth with blazing eyes. He indeed had a temper to match her own. He was magnificent, as was she.

The Queen glowered at him. "Do you forget your position within this court and country, sir?" she growled. "Do you forget whom it is that you address?"

"What has happened?" I asked Death.

"She found something of great importance happened when she was out riding, and blamed your husband for keeping her away from her duties," he said. "The King of France was injured jousting, and not long after died, putting her cousin of Scots on the French throne."

"I forget nothing," Robin said coldly. "Not the bonds of duty to my Queen, nor the ties of friendship and affection which seem to have escaped *your* own understanding at this time."

"How *dare* you?" The words hissed from Elizabeth's mouth as she gritted her teeth at him like a cornered vixen. "Who do you think you are to talk to me as such? I am no wife of yours, sir, nor maidservant, or tavern wench! I am your *Queen* and master. You will apologise immediately or see yourself banished from my court for good for your insolence!"

"I would rather be banished from your side forever," he protested, his great height towering over hers, "than be at your side and never speak my mind, madam! Although others may pander to your temper and fawn at your rages, I am not made of such stock! I will speak my mind, even to my Queen and master."

I looked up to see St Loe, head of the Queen's guard, glancing hesitantly over the clipped hedges at the Queen and Robin arguing. It was quite clear that he could hear every word they were saying, and was disturbed, worried. Elizabeth held up a hand without pausing in her flow of furious anger directed at Rob, and St Loe paused, not taking his eyes from the two, but waiting at his Queen's command. He looked astonished she had not called for Rob to be dragged away.

"I could cast you down, Robin," the Queen threatened, her voice cold. "Just as easily as I raised you up. Think you that you are the only pretty face that I might entertain myself with? Think you that you have the only merry jibe to court my humour?" She laughed mockingly. "You are not as special as you like to think, my lord. For every Robin Dudley there are a thousand appealing boys to dance attendance on me, and each and every one of them would be more sensible of his position than you are presently."

Robin's face grew even darker, this time as much with jealousy as with anger. "I know well enough," he said bitterly, "only *too* well that Your Majesty may court the hearts of any and all she pleases. Dancing here with one and there with another. Casting the feelings of your loyal subjects and those who love you to the floor and grinding her heel through them to turn them to dust!"

"He calls her a whore, without calling her one," I noted. The Queen evidently thought the same.

"How *dare* you?" she shrilled, walking towards him, hands raised as though she might strike his handsome face. "Tell me who amongst those you describe truly ever risked their heart? Tell me which of those men I dance with or smile at ever honestly offered their love to me?" Her hair was falling from its pins and ribbons as she shook her head furiously at Rob.

"None, that is the answer, my Lord Dudley, none! They do not see a woman to whom they give their hearts in love or friendship; they see a crown to which they aspire. You condemn me for cruelty? Is it not crueller to pretend love to a woman in order to gain her power? I have no cares for damaging the feelings of their hearts, for they have none!"

"There is one who offers his heart to that woman truly," said Robin quietly, rage slipping from his features. "There is one who cares nought for the crown she wears or the chair on which she sits. There is one who truly does risk his heart, and feels it break when he sees the object of his love offer her graces to others who do not deserve her."

"You speak of yourself?" she exclaimed, throwing her hands into the air. "You would be my suitor? What good is that to me, Robin? What good? *You are married*. You have a wife! Queen I might be, but I cannot change the laws of God and man to suit my own ends. My father spent his time dismantling the institution of marriage for every new and fair face that smiled at him, and what did that bring to our country but fear and unrest? I am Queen of a country that finds itself without money or allies in Europe. We are surrounded by enemies most dangerous; the French covet my throne and the Scots linger hungrily at our borders. The Spanish hate all that we stand for and all that I am. I am a Queen, unmarried, and so my greatest weapon is to use that state for my country. So, yes, my lord, I dance and I smile and I keep every ambassador guessing; their princes court my hand and advance the interests of my country and my people. As long as they all woo me then England has power still, but do not think for a moment that they risk their hearts any more than I risk mine. This is politics, my lord, not passion, leverage, not love."

She turned from him and cast her eyes upwards, staring at the blue skies with their ruffled clouds bobbing along peacefully, unaware of anything wrong in the world or complicated in life.

"What if..." Robin's voice haltered.

"What if *what*, Rob?" She breathed in shakily, her voice soft and low. Anger was draining from her, I could see it.

"What if..." he stepped closer, until he was just behind her "... what if there were a time when I *was* free to offer myself to you, my lady?"

She turned around. His body was close to hers; a bare whisker of propriety remained between the Queen and my husband. "What do you mean?" she asked. Her hand reached up and set itself on his chest, half as a gesture of affection and apology, and half perhaps to hold him just a little away from her, an attempt to try to retain that control she needed. Elizabeth looked up into his warm brown eyes, seeing them soften as he gazed at her. His pupils widened. One hand wrapped itself around hers at his chest, and the other reached out to smooth errant hair from her forehead.

"You look so very beautiful, Elizabeth..." he smiled warmly, "... when you are at your most furious."

"You too, are rather handsome when you storm, my *Eyes*," she said with affection.

"Elizabeth," he murmured, wrapping his fingers about hers. "My wife is sick."

"What do you mean?"

"She has a growth, a canker, in her breast," he continued, his words purring out almost in a whisper. "The doctors say that she cannot have more than a year or two left, perhaps less. It is mortal, and she will die of it."

"Does she know?" the Queen asked. Rob nodded.

"The growth has made her sick for some time now." His free hand gently tucked her hair back into her hood. "She knows that she will not have long for this world."

"You pig," I whispered. "You used my death to propose to her!"

"Why do you tell me this?" The Queen did not seem as excited as I might have thought she would be. She looked worried, in truth.

"If there were to come a day when I was free to offer myself as your husband," Robin said, "would you have me, my lady?"

"I cannot answer something like that." She tried to pull her hand away from his. He held on to it, stalling her from escape.

"Why can you not?" he asked, pulling her closer. "I ask not to become a consort or a king. I want nothing of politics in my marriage bed. What I want is to be with the woman I love, the woman I have always loved. I want to pledge my life, my body, my soul, my *world* to you, Elizabeth. I love you."

She wrenched her hands free and he released them, standing before her, looking so sad that I felt as though my heart might break to look on him. But my heart could not break anymore, it was stone. "He is lying," I whispered, "and she sees it. Look at the way he just spoke to her, such contempt and disrespect. The moment she is his, he will treat her like that all the time, and she knows that. If she married him, he would seek out all her power and take it from her."

"Robin…" Elizabeth spoke falteringly, her voice unsure, confused. "Robin, *please*. Your wife is yet living. I cannot answer what I may or may not do should there come a time when you would be free to become mine. How can I? Can I court the bed of another woman before she has left it for the grave?"

She looked at him steadily. "Another man once offered me his hand in marriage before he was free to do so, and when I turned his suit down, he married within weeks to another. I do not like promises made for a time in the future when all may be garlanded with roses and shining with fairy-dust." She tossed her head, holding her hand between them. "If there comes a time when you are free to become the husband of another, come to me then, and we will see if the love you have for me remains as strong when the choice of all maids in England are open to you." Her hand alternately was clenching itself into a fist and into a flat hand, over and over as it stood between them.

"Elizabeth," he protested, trying to step closer.

"Stop, Robin! For this time and all times, my lord." She drew herself up, hand outstretched now before her like a shield. "*I am your Queen, first,* and you will address me as such!"

"Your Majesty," said Robin stiffly, as he bowed.

She turned to leave, but stopped. She did not turn back to him. "Think not, Robin," she breathed, "That your words have not had effect on me. Should I be willing to set aside all other considerations, should my heart have the say that my head reserves first, should I ever be free to choose with the eyes of love rather than the need of necessity, then I would perhaps choose a different path." She turned back to him; there were tears in his eyes.

"It is not a 'yes'." Her voice was very quiet. "But it is not a 'no' either. That is the best answer that I can give you, at this time."

He smiled. "You give me hope," he murmured.

She nodded. "I must go now, Robin. But I will think on all you have said to me." She paused. "And I am sorry for shouting at you, I was angry on another matter entirely, and I should not have sent such a message to you."

Robin bowed as the Queen spun on a heel and walked swiftly from the gardens, indicating to the still watchful St Loe to follow.

"She promised him hope," I said. "And he abandoned me that day."

Chapter Twenty

Progress

July 1559

People were rushing everywhere around us, dismantling furniture, packing cases. Court was on the move. It was the Queen's first royal progress. A chance to move from house to house across the counties of England and to stay with honoured hosts who would welcome the expanse and the expense of entertaining the Queen and her court. It was a chance for the new Queen to show favour to those houses visited, and to show herself to the people.

"They would wend through Eltham, Dartford, Cobham and Nonsuch," I said, watching as the Queen and her ladies walked to the front of the palace. "I was not invited, of course. People said the Queen was saving money, asking others to feed her and the court all summer, and it might have been true but they all vied to be one of the ones she called on all the same."

"The horses are ready, Majesty," Rob's voice rang out in the courtyard. She turned to him, smiling.

Elizabeth was merry, and for good reason. Although dangers still lurked at our borders, the threat of immediate invasion had perhaps paused by that time. Plans for disruption in Scotland were going ahead; the Earl of Arran was being shipped secretly to England as we later found out. In France, Ambassador Throckmorton reported friction developing between the Guise family and the Dowager Queen, Catherine de Medici. King Henri's death had not led to the Guise immediately turning their eyes on England, but instead had brought confusion as the mantle of power was scrapped over at the French court. Catherine de Medici had emerged suddenly as a strong combatant in this match, and the Guise were struggling with her. Each side seemed to think that they should be the ones to rule the new King and his Queen. None of them thought that the new King and Queen should rule, of course. Such a possibility had clearly not been considered by anyone.

"You have mounts ready for my ladies?" the Queen asked Rob.

"Of course, Majesty," he said, nodding to Bess, Blanche and fair Geraldine, who all smiled at him. "Follow us as promptly as you can, Kat." The Queen gazed up at the summer skies with longing. "I will go on ahead."

Kat curtseyed obediently, but I saw her eyes stray to Robin with a strange and wary expression. He was watching the Queen as she put on her riding gloves, seemingly oblivious to the vigilant, mistrustful eyes of Elizabeth's oldest friend.

I could read that face.

Kat Ashley did not like the manner in which Robin was looking at Elizabeth. She disapproved. My heart warmed to her.

"Come then, Robin." Elizabeth, apparently oblivious to her friend, batted him lightly with her riding whip and laughed at his affronted face. "Get my ladies and me to our horses and let's be away."

"Kat Ashley did not like Robin to be so close to her mistress," I said and Death shook his head.

"Indeed not," he said, pointing.

It was Eltham, I knew it well by the tiny castle and ancient moat. It was romantic in its antiquated way; a place where ladies should sigh, and gallants should pursue. Eltham was amongst the oldest of the royal palaces, surrounded by the finest hunting grounds. I had come here with King Edward's court once. Wide open parks rich with deer were dotted here and there with patches of woodland where imported boars were loosed for the monarch to hunt. Court was apart from the clamour of the city here, and could wake to ride through glen and over hill, seeing only a few souls on the way. Eltham was a good palace for the summer, but too draughty to use much in the winter months.

We watched day after day pass, flitting shadows and fragments of memories flying past, of Robin and Elizabeth riding out before dawn with her ladies and guards, hunting or riding through Eltham's parks, eating under gnarled branches and full leaves of English oaks, and dancing long into the night. They rode through the countryside, hearing the call of the corncrake in the fields, and the slathering baying of the hounds that ran gamely at their sides on the hunt. Flag, bulrushes and reeds tossed and whispered at the edges of ponds and lakes, and sweetbriar roses twisted thorny beauty through the wilderness, spreading a sweet scent of ripe apples. Wild thyme grew over chalky hillsides, clustering together in rose-coloured mounds, and sharp tempered nettles tarried in the undergrowth longing to sting unwary ankles. Even when light rain fell, and the ground beneath them was churned red-brown with mud, they did not mind.

We watched Elizabeth turn restless when Robin was not with her, tap her feet with displeasure, and then her face would beam when he appeared. Then one day time slowed, no more speeding past, and Kat Ashley was there to greet her mistress in from the hunt.

Kat shooed the other ladies to the back of the bedchamber, and started to undress Elizabeth herself. "A good ride, Majesty?" she asked.

"Indeed, Kat," the Queen sighed languidly. "My Lord Dudley knows a fine horse when he comes to it. He chooses well for me, as he is attentive in all ways."

"Yes, Majesty." Kat's voice positively dripped with the urge to say more. "Some may say that he is *too* attentive."

The Queen turned, the gown mostly removed from her body so she stood before Kat in a long kirtle. Elizabeth scowled at her, anger flashing in her black eyes. "What mean you? *Who* would say?"

Kat surprised the Queen by suddenly falling to her knees before her. She held her hands up as if she were praying, her face wrung with worry. "Majesty," she said earnestly, "I have known you since you were little more than a babe, and you have always trusted my counsel, even when you did not take it. But I implore you to think on the manner of your behaviour with Lord Dudley. There are many rumours that abound about any noble or Queen, but his behaviour towards you, and yours towards him have started to give rise to rumour most damaging and dangerous. The people of this country love you, Majesty, but they will not love a Queen who they fear has given her dignity away by, by taking a lover!"

"I have taken no lover, Kat," Elizabeth said slowly.

"Majesty…" she wrung her hands like a wash cloth before her "… I know that, as well as do all your maids and ladies. As well as does any who truly knows you. But when those who do *not* know you see how you act with Lord Dudley, they have cause to suspect. A king may tarry with many ladies, he may take them into his bed and all men will merely look at him with esteem, but a queen cannot do the same. If she tarries too long with a single man, then tongues will wag about her. You are opening yourself up to dangerous rumours, my lady. And I fear for you!"

"If I have shown myself gracious to Lord Dudley then it is due to the honourable nature of his character and my *platonic* admiration for him. I have taken no lover, Kat. I am a virgin, as ever I was."

"I know that, Majesty," said Kat, "and will swear it to all and any who ask, as ever I have done, many times, already."

"People… ask that often of you?" asked the Queen looking at her with narrowed eyes. Kat blushed and nodded. "Do they ask this, too, of my other ladies?" Kat nodded again. "And do my other ladies answer the same as you, Kat?"

Kat nodded furiously, and the Queen turned from her worried eyes. She looked as if someone had punched her in the chest. "I wonder that such an opinion of me could have been formed," she muttered sadly, walking to the window and placing her hands on the stone sill, "when I am surrounded day and night by the ladies of my bedchamber and members of my Council. All who surround me can see that there is nothing dishonourable between myself and my Master of Horse."

"It is not those close to you who are the ones to suspect anything, Majesty," Kat went on, her voice miserable. "It is the people who float on the periphery of the court, the people who seek to make mischief for you and your reign. This behaviour is rich food for your enemies."

"And to those types of mischief-makers you think I should have to prove my own virtues?" She turned and glared at Kat. "To people who know nothing of me but simply want to create problems for me, those are the people you think I should pander to?"

"A queen does not have the luxury of discounting gossip about her doings," Kat counselled softly. "She must be beyond reproach on every score."

"And you, the woman who encouraged me to court the bed of Thomas Seymour before his wife was truly within the ground, *you* are the one to talk to me of behaviour beyond reproach?" Elizabeth asked, her voice rising. The ladies at the other end of the bedchamber were glancing at the two women, their faces pale.

Kat flushed crimson. Dark sparks of anger flashed in her eyes, but she held the Queen's gaze. "I am your servant, my Queen," she said in a stout tone, "and it is my duty to advise you where I see danger for you. For my part, I would rather have strangled you in the cot, than see you disgraced before your people!"

"And what do you advise I do, Kat Ashley? Since you have, this day, apparently become a member of my Council?"

"Marry, Majesty," she said, putting her hands out to Elizabeth, who did not take them. Those outstretched hands dropped to her sides as the Queen glared at her. "Put an end to the rumours with Lord Dudley and choose a consort who will aid your rule of this country and bring you the joy of children."

"Kat," the Queen spoke gently. "You know as well as I do that I cannot marry without first weighing up all the consequences of each match. The state we are in presently would mean that any outright declaration would be premature. My marriage is not something romantic, it is politics."

"I speak from fear that these rumours might cause your people to love you less well, Majesty. It could even spark a civil war, and we want no more of that evil unrest in our country."

"My people will not rise against me," Elizabeth protested, her voice solid as stone, "as you yourself have said, and as for these rumours, any who know me as God knows me, will know that I am innocent of them."

"Innocence matters little to rumour, Majesty," warned Kat.

"As well you should know, Mistress Ashley. After all, rumour is the master for whom you have worked the longest, is he not?"

Kat ruffled like an indignant goose. "All I have ever done has been for you, my lady, including when I went to the Tower as a prisoner to protect you, including when I spoke of nothing that would harm you even when they threatened me with death and pain." She gazed upon Elizabeth with fearful eyes. "Will you not consider, for the sake of propriety, merely *distancing* yourself from Lord Dudley?"

The Queen heaved a sigh. "Kat, my life has been made up of so much sorrow, and so little joy and you would ask me now to give up the small joys that I have?" She tossed her head defiantly. "I will not be deterred from the honest company of friends whom I admire and trust because of the malicious words of those who would seek to destroy me by underhand means. If I gave up such friends because of the words of those who only wish to defame me, then my enemies would only find another way to try to attack me, and another after that, until I have no friends. I would rather stand as I am and be seen, unashamed in my behaviour for I am as innocent as the first spring lamb, and as unsullied.

"I thank you for your devotion to me which I know was the cause of this advice," the Queen continued in rather a formal tone. "But I want to remind you also, that there was a time when vicious tongues worked rumour around you and me, and you were taken from me because of it. At any time in our parting I could have given in to the force of those evil tongues and abandoned *your* friendship to better secure my own reputation, but I did not. And do you know why?"

Kat's cheeks were flaming.

"I did not abandon you, Kat Ashley," the Queen went on, "because I knew the rumours that others spoke about you and me were untrue. I knew that within you beat the steady and loyal heart of a true friend. I will not live my life as a slave to the cruel tittle-tattle of wicked tongues of the court or the world. My friends are *my* friends, chosen by my judgement and they will remain as such until *I* decide otherwise. That is as true of you, as it is of Robin Dudley." The Queen touched her shoulder gently. "Now, we will say no more on this matter and you will prepare my bath."

The Queen stood staring from her window a long time before she went to that bath. "Kat has scared her," I said, standing beside her and Death. We stood at the Queen's side. "She knows what her lady says is true. Robin will ruin her."

Chapter Twenty-One

Eltham Palace

Summer 1559

We were in the woods. Rain had fallen not long before, for the world smelt fresh and damp. Leaves were dripping, an uneven *pit-pat* melody which was oddly comforting. Next to where I was standing the Queen pulled up her horse at the edge of the woods. Close behind her was Robin, and he too pulled his horse to stand.

At their feet, the horses' hooves churned green stems of wild onions into a paste with the mud, releasing a sharp tang into the air. Briar and bramble clustered, crowding at the edge of the woods, their pretty white and pink flowers fresh and lovely. Robin was looking at Elizabeth with a question in his eyes, and she shook her head with impatience.

"They want me to give up your company, Rob. They say that it is unseemly for a queen to spend so much time with a man whose company she enjoys." She twisted in her saddle to look at him, his face furrowed with annoyance. "Do you think I should do so?"

"Do you *want* to do so, my Queen?" he asked, his eyes not meeting hers, but looking past her and into the trees.

Elizabeth exhaled morosely in answer. "I will not abandon the pleasures of friendship with those I love," she said grimly, "so I might win the approval of those I despise."

Rob looked at her with surprise, and beamed. His handsome face was so boyish I almost smiled.

"You are my friend, Robin. I do not turn from my friends unless they turn from me."

"I am glad to hear that, more glad than I can say, my lady," he said, patting the side of his horse.

"It does not help that you carry yourself in court in the manner that you do though, Rob," she huffed with sudden petulance. "You take my friendship as an excuse for your haughty manner over others."

"I cannot be any other than what I am." He adjusted a strap on his saddle and looked up with eyes still sparkling from her avowal that she would not abandon him. "And if I show pleasure at having the ear of my mistress, and others are offended by this, there is little I can do."

"There is much that you *could* do," she disagreed. "Do you truly not care what others think of you? What others say of you?"

Robin shook his head. "There is but one opinion in the world I care for, and as long as she thinks well of me, in general, and despite my faults, then all is well with my world."

"I do think well of you, *Eyes*. Your friendship is the most important of my life."

"It is yours, Majesty, and always will be, much like my heart."

"Even if I marry another, Robin? Even if I take another man as my husband and consort?" Robin glowered and tore his eyes from hers, staring into the darkness of the woodlands again. "Answer me," she insisted.

He snapped his dark eyes back to her face. "I would that I could take every man that courts your affection," he declared bitterly, "and run a sword through each one. For not one of them is worthy to have you!"

"But you are?"

"If you would have me, I would make it my task to deserve you every day for the rest of our lives."

"And what of your wife still living? Have you forgotten her, again, my lord?"

"I would ask the same," I said, leaning against a tree.

Robin scowled. "I have said to you that she is sick, Elizabeth. There may soon come a time when I would be able to ask for your hand honesty and nobly."

She looked away from him.

Behind us I could hear the galloping hooves of the rest of the party as they sought to catch their Queen. Robin and Elizabeth were always far ahead of the others. "I will talk no more with you on the subject of your wife," she told him quickly. "And I would urge you to make friends at court rather than enemies, even if the only reason is to please me."

Robin bowed his head. "I already have many friends at court, Majesty. Though none of whom are within the party of your dear, loyal Cecil."

"Cecil dislikes you," she agreed.

"He dislikes another man coming close to you, Majesty."

"Cecil does not think on me in that way, Robin," the Queen snorted. "He has a wife and a family, and I hardly think that we would be suited to each other."

Robin laughed at her jest. "It would certainly be an unexpected move, my Queen!" he chuckled, shaking his head. "But that is not what I mean. Cecil is jealous that you may take advice from any other but him. He does not like that you might listen to me over him."

"Men are ridden with jealousies born of their imaginations and fantasies," the Queen mused. "And they are so often unfounded. Although I love you, Robin, I would never abandon Cecil's counsel. He is one of my wisest men, and has served me loyally both now and in the past."

Robin was suddenly quiet and she glanced around at him. "What?" she asked, looking at his strange face.

"You said that you loved me," he said quietly, "and yet, with the same breath, dismissed me. It is a heady and confusing mixture for a man to deal with, my Queen, to be brought near to your heart and then denied it all at the same time. You keep me ever wondering, wishing, hoping."

"I cannot be other than what I am, Robin," she teased, smiling, echoing his words. "And I will not flatter you with lies and pretence. I need Cecil, but I need you also. Find a way that I can keep you both peaceably at my side, for I have had enough of strife."

Robin nodded. The rest of the group rode towards them. "Do we have to wait all day for you to catch us up?" the Queen chastised with a smile, shaking her head. "You are all too slow!"

"Forgive us, Majesty," panted the Queen's cousin Catherine Carey, her cheeks bright and her eyes darting from Robin to the Queen. "We are not all as brave as you and your Master of Horse."

"Muster some courage from the depths of your spirit, cousin," the Queen cried boldly to Catherine. "The day is young yet, and there is much ground to cover before nightfall." She dug her heels into the sides of her restless mount and he reared in the air, then plunged downwards across the field at terrific speed. There were a few short screams from the Queen's ladies. She often terrified them by the daring manner in which she rode, but she was a skilled rider, as good as her father had been.

I watched the Queen as she plummeted down the hill and into the open park. "She wanted to outstrip them all," I said. "Even Robin."

I looked at Death. "I think she liked him better when he was safely married, not when he was unsafely free."

Chapter Twenty-Two

Nonsuch Palace

Summer 1559

Nonsuch was a palace beyond all others, a palace of the imagination. Standing before it, you could not imagine yourself in any other place. It flooded your mind and heart, so it was all you could see. Though petite, it was built as if it had stepped from a fairy tale; a mass of towers and elaborate stonework, encrusted in carvings of angels, gargoyles and saints. The miniature moat was unsuitable for any sort of defence, but had not been constructed for such. It was made to delight the eyes, and twinkled in the summer sunshine, surrounding the palace with a ring of sparkling waters. It was a palace of pleasure. Nonsuch was then in the keeping of the Earl of Arundel, one of the Queen's many suitors.

As all of court rode towards the house, minstrels and dancers in antique gowns of flowing white and silver emerged from the front of the house and from around its sides. Robin and the Queen pulled up their horses and the rest of court clattered up behind to watch what entertainment Arundel had laid on for their arrival.

"Arundel was courting her," I said. "Everyone said he would make a worthy husband, but he was not the most attractive or intelligent of men." I paused as a female dancer whirled past me. "Perhaps he would have suited her," I went on. "She could always have outwitted him, always kept him under control."

"Yet there is a danger in foolish men," said Death. "They grow overconfident where they are given no cause to be so, and bring about plans that, by their sheer rashness, sometimes succeed."

I looked to the dancers, all comely young women, faces part-covered with simple masks of white and gold. Across their chests they wore loose pennants inscribed with virtues; *Love, Charity, Mercy* and *Peace* danced past *Loyalty, Munificence,* and *Perseverance* as the musicians took up a lively tune. Around the side of the house came the noise of young voices singing and the visitors turned to see a company of children walking around each side of the palace, voices chanting in exquisite harmony. The virtues danced around them, joined by male dancers who burst from the palace and leapt around them bearing similar mottos on their strong chests. They lifted the girls in pretty spirals through the air around the groups of singing children.

As their lovely display came to an end, Arundel himself rode from the mouth of the castle towards the Queen with a volley of men in his wake. There was a great smirk on his over-proud face. The Queen stifled a giggle.

"Arundel's people dance a pretty dance for you, Majesty," Robin whispered into her ear. "Perhaps later he will give us his own rendition of that graceful performance… Dressed as '*Improbability*', mayhap?"

A laugh escaped from her mouth before she could stop it, and she cast a disapproving eye on Rob which was more than slightly marred by the smile she could not hide from her lips. "Behave yourself, Robin." Elizabeth lifted a welcoming hand to the fast-approaching figure of Arundel galloping towards her.

"Where would be the enjoyment in that, Majesty?" asked Robin, also raising a hand to wave at Arundel. I saw Arundel's face darken as he approached; he did not like Robin daring to welcome him as though he were an equal.

"No wonder such men loathed Rob," I said, "he goaded them."

The Queen was suppressing another snigger. "You are a bad and naughty man," she chastised.

"Will you spank me to make me behave, as my tutors did, Majesty?" Robin asked, causing the Queen's cheeks to ignite. She shook her head warningly at Rob as Arundel stopped his horse before them and dismounted.

Arundel was not a graceful man, and the time it took him to unwind his legs and generous backside from his saddle brought amusement to many of the party. Arundel's ungainly bottom wobbled in the air. Elizabeth was struggling not to laugh.

"Most gracious Majesty," he cried in a booming voice filled with pride, rushing to her horse, "I am honoured to welcome you to my house; never will the stones of Nonsuch forget the glorious presence of Your Majesty. Never before will it have felt the magnificent excellence of such exquisite company within its halls. Never will the people of my lands forget this time when their most beauteous Queen came to grace our house..."

"You are gracious indeed, my lord," Elizabeth said, trying to stop him from launching into further ridiculous platitudes. "Please rise, and convey us within the palace of Nonsuch. It has been many years since I saw the halls that my father created, and I am anxious to view them once more."

"I shall escort you at *once* within the safety of my household, Majesty," proclaimed Arundel, as if the Queen might be assassinated at any moment.

He rose laboriously from the ground and snapped his fingers for his horse. His servant rushed forward and pushed Arundel's large bottom once more up into his saddle, somewhat marring his overstated gallantry. The lips of the Queen were twitching with amusement. But, eventually, the Earl was seated on his mount and started to lead the procession into the castle. As they rode, Elizabeth's clearly aching face broke into a smile, for now it could appear as though she were overjoyed with Arundel and his house, rather than overcome with mocking glee at the sight of his cumbersome bottom. As they rode to the gates, the dancers and minstrels started up their refrain once more, welcoming the party with a stream of graceful, flowing bodies and notes.

As he rode ahead, Arundel had pulled his horse to the side of Katherine Grey, sister to the dead Jane Grey, speaking words of welcome to his niece. Many considered her heir to the Queen. The Queen, however, did not.

"*Thank God* for the *protection* of Arundel, Majesty," whispered Rob naughtily to his Queen as they passed through the gatehouse. "Think what may come of us should we not have him to shelter us from danger!"

Elizabeth snorted with laughter.

"Forgive my brother, Majesty," said Lady Mary Sidney, shaking her head at her brother Robin as she heard his whispered words. "He speaks only with disrespect to amuse you, he does not mean it in truth."

"It is sweet to me that you attempt to shelter your brother from harming himself, Mary." The Queen twisted in her saddle. "For your brother thinks not at all about the words that come from his mouth before they have escaped. It is well he should have someone to mind them for him."

"I had not seen Mary for years," I said, standing in the courtyard, watching them. "She had as much charm as her brothers, and a pretty face to match."

Robin shrugged. "It is true enough that I prefer to speak my thoughts aloud, my lady," he agreed. "And if I sometimes poke laughter at another, where is the harm in that? There are many who spend their time laughing at me, but it does me no harm."

"A good resolve, Rob," Elizabeth concurred, somewhat sardonically as Arundel's men rushed forward, garbed in their best livery with even their boots shining bright, to aid her. "I prefer to find the lighter side of life, for there have been too many times I have had to linger in the darkness."

"I will be more worried when men cease to laugh at me, Majesty," Robin continued, "for then I will either have passed from the centre of their gaze, or become too pitiful for them to find humour in." He sighed dramatically. "I do in fact, do *honour* to those I tease, Majesty, for I allow them to know that I still hold them as worthy targets for amusement, rather than forgotten bystanders in life."

"You do them much honour, indeed, Lord Dudley!" The Queen nodded mockingly, unhooking her leg from its side-saddle as she swung from her horse. Her riding boots hit the cobbled floor with a clatter and the Queen reached up to stretch muscles that had become sore and rigid from much time in the saddle. "Do not fear, my lord. When all others have ceased to titter at you, you may yet always be assured of my mirth. I will *always* be laughing at you, I assure you."

"And for what do I live but to make you smile, Majesty?" Rob swung gamely down from his horse in one fluid, graceful move, so different to the ungainly Arundel. "As long as I always have the ability to make you smile, Majesty..." He bowed to her, "... then I have my place in life happily set for me. Laugh at me, or with me, I mind not, but always have joy on your lips when I am near."

Arundel had left Katherine's side and was waiting to take the Queen within the palace. Arundel did not look pleased that she was jesting with Rob when she should, obviously, have been raptly gazing at *him* with adoration instead. Elizabeth smiled at Arundel, but looked at Robin once more. As their eyes met, he took her hand, bowed his head and kissed the glove that covered her white fingers. Their eyes locked for a moment which stretched in silence, making the others uncomfortable.

Kat pointedly cleared her throat. "Arundel waits, Majesty," she said.

The moment was broken, and the Queen blinked and snatched her hand from his. Rob's small sideways smirk as he stepped away from her was as cheeky as the wink he then threw at Kat, and the grin that met Arundel's waiting face. I shook my head. How quickly he made enemies, without seeming to care about it. I had never realised he could make foes as easily as he made friends. Elizabeth stepped forward, taking Arundel's arm, and started to talk to the Earl in a most animated fashion about the palace and all that she remembered of it. Arundel's standoffishness softened as the Queen turned her full attention to him.

"You can see why she favoured Robin, when you note what other fools thought themselves worthy to be her husband," I said, watching Arundel prance about her like a devoted imp.

"Arundel proposed, and she all but refused, although not quite," said Death.

Time spun, and we were with the party riding away from Nonsuch for Hampton Court. Death and I sat on a wagon, riding close to the Queen. She had been chatting to the driver, displaying that same easy familiarity that her father, too, had possessed by conversing with all of her people, even those of the lower orders. I ran my hand over a leg of furniture in the cart at my side; was it a bed or a table? There was a dragon engraved on it, and I wondered if it had once belonged to her grandfather. A stream of silver thread seemed to dance from my fingertips, vanishing into the wind as it reached the wood I touched.

"What said Arundel to you, Majesty, as we left?" asked Robin, with ill-disguised jealousy as he took his customary place at the Queen's side.

"Nothing of import, my lord," she said breezily, "and nothing that should concern you, though I saw you try to crane your neck and overhear us."

"I take an interest in all matters that concern my Queen." He widened his eyes at her, as though entirely innocent, making her grin. "It is surely part of my duty as your Master of Horse, to have a mind for your welfare."

She chuckled. "Then, by that reasoning, Rob, it would seem that none of my gossiping, intriguing subjects are meddling in any of my affairs at all, but simply having a care for my wellbeing. For every member of this court seems to take more care to overhear my conversations than they trouble to make conversation themselves!"

"Rest assured, Majesty," replied Robin, "I make it my office to know of any affairs that may endanger Your Majesty's happiness."

"And see you any arising?"

Robin stared out before him at the miles of good road. Yeomen rode before and around them. The Queen's ladies and courtiers were chatting and laughing behind us and for miles at the rear came the other baggage carts, creaking and groaning on the hot roads as they hauled the Queen's gowns, chairs and bed, and other such luxuries. "Luckily enough for my own peace of mind," Robin replied boldly, "I see nothing in Your Majesty's future that makes me fear for your happiness. When you have the fortune to join with the best man for you, then I see your happiness becoming complete, and lasting."

"So you have become a soothsayer, my *Eyes*? Have you taken instruction at the hands of your former tutor, John Dee, then? Tell me, does the face of the man I am to marry appear to you? Or perhaps his name? For all my lords say one man and then another, I know not best how to please any of them, let alone myself."

"You should marry the man who will make you happy, Majesty," said Robin. "And let all others be damned!"

"And who is that, Rob?"

"The man who loves you more than he loves anything else in this world." He turned in his saddle, his brown eyes earnest. "The man who knows that there is no jewel or land or empire or gold that could compare to a moment caught in your eyes. Everything else fades into dust when you are near, my lady, for the man who knows your true worth."

"Does this not get tiring?" I asked Death. "All this flattery, all the time? It becomes as birds chirping in the undergrowth, as words become meaningless when they are said over and over again. If I were her I would suspect all those who flattered me so much, so constantly, were not honest."

Indeed Elizabeth had looked away from my husband. "You must take care with what you say, Rob," she whispered. "Someone will overhear."

"I would not care if they did, my lady," he retorted. "I am not ashamed of my love for you."

"You are married," she said bluntly.

I looked at my feet, dangling over the back of the creaking cart. "She wanted the illusion, the fantasy. I gave him reality of love and it was not enough, but *his* reality of love was too much for her. It scared her," I said.

"There is truth in what you say. Humans live in fantasy, it is how you make the world." Death lifted a spider, catching a ride, from his cloak and placed it on the cart where it scurried away.

"Was the world always so bright?" I asked, shading my eyes. "It hurts."

"There is another place, waiting for you," said Death. "The light there is dim and cool, more silver than gold, more night than day, and there your eyes will not hurt."

"You are saying I do not belong here anymore?"

Death did not answer.

I looked again to the Queen and Robin. Rob's face had clouded over with a queer darkness. The Queen stared at him. "I am sorry, Robin," she rushed in, in a low tone. "That was tactless of me. Your wife, does she do well or ill?"

"Ill, Majesty," he replied, the previous playful flirtation entirely vanished from his face. "According to missives I received yesterday, she sickens each day. It will not be long …" He trailed off.

"I was not so sick I would die right then!" I exclaimed. "He lies! He lies to get her to promise herself to him!"

"You feel for her now?" asked Death.

"Perhaps," I said. "Perhaps she did not steal, perhaps the object in question leapt into her hands."

"Elizabeth," Rob whispered urgently, "my wife is a good woman, and once there was a love between us, but it was the love of children who know not what real love is. It was not the love of a man who knows himself and his own strength. I loved Amy once, but it has been many years now that I have only loved one woman, and that is you. But before this time, before this year, I never had cause to hope that you might return my love in truth. But if it should come that my wife may die, I need to know that you might consider, that you might think, to love me as well as I do you."

"I have said before, my lord, that I will have none of this conversation." The Queen pulled herself up and snapped her eyes away from him.

His shoulders sagged. "I understand," he said. "I will speak on it no more."

I blinked hard, feeling tears in my eyes. "We can go on," said Death. "If this place hurts your eyes."

I nodded, not wanting to say that whilst the light hurt me, the callousness of Robin hurt more.

*

At Hampton Court, in the chambers of the Queen, there was another with words the Queen did not wish to hear.

"*Alright,* Cecil," Elizabeth snapped, exasperated, as he dogged her about this matter and that which had not been attended to in her absence. "It is as though you wish me to refuse the traditional right and office of my forebears, to refuse to go on progress. You could have brought these matters to me when you visited me!"

"No, indeed, Majesty." Cecil looked up at her in a slightly startled manner from his many, many papers all competing for room on the oaken table. "Progress is a vitally important task for any monarch; to allow the people to see you only adds to your popularity with them. Still, there are many details on various matters that I would call your attention to."

"Consider my attention *well called,* Cecil!" she snapped in a dangerous voice, flaring her nostrils like a dragon. "I woke in a pleasant mood and am quite swiftly becoming entirely out of sorts."

"I apologise, Majesty, for any offence caused." Cecil blinked. "But you would not wish to be left in the dark on these matters, I think?"

"The darkness may well bring more relief than the light, Cecil," she sighed. "Alright, Cecil, get to the point on these matters and I will listen. But do not spend any more time rattling on, wearying me with how you have struggled in my absence. If you struggle too much in the office I have granted to you then I could always replace you with another? If the tasks are too burdensome?"

Cecil's face blanched as he shook himself like an old dog caught out in the rain. "I would not wish that, Majesty, and nor do I think would you."

"Don't test me, Cecil," she warned, waving a finger at him. "Although there may not be one man to match your wits about my court, I could replace you with several who *between* them might together make up a mind as good as yours. Many, you know, do not like that a relative commoner should take such an important post at the side of their Queen. There are others, waiting, longing for the post which you hold now. And if they could be prevailed upon to let me have the facts without twittering on about their own struggles in life, then perhaps I will have you replaced." Elizabeth sniffed. "I cannot stand the sound of self-pity. When any have had a youth such as mine, they would find that such an emotion is self-indulgent and self-destructive; it does no good to sit around moaning about the throw of the dice that life has cast for you. Much better to get on with what you have to work with."

"Yes, Majesty," agreed Cecil. "I will seek to tire you no further with any of my own pains."

"Perhaps I too should listen to her words," I muttered.

"Good!" the Queen cried in her curt voice, and then her face broke into a smile at his most serious tone of voice. Elizabeth laughed.

"She is most unpredictable." I said. "It is what people are drawn to."

"It protects her. If people do not know what she will do, they cannot catch her out." Death was standing by the window, but I was in the shadows. My eyes were soothed by the darkness.

"Dear *Spirit*," Elizabeth cried warmly. "How I do miss you when you are not boring me to death."

His face crinkled into a smile. "I live to amuse Your Majesty, of course."

"She spends her time with Rob, and Cecil worried this would affect her marriage proposals," I said.

"He worries for her a lot. She is the ship he chose to sink all his fortune in, but more than that, he loves her," said Death.

"I must warn you, there are rumours, Majesty," Cecil said in a serious tone, all traces of former humour gone. "Rumours that you and Lord Dudley are secretly lovers, and that you carry his child. That Lord Dudley means to poison his wife and then you will marry him. The stories get more fantastical as they go on, and they grow in number every day." He spread his hands as the Queen glowered at him.

"Soon enough they will say that he can command the sun to dance, teach horses to fly, apes to joust and has me under a spell to take my throne," she muttered.

Cecil spread his hands. "Majesty, those of us who know you well know that you would never endanger your reputation or forget yourself to allow any such intimacies as these rumours suggest. But your suitors and your people, who do not know you personally, *will* listen to such rumours. If you would stop seeing Robert Dudley so *much* then perhaps it would give these rumours a chance to subside. It would certainly help our case with your other suitors."

"I will not abandon my loyal friends because others choose to think ill of them, or of me! And should I bow to the will of those malicious tongues this time and in this matter, then I will have to do the same for every rumour that may come to be spread about me. I will be master within my house, Cecil. I will not bow to the wants and wills of others."

"What of the wants of your people, Majesty?" Cecil asked quietly. "What of the love of your people?"

"I am sure that the people will not cease to love me because I have one, or many, close friends, Cecil," she said. "My father had many intimates, and although there will always be jealousy, and rivalry between people in such positions, there is no call to abandon friends at the passing whim of the people."

Cecil nodded. "As Your Majesty wishes." He looked at her with sorrowful resignation. "I just urge you caution in your dealings with Lord Dudley. I do not doubt his loyalty to you, but he has a talent at court and without it for making enemies rather than friends. People do not like it when others rise higher than they for no discernible reason. They look about for a reason and will find it in the crudest places."

"People do not like it when others rise higher than they do, Cecil," she spat. "*That* is where that sentence should end. Those people have not the wit to see the *reasons* that others may rise higher than they. They do not see that others are cleverer, wittier, smarter or more talented than they are. It is just those kind of people who will never get anywhere in life, for they will spend their time wallowing in self-pity for the things they believe they *deserve* to have. They do not see that all that is in this world is within the grasp of any man, should he have the nerve and the pluck to get up and grasp it. But those who are weighed down by their own self-pity will never attain the heights they long for. We, all of us, have things that we are good at and things we are not. If we work on the talents we have, rather than twittering away our lives moaning about the ills life has granted us, then all would be better in this world! Look at me. There was a time when I believed I had lost everything of value in this life; power, freedom, and my own life was in peril more than once. But I did not allow myself to dissolve in a pit of my own misery. I used the best that God gave me, and all I had within myself, and I survived, and I prevailed."

The Queen stuck her chin in the air in defiance. "It is not the best man who wins in this life, Cecil. It is the man who knows how to make the best from what he is given."

"How does one make the best of death and being discarded?" I asked.

"Embrace death," Death said, with that hint of a smile in his voice again, "and know that in casting you off, the one who cast lost much too. They failed to see the worth in you, and so that worth was lost from their life."

Elizabeth let out a short noise of irritation and tossed her head like an angry horse. "I will not give in to those who would destroy my friend through jealousy. Enough of this! What more do you have to tell me? I wish to go on a walk this evening."

Cecil glanced hurriedly at his papers, although I was sure he knew all the news upon them by memory. "Erik, Prince and heir of Sweden sets sail for England this week, Majesty," he said with care, not daring to look up at Elizabeth. "Hoping to impress Your Majesty with his marriage suit in person, where he failed to succeed on paper."

"Another one," she groaned. "Will we have a bed left at court if any more of these suitors arrive here? I swear I will start to misname them in no time at all if any more arrive."

Cecil smiled a tight smile. "He believes that as a fellow Protestant, his suit will carry well with you, Majesty, and he writes of his most desperate love and affection for you."

"On the basis of seeing my portrait? I remember how well that worked for my father once also." She played with one of the ornate pins on the front of her gown, sending its tiny head spinning. "When he arrives, we will welcome him, and I will meet in secret with the Earl of Arran before he heads off to destabilise the rule of Mary of Guise for us. But I promise to marry none of them, Cecil, until I find such as man as will do for both me and for the country."

"I hope Your Majesty may someday explain to me exactly where to find a man acceptable to both you and the country," Cecil said dolefully, "for soon I should like to see an heir to the throne of England, as would your people. All would rejoice to see the continuation of the Tudor house on our throne." He smiled at her with affection. "I should dearly love to see a babe in your arms, my lady."

"Find me the man who can hold the wind in a net, and I will make him my husband, Cecil," she murmured.

"Majesty?" Cecil gazed at her, frowning.

"It does not matter. That is enough for today. I will meet with you and the Council tomorrow to continue on matters of state." She stared longingly from the window at the gardens bathed in the last warm glow of the day's sunshine.

"We are done for the day, Cecil," she commanded. Leaving him to gather his papers, the Queen of England almost ran from the room. She wanted to be with her friends.

"I pity her for that," I said, watching her gown billow as she strode fast into the hallway. "I had all the free hours she wished for, and she all the life I wanted to have."

Chapter Twenty-Three

Hampton Court

1559

"The country longs to see you settled, Majesty," Cecil was saying disapprovingly as we stepped from silk and silver into the world of the living. "And with a babe in your arms to bring security to the realm."

"Tell me, Cecil." The Queen leaned forward, her eyes sparkling at him dangerously. "Did my father's quest for a male child bring security to his realm? Did my sister's attempts at breeding ever bring peace and harmony to this land?"

Cecil looked unhappy. He glanced at Parry, trying to gain support. "The production of an heir is the best chance to secure the future of Your Majesty's country," he insisted.

"Indeed, so I hear, often," Elizabeth growled. "Never mind all that is within the power of the Queen *herself* to do. Never mind what may come, apart from an heir, from the reign of *Elizabeth,* Queen of England."

She looked impatient. "I have lived as the heir to the throne of England, and it was not a position that I would wish on any, my friends. How can a parent love a child while at the same time wondering if the child resents them for living long and keeping the throne? How can a child love a parent while living in terror of their parent's suspicions of disloyalty? And if there is more than one child, can royal siblings ever live at peace with one another, when the death of one may secure the future of another? Where the desire for power may outweigh the love that should come from sharing blood with another person? It seems to me that there is no security in a family of royal blood. I have read much history, my friends, and I have lived the life of the heir; neither experience speaks to me of security or love in the families of the powerful. Bringing an heir to the throne often only brings more problems, and more struggles."

Parry and Cecil both gaped at her, unsure of what to say.

"She went too far, revealed too much," I said.

"You are excused, both of you." She turned from them, cheeks pink. "Bring the Earl of Arran to me later this night," she snapped, her back still turned from them as she gazed out of the window. "I would have you both in attendance with him as I send my ladies away for the night."

Parry and Cecil left, bowing to her. Elizabeth walked to the window and put her hands to the cool whitewashed stone at its edge. She sighed.

"They were all chasing her to marry," I said. "But I understand why she did not want to."

"Arran, Erik of Sweden, Arundel, and your husband," said Death.

"She did not want to surrender power to a man," I said.

"There is truth in that. Her father showed her what a husband might do to a wife. Her sister showed her what might happen to a Queen who married." Death lifted a hand and the world spun, soft and silver. We were in the same chamber, at another time.

Cecil spoke. "You know that in reality, if Sweden is an unrealistic match, English unpopular, French impossible and Scots unattractive, then there is only one realistic match left for Your Majesty's hand."

"If I should think to marry at all, Cecil," Elizabeth reminded him, standing at the fireside and watching the flames of sea coal writhe and dance.

"Your Majesty *must* marry to secure the throne and an heir," said Cecil.

"*My* Majesty will decide what is best for the future of this throne and my people," she said, setting her shoulders back. "We are in agreement that if France and Scotland have turned enemy to us then the house of Hapsburg is our natural ally, and in order to have them fully on our side, we must of course reopen negations on my union with the Archduke Charles." She glanced over at him. "How go the Hapsburg negotiations?"

Cecil's face twisted unhappily. "They would go more easily and smoothly if you would meet more often with the Spanish and Imperial ambassadors rather than dancing away from them each time you meet, Majesty," he said glumly. "The new ambassador, Bishop de Quadra, is a proud man and he cannot seem to get a word in when Lord Dudley is at your side."

"The Ambassador does not like or trust me. He will not trust that I am serious about the Archduke's suit if I simply turn to him now. We need something to lure him in, someone he would trust more than me."

"Then what would Your Majesty suggest?" Cecil poured some wine and handed it to her.

"I could send you, *Spirit*," she pondered, looking at her old friend. "But I think the ambassador would prefer some signal of a more intimate nature to give him real hope for this match, and to secure our friendship with Spain and her cousins."

"Whom would Your Majesty suggest then?"

She smiled. "It is time, I think, for a new spy in silk stockings to further our cause with the Hapsburgs."

Cecil frowned. "You would send one of your women?" He lifted his eyes ponderously to the gloriously carved, gilded ceiling. "That would give it a certain… familiarity that de Quadra might suspect less."

"I will send the Lady Mary Sidney to him, and ask her to relay a secret message that I am keen on the match but unwilling to show it, due to a deep sense of maidenly reserve. And I will ask Robin to confirm her words."

Cecil frowned deep. "You would ask… Lord Dudley to confirm your interest in a Hapsburg marriage?" he asked, incredulous.

"De Quadra will believe us utterly then, and we shall have the Hapsburgs as allies."

"She uses Robin as a toy in her games," I said with interest. I did not feel bad for him, strange as it might sound, but merely interested in what Elizabeth would do next.

"Your Majesty," Cecil spoke haltingly, "I do not think that Lord Dudley will do as you ask. It is clear that he has a great deal of affection for you. Surely this would be taken as an insult to his pride?"

"Robert Dudley is as good a statesman as any other," she stated with heat in her voice, "and if I ask him to play along with this then he will do so." She paused and stared at Cecil's doubtful face. "He *has* the capacity to put the good of his country above his personal wants, Cecil. I am sure of it, and so shall you see it come to pass."

Cecil lifted his bushy eyebrows, obviously unsure of the idea. "Your Majesty trusts him in this, and so will I, but I must tell you as a friend and an advisor that I do not think he is capable of hiding his own feelings in this matter."

"He can hide them, Cecil," she assured him. "If there is enough at stake, he can hide them."

Cecil nodded, placing his goblet on the table. "It will still take a lot to convince the Imperial Ambassador that Your Majesty is in earnest," he mused. "There have been so many other suitors and so many times he has been fenced and parried away from you that he will still suspect you play a game with him. He is a proud man, and will not take well to the suspicion that you play him in order to win friendship."

"We are all playing games, Cecil; every man, woman, child, country and king is playing their own games and hoping to win before the others master the rules." Elizabeth paused. "We need the Hapsburgs on our side, so we will convince the new ambassador that we are in earnest. I will not have my country threatened for want of friends and allies, and if I must offer a hand to every one of them to secure that, then I will."

"Majesty," urged Cecil, that old, desperate note growing again in his voice. "It could be a good match in truth for you and for the country. De Quadra says that the Archduke may well convert his religion, or at least modify it so that it would not become an issue for your realm. It would mean we were allied with the Hapsburgs and you would have a husband, finally, and all rumours brought about by your unwed state would end."

"Let us see where this path takes us, Cecil, then decide where our next steps should lead. Each challenge requires a new vantage point, and each road requires a new set of shoes. Let us not tie ourselves to one course until we can see the lay of the land."

"Majesty." Cecil bowed to leave, sounding once more frustrated with her.

"Cecil?" she called as he walked to the door. He turned, eyes dark in the dim light. "Let Parry know of this plan, too," she said. "I can see de Quadra checking my credentials at all points. When he comes to ask, all my servants will answer in the same voice."

Cecil inclined his head in agreement, bowed again, and left the room.

"He does not wish to be played with," the Queen murmured, sipping her wine. "But he will compete in our game nonetheless."

A day whirled away, and there was Robin glaring again at the woman he loved.

"Well?" asked the Queen.

"You are going to marry the Archduke?" he asked, his measured tone carrying a dangerous undercurrent.

Elizabeth tilted her head sideways, playfully. "I think you must have only listened to half of what I said, my *Eyes*." She pursed her lips in mock irritation. "Why is it that no matter how many words a woman says, the men around her only seem to be capable of hearing a fraction of them?" The Queen threw her hands up in the air. "It is as though God should have only given you one ear in truth, for you only seem capable of using half of your hearing."

His face darkened and he made for the door, but she grabbed at his arm and pulled him back. "You fool, Robin," she teased. "You let your anger cloud your senses."

"Your Majesty should allow her Master of Horse to leave," he said coldly, "since you are to have a new husband soon enough. He may wish to replace me at Your Majesty's side."

"Rob," the Queen purred. "*You* have a wife and yet I do not speak to you like this, with the green fog of jealousy clouding all before us. Now, calm that temper and listen to me properly. I am *not* going to marry the Archduke."

"You are not?" His face turned back to her, brighter than the first light of the dawn over the horizon.

"Of course not!" she exclaimed. "I am going to reopen the marriage negotiations with the Hapsburgs because we need an ally against the French and the Scots. The house of Hapsburg is the natural choice. A potential match with Phillip's cousin is the best way to ensure friendship between our countries."

"Why cannot you have an alliance with them that does not involve marriage?" he asked, sullen with jealousy.

Elizabeth tossed her hands in the air. "If I had a coin for every time I have asked myself that question, Rob, I would be the ruler of the world and all her wealth by now. You know yourself that every single negotiation about my realm seems to involve my marriage in some way or another. This is no different, and in the end, it will have the same outcome as all the others."

"You will not marry," he said, looking at her with gentle, hopeful eyes.

"I will not marry… yet. I do not say for the future. That is not a realm into which I can see."

Robin reached out to take her arms, his eyes soft and his embrace eager. "I was a fool."

"You *are* a fool," she agreed impishly, holding him at bay with a hand on his chest. "But you are *my* fool at least."

He breathed in deeply and let the air out again through his nose. "I do not like the thought that you would marry him."

"Indeed?" she asked, laughing. "Your displeasure quite escaped my notice. Is there anyone you would be happy for me to marry?"

He nodded. "One alone, one who strives to last long enough to make you an offer, should he ever prove brave enough to try!"

"I never thought you were a man who lacked in courage," she whispered.

"No man's courage is ever truly put to the test until he gazes into the eyes of the woman he loves, holding his heart out to her in his hands." Robin's eyes were serious.

"Battles and conflicts do not worry you overmuch then?" she asked, walking away from him, across the room to the window. "Those long months in the Tower, as you waited to see if you would face the same fate as your brother and father. They did not strike fear into you?"

Robin shook his head, walking to stand behind her. Standing beside her, I could feel his breath on her neck. "I lost my fear on the day I first saw you wandering those paths in the Tower gardens." He placed his hands on her shoulders. "Sometimes, I would see you talking to yourself, mulling over thoughts, your lips moving but your words kept hidden from those around you." He paused and turned her gently, so her eyes met his. "You never knew it," he whispered, "but you were my courage in that place. You were the spirit that kept me fighting. I could see the future of our country in you. I could see a future for myself, in you."

She smiled. "I hate to think what you might have thought if you could have seen the thoughts in my head, my lord. I was not as brave as you thought I was."

Robin scowled. "Yes, you *were*, Elizabeth. You could not be cowered by your captors; you could not be overshadowed by your sister. You were a princess, the true daughter of the King, the heir to the throne. You were magnificent, courageous, they could not bring you low." He shook his head, frowning as though she was a child he could not explain a lesson to. "You do not see yourself, so I think it is hard for you to see just how special you really are."

"Enough!" The Queen laughed, pushing him back. "You flatter me, Rob, and yet there are important things for us to do now." She held up a hand to stem his praise.

"I need your help, my lord, and that of your sister, if the Hapsburgs are to believe that I wish to marry the Archduke in earnest. Now listen to me closely. When we leave for Windsor at the end of this month, you will do as I say..."

As they went into whispered conversation of her plan, I turned to Death. "Sometimes I think she loves him, sometimes I think she holds him at bay," I said.

"Both can be true at the same time," he said. He took my hand and into soft silver we walked, emerging on the other side. Days flew by, until Elizabeth was in conversation with Rob's sister.

"I do not wish to marry at all, Mary," the Queen was saying to Mary, her voice soft. "A woman, in marrying, must give up whatever personal power she has in favour of her husband. Perhaps other women do not think of it as a curse, as I do, because they have less power than I do, they come to their husbands usually as an advance in power and influence, and so they have more to gain and less to lose. But I only have power to lose, as far as I can see. For all my years as a princess of this realm I fought to survive, to come to the place where I am now, to be Queen, to hold the power over my own life in my own hands, to decide what is right for my people and for myself as God gave me licence to. Now that I am the Queen, I do not want to hand that power, those rights, over to any man, no matter who he is or how much I might care for him." Elizabeth looked up at Mary, who was standing by her side. "I do not want to give up who I am, in order that I might know the happiness of marriage. I do not want to surrender my own freedom, in return for love."

Mary rushed to Elizabeth's side and knelt at her feet. "It does not have to be that way," she breathed, looking up with her large, beautiful eyes. "Not with the right man, the man who would love you and would only want to have you."

Elizabeth took her hands. "There is no man who could ever see me without seeing my crown first. There is no man, no law that would protect my power within the bonds of marriage as well as I would be protected by remaining unwed. As soon as I give my hand, I will cease truly, in the eyes of my people and in the eyes of the law, to be an independent person and Queen in my own right. My sister chose to limit herself by giving herself up as a bride, and she broke her heart trying to believe that Phillip loved her for herself. I do not want my illusions shattered so."

The Queen reached out and touched Mary's lovely face. "Go now," she commanded. "It is late, and my mind wanders in my tiredness. Send Kat to me for the night so that she might watch over me."

Another day, or more. How they flew now, racing past me.

"Your move, my lord." Elizabeth sat back, fixing her eyes on Robin over the chessboard between them. "And tell me of what passed between de Quadra and you on the subject of my marriage to the Archduke."

Rob's eyes shifted reluctantly from the board. "If Your Majesty was not the stalwart and honourable Queen I know you to be," he commented, with a sly look, "then I *might* think that you were attempting to distract me from our game, by bringing this subject up at this time."

She opened those black eyes wide and spread her hands as though innocent. "It would not speak highly of my honour to do so," she said, laughing. "Although it might be of credit to my war craft."

"Then you admit it is a ruse?"

"I neither admit nor deny anything, my lord, as usual." She offered him a lazy smile. "Of course, if you find our game too taxing on your wits to simultaneously consider the affairs of the country, then I shall separate the two into manageable mouthfuls for you, like a wee babe being fed his dinner." Elizabeth smirked, a challenge.

"I believe I have the capacity for both, Majesty." He frowned at the board for a moment, then took hold of his Queen, deftly moving it into an aggressive stance. "I always had a goodly appetite."

"Then, answer me. De Quadra came to you seeking confirmation of my words to Lady Sidney, yes?"

"The Ambassador came slinking into my chambers, Majesty," said Rob. His eyes shone in the light from the window, and in them, I could see the storm clouds reflected in the blackness of his pupils. He looked far too happy with this latest move. "He seemed to want a second opinion on my sister's word."

"He did not believe her?" Elizabeth asked, moving her Queen to safer ground.

"Oh, I think he found her most persuasive." Rob scowled at the board, unable to hide his frustration. Despite his protestations that he could both talk and play against his Queen, he was, in fact, finding the two challenging. "Men often find the words of women a great deal more believable when they are also entranced with their beauty. But I think the ambassador believed that my poor innocent sister might have been duped by her wily mistress and sent to confound him." He looked up at her with steady and amused eyes, and as he smiled the edges of his eyes crinkled slightly, something I had always loved. "You were entirely right that he would seek me out to confirm your words."

"And did you?"

Rob sat back, leaning so that the strain of sitting before the board was pulled from his muscles. He lifted his arms and winced pleasurably as bones cracked in his back and shoulders. Rob was never very good at sitting still for too long, he was a creature of movement and action. "I told de Quadra that you were indeed deeply in earnest, Majesty, and, that I supported the marriage wholeheartedly. I told him of my deep gratitude to his master, Phillip of Spain, in securing my release from the Tower when his wife held me captive. I told the ambassador that in my eyes, there was no match for England but to return to the might and security of union with the Hapsburg Empire, for you to marry Phillip's royal cousin, the Archduke Charles of Austria, and that all honest Englishmen would come to see this in the end."

"And he believed you, Rob? You must have said it more convincingly to him than you relay to me."

Robin smiled. "I can be most convincing when I want to be, Majesty."

"Of that I am well aware, my lord," she said, somewhat ruefully. "Continue."

"Well, de Quadra still looked somewhat sceptical, and said to me that there were many rumours concerning Your Majesty's feelings towards… me."

"And what did you say to that, Rob?"

"I told him that Your Majesty and I have been friends since childhood." He shrugged. "That we shared many interests and were close friends, and that such platonic friendship between a man and a woman might often be misconstrued as a more lasting attachment, especially by those who would want to disrupt an alliance between two great powers in Europe. I said that you were as my own sister and I valued your friendship so dearly that I longed to see you married with equal felicity as I have had in my own marriage, but I was aware of your deep commitment to only marrying where was best for your country. I told him this was why you had taken a long time, a good deal longer than your sister did, in deciding whom to wed."

"My sister decided she would marry into Spain when she was still within her mother's womb, I think," Elizabeth muttered. "After being promised to Charles V when she was a child, she worshipped his house for ever after. I do not think that she would have cared *what* prince marched from the Hapsburg Empire to be her husband, as long as he was in some manner related to her mother, and when Phillip was offered, oh! She could not help herself! The son of her idol Charles, and a handsome man as well? No wonder she believed the Holy Spirit wanted her to marry with Phillip, he must have seemed like a gift from the Almighty Himself!" She paused. Rob was entirely distracted by their talk. He was playing carelessly. "You think the ambassador believed your protestations of our friendship?" she asked.

Rob nodded. "I think he was *willing* to believe. He wants good news to give to his master, after all." He frowned and moved a knight sloppily across the board. He was not paying attention. "He was even more convinced when your Lord Treasurer, Parry, also confirmed my sister's words, and said that the marriage was a necessity." He looked up at Elizabeth as he took his fingers from his piece without thinking, committing himself to the move.

"So you think that we have him?" she asked, stretching her arms by her side.

"I think he is ready to resume chasing Your Majesty in the name of the Archduke once more," Rob went on, leaning on the table and interlacing his fingers. As he thought, he unhooked two of them to point at her; they bobbed up and down, the rings on their fingers sparkling at her. "In fact, my men tell me that he has sent word to Spain in this vein already, and that he is conferring with Baron Breumer, the Ambassador of Austria, at this very moment, in order to proceed. I think you have your alliance with the Hapsburgs, my Queen. The French and the Scots will have to consider the power of Spain and Austria if they should think to invade our shores."

"I will make sure it does not come to that." She turned her head and looked out the window at the golden-leaved countryside. "As long as I am Queen, no foreign lord will ever step with hostile foot on my shores."

"They would never dare, Majesty, they would know themselves beaten before they set sail."

"Oh, they would dare, Rob, they would dare." Elizabeth smiled sadly, looking back at him. "When men look at a woman in power they do not see her mind or the strength in her blood. They see her frail shape; they compare her to the strongest of their own sex and see her come up short. They look at the weakest of her sex, made weaker still by ill education and supplication to the image of woman that most men hold, and they laugh to see such a creature play-acting at the role of king. They see her beneficence as feebleness and they will attribute her successes to the counsel of the men around her. And do you know why they do so?"

Rob shook his head.

"Because all men fear that which is different," she said. "They fear that which they cannot control, that which they cannot predict. All their lives, men have been told that they *own* the world, and so to have a woman in a place where a man should be is both confusing and terrifying to them. They name me therefore as unnatural, strange. They try to claim that I am of the Devil, an aberration of nature. They fear me. That is why they try so hard to force me to marry, because a woman with a husband, or a queen with a king at her side, these are things they can understand. Once they understand me, they reason, they will need to fear me no longer. But as long as I remain strange to them, they will fear me. That is why they will try to take my country from me if they fail to marry it away from my hands, and that is why they will always seek to degrade me in the eyes of the world. They would dare to invade our shores, my lord, never think that they would not. But they will find that as well as having the bravest of men, the best of soldiers and the most daring sailors of this world, this country also has a Queen who is equal in spirit and in mind to any man or prince. And whilst I have breath in my body, I will keep the lands of my father and forefathers safe from them."

There was silence between them for a while. Then, the Queen grinned wickedly and leaned forward. She took hold of her ivory Queen and shifted her to her last position. "Checkmate, Robin!" Elizabeth announced, sitting back with her lips twitching as he stared in dumbfounded confusion at the board.

"He thought to best her, but she was always playing him," I said.

"If he supposed he could beat her, perhaps he deserved to be beaten," said Death.

"I agree," I said. "He deserved to be beaten. I was not the one to do it, but she was."

Chapter Twenty-Four

Greenwich Palace

Autumn 1559

"As I said, Excellency," the Queen's voice snapped, curt and tart of tone as we stepped from realms of silver light into the bright harshness of the world. "I cannot invite the Archduke to my court; as a maiden it would be improper. If the Archduke chooses to come to my court then he will be made welcome. But it must be made plain that I have issued no invitation and that I cannot commit to giving him my hand."

I blinked. The Queen's audience chamber at Greenwich was where we stood. Even inside the light was too bright for me now. I winced at the soft hum of voices about the chamber, all of them intruding into my ears, and the Queen and de Quadra, the Imperial Ambassador were almost shouting. I shied back from them, but I could not escape the noise of the world.

"It becomes too loud," Death said, in sympathy.

I nodded, but then I sighed. "But I want to know," I said, brushing the threads of the other world once more from my gown. Eventually I stopped; why should they not remain?

"Majesty…" de Quadra was screeching, his face aghast, "…there must be some kind of invitation if the Archduke is to visit!"

Elizabeth held up a hand. Even though she was a queen I marvelled at her audacity. That I could have had such authority in my own life! "The matter is in the hands of your master, Excellency. I cannot be involved in this matter any further. It is uncouth for a maiden to be so much involved in the manner in which a man is sent to woo her. Have some regard for the frailty of my feelings and take this matter to your master. I am sure that you and he will find a way to proceed. Now, you will excuse me. I am due to take my exercise in the parks at this time."

I laughed aloud. "The frailty of her feelings," I snorted.

De Quadra stared at Elizabeth, so furious he was barely able to even make his bow as the Queen's ladies and the Queen herself swept from the room, but I saw him eye Katherine Grey with renewed interest as she scampered to Elizabeth's side. As they left, the ambassador remained, and turned to Cecil.

"Do they know the Queen is outside, listening?" I asked Death.

He shrugged.

"She is entirely at odds with herself!" cried the ambassador heatedly. "She will not enter into discussion on her marriage for fear of offending her maidenly pride, so how is she meant to marry at all?"

Cecil's quiet voice sounded strained as he answered. "The situation is unusual, Your Excellency. The Queen has no wish to leave her marriage negotiations entirely in the hands of others because of her love for her people, and yet she is not a man with whom negotiations might be conducted without fears of offence. She wishes to marry, her people wish her to marry and her Council wishes her to marry, but woman that she is, she also needs to feel loved and desired."

"She is a spirited and obstinate woman," spat de Quadra. "We must take into account her passionate spirit." It sounded as though he mused on a problem most complex.

"Your master must know that *I* above all people wish to see this marriage occur," Cecil's voice had turned soft, cooing, wooing the ambassador's splintered spirits. "The Queen *must* marry for the safety of her realm, and she must produce heirs to her throne. The Hapsburg offer is the only sensible choice left open to her. Ask your master to come to the court, Excellency… upon invitation of the Queen's Privy Council."

I know not how, but at the same time as I could see these men, I could too see Elizabeth. She was in the outer room, but in my mind I saw her, and saw her face fall. She had been grinning, but that fell from her lips as she heard what Cecil said. He meant to go around her wishes, undermine her. I could understand why she was displeased. She had trusted him absolutely and he had just betrayed her.

"Is there no one she can trust?" I asked.

"Many people she cannot, for they hate her," said Death, "and even those who love her frequently take it upon themselves to act for her, thinking it for her own good, and yet they act against her wishes."

I nodded. This was certainly against her wishes. An invitation from the Privy Council was almost as good as that of the Queen. I could understand what Elizabeth was up to for she hardly wanted to insult the Hapsburgs by refusing their candidate for her hand when England was surrounded by hostile French and Scots. Her games with de Quadra would have given more time for negotiation. Cecil appeared to be ending that, without reference to her wishes. If the Archduke came to her court it would be hard to turn him down as a suitor without insulting the Hapsburgs and thereby making dangerous enemies.

"Cecil wants her to wed," I said, understanding. "And he tries to force her hand."

"Once my Queen has seen your master in the flesh," Cecil continued in a low, calm voice, "I am sure that she will not seek to turn him away. They are well matched in education, and all reports say he is young and handsome enough to tempt even the most maidenly reserve. Invite him here, my lord ambassador, and I will ensure that this marriage goes ahead... as long as all that has been said on the matter of religion still stands true."

All colour drained from the Queen's face as she heard that. She backed away from the door, numb disbelief on her face.

"There will be but one mistress here, and no master!" Elizabeth muttered as she marched in anger towards the stables. "I will not be made to do the will of others, *I will not*!"

A slip in time and we were in her chambers at Whitehall. My husband was there, looking like a prize peacock in a new doublet. "*More* new clothes, Robin?" the Queen asked, extending her hand for him to kiss. "You are a fine bird this autumn with your ever-changing plumage!"

He chuckled. "Your Majesty's generosity has allowed me to purchase some new items of clothing, it is true." He put his hands out and twirled like a girl with a silly pout on his face. My lip curled. "You do not disapprove, I hope?"

The Queen's ladies started laughing at the ridiculous face he was pulling, and the Queen joined in. Only Kat seemed uneasy as she looked him up and down. Kat's disapproval was causing a great deal of friction. I could feel it crackling in the air.

"I think it would be hard to find one to disapprove of you, Robin," Elizabeth said warmly. His doublet was bright white, a most becoming shade when contrasted with his dark colouring. His chest strained against the tight-fitting velvet, and large gemstones twinkled at his neck, making his fine eyes shine. His beard and hair were newly trimmed, I saw, and was annoyed to see that he had trimmed too the slight curls at the back of his neck. I had loved those curls.

"Oh, I could find you one or two who heartily disapprove, Your Majesty."

"Of whom do you speak?"

"The Duke of Norfolk, my Queen," Robin said with an unconcerned grin.

Norfolk was young and brash, also rather trying from all I had heard, much as his father and grandfather had been. Obsessed with the nobility of his line, and determined to always be seen and heard at court, he was a man who was never silent and yet had nothing to say. Or, at least, that was what Rob had told me once.

I was not surprised that he disliked Robin. I had heard the rumours when alive, and Rob had spoken of it more than once. To Norfolk, Rob's family were common upstarts who had turned traitor to the Crown more often than they had worked for its good. Norfolk did not see, of course, that although his blood was noble, royal even, his own family had found themselves in hot water with the Tudor line almost as often as Rob's had, but rationality and sense do not matter to men like Norfolk. He saw Rob as barely better than a ploughboy, and hated him because of his rise in favour and power at court.

"He finds me entirely annoying, I think," Rob went on blithely. "He believes that I interfere with affairs of state which Your Majesty should, of course, leave entirely in his hands. He thinks that I am unfit to counsel, or serve Your Majesty and should be replaced by one higher in blood and closer in station to you. In fact, I believe that he only really approves of *himself* being your closest friend and advisor!"

The Queen wrinkled her nose at Rob. "If my kinsman Norfolk wishes to become my friend, then he should be friendlier," she quipped. "And if he wishes to advise me, then he should have advice to give. I cannot bear courtiers who spend their time moaning over the advancement of others when they make so little effort in advancing themselves. Those who spend all their time bemoaning their fates rather than taking control of them are entirely useless to me. If Norfolk wants advancement then he must earn it, like everyone else," She flicked her fingers out before Robin playfully. "And besides, he shows poor taste in disliking the best-dressed man at court."

Elizabeth put a hand out to Robin and he kissed it, his eyes flashing at her with pleasure. "To other business, my lord." She took her hand from his and turned to walk to the fire. "The Duke of Finland arrives this week to woo me for his brother, Prince Erik of Sweden, who now cannot come in person. I wish for you to greet him and make him welcome when he lands on our shores."

Robin was clearly pleased. It was an honour to be chosen to meet foreign dignitaries on the Queen's behalf, an honour that Norfolk would have liked a great deal. "It will be a pleasure, Majesty. May I ask of any further news on the Archduke's suit?"

The Queen frowned, and beckoned Rob to her. She told him of the interview, and of what she had heard afterwards through the door. "After I left the room, I heard Cecil heartily encourage the ambassador to invite the Archduke to court. If the man actually comes here it will be very difficult and potentially dangerous for me to refuse him. Cecil must know this. I fear, Rob…" she trailed off and bit the side of her finger.

"Cecil wants you to marry him in earnest." Robin looked concerned. "You are right; Cecil would not mistake something as important as this. He must want the Hapsburg marriage to go ahead."

"How can I refuse the Archduke if he is actually sent here to me?" Elizabeth threw her hands into the air in annoyance. "It would be a scandal, an affront to the dignity of Austria *and* Spain. We cannot afford more enemies, Rob."

"Then we must ensure that the Hapsburgs remain unsure," mused Robin. "If they think there is a chance the Archduke would be turned down, they would not send him and risk such an affront to his dignity."

"What do you recommend?"

"Majesty…" Rob's face was sly, "… you are the very best of dancers. This just requires more of those famous quick steps of yours." He leaned in to her. "The arrival of another emissary is most timely. Pretend intense interest in the Finnish Duke; pretend you have fallen in love with your new suitor's brother. If the Hapsburgs believe you have fallen for the charms of another, they will not send their Duke to England. We will beat Cecil and the Hapsburgs at their own game."

She breathed out. "I admit, the same thought had come to my mind, but it does me good to hear you say it, my *Eyes*." Her brow puckered. "Does it not seem to you that all I do is play games? My hand is given here, and there, and everywhere, and yet nowhere at all. I grow tired of these games, all these toys."

Robin reached out and took her hand. "Elizabeth," he whispered urgently. "My wife is sickening rapidly. The doctors say she will not live the year. If you could but hold on for a while longer, then it may be that another suitor might be able to enter his hand to play for yours. One that you might like better than the others who have come before."

"You know I do not like such talk, Robin." She started to pull her hand from his. He held on. All I wanted in that moment was to clap the Queen of England on the back, and give my thanks. At least one of them thought it unseemly to gloat over my supposed imminent death.

"I know." His eyes were intent on her face. "But I only tell you this so that you may consider that one day there may be another option. Not some foreign prince or inbred duke, but a man of England, a friend you have known since we were children, and a man who would honestly love and cherish you for yourself, from now until the end of time." He kissed her fingers and released her hand.

"I know, Robin," she whispered. "You must not think that you are not very special to me. I do think about what might happen if the right man was granted to me. I do think, I do wonder, what it might be like." She stopped and looked around. Her ladies were apparently engrossed in conversation, whilst certainly straining to hear her words.

"She wanted so to be able to trust," I said.

Elizabeth pulled back from Robin. "These are questions for another day. But I do think on them, the same as you, Rob. I do wonder about the future. I do wonder about you and me, about what might come."

He smiled. "That must be enough for me, then." He stretched his arms out and sighed, making a slightly disgusted face. "As for the present, I will retire to my damp apartments to pack so that I might greet the Duke in style."

As he bowed to her she stopped him. "What do you mean, your *damp* apartments?"

Robin grinned with good humour. "The chambers allocated to my household at Whitehall are very spacious and fine, Majesty, but they are close to the river, they are damp, and the smell of fish pervades them."

The Queen's nostrils flared with disgust. "Why did you not say? Well, this will be rectified immediately. I will not have my Master of Horse living in a fish market. You will move to the apartments next to mine," she ordered, "on this floor. There are quarters to spare here and we can accommodate your servants too."

Robin beamed. First-floor apartments were the very finest, generally reserved for royalty. I saw a shadow of disapproval float over Kat's features as she overheard her mistress. "Have your things moved up immediately, Robin. I will not have my Master of Horse bringing offensive scents into my chambers. You know I cannot abide ill smells."

"At once, Majesty," said Robin with great aplomb.

"He engineered that," I said. "The Queen would never want him somewhere unwholesome, and knowing that he played her."

"Perhaps she too wanted him close," said Death.

Chapter Twenty-Five

Hampton Court

Summer's End – Autumn 1559

"How many suitors is that now, Cecil?" Elizabeth asked flippantly as they sat in the Privy Chamber together after she had welcomed yet another party of envoys bearing messages of eternal love to her court that afternoon.

"Around twelve, Majesty," Cecil glumly muttered, refusing to look at his Queen.

"You seem so sad, Cecil!" she cried merrily, clearly up to something. "Do you not think it *marvellous* that we have so many friends in the world? And all of them love us so well!"

"I would rather see that Your Majesty had one and the rest were let go with dignity," he said, his voice gentle but firm. "The Hapsburgs begin to tire of the games."

Elizabeth knocked her knuckles on her armrest, a sharp short beat, making him start and look up at her. "But this was the plan, was it not, Cecil?" she asked in a dangerously casual tone. "That we would continue to seek the best match for our country and would not settle until we did? That we would gather friends to protect us against our enemies? That we would enter talks with the Hapsburgs, but not offer them anything in truth. Unless, old friend, you had been thinking of *another* plan without telling me?" Her tone sounded light, but Cecil could read the ominous undercurrent.

Cecil's eyes widened just a little and he started to rearrange his papers briskly. As he peeked out over his whiskers a light flush was on his cheeks. "All the world, Majesty, knows that the choice is yours. But you know well my mind on the subject, since I have spoken it enough. I would like, as would many of your subjects, to see you married and…"

"Yes, yes." The Queen snapped her fingers at him. "*Breeding.* Yes, you have made yourself perfectly clear, Cecil. You wish to see me heavy like a broody cow, for that is the only good I can do for my realm, is it not? That is the only virtue I have? To do as every other woman does in the world and get with a *child* by a *husband*. That in *your* mind is the only worth I have, yes?"

"Majesty." Cecil rose to his feet and shook his head rapidly, leaning on the table. "That is not my thought at all. You know of the very great respect and admiration I have for the strength of your mind and intelligence. I would never think of you as a mere woman."

"Then do not think you can try to trick me or sell me off to whomsoever you think should be my husband, Cecil." Her voice was treacherously calm and she stared at him with glittering eyes brimming with restrained anger. "You may think that you are too valuable to be dismissed but I can make you fall much further than you have risen if you displease me again."

"How have I displeased you, Majesty?" he asked, staring at her as the flush on his cheeks grew.

Her lips twisted with anger. "Your cheeks know the answer even if your lips claim innocence," she hissed, "so do not pretend to me that you were not attempting to get the Archduke sent here so that I might have no honourable way to turn him down. I will not be duped, Cecil, not by you, not by anyone. It may have escaped your notice in all the *respect* you were doing to my intelligence, but I am the Queen, placed here by God to be your master, and by God! I will take none as *my* master *but* God!" The Queen thumped her fist hard on the table, her voice rising to a shout.

Cecil was staring at her in horror, his face swiftly turning from faint flush of blood to a deathly pale grey. "Majesty," he stammered, "I know not who has told you such things of me, but it is not so! If Lord Dudley has said anything against me in this matter…"

"Robert Dudley has said *nothing* of this matter to me, Cecil, nor does he need to!" She jumped to her feet, slamming both hands on the table and glaring ferociously at him. Cecil started backwards, staring at his mistress in fright. "I *heard* you with my own ears, Cecil! Do not seek to place blame which rests soundly on your shoulders onto those of others. You overstepped your authority, sir, and tried to treat me like a fool! It is not to be borne! For your many services to me, and your great skill in your work I will not dismiss you for this action, or send you to the Tower for betraying my trust, as perhaps you deserve. Although do not think I have not considered it! I will forgive you this time, but do not believe that I will ever forget." She lifted her hands from the table and stood tall, magnificent in her fury. "A woman's memory is long and sharp, my lord Secretary," she warned, "and it never forgets a thing."

Cecil's face was pale as pudding, eyes alight with fear. "I can only apologise if I have offended you, Majesty," he spluttered. "But please believe that in all I do, I try to do good for this country and for you."

"I will be the judge of what is good, for England and for Elizabeth," the Queen said imperiously. "You can go."

Cecil walked slowly from the room, and as he left he turned his head to her. I saw such an expression of sorrow on his face. He said nothing, and left.

Elizabeth was still clearly in a rage, pacing her chambers until she abruptly left, stalking to Robin's with a face like a storm. She barged into Robin's rooms without announcement. Robin looked up, surprised, from a heap of papers that he and his sister were leaning over at the table. They both bowed and I could see amusement on Mary's face at the Queen's unorthodox entrance.

"Majesty," said Robin, smiling as he kissed her hand. "I did not expect to see you."

"As my Master of Horse, my lord, I would expect you to be ready to see me at any time." The Queen snatched her hand back and paced towards the table. "What is this, then, that has you so engrossed?" Her words were clipped. It was easy enough to tell that she was in a foul mood. Mary shrank back and let her brother approach instead. Clever girl.

"It was to be a surprise," he rebuked, teasing, "but you have caught us. We were planning a joust next month, a surprise for your entertainment."

"You were planning a surprise for me?" Elizabeth asked, suddenly happy. "How sweet." She looked around contentedly at her ladies, and every one of them looked relieved to see her temper calmed. "How is it, Rob," she asked, linking her arm with his as he showed her his plans, "that you always know how to soothe me?"

A rush of air moved us, and it became autumn in truth. We were outside, standing in the stalls of the jousting rings, watching. Robin was competing. Unwittingly I moved forwards to see better. It had been years since I had seen him in the lists, and he was magnificent, there was no denying that. From the look on the Queen's face, she at my side, she agreed too.

The cold November air was chill and harsh, yet the Queen leaned forward, not heeding its bite as she watched Robin and his mighty horse charge into the fray. The frothing spit of the horses flew through the cold air, their hooves like thunder as they churned the soil. The crowds screamed with excitement and fear; maids clenching their hands together and men bellowing in support of the riders. As the riders came closer, their horses flying as though the Devil were behind them, I watched Robin lean in, bracing the side of his body that held the lance with all of his strength. Lance met metal with the crash and the bash of impact, shards of wood soared and flicked in all directions as Robin drove his mighty weapon into the side of his opponent.

Robin stayed firmly on his charger, still riding fast, even as his opponent was thrown from his saddle, landing with an ignominious crash upon the floor.

"Norfolk," I said, gazing at the man's banners, now held by a horrified-looking page.

As the Duke of Norfolk rolled on the dirt like a woodlouse seeking to right itself, Robin slowed his mount and trotted to the gallery where the Queen was clapping. She was not the only one. All people in the stands had risen to applaud him. It was a feat worthy of applause, in truth. Next to her was a man I had only heard of, Duke Johan who had come wooing on behalf of his brother Erik of Sweden. I knew the man from a copy of a portrait I had seen, notables of court there that season.

To the Queen's other side, de Quadra clapped with the slow and deliberate smack of one who is not admiring, but contemptuous. I held up my hand, soft tendrils of the silver smoke wending through my fingers and shimmering on my gown. I left them. They did no harm. I even found this touch of the other world comforting now.

"Majesty," cried Robin, lifting his visor, his face lighting up with that easy, charming smile. He came to her on his horse. "I claim the match." The sunlight shone from his armour, winking. Robin looked like a knight of old, like a warrior-saint brought to this Earth by God.

"Three points well won there, my lord," Elizabeth heartily agreed, "an honour to my colours."

Robin pulled his arm about to display the green and white Tudor colours that were bound to it, entirely unscathed in the messy operation of unhorsing one of the premier noblemen of court. Norfolk's servants were pulling him upright as the noble Duke muttered curses like a fisherman lost in a storm.

"You only needed to break the tip of the lance to win, Rob," the Queen reminded him in a teasing tone. She sounded delighted he had bested Norfolk.

Robin shrugged, making his armour clank. "I do not believe in only doing what I must, Majesty, when I am capable of more."

Duke Johan burst into laughter and clapped his hands with vigour. "Well said, my lord!" he cried with infectious abandon. He gazed at Rob with great admiration, not seeming to be affected by the envy that I saw glisten in the eyes of many other courtiers.

"It is a secure man who celebrates honestly the victories of others," I said.

"Indeed, most cannot achieve it," said Death.

Elizabeth put a gentle hand to the excitable Duke's arm. "My comment was not censure against my Lord Robin, I assure you, Your Highness." She smiled at her guest reassuringly. "I am most pleased to see my own colours so honoured by the win of my knight."

"And *what* a win, Majesty!" the Duke almost shouted appreciatively, still clapping his hands as though he had quite forgotten he was doing it. "See the Duke of Norfolk, how red his cheeks have become!" Johan started to chortle gaily at Norfolk's clear discomfort. I smiled. The Duke was infectious in his enthusiasm, almost childlike in his enjoyment.

"If only we could stay that way forever," I said.

"Some do," said Death. "Humans so often think they have no control over how they feel, but they do. To be happy or sad, to see the good or the bad, each are choices."

"Some learn to be sad, for that is all they are granted," I said.

"The happy are not happy because all they ever are given in life is joy," said Death. "Often the opposite is true. Yours are a resilient kind, and all people are granted sadness of one type or another. No one escapes. Those who learn to be happy choose a harder path; to note the good in life, and note that it occurs at least as much as the bad. Often those most able to find joy are the ones who have seen the most sorrow. They find joy because they seek it out, because they pay attention to it, knowing how bitter sorrow is if we allow it to win, clouding our eyes so all we see is sadness and pain."

I looked to the Queen, who was busy frowning. "Norfolk will not thank you for this, Rob," she warned. "He already seeks to make trouble for you at court and beyond. Perhaps it would have been better to take a narrower win and save him the dignity he so treasures."

Robin shook his head, dark hair waving in the light breeze. Some was plastered to his forehead with sweat. "Majesty, the Duke has seen today that the better man prevailed," he said flippantly. "This is something he will have to learn, so why not begin his lessons now?"

"You play with fire, my lord; enemies are not lightly made or lost at this court."

"Then it is good that I have the loving eye of my sovereign lady to watch over me," he said cheerily and bowed. "My Queen…" he announced loudly, as much for those in the stands as for Elizabeth "… I have won the match in your name and I present you with all the honour it is possible for a loving servant to offer his Queen. And now as the matches are done for the day I beg leave to go and bathe before the entertainments this night."

"We thank you for your pains on our behalf, my lord, and give you leave to retire in all honour, and to wash before you partner me in the dance this night." She wrinkled her nose. "Wash well, Robin," she whispered, leaning in towards him, "I do not wish to feel as though I am dancing with a cooking pot this night."

Robin laughed, and bowed from astride his horse. As he rode off, Norfolk rode over to excuse himself. "Well fought, Your Grace," Elizabeth consoled. "It is a pleasure to see one of my own kin with such martial skill as yours. Only a shame that you, perhaps, met the better horseman in this match."

The Duke bowed his head. "Luck, Majesty," he said grimly, wheezing as he tried to recover his breath, "is an ever-changing and fickle friend."

"You think Lord Dudley was merely lucky, then, in besting you this day?"

"Norfolk is a poor loser," I said.

Norfolk nodded to the Queen's question. "Fortune's wheel is ever fond of turning, Majesty," he said. "Those that ride high in the estimations of the world one day may fall as low as sin the next. Those who rely on their luck alone are sure to fall." He sniffed. "I will allow that Lord Dudley is a good horseman, Majesty, and you are obviously… lucky to have him as your Master of Horse."

The Queen started just a little, aware there was a veiled insult in the words of the Duke. Her smile became strained. "It seems that there is much in this life that you would attribute only to luck, Your Grace. I find often that those who do so, preferring to attribute their rival's advancements to blind luck, ignore to their peril the qualities that allow one to advance in life."

The Duke smiled wryly. "We all know well enough, Majesty, of the… *skills* that Lord Dudley has mastered."

"I am pleased to hear you so magnanimous on the subject of your rival, Your Grace," the Queen praised loudly, unable to keep sarcasm from her voice. "So many *lesser* men would hold bitterness against a worthy opponent who had unhorsed them, *so* magnificently, in honourable and fair combat. It is good to see that you, Your Grace, are above such small, petty, unmanly, I might even say, *ignoble*, expressions."

To her side, Duke Johan let a small guffaw slip through his lips and then stared suddenly in the opposite direction, as though distracted by something. Norfolk glowered for a moment, not enjoying the idea that the Queen and her Finnish friend were laughing at him, and then bowed again. "Majesty," he said pompously, "I beg leave to retire for the day."

"Granted, happily, Your Grace, with the utmost pleasure."

As Norfolk rode off Johan grinned openly at Elizabeth, eyes warm and full of esteem. "Your Majesty has a playful wit. Something to be much admired in a woman and a queen!"

She widened her eyes in innocence. "I have no idea what you mean, Your Highness," she lied smooth as a snake. "I was merely congratulating the Duke on his fine sportsmanship."

"Of course, Majesty," agreed Johan with a barely straight face, looking as though he might fall about with laughter. "Of course!"

"Your Majesty often seems to favour lords of lesser blood over the established nobility of the realm," de Quadra drawled from her other side. "A curious notion, one might say."

"I favour where favour is due, Your Excellency," she said, turning to him. "My father thought the same as I; that nobility and blood are to be honoured by duty, but this should never blind us to the merits of other men. Besides, my lord ambassador, the Dudleys *are* of the nobility."

"But not of as noble a house as that of the Duke of Norfolk, Majesty. One must remember that," he said, his smile oily.

"Lord Robert's father was also a Duke, Excellency."

"And was executed by your illustrious sister for treason, Majesty, was he not? As, before him, the Lord Robert's grandfather was also executed for treason, by your great father?" De Quadra's face was impassive, but his tone was not.

"I don't know if you take a close interest in all those whom my father had executed for treason, my lord ambassador? Perhaps you are aware that the Duke of Norfolk's father was also amongst their number? His father, the Earl of Surrey, was executed a bare few days before the death of my own father, on charges of treason, and his grandfather only escaped the same fate because my great father died before he could sign the warrant."

The Queen's smile was a snarl now. "I do not judge men on their pasts, or their families, Excellency, be they of good stock or bad. I judge them on their virtues and talents and on the loyalty they show to my rule and my throne. Any man may have a father or grandfather who was condemned as traitor to my ancestors, but as long as he shows loyalty and love to me and to my crown, then he is allowed to make his way at my court on the back of his own skill, talent and determination. As all have the same chance to do so, my judgement is fair and just."

Elizabeth rose briskly and extended her hand for de Quadra to kiss, almost shoving it up his nose in truth, and then turned to her charismatic Finnish Duke. "Come, Your Highness. I believe you will enjoy the evening's entertainments. They have been organised by my Master of Horse, the Lord Robert Dudley."

"The more they tell her not to love him, the more she does," I said to Death, lifting my hand again so I could see the smoke twisting like an affectionate snake through my fingers. "And yet, when it comes to just the two of them she sounds unsure. I do not think I am the only thing standing in the way of them loving one another."

Death nodded. "You start to understand," he said.

"What does she fear?"

"Perhaps love itself is enough to fear." Death stared after the Queen. "Perhaps she simply wishes for a life unfettered."

Chapter Twenty-Six

Greenwich Palace

Autumn 1559

"What news today, Cecil?" the Queen asked as she sat down on the throne upon its dais in her Presence Chamber. Gathered supplicants milled along the walls and in the hallway outside, each waiting for a chance to talk to their Queen.

The hum of many mumbling voices thumped in my ears. It was hard to turn all my concentration on the Queen. Suddenly I wondered how I had done it when alive. How did I walk through the world with such ease when there was so much noise? When the light of the sun or even candles was so bright? How did I continue on, so blithe and uncaring most of the time, with all this din, haste and distraction? How had I shut it all out and become so concentrated on nothing but the inner world within me? It seemed almost impossible now.

With a wrench to my mind, I turned my eyes from darting back and forth at all the people and their talk. At the edge of the chamber I could see Katherine Grey conversing quietly, passionately, with young Hertford. If this was mid-autumn, Katherine's mother, Frances, had died the month before and the Queen had been obliged to pay for a state funeral in Westminster Abbey. No matter how much Elizabeth disliked all the Greys left living in this world, Frances had been of the blood royal, and the Queen had to honour her passing. I looked to Elizabeth and saw her eyes on the pair too. Hertford was a dangerous match, if that was what Katherine was thinking. He was the eldest son of dead Edward Seymour, and was named for his father. Katherine was of royal blood, and he of blood most ambitious, blood which had ruled in the past. From the steady way Elizabeth was watching them, I could see she was considering the same thoughts I was, and did not welcome them.

"Trouble rears its head between two members of your court, Majesty," Cecil murmured to the Queen from the side of his mouth whilst smiling out at the gathered masses.

"How so?" Her face too did not move from a gentle look of beneficence. It was a talent, the mask she wore.

"Rumour has it that Norfolk and Lord Robert Dudley are less than friends in these past months, Majesty," continued Cecil. "The Duke confronted Lord Dudley openly, accused him of standing in the way of your marriage to the Hapsburgs. Norfolk told Lord Dudley he would do all he could to help bring about the match and thwart his plans."

The Queen sighed wearily. "And what did Robin say in return to this slander?"

"Lord Dudley was heard to say loudly that '*He is neither a good Englishman, nor a loyal subject who advises the Queen to marry a foreigner*,' Majesty."

"It would seem that my Lord Dudley speaks for many in my court and country. There are few people, it seems, who welcome the idea of a foreign prince on the throne of England."

"But there are many who would wish to see Your Majesty honourably settled," argued Cecil, his voice low, but tense.

"I cannot please everyone, Cecil," Elizabeth whispered, "and it seems to me that anyone who is picked to be my consort will displease some of my people in some way, even if they please others. I do not believe the time is right to secure one match over another, not whilst there is such divisiveness in my realm on the subject, and the demands of the Hapsburg are ridiculous! That, should I die, the Archduke Charles would inherit my throne? No English man will stand for such an arrangement, the Hapsburg must know that! No, Cecil, I will leave the subject of marriage for a while. Perhaps if I do, then the men of England will find a candidate they can all agree on, and I will see if I like him or not!"

"No one man will always agree with all others, Majesty." Cecil rubbed a hand over his beard, covering his mouth with his hand. "Eventually the time must come to choose a husband, even if not all are pleased with him."

"It seems that within England, no man will agree with any other at *any* time," she said, shuffling back on her plump cushion. "And so, I am stuck, do you not agree, Cecil?" Her Secretary looked at her with wearisome eyes, but did not continue to fight. The Queen turned back to the milling crowds. "Look, Cecil, here comes de Quadra to brighten our day."

The dour, black-garbed bishop was making his way towards her, and the Queen inclined her head to allow him to begin speaking. "Majesty," he announced, bowing fluidly. "I am happy to relay good news; the Archduke may well be able to honour your court with a visit soon."

She waved her hand airily and he looked annoyed. "She does it on purpose," I said. "Acts the flowery, vacant maid to irritate him."

"It keeps them off guard," agreed Death.

"I am not much in mind to take a husband at this time, Excellency." Elizabeth sighed a trifle dramatically, fluttering her hands at her chest. "There are so many other considerations in my realm that I find my attention has quite been taken from the subject."

De Quadra blinked and his mouth dropped open. Cecil also did not look best pleased, even though I knew that by this time he had lost some interest in the Hapsburg alliance for the same reason the Queen had stated, the demand that the

Queen name the Archduke as her heir. No man of England had wanted that. Many said the Queen herself had leaked that information to the people, for it pitted them against one of her most ardent suitors and then she could claim she could not wed him for fear of losing her people's love.

In an airy tone, the Queen went on. "Of course, if I saw the Archduke I may change my mind, if I fell in love with him." She spoke in such an off-hand manner I could see the Ambassador trembling to keep from losing his temper. "But I cannot make any promise of meeting with him immediately, due to the pressing needs of my country and my people."

"The Archduke was to be invited, in honourable estate, to your country and court, Majesty," protested de Quadra, simmering with anger.

"Oh, of course, my lord Ambassador," she agreed, "but I only wished to meet him in case I decided to marry at some future date. I cannot possibly think on the matter now. There is so much else to be done."

De Quadra spluttered and glanced angrily at Mary Sidney, who was hovering behind Kat with the rest of the ladies beside the throne. "Your servants seemed convinced that you were amenable to the idea of marriage at this present time, Majesty," he stuttered, glaring at poor Mary. "In fact, they seemed convinced that for the security of your realm and people, you were eager to marry."

Elizabeth flicked her fingers in the air. "Servants often say things, Excellency," she noted dismissively. "But I gave no one licence to speak on my behalf, nor encouragement to enter their thoughts into my affairs. I do not say that they do not have the best intentions, for their love for me is as honest as the break of day, but that does not mean that when they talk, they speak with my tongue."

De Quadra glowered at the Queen, then at Mary, and went on to frown at Cecil. He was being made to look a fool, and he did not have the wit to retire from the conversation. Some men cannot bear someone having the last word, particularly if that someone is a woman.

"We will honour the arrival of the Archduke, if he comes, with all the dignity he deserves at our hands, of course, Your Excellency," the Queen continued. "But in matters of marriage, it must be clearly understood that there has been no promise made, and besides…" She paused and gazed lovingly at Duke Johan who was standing at the edge of one of the crowds of people, conversing with others. "I have reason to think that perhaps a suitor may come forward who is already at my court, and would be most welcome to my heart, and my eyes." Elizabeth waved a hand at the Duke who bowed to her, smirking. De Quadra looked as though he might explode.

"Majesty," spluttered de Quadra, "I beg leave to retire."

"Granted, Excellency, with pleasure." Elizabeth beamed at him, well pleased to see him caught so off guard. She had not refused the Archduke, but had given the Ambassador reason to at least delay his imminent arrival. "As you can see there are many supplicants requiring my attention this morning. The work of a prince is to be ever aware of their myriad of responsibilities."

De Quadra bowed and left, glancing at Cecil as he went.

"Get no ideas into your mind on this matter, Cecil," the Queen warned in a tone soft as honey. "Once you have gone behind my back I am ever anxious to glance over my shoulder. I want to find no further meddling in my affairs. Nothing shall come to pass that has not been sanctioned by me."

"Majesty," said Cecil in a stout tone. "My loyalty is to you and England alone."

"Take care to remember it, Cecil, for I find that men have a habit of forgetting much, whereas women remember all."

"Majesty." He bowed. "There is one more thing, and I am sorry that you have to see this, but..." He passed her a letter, with the seal of the ambassador to Brussels, Sir Thomas Challoner, on it. I read the missive over her shoulder.

It reported on wild rumours gathering in other courts, that the Lord Robert Dudley intended to poison his wife in order that he might marry with the Queen of England. My face flushed as I read it, and I glanced at Death, who said nothing. The report stated that rumours did say that Elizabeth might or might not know of the plan. Challoner begged that Cecil relay the rumour to Elizabeth, and urge caution in her actions towards Rob.

She read in silence, and passed the parchment back to Cecil. "Men in high positions often attract the jealousy of others, but it does nothing to our credit to humour such wicked slander."

"I do agree, Majesty. But still I would urge you to caution, for the sake of Lord Dudley, if not for yourself." Cecil looked desperately uneasy. "Your continued favour of him, and your refusal to make a match with another suitor, is what leads people to fear that you may abandon a glittering union with a prince or king, and take instead one of your subjects to be your consort. Your Majesty, this type of rumour places Lord Dudley's reputation in great peril, as a knight and as a nobleman, and especially as a married man. This kind of rumour may destroy him. It also bears on Your Majesty's own reputation without favour."

"I am well aware of that, Cecil," the Queen murmured in a heated whisper. "But I refuse to bow to the envious ramblings and nefarious gossip of those who would have me abandon my friends at their whim. No, my friends stay as they are, and those who would spread such evil in this world will come to see with time that their accusations are groundless. They have no proof, no reason to suspect him, or me, of such wickedness."

"Many would see his ambition alone as grounds for suspicion," counselled Cecil. "Men have done much more than simply get rid of a wife, for the chance of a crown." He shook his head at the Queen's angry face, which was growing redder by the moment. "Majesty, I do not believe this of Lord Dudley for a moment, but you placed me here not to always tell to you the sweet and good things in life, but to counsel you on *all* your matters. I will not hide this from you, nor attempt to honey-coat the poison held within here. I advise you only to remember these rumours and the damage they may do to the Lord Dudley and to yourself."

"I understand, Cecil, and will as ever think on your counsel carefully." She waved the next petitioner forward.

"Were they poisoning me?" I asked. "I asked at this time, again, to come to court and Robin said I could not."

A slip of time and I was moving house, the younger me that was. I had stayed at Cumnor before, several times, and now I had been told to move there as a permanent residence. "As permanent as I had," I said, walking through the chamber over the great hall that would be mine until I died. "I feel like after I left my father's house, I would have done well as a traveller. No room was mine, truly, no house. Had I had a house to keep I might have had more to do."

I sighed, watching myself. I was ill, weight had dropped from me. There were shadows under my eyes, for I did not sleep well, a few hours and then I was awake and pacing the room, then a few more and I was up again. Long hours I spent in the chapel, asking God to save me, shrink the hardness in my chest, near my heart, and return my husband to me, return some life to me. I had none. God did not answer me.

"I came to think he did not, in truth, want me at court, and that thought pained me as much as it haunted me. Did he truly want the Queen? Did he think he had a chance with her, to become a lover to her or perhaps, should anything happen to me, or should he think to annul our marriage, to marry the Queen, and become King?" I sighed, watching myself sit down on a chair to recover some strength.

"Were they poisoning me? Was he alone doing the deed? I come to think the Queen could not have, unless you do not show me all that happened."

"I show you all that is important," said Death.

"Then you would surely show me if he was slipping poison to Mrs Picto or others?" Death did not answer, and I watched a younger Amy stand from the chair, carry on with her day. Pale and wan I was, depressed of spirits, but I went to that chapel each day and prayed for hours to live. I did not want to die.

"It was enough to tempt any man, surely, and we had been married long and without a child appearing in my arms."

I stood by my younger self as she prayed. "I wished for a child, and, God forgive me, not in truth because I wanted a child but because I wanted something to occupy me here in the country, because I wanted company, and because I wanted a secure and solid reason that my husband could not abandon me."

To the altar I walked, wondering why I did not resent God more for not answering my prayers, but it seemed to me then that if God answered all prayers this world would be chaos more than it is now. "All men want to best their fathers. Robin's father had been a kingmaker, or more accurately a failed queen-maker. Robin would be King."

I turned from the altar and walked back to my kneeling, muttering self. "And when he came home, occasions which became only more sporadic as time went on, I would be elated and then deflated. As happy as once he had looked to see me, now he looked displeased."

I looked at Death. "I was standing in the way of the life he thought he should have. I wonder if he did love her, as he protested? I am sure she was, to him, all things that he thought should be his, power, influence, riches, but did he love her true? He wanted power, safety, ambition satisfied, and marrying the Queen would do that, would it not?"

Death was silent, allowing me to speak, my thoughts tumbling from my lips.

I stood beside my kneeling figure in the cold chapel, and I put an unseen and unfelt hand on my own shoulder. "I think he loved ambition more than any woman, and I think Elizabeth sensed that. She only had cause to suspect it, but I, who had already been so abandoned, knew it."

Chapter Twenty-Seven

Cumnor Place

Winter 1559

"A seat in Parliament!" Rob exclaimed. "It is good, but I need a seat on the Council."

"Can you never be happy with what you have?" the younger me asked.

He glanced at her, but I knew even then he barely noticed I was there. My question at that time was poignant, as much about me as about his career. Rob always wanted more, he never was satisfied. That meant also that he never was happy. Lusting after a woman who was untouchable, out of his reach, when he already had a wife who would be dedicated to him alone if he but reached out with his heart, was a prime example of this.

"The Queen takes my advice when she asks for it," he said. "But on the Council, how much I could have done!"

"Perhaps she does it to protect you," the younger me said. "You are making enemies fast, so I hear, husband."

"He was," I said to Death. "In the early part of that winter, as the first gales blew wild over the hilltops and rushed through the streets, two men had been sent to the Tower for plotting to murder Robin. A soldier named Sir William Dury and his brother, a gentleman server of the Queen's own Privy Chamber, were arrested. They had been planning to waylay the Master of Horse in the streets of London and stab him to death. They were discovered by informants of Parry hidden within the court, but it was a narrow-won thing. They were but a few days from acting on their plotting when they were discovered. Not long after this plot was uncovered, Rob asked the Queen to pardon the men."

"They would not have told the Queen's men who was behind the attack, or planned attack anyway," he had told me. "The captured men were not the ones who wanted me dead, in truth. They were just the daggers other men, men of power, would use. I told the Queen that executing these men would do nothing, but releasing them might, for the people would know I was merciful and kind…"

I had thought how arrogant he sounded then. He thought himself a King already.

"… and the Queen agreed."

"Of course, she is infatuated with you, is she not?" The younger me was clearly annoyed with her husband.

"Does every trip here have to end with us shouting, Amy?" he asked.

"Does every trip here have to be filled only with conversation about the woman you ride off to leave me for, even when I am ill?" Young Amy shook her head and looked from the window, tears in her eyes. "And I hear how ill I am from others, how near death I stand, how lost my cause is. Are you spreading it about court that I will die and leave you a free man soon, so you might wed the Queen? That is what I hear!"

Death and I stepped away as the shouting began. "I do not need to hear it again," I said.

"Then let us see another conversation." He lifted his hand, and we were at court, beside the Queen and her ladies. They appeared to be eavesdropping. There was a little balcony overlooking a hall, and in the hall were raised voices. Norfolk, and Robin. No one had noticed that the Queen and her ladies were hovering in the darkness above them. "Don't let them see you," Elizabeth cautioned her women. "I want to hear for myself what is occurring here."

Her ladies nodded, shuffling behind her. I could see fidgeting anxiety on Mary Sidney's face. She would not wish to see her brother displayed to the Queen in any way that might make Elizabeth less affectionate, but the Queen, who crept forth, clearly wanted to know what these men were bickering about, was keen to listen.

"… And you interfere constantly in the Queen's business!" brayed Norfolk. He sounded like an outraged donkey. "You have not the right to do so. You are no member of the Council. You are no member of the *nobility* in truth!"

"If the Queen asks questions of me, I do my best to answer, Your Grace," Robert defended himself, his voice rising in volume but, as yet, under control. "And if it happens that the Queen cannot find the advice she requires within her Council, then why should she not seek it elsewhere?"

I could hear Norfolk sputtering. "You think that you are better placed to advise the Queen than all the learned members of her Council?" Norfolk screeched, his voice leaping toward the heavens. "You go too far, you foolish upstart! You, you vainglorious little *bastard*!"

"My parents were legally married, as well you know, Your Grace," Rob quipped smoothly. A few bystanders tittered. "And they were of the nobility. My blood runs as rich as yours does on that score."

"Traitors!" shouted Norfolk. I leaned forward to see the Duke pacing towards Rob, his hands flying out. "Tell me, my Lord Dudley," Norfolk hollered into Rob's face. "Tell me, which of your ancestors has *not* been executed for treason? For those members must be in a minority in *your* hallowed family! Your grandfather? No. Your father then? No. Brothers? No, I think all of them but you and your brother Ambrose were sent to the block for treason. You come from a mighty line of betrayers, deceivers and traitors, my lord. London Bridge is kept a rich dark red by the blood of your family ever dripping upon it!"

Rob drew himself up before Norfolk. "And their blood was joined by that of your own father, Your Grace," he said boldly, "and almost that of your grandfather too. Wasn't it only by luck that the great King Henry VIII died the day before he meant to sign your grandfather's execution order? And was it not one of your cousins, the Queen Catherine Howard, who was given to that same King as wife, and betrayed the King in a privy with his own serving men?" Rob shook his head at Norfolk and snorted. "Mine is not the only family with stains upon its honour, Your Grace."

"He does not mention that only one of his brothers died on the block," I whispered to Death.

"I would think he realises there is small point arguing the details with Norfolk," Death told me.

"How dare you question the honour of *my* family?" screamed Norfolk. "How dare you question the honour of my blood?"

"You do the same to mine, Your Grace," cried Robert, his voice rising. "And you dare a great deal more when my back is turned, I know well."

"What mean you?" asked Norfolk, staring at him. Something in Rob's tone pulled the nearly hysterical Duke up short.

"I believe you know well what I mean, Your Grace." Robert's eyes were dangerous. "You are a wealthy man, with coin ready in his purse to buy all kinds of things; a fine bolt of cloth, a favourable jewel, or even, perhaps, the direction that a man might cast a knife in the darkness."

Norfolk paled, and in that moment I was sure that Rob was right. The Duke hated Robert and had the most to gain, at least so he thought, by achieving the removal of the Queen's favourite. "And I have no doubt, also," continued Rob, standing imposingly in front of the Duke, "that you were not alone in your plotting." His head turned, just for a moment, towards one of the men standing behind Norfolk, watching the confrontation in horror.

It was Cecil.

I stepped back in shock. I could not say whether or not Rob was right, but he was no fool, certainly. If he had reason to suspect Cecil had been involved in the attempt on his life, in conjunction with Norfolk, then perhaps there was indeed reason to suspect.

Perhaps Cecil thought that if Robin were removed the Queen would more easily agree to marriage. Cecil would bring security to England by selling Elizabeth to the highest bidder and getting a babe in her royal belly. If Robin were removed, the Queen might listen to Cecil alone.

"You have no right to accuse me of any of these crimes, my *lord*," Norfolk spat angrily. "I am a man of honour and of the nobility. Your upstart pretensions to cloud the Queen's head with your... your *devil's* talk will never succeed whilst I am within this country. I will see you fall, my lord, and fall faster and lower than any man thought possible."

"Whilst I have the friendship of the Queen and the love of her people," replied Robert, "I will fear nothing from you, Your Grace." Rob shook himself, ruffling his shoulders at Norfolk and standing tall. "And my heart has ever been with God, Your Grace. I bring no evil with *my* thought or action."

"You bring the Devil into the presence of the Queen every day!" Norfolk roared, almost insensible with fury. His red face shone like a beacon, and flecks of white spittle flew from his mouth. "You confound her with witchcraft and cloud her senses with your spells. You are a creature of darkness who will lead our Queen and country into destruction with your wiles! She is but a woman, though she be a queen, and women are easily corrupted by the powers of evil!"

Clearly, judging by her expression, the Queen had heard enough. Elizabeth stepped out onto the platform. Trumpeters who had been standing, staring open-mouthed at the heated argument, leapt to attention and sent out an ungainly blast of noise to herald the Queen's arrival in the hall. "The Queen!" heralds shouted and all below her hurriedly bowed in surprise.

Norfolk's face was rather red as he straightened up.

"I was enjoying a morning thinking on the delights of the season of the birth of our Lord Jesus Christ," the Queen announced smoothly and loudly, her voice ringing through the hall, "when I was distracted from those thoughts by a great commotion. For a moment, I thought two street hawkers had entered my palace and started a market within its walls to sell their wares." She paused and gazed down at Robert and Norfolk, both of whom were blushing now. Around them were many faces smiling at their discomfort.

"How then, was I further amazed to find, instead of the screeching harpies I had expected, that it was the Duke of Norfolk and the Lord Lieutenant Constable of Windsor conducting themselves as though they were squalling, brawling infants!" The Queen lifted her eyebrows and shook her head. "And here I find you, in a public contest, it seems, to find which of your family contains the most members to have flouted the will and law of my royal line. A most illogical competition to my mind, my lords." She held up a hand haughtily as each of them attempted to defend themselves.

"I will hear *no more* of your voices on this day, my lords," she cried imperiously. "Quite enough I have heard of you and rather *too* much on some counts, to be sure." Elizabeth glared at Norfolk and watched him turn a most unhealthy shade of scarlet. "I would offer each of you this piece of advice, my lords," she continued, her voice as cold as the wind wailing outside the palace walls. "Perhaps rather than seeking to contest which of your families has more or less often disappointed *previous* monarchs, you should work to ensure that your behaviour does not dissatisfy your *present* monarch. Succeeding in that task may allow you to keep your heads where they belong; on your shoulders. Do think it over carefully, won't you?"

She gazed around the hall at the others and scowled at them. Many faces which had been smirking to see her scold Rob and Norfolk dropped their eyes and their smiles. "And for all the rest of you, grinning here. You would do better to go about your own business rather than hang about idly watching others disgrace themselves. It would do better to your own ambitions and the wealth of your characters not to indulge in such a spectacle of idiocy. There is ever much competition for the places of privilege at my court, and there are many that would be glad to be offered a post here, should any of you disappoint me again."

The crowd below shifted uncomfortably. Many a mortified nobleman stared wide-eyed at his shoes. "You can go now, my lords," the Queen ordered, but as Norfolk bowed and turned to leave she called to him.

"One final suggestion, from a loving monarch to her subject, Your Grace..." Norfolk turned and looked up at her, his crimson face wary and deeply shamed. Under the redness of his cheeks I could see anger at being reprimanded so, and in public. "... Although I be *but a woman*, forget not that I am also your Queen," Elizabeth called, her tone scathing. "And I am led by *no one and nothing* other than the conscience within me and the guiding hand of *God* who placed me on my throne. Forget not that, Your Grace, even if you fail to remember aught else."

Norfolk's already ruddy face burst into flames as he bowed, mumbled something incomprehensible and fled from the room. Elizabeth turned to her ladies and sighed. Mary Sidney looked most uncomfortable, whereas Kat was grinning from ear to ear. "My court is become a nursery," the Queen said to them. "Come, let us walk once more through the halls and find a way to forget the foolish prattle of overgrown infants unable to restrain their tempers or their tongues." She shook her head. "And they, ladies, would be the first to call women hysterical creatures, unable to govern themselves. It makes one wonder if men have ever gazed into that contraption we call a mirror."

I watched them walk away, Elizabeth's ladies laughing. "The plan with footpads I could see Norfolk being in on," I said to Death, "but Cecil? I would have thought he would be more careful, more cunning." I looked at the decorations, ivy and holly bound around the windows. If Norfolk had been part, or indeed the author of this plot against Robin, could he have been involved in my murder too? "Later that week Norfolk was sent from court. Rob wrote of it. Norfolk went north to serve as Lieutenant General on the Scottish border. He was a good general, coming from a family most experienced in the art of war, so the Queen needed him in such posts, but Rob said the Queen wanted the man gone from court, too, and this was a way to do it without disgrace. Arran was working for the Queen too, trying to unseat Mary of Guise. The regent of Scotland had French troops coming to aid her then, I think."

I trailed a hand over some ivy, brought in to decorate the palace. Threads of silver danced from my fingertips to stroke the bright red berries hanging there. "As Christmas drew nearer, England declared an outright alliance with the Scottish Protestants."

"It was then other plots for the heirs to the throne were afoot too," said Death, pointing.

I looked around. Elizabeth was in her rooms as Kat came to her with a harried, grey look upon her face. "What is it?" the

Queen asked, drawing her aside to a corner of the chambers as the other ladies gathered about the fire.

"Those… items you wished watched over, Majesty?" Kat said, something I seemed to know without asking was code for the Grey girls, Katherine and Mary, the surviving sisters of Jane Grey. "Well, I believe that I have found out something deeply troubling," Kat went on. "There is word of a plot afoot for the Spanish to take Katherine from England, and ship her to Spain. There she would be married to Don Carlos, the son of Phillip, and brought back at the head of an army to claim the throne of England."

"She would place herself on my throne!" Elizabeth hissed.

Kat shook her head quickly. "The Grey girl knows nothing of the plan, Majesty, at least if my informant is to be believed. Katherine has been courted by the envoys from Spain and the Hapsburg Empire, yes, but apparently they wish to make friends with her so that she will not suspect when they carry her off. They say that when Feria was still here he tried to test her, to see if she was willing to voluntarily leave England, or marry out of it, and she said that she would rather die than leave England." Kat's mouth twisted. "Evidently the girl had not the wit to understand what he was really asking her, Majesty. She thought it was an innocent conversation, when in fact he was trying to discover if she would be willing to marry into Spain!"

"You really think that she is that foolish?"

"I think it is indeed a possibility, Majesty," she said.

Elizabeth ran a hand over her dress of purple and silver cloth. "Well, either way, we must make sure that Cecil and Parry keep an eye on Katherine," she said. "And if the plot is indeed kidnap, how unoriginal the Spanish are! Do you remember when they planned to do the same to me? To marry me off to Philibert when I was but a princess. And now they would think to do the same, that is if Katherine truly knows nothing of it." She bit her lip. "We will have to make some changes in the royal apartments. If Katherine *is* the victim of a plot, then I want her as close to me as possible so that she cannot be carried off without me knowing of it in a moment. And if she is in cahoots with the Spanish, I will give her something to think upon which may outshine any promises they have made to her. Either way, I will not have her driven into enemy hands and used as a weapon against me."

"What do you mean to do, my lady?"

Elizabeth curled her lip. "Something I will have no love for at all; promote the Lady Katherine Grey to my Bedchamber."

Kat looked astounded. The highest of the ladies-in-waiting served in the Bedchamber, usually only women the Queen trusted without question, and she did not like Katherine. "It is the only way to keep her close, Kat," the Queen rushed on. "I will make a show of flattering and fawning upon her, and you will spread it about the court that I love her so much I cannot do without her. Let us make all believe that I intend to make Katherine my heir, legally, and then we shall see how easy it is for the Spanish to kidnap her, or tempt her into treachery!"

"The Queen had a ready replacement, standing close," I said. "Another woman, one more foolish and malleable, younger than her too. I never met Katherine Grey, but if she was fool enough, as this evidence suggests, she could have been used against Elizabeth with ease."

Death nodded. "The Spanish were growing desperate. That December, Baron Breumer finally left England. He told Cecil before he left that he believed he had failed in his mission to bring about a union between the Archduke Charles and the Queen." He pointed to the Baron, writing a letter.

"The Queen is too changeable of spirit," the Baron said to Cecil, handing him the letter. "It is explained by her youth, for sometimes she was regarded as legitimate and at other times not; she has been brought up at court, and then sent away, and to crown *all,* she has even been held captive. Since she attained the throne, almost by luck as much as anything else, she is like a *peasant* on whom a baronetcy has been conferred and is now so consumed by pride that she imagines she can indulge her every whim. But here she errs, for if she takes my Lord Robert, she will attract so much enmity that she may one evening lay herself down as the Queen of England, and the next rise as plain *Mistress Elizabeth*."

We watched as Cecil dared to read this letter to his Queen. The man had courage, that was certain. Cecil was determined, now, at all times to impress Robin's inadequacies upon his Queen, and the dangers of her choosing him as her husband. Although nothing had been said, either publicly or privately, about a possible match, Cecil was obviously certain that this was the path Elizabeth was intending to take.

"Do you think she was?" I asked Death. "I cannot see from one moment to the next what she intends. The Baron was right, she changes and shifts as the sky does through a spring day where it may be summer one moment and winter the next. It is not only that he is married, or was, it is her."

"She has trouble trusting. A King could wed and not surrender power, but she, a woman could not. Any husband would be a danger to her, in one way or another."

"They could put restrictions on his power as King, there were the same for Phillip of Spain." I sat in a window seat, swinging my legs along the dark wood panelling.

"Would she trust that Robin Dudley would keep to such restrictions? She knows him well, and she knows his ambition. You said it yourself, he never was happy with what he had. He always wanted more."

"She might marry him for love, but she would want to be sure he was marrying her and not her crown." I nodded. "How could she ever be sure of that?"

"How indeed. Power changes your kind."

Cecil had finished reading the Baron's letter to his mistress.

"The Baron is a lot clearer in his speech to you than he ever appeared capable of to me, *Spirit*," Elizabeth said, running her fingernails down the sides of her dress, sending the purple silks and gold lace quivering on her skirts.

"I understand, Majesty, that some of the sentiments in this passage will not have been to your liking," agreed Cecil, a tad warily, as he watched the Queen's eyebrows shoot upwards again on her pale powdered face.

It was the latest style at that time for women to wear a pale lead cosmetic that made the skin shine like a pearl. Rob had sent some from London for me, but I did not wear it. I did not want people to think I was aping the Queen, the woman who had stolen my husband, although, being fair and after watching all I had seen, I knew now he had leapt into her arms to be stolen.

"I only wished to draw Your Majesty's attention to the concerns he raises, which many others do also hold," said Cecil.

"Yes, yes," the Queen muttered irritably. "That if I run off and marry Lord Dudley then all the country will rise about me and I will be put off my throne." She shook her head, weary, little pearls rattling amongst her red tresses. "Cecil, Robin is married and I have never once made any public nor private statement that I would marry him. All this supposition is just to undermine Robin's character and position at court, of which many are jealous."

"They are jealous, Majesty, because you make them so," Cecil gently censured. "Because you show such favour to Lord Dudley, these assumptions are made. But it is more than that. The country is not rich, it is still beset by enemies on all borders. A union with a prince of another country would bring wealth and protection to the realm, and also give an heir…"

"Yes, yes," Elizabeth interrupted again, holding up her hand. "An *heir*, so that we might all rest well in our beds at night since no doubt the squalling infant will be entirely capable, singlehandedly, of holding off the French and the Scots and the Spanish and restoring the treasury to riches." She frowned at him. "Perhaps also this miracle babe I am supposed to produce could end all wars, make England the master of the world and cure all disease and pestilence too?"

"Majesty," sighed Cecil in that now-familiar despairing tone.

"Cecil," the Queen snapped. "Enough of this. I will not abandon my friends, as I have told you before. As to when and whom I shall marry, if I marry at all, that will be down to my choice and that of God to decide."

"Majesty," he acquiesced, bowing his head.

"That winter was so cold," I said as we went back to Cumnor. I was by a fire, wrapped in blankets. "I was not hale, and the wind was so cold, the air was harsh. Snow fell early and kept coming. I could not get warm. The only time I felt warm was when I ate, I could feel then the pottage seeming to travel to the ends of my fingers and toes, steaming the blood and the flesh. But I did not want to eat. I never did when I was unhappy. I went to the chapel and I prayed, prayed until my fingers turned blue, that I might get better and live. When I could not feel my hands, I came back to the fire."

I gazed upon the forlorn figure by the fire. "The fire kept me warm, my maids too, but my heart was cold," I said and looked at Death. "I wasted time. In my head I played out conversations we had had, and I would talk him around into loving me again. I would win every argument. I went over fights we had had, time and time again, growing only more bitter every time I replayed that fight." I watched as the younger me wrapped her blankets about her tighter, a frown on her face. "If I could tell her now what I know, what comfort I might bring her!"

I put my hands on Amy's shoulders, but she could not feel me. She shivered. "I thought I had no choice at the time, but you are right, I did waste what time I had. Had my heart not been consumed by Robin, by feeling betrayed, if I had chosen to spend my days trying to do other things, living a life no matter how bad or well I did, I might have not wasted the time I had left."

"You did not know it was so little time," said Death, compassion in his voice.

"Did I not? We all know we must die, it is the one thing we all will certainly do with our lives. We all know an end will come."

Chapter Twenty-Eight

Cumnor Place

February 1560

We stood outside, the air biting and cold. Not far from the house, fenlands sounded with the echoing calls of duck and geese. Slate-blue kestrels swooped from great heights to dazzle brown-plumed females with feats of flight. Rooks sought to pickaxe through hard and frozen ground, often giving in, leaving to hunt unguarded baskets of women bringing wares to markets. Swans came to rest in great swathes on the rivers, and we watched time turn as spring started to break from the bonds of winter, bringing the bleating cries of new-born lambs to thread through the countryside.

I looked to the house. "As the winds ceased to wail, I started to think that with the spring, came new hope, for I felt better. I was swiftly proved wrong."

"I grew sicker," I said as we appeared in the frozen chapel where I was praying again. Mrs Picto was with me, her nose pink, blowing on her fingers to try to bring life back into them. "My prayers more desperate. I felt unheard and abandoned, bitter, set into the country to rot away from the inside out. It felt like Rob was just waiting for me to die, and something in me did not want to, just to spite him. Every day there were more rumours about him and the Queen."

I looked to the plain altar. Light was coming in through the window, making it sparkle. I stopped in wonder a moment at this tiny little joy, and looked at myself. The Amy who had been me did not look up, did not see this little wonder, this tiny beauty. Her eyes were closed as she prayed, prayed to God to preserve a life she was miserable in. "I wish I had made more of the time I had," I said again.

"There is still time," Death said. "Life is done, but your existence is not."

I gazed up his face, something that should be fearsome and yet I now found so comforting, and I nodded. There was silence a moment, and then I went on.

"We heard that, that winter, the ambassador to France, Nicolas Throckmorton wrote to the Queen warning of grave plots on her life. Rumours had reached him that the Guise planned to send an Italian to poison our Queen. Cecil decreed that all the Queen's food must be tested, and she was to accept no gifts of sweets, marmalades, perfumes or perfumed gloves, even from people she knew well, for those bent on killing her might manage to trick those whom she trusted into delivering their poisons to her unawares. Her guard was doubled, people said she was not safe. People said she needed to marry, for a husband would keep her safe. It seemed to me more often a husband was the thing to fear."

From Cumnor we found ourselves at court.

"We have no true heir to the throne, Majesty," warned Cecil, looking distressed. "Even if we were not motivated by love and respect to ensure your safety, if one of those men were successful in their wicked plots chaos would reign in England. Some would back Katherine Grey, and some your cousin of Scots, some might even support the dullard sons of the Lennoxes for the throne, but what surely would happen is that the country would descend to chaos and then our enemies will have truly won. I know, Majesty, you would never wish that for your country, so it is imperative that you remain alive, and remain our Queen."

Elizabeth smiled. "All my life, Cecil, people have wished me dead and they have failed in their task, for I am still here. I will preserve my life. I will try not to complain, my friend, of the measures you and St Loe have put in place for my safety, although they irk me. I understand your fears are for my welfare and my country's welfare also." Elizabeth put a hand to his shoulder. "I cannot promise I will never complain again, *Spirit*." She smiled wearily. "But I will try to remember the reasons for this, and control my irritation."

Cecil looked grateful, but despite his warnings the Queen and Robin were still out riding each day. We stepped into another day, another hour. "He is a poor influence on her!" Cecil shouted to Parry, pacing up and down in Parry's chamber. "When Lord Robin is with her, she is listening only to him."

"She takes all the guardsmen you insist on with her," Parry said. "And you know our Queen, if she cannot ride and exercise she will come unhinged."

Time swirled, and Death and I stood upon grass. It was a chilly early afternoon in March, I would have guessed from the trees. We were outside, in a royal park. The wind was bitter and sharp, so the Queen's many guards had built a fire at the edge of the woods so they and their mistress could shelter under the trees. Rugs had been made to make seats on fallen tree trunks. The men were warming wine at the fire, and toasting bread. Smothered in yellow butter and new, white cheese, it was served with slabs of beef and venison, as well as wild leeks roasted on the fire. Celandines were peeking bright yellow eyes from the leaf mould. Elizabeth set her plate on the ground and smiled at Rob, who was, as usual, eating too much.

"You'll eat yourself to death like that, Rob." She smirked at him, and then frowned. "Soon enough the spread comes to the man and his appetite becomes too big for his body to bear."

Rob glanced sheepishly at his swollen belly. There wasn't an ounce of fat on him, to be fair. "Then I shall put down my knife for love of Your Majesty," he said, still looking hungrily at steaks sizzling over the fire.

"You can't still be hungry!" she exclaimed. "You have eaten more than all my guards put together!"

Rob and the guards chortled. "I always hunger for more." He nodded. "It is in the nature of a man to always want more."

"Something that is understood with heavy hearts by all women. They understand that their own husbands will never be satisfied with what they have!"

"She knows him," I said.

"Well, as to that, it entirely depends on the woman." Robin stared at the fire with those dark eyes. He turned to her. "If a man had the right woman at his side, he would never need to look anywhere else to satisfy his hunger."

Elizabeth flushed a little, gazing at the guards who all appeared now not to be listening.

"Elizabeth," whispered Rob, also looking at the guards. "I have something that I would ask you."

Elizabeth sipped wine and stared at the fire. "What is it?"

"I am thinking of pressing Amy for a divorce, or rather an annulment of our marriage." His words came quickly, falling over each other. "I wanted to know your thoughts on the matter."

She stared at him. "You do this for hope of marrying me, Rob?"

"I will not deny that as one reason," nodded Robin. "You know that I love you. You are all that I think of and all that I want. You are my Elizabeth. I have known that we should be together since we were children, but the possibility of anything between us was so remote that it was only a dream. But when

I found that you perhaps felt the same as I did, then I dared to hope."

"Marriage is a sacred institution, not to be laid aside or entered into without thought." Her voice wavered. I wondered if she was thinking of her mother.

"Marriage is so," agreed Rob, "and should not be treated lightly. But I believe I am within my rights to think on separating from Amy, to seek another wife." He leaned towards her. "Elizabeth, I am a man. I have titles and wealth and I wish to have children, to have a son to hand my name and my rights to when I die. Amy and I have been together for years and never once has she given a sign that she is fertile. I wish to have children. I am within my rights to separate from my present wife on the grounds that she is infertile, and marry again." He reached out and put his hand over hers. "Amy is sick, and I could wait for her to die. But as you have said so often, talking of replacing her, waiting for her to die, it is all so morbid, is it not? And it is not fair to the woman I married."

"And you think that divorcing her will do right by her instead?" There was an edge to her voice. I wondered if he remembered Elizabeth's father had separated from women who had not given him a son, too.

"It would be *honest*, which is what I think is right, and it is what I think you objected to when I offered you my love before. I could not offer myself to you as a free man, and you liked not the idea of hanging on for the death of a sick woman as it made you feel ghoulish." At his words, she shivered.

Rob nodded. "There, you see? I am right, am I not? If I press Amy for a separation then she can retire to a convent or to her family estates. She will be free of a husband that she never sees. I will be free to marry again, to finally have the wife that I long for, and the family of which I dream."

"Retire to a convent," I spat. "What more could I do to retire from the world than what I was then? He grew impatient!" Something clattered in my soul. Just how impatient had Robin been? Divorce, annulment… these things could take years. Death was quicker.

"I do love you," Elizabeth whispered. "I cannot deny that you are ever-present in my heart, and if I were ever to marry you would be the only man I could consider in truth. I would share my life with you. I would share the care of my country with you."

For a moment it looked as though Rob was about to grab her in his arms and kiss her. But he stopped himself, remembering the guards. It would hardly be done to kiss the Queen as though she was a tavern wench.

"But there will be much opposition to our match, my *Eyes*," Elizabeth whispered urgently, her cheeks burning. "There would be many against it."

"Then we will convince them," he murmured, taking her hand once more. "Just let me know, Elizabeth; if I should bring this to pass and leave Amy, would you take me as your husband? Would you let our love come to life at last?"

She swallowed. I wondered if she wanted to answer at all. "I will marry you…" her voice was soft, low, and throbbed with all the fear and the excitement of her choice… "When you have divorced your wife, or rather annulled the match, and when a decent space of time has passed, I will marry you, Robin."

Again, Robin moved to gather her in his arms but she held up a hand, blushing furiously. "Until that time, though," her voice squeaked with sudden fear, "none can know, Rob. You must promise me that. If it comes out, I shall deny it utterly. You cannot say a thing, even to your sister or brother, you must promise! The Queen of England cannot become engaged to a man who is still married to another. The shame would be unbearable. I would risk the love of my people, risk my throne, even. You must promise me."

He lifted her hand to his lips and kissed each finger on it. "I swear to you with all my heart that I will tell no one of your promise to me, and I swear to you also that I shall play this scene to myself every morn and every night, for the rest of my days, to remind myself of the happiest day of my life."

His face glowed with excitement. I wondered if he was more excited by the woman or her throne. "I swear to you, Elizabeth," he promised ardently, "you and I, our love, we will be the envy of the world. We will have beautiful daughters and strong sons, and I will love you until the end of my days. We will make England greater than it has ever been; the envy of all other countries." He kissed her palm. "And I will make sure you know every single day that you are the most beautiful, most wise and most wonderful woman in the world!"

She laughed. "I do not think I am any of those things, Robin." Elizabeth leaned in against his shoulder. She looked at peace with him in that moment, but her eyes still were unsure.

"You are all those things to me and more," he murmured, and shook his head. "You are my love and the master of my heart, my hopes and my happiness. My life can never be complete without you in it. You have the ability to make me angrier than any other person I have ever met, and yet you make me happier and more peaceful than any other too. When I am sad you lift me up, and when I am pompous you cut me down. You are my confidante and my friend, Elizabeth, and when I die, if they look at my heart, they will see your name alone carved into it."

Tears sprung to her eyes as he spoke. "You are my best friend, Robin," she stuttered. "You, you make me laugh. You surprise me. When I think I have lost all faith in the world, you, you come to me to offer me more. I have loved you since I was a girl, I think, although I never dared to hope that there was a chance you could be mine. I have not had an easy life, and my life is not easy now. But if you, if you will take the good with the bad, then I will offer my heart to you freely, Robin, and love you with all of my heart, until the day I die."

Robin clenched her hands. "Then, I am engaged," he whispered. "But none shall know until the time is right, I promise you, Elizabeth." He frowned in concentration. "I will ensure all of this goes smoothly and there will be no opposition to our marriage when all is done."

"How did you ensure it went smoothly, Robin?" I whispered.

The fire had grown low and the wind was picking up. The woodlands started to look dark, shadows creeping through the twisted ivy and rustling briar. "We must head back to the palace," Elizabeth said, sadly. The guards stamped out the fire, and poured water from a stream on the embers.

My husband beamed at the woman he had just become engaged to. "I'll wager Your Majesty a silver noble I can beat you back to the palace."

Her lips curled upwards. "Wager accepted, my lord. Although you know you will never win. My horse carries but one slight woman, whereas your poor mount has to carry you *and* all that food you consumed."

They went to mount horses, as the wind was tumbling fast from the skies. "A storm is coming," I said and Death nodded.

Chapter Twenty-Nine

Hampton Court

Spring – Summer 1560

From sheen of silver spider web, not sticky but clinging to my skin all the same, as if it wanted me and me alone, we stepped into the bright, hard world, and came upon the Queen making plans most sly and careful. I gazed back, with a sense of longing and loss, at the soft light of the grey-silver world we kept leaving in order to come back to this one. The shadows that moved there, they seemed to hold out their hands to me in friendship. I took comfort in the threads left on me. They had grown in number now, so when I looked down, I seemed a thing of silver myself.

"In the late spring of that year, news came that Pope Pius IV was sending a delegation to England to command our Queen to return to the Catholic faith, and bring England along with her," I said, turning from the other world and feeling a sadness I could not explain pervade my blood. "The Queen sent word the delegation were to not enter England."

"If they cannot deliver the Bishop of Rome's commands to me, then I cannot refuse, can I?" Elizabeth asked Parry breezily. "Therein, the Bishop of Rome can have no cause to be angered, as his delegation was simply unable to present his wishes to me. Tell them whatever you want; disease is prevalent in England, or there are fears for their safety from Protestant fanatics. I care not. Just keep them at bay." Suddenly she stopped, peering at him. Elizabeth had poor sight, Robin had told me long ago. It gave her a most piercing gaze, much like her sister Mary had possessed. The eyes of the Tudor sisters seemed to gaze into the souls of men, but it was an illusion cast by frail eyesight. "Are you well, Parry? We are not overworking you in your present duties?"

"The man is pale, it is true," I said, looking close at him, the shadows under his eyes.

Parry's eyes lighted on his Queen with affection and he smiled. "No, Majesty," he assured her. "I am well. I have ever thrived on hard work."

"Well, you must take more care for yourself," she scolded. "I will send my doctors to you to bleed you or recommend a tonic for your present pallor."

"My Queen's concern for my health is of great comfort to me, and is, in itself, the best of tonics." His eyes were warm. "But send no doctors, Majesty. I have often seen hale men fall into sudden death at the hands of a doctor. I will take more care for my own self, I promise you."

"It is true," I said, turning to Death. "Often I felt sicker and weaker after I was bled, and especially after they purged me. The herbs the cunning woman of the village sent helped, but nothing the doctors tried on me did."

"You should eat and drink more sparingly," Elizabeth was telling Parry. "I often find that men at court are apt to eat themselves into an early grave. If you will not see my doctors then at least avail yourself of the healing herbs in the physic gardens. I do not like to see my friends in fragile health."

He promised again to care for himself, and was just on his way out when Cecil arrived and asked if Parry might stay as he relayed some news. Cecil was beaming. "The regent of Scotland, Mary of Guise, is departed from this life," he announced with glee. "The French sent word at this news that they are willing to sue for peace with us and the Scottish lords."

Elizabeth snorted. "As well they might, Cecil!" She sat back on her chair and exhaled deeply. The sense of relief falling upon the chamber was palpable.

"A woman is dead and they care only that she is not a threat to them anymore. That is clear enough," I said.

"The woman was their enemy more than ever their friend," said Death. "Humans choose to protect their own rather than loving their enemies."

"Is that not reasonable?"

Death almost seemed to chuckle. "Perhaps, yet all these people would say they were Christians, and Christ said they should love their enemies just as well as friends."

The Queen was still talking. "Without the Guise she-wolf the French will lose the country entirely to the Scots lords. They will not be able to place our cousin Mary Stuart on this throne, or advance her claim to be named as heir of England, unless they make peace with us."

"We have them, my lady!" Parry sang joyously, his previously pale face now pink with excitement. "England is freed from the threat of invasion!"

"It was true; England was safe at last," I concurred. "This death, the death of but one woman, now meant that Scotland was without a regent, and the Scottish lords could now take control. Without Mary of Guise holding them together, the Catholics and the French would lose their power in our neighbours' country. The French were unable to send troops into Scotland because of our English blockade in the Firth of Forth, and so they would be unable to press their Queen's claim on the throne of Scotland without English help." I shook my head. "One death of but one woman, and all changed."

"If the French are willing to sue for peace," Elizabeth mused thoughtfully, "then perhaps they might be willing to enter into talks for the return of Calais."

Parry and Cecil both looked at once doubtful and interested in the idea. The loss of Calais had gravely wounded England's pride. Perhaps now there was a chance to reclaim it, to bring lost glory back to the English.

"We must think carefully on the terms we wish to present to the French," the Queen said to her men. "I will wish to think alone for a time, both on what to press for and demand, and on whom to send to bring our wishes about. Leave me for a while to think."

As they left, she called for Robin. "Rob!" she cried as he entered her chambers. Her women were there, as usual, and Lettice Knollys looked up as Rob entered. Pure admiration swept from under the young girl's dark lashes as she gazed on him.

My brow furrowed, as did that of the Queen. "Another one, Robin?" I asked. "And your true love just here in front of you?"

"He had an eye for pretty women with red hair," said Death.

"We are freed of the threat of war, Rob," Elizabeth announced joyfully as he turned all his attention to her, and she told him of the death of Mary of Guise.

"Of what did she die?" he asked.

"Dropsy, or so I am told," Elizabeth replied. "But for whatever reason, our enemy in Scotland is gone! The rebel lords there wish for us to continue to help them complete their conquest, and the French know they are beaten and wish to sue for peace."

"Have you thought much as yet on your terms?" asked Rob.

"Are you not even to take one moment and rejoice for England's happy fate?" She poked at his tunic with a sharp finger, and giggled like a girl. Rob chuckled at her buoyant mood. Behind him I could see Kat looking at the Queen as the Queen had done at Lettice, with disapproval. Kat dropped her eyes as Elizabeth glared.

"Of course, Majesty," said Rob. "I am overjoyed to hear of the safety and the benefits that might come to our nation through this event. It has been a heavy threat hanging over us."

"Dear God, he is already preparing to be King, listen to the formality in his tone!" I said, shaking my head. "Ridiculous."

"You do not think so well of him now?" asked Death.

"I did not think well of him for some time."

"But you do not admire him, want him as once you did."

I stared at my husband. "Perhaps not," I said, and was surprised that I felt not like weeping for him, but like laughing.

Elizabeth went on. "Perhaps now the French will think twice about their plans to poison me also, they hope to have a friend in me now, to negotiate with those who would remove Mary Stuart entirely from any claim to her native Scotland."

Rob took Elizabeth's hand and kissed it. "Thank God for all graces we are given in Your Majesty's safety."

She led him to a more secluded corner. "How go plans with our other matter?" she asked quietly. Rob's face fell and he shook his head.

"I have started to enquire on the technicalities of gaining an annulment," he murmured. "But in trying to keep this matter as quiet as possible, my task runs slowly." His brow grew darker. "I had thought that her death might release me from my bonds by now."

"I have not even a name anymore," I said angrily.

Elizabeth at least looked uncomfortable at the notion of waiting around for me to die. "I will pursue the means to separate from her," he went on swiftly. "We must not wait any longer. It is torture."

"It is, for me too, Robin."

He lifted her fingers to his lips. "Soon, my love, all our waiting will be over and we will be as man and wife. How I long to hold you in my arms before the world, free to let all see the love between us!"

She shook her head in warning and yanked her hand away from his.

"Too far, Robin," I jeered, walking about him. "You gloat too much about the death of the first wife for the second to rest easy! How is a woman to feel safe, seeing how you treat someone you once protested to love for the rest of life?"

"Have you thought on your terms for France, then?" he asked, going from romance to business with swift ease.

"I have thought a little. I want the French entirely removed from Scotland, no standing armies or anything similar. I want the French to publicly recognise my title as Queen of England and to stop pretending that Mary Stuart is the true Queen."

Rob nodded thoughtfully. "Those are all good things," he agreed, adding mischievously, "it would be nice to see the look on Mary Stuart's face when she is told to stop calling herself Queen of England."

"Something I should dearly love to see in person," the Queen laughed. "She and her foolish husband will see now that all their spiteful insults against my throne and my title will be remembered. They will have to remind themselves not to underestimate the English."

"I wouldn't have thought they would dare to, now they have lost their leader in Scotland."

"I want the government of Scotland to be handed to a ruling Council of the Scots lords," the Queen continued, "men who support my title as Queen of England. The French will take no more part in their destiny, but my cousin will remain their sovereign. However much I personally dislike the woman, she *is* the rightful heir to that throne. If the French agree not to interfere with the Scots, then I will promise England will not either, unless asked for help by the Scottish Council."

"Perhaps you are more generous to Mary of Scots than she deserves," Rob mused, looking over the gardens.

"A mere war or disagreement cannot change the right of succession, Rob." Words came from Elizabeth with passion. "My cousin has no right to *my* throne whilst I live, but she is the only legitimate heir to the Scots' throne, and she is their Queen. Whilst I will not have her lay claim to my England, I cannot deny that she was chosen by God to inherit the royal house of Scots. For better or for worse, she is their Queen. Her legal right to that crown must be respected, even if she never takes it up in truth. I see small chance of her leaving her comfortable place in France. Her husband the boy-king seems sure enough in his crown, even if his power is wielded by others. In all likelihood Scotland will be governed by the Council we will install there for the rest of our lifetimes. Mary Stuart will be a distant figurehead at best, and our neighbours to the north will be eager to deal peaceably with us, as we helped their country to freedom and concord. The French will be willing to deal with us in peace as they know they cannot beat us. This solution brings the best of all our plans together," she smiled, "and I did not have to marry anyone, for such a thing to come to pass. A miracle in itself, according to my Council. They think the solution to every problem is to have me marry!"

Rob let out a small snort of laughter. "And what of Calais?"

"You and I are of a mind, as ever, Rob." She was grinning. "Calais was the first thought that entered my mind. How I would love to have it returned to us! I think of how it would grieve my father to know of its loss and that thought shames me still. How my sister could have sat back and let it be taken, I will never understand."

"Forget not, I was in France when it happened," Rob reminded her, his face betraying deep shame, and sorrow. "The Spanish we were allied with would not send the men needed to take Calais back from the French. All Englishmen there were willing, but all dispatches from England told us not to go." He turned his eyes on her and gritted his teeth. "For all English men who served in those wars, and all who died for our then Spanish overlords, such as my brother Henry, we must see Calais returned to our territories."

"I agree, Robin. It must have been a terrible time. I cannot imagine what it would have felt like to be a soldier there, or to lose one of your own brothers to such a pointless conflict."

Rob looked sadder than I had ever seen. "It felt as though we had come to the end of the world, Majesty, for there was no horizon. The end of that engagement felt so pointless. There was no honour to be had for England; it was all taken by Spain. Mary, your sister, wanted to hear of nothing but the glory of her husband Phillip. She cared nothing for her own men." His face was bitter for a moment, but it cleared as he looked up into her eyes. "But then," he went on, "then there was a brighter time when we came home to find there was a fresh, wise young princess ready to take up her sister's mantle and heal all of the wounds we had endured." He kissed her palm tenderly. "You gave us back the hope I thought had been lost forever in the fields of France."

"Perhaps that is the truth of it. He seemed changed after that time," I said, thoughtfully. "One man I was married to went to war, and another came home. No wonder he loved me no more. He was not the same man." I thought for a moment. "But the Tower changed him too," I said.

"All things may change, and change us," said Death. "What we change into is up to us."

"Hush, Rob." Elizabeth took her hand away, ever aware of her ladies' watchful eyes. Rob swept a charming grin over the women in the chamber. Their eyes dropped to their work and their cheeks flushed to be caught staring.

He turned back to his Queen. "Who will you send to deal with the Scots?"

"At the moment, I am unsure. It will need great tact and strength."

"So… Norfolk, then?" Rob asked impishly, making the Queen titter. She slapped his shoulder. "What about Cecil?" he asked.

She looked at him sharply, but there was only innocence on his face. "Would you have me send Cecil because you think him best for the job? Or because you think he was in league with Norfolk and wish him gone from the court?"

Rob looked surprised as Elizabeth went on. "I heard much of that childish spat between you and Norfolk at Greenwich," she told him. "It seemed then you suspected Cecil of wanting to do you harm."

Rob shook his head. "I did wonder, at the time, if he had supported Norfolk against me, but back then I was seeing shadows with knives at every corner. I do not believe Cecil capable of that type of deceit now. But I do not think he looks favourably on my friendship with Your Majesty, and I wonder if he is a friend to me."

"He has been a friend to me and my most valuable of servants. Would that be enough for you?"

"Only if, in being that friend, he has sought to offer you advice and counsel, rather than seeking to force you to his way of thinking." Rob spoke quietly. "Tell me truly, can you say there has never been a time when Cecil has overreached his authority? When he has sought to alter your mind to agree with his?"

Elizabeth said nothing, which spoke volumes.

"But I do not recommend Cecil for this task because of anything to do with that matter," Rob went on. "He is your most skilled counsellor, he knows the politics and he argues shrewdly. If you want to get the best out of these negotiations, you should send Cecil."

"It is strange to me that you speak so warmly of one whom you so obviously distrust."

Rob grinned wide, like a wolf. "How many people in this world can one truly trust, Majesty? I may not agree with everything Cecil says or does, but that does not stop me viewing his talents with admiration. He is a most able man, the cleverest you have, and I believe that you see him in the same manner. This is the court. One cannot trust everyone who walks its halls, but one can still appreciate them."

"It does you credit, Rob," she murmured, "that you can view such a situation thus, looking on it objectively, without personal feelings involved. I will think on what you have said."

"Cecil did not want to go to Scotland," I said. "I heard that, even in the country."

"He did not," said Death.

"He must have known Robin had suggested him," I said. "He must have thought Robin was stealing away his place with the Queen." I laughed a little. "Cecil was me, not wanting to be the one left behind, unheard, as Robin stole away his Elizabeth."

Death nodded his great head to a conversation on this matter between the Queen and Kat Ashley. Had we moved days, or hours? I could not tell. My gown was grey now, with all the strands of the other world clinging to me.

"Cecil has written to Throckmorton that he suspects this is a plot by his enemies to distance him from Your Majesty." Kat looked unhappy. "He thinks that he might be betrayed by some other whilst he is far from Your Majesty's side."

"He is the best man for the job, that is why he is being sent," Elizabeth replied, annoyed. "Whatever Cecil thinks is afoot is clearly not. Rob recommended that Cecil do this task based upon his skills and knowledge, not in an attempt to remove him from court, or from my side."

Kat agreed, but I could see she did not believe Elizabeth, or thought she was deceived by her belief in Robin.

"I do not abandon my friends, Kat," the Queen said, "as you should well remember."

"Your Majesty never gave me cause to think so," she agreed, raising her hands as though the Queen might shoot her. "But perhaps it would do good for Cecil to hear such sentiments from your own mouth."

"Cecil has had proof enough of my loyalty. He would do well to think on the honour of this position and the mission on which I have sent him, rather than dally with such dark suspicions as those which now reach my ears. It is not just any man whom I would entrust to negotiate for the security of our reign."

We stood in Essex suddenly, I knew for Death told me, as an old woman was arrested for talking of the Queen with disrespect. "Cecil left for Scotland, and Elizabeth and Robin went hunting every day," said Death, and pointed at the woman and the crowd.

"Old Mother Annie Dowe was a village gossip," Death told me, "ever fond of repeating all she heard to any willing ear. She had told one of her fellow cronies that Robin had given the Queen a present of a red petticoat. Her friend had chuckled and said, 'Think you he gave her a petticoat? Nay, it was a *child* he gifted to our Queen'."

Mother Dowe repeated this snippet of gossip to all who would bend an ear to her, further flavouring the tale as she went along with spices all her own. "They have played at *games* together," the old crone cackled gleefully to her listeners, "and he is the father of her child!"

"But she has no child as yet," wondered astounded villagers.

"Not as *yet*…" replied Mother Dowe, licking her withered lips. "But soon there will be proof, for they have put one to the making within her."

"Mother Dowe was not the only one," I said, watching as she was taken away, weeping and protesting. "Other tongues spoke, other people were arrested. There were pamphlets confiscated and burned which called the Queen a whore and a heretic. I thought Rob might be sent away then, but I was wrong. Despite the rumours, the Queen refused to stop seeing Robin."

We stood in summer, at Whitehall. Dog roses danced on the edge of the woodlands. The Queen was reading a letter in the sunlight, and then she screwed it up and thrust it in her pocket, an angry look on her face.

"Cecil wrote from Edinburgh to tell the Queen that he had secured peace with the French and the Scots in an accord known as the 'Treaty of Edinburgh'," explained Death. "Some terms of the treaty were entirely agreeable to the Queen: Mary Stuart was to revoke her immediate claim to the English throne, although she would, as a cousin of the blood, be recognised in the line of succession. Mary and her husband, François II of France, would cease to quarter their arms with those of England. All French and English forces would withdraw from Scotland leaving it in the hands of the Scottish nobles and their new Council. The cessation of hostilities was proclaimed by two cannon shots from Edinburgh Castle."

"But Cecil pressed not for Calais," I said. "There was much talk of it."

"You have heard?" Elizabeth asked Robin, finding him at the stables where he was preparing horses for them to ride out that day. The Queen's ladies stood back a little, allowing their mistress a touch of privacy.

Robin inclined his head. "Cecil has brokered a peace."

"But left out all that I importuned him to seek!" She flung her hands into the air with frustration. "I thought that he would prove to be the best man to see our territories returned. He knew how important Calais was to me! Why would he not seek to push our advantage when we have it finally?"

Rob shrugged. "I, too, am disappointed, Majesty," he conceded. "The return of Calais was, I thought, one of the priorities of the negotiations."

"Perhaps the French thought it a push too far," she mused bitterly. "They like that little slice of England they have stolen from us; it allows them to stand at a distance now and taunt us. The failure to return Calais makes me look weak as a ruler." Elizabeth dropped her hands to her sides, frustrated. "If my father were still here," she mourned. "He would have ensured its return, or he would have had the head of the one who did not achieve it."

"Cecil has managed to get them to acknowledge you as Queen, my lady," Rob reminded her gently, taking her hand.

"Something that was mine by right, whether they agreed to it or not, as is Calais. That land was *mine*, Rob. It was conquered by my forebears and held throughout the reigns of my grandfather, father and brother. I think of what my father would have done. I believe that he would have mounted horse and invaded France once more, and all of England would have risen at his call!" She exhaled sadly. "Sometimes I think it is indeed a curse to be a woman. If I were a man, would I have already started amassing an army to take back our lands again? If I were a man, would I not have mounted horse and strapped on armour by now?"

"If you were a man, Majesty," he said, his eyes sparkling naughtily, "then perhaps my heart would be quieter within me, but it would also be less than whole. God made you a woman, and I am glad He did so."

"My mother was not so glad, I think. If I had been born a boy, she would have lived. Her place would have been secure. Had I been born a boy, she would not have died."

"We cannot change the past." He held her at arm's length. "Nor can we change God's design for this world and our own paths on it. He made you as you are. He protected you through battles and strife that would have killed a lesser person twice, thrice over. You are His chosen, His sovereign of England, and He made you as you are for the betterment of His own plans. Do not seek to alter that which I have come to love so well. If you were a man, Majesty, my heart would have remained a closed volume on the shelf, never to be opened, never to be seen. You are the light that illuminates us all. You are the rightful choice for England at this time. If that means that you pause before war where a man might not, then perhaps there is reason for that. If you cry to see the lists of the fallen in battle, then perhaps there is reason for that. God picked a woman to rule us, and He has a plan for you as He does for us all."

Robin's eyes were warm and gentle. "Seek not to alter the woman I love," he whispered, "in wishing her to be any other than whom and what she is."

She leaned forward and kissed his cheek. "You always know what to say, Rob, to soothe my soul."

He looked at her wide-eyed and glanced about. It was the most intimate gesture she had made in public. Although every eye, it seemed, was looking intently elsewhere as their Queen kissed her Master of Horse on his cheek in public.

Robin blushed, a charming flush. "So, Rob," she chuckled, "show me which horse is mine for today. Even if Cecil has not succeeded as I would have liked, we still have cause to be merry. England is freed from threat of war, and the sun is shining on our lands. I would be out in it, rather than cooped in a stuffy castle for another afternoon."

Robin laughed and took her to look over the horses. "You and I have ever thought alike, Majesty. Better a poor day's riding in inclement weather, than a day spent inside huddled near the fire." He looked over a few mounts with the critical eye of the expert horseman he was. "This one, I think." He gestured towards a fine white stallion. "He is just come in, but I have tested him for Your Majesty." He raised his eyebrows at her. "I think you will find him restless to be let loose," he said, and then dropped his voice, "as am I…"

"Any news on, our matter?" she stuttered, trying to cool her cheeks.

The mischief dropped from his face. "Amy sickens by the day," he said wearily, looking rather old suddenly. "I think it will not in fact be a separation that releases me, but death. Her breast pains her, as do her bones, and her servants tell me she is brought low with it. She is depressed in spirit, they say."

"I am sorry, Robin."

He shook his head. "There is no love between us now," he assured her. "But I would that she would depart the world remaining a friend to me." He looked at Elizabeth, chewing his lip nervously. "In view of the fact that she will not live long, my doctors tell me no more than a few months at the most, I was going to put aside my quest to procure an annulment. It does not seem right, to leave her upon her very deathbed. Perhaps she could die in peace and be buried as a wife of the Dudley family, without the shame and trial of legal separation?"

"I do agree, Robin, I do. I would not have you cause her further distress at this time. If you think she is not long for this world, then I can wait. I have waited for a long time now to offer my heart to you. I can wait for you."

Robin flushed again. "Thank you, my lady."

"You blush like a maiden, Rob," she teased. "I do hope that when the time comes you will not be so humble, so modest."

A grin spread over his face. "When the time comes, Elizabeth," he whispered. "I will not be humble. Of that, I promise you."

"And just like that, I am dead," I said.

"Not for a time," said Death.

"But to them, I am already gone," I said.

Chapter Thirty

Windsor Castle

Summer 1560

At the end of July, we watched as Cecil arrived back at court. Due to his supposed failure over Calais, when Cecil came to his Queen he received a cool reception.

"Cecil fears that you have become distanced from him," Parry told Elizabeth as he handed her another stack of papers to sign.

She gazed at Parry with cold eyes. "Cecil will have to remember better what his master wants of him, if he wants more favour of me."

Parry closed his mouth.

"You still look pale, Parry," the Queen clucked. "You have not seen my doctor, or availed yourself of the herbs of our physic gardens?"

He bowed. "I have had great help and relief from Your Majesty's gardens. You have many fine physicians working for you. They have given me some cures for my ailments, although they tell me they may take time to work."

"I have never had faith in any who said that a cure would be instantaneous." She smiled affectionately at Parry. "I am glad that you changed your mind, then, and saw my doctors. There are many false leeches in the world, but the men working for me are clever and true. If they have prescribed you tonics and potions to take, offering health over time, I believe in those more easily than any who offer a quick fix."

"I too, Majesty," he agreed.

"Well, have a care for yourself, Master Parry. I find that there are fewer and fewer people whose opinions I care for at this time. I would that those I do want to hear are well and able to offer counsel to me."

"Majesty," he bowed. "If that is the case, Majesty, I would offer something to you that you might not wish to hear."

"We have ever been good friends, Parry. I do not forget how you worked for my survival when I was a prisoner in the Tower, nor your many years of service to me before and since. But if the advice you make to me is to say aught of Lord Robin Dudley, then I would bid you to bind your lips. I have heard more than I would wish from people who think they know better than I of what is good for Elizabeth, and good for England."

"I would not seek to say such, Majesty. But I would offer you a thought of caution, for the sake of Lord Dudley, if not for yourself. The people are restless on the matter of your favour to him. Actions done in private at court are spreading through the land as gossip. All the people of England know of your affection for him, and it makes them nervous."

She sighed. "They were unhappy when I did not marry. They were unhappy with a foreign bridegroom and now they are unhappy with the favour I show to a friend. Tell me, Parry, whom might I be friends with, and whom might I marry to appease everyone? It seems to me that I ought to marry where it might make me happy, rather than seeking to please every man, woman and child of England and Europe."

"That is what your sister thought also, my lady," Parry said quietly. He looked nervously at her face, which flushed with both anger and shame to be so compared to her sister and her disastrous match with Spain. "Majesty," he continued, "please remember that I say this only for love of you. My loyalties are to you and have always been so, and in times when you faced the most peril I was at your side to help defend you. There are rumours at court that some of your Councillors have declared that they want no further women rulers, stating that they bring only trouble to the realm. I tell you this so that we might be prepared should anything come of it. Some may be the ranting of men disappointed that you did not heed their choice of suitor, some may come from men who fear Lord Dudley and resent his rise, but none should be ignored."

"And think they that my father, who was a man, after all, brought rest and calm to the country in his many marriages?"

Parry shook his head. "Your father, God rest him, is dead, Majesty," he said. "Whatever flaws and faults he had, whatever mistakes he made as a ruler, are forgotten, this was so as soon as his spirit left this earth for heaven. Those who live are criticised, those who die become more perfect than they ever were in life. That is the way of things. It will not matter what the truth is; they will compare you to your father, and your father will always come out the better of the two of you, not because he was a man, but because you are alive and he is dead." Parry smiled sadly at his Queen. "The eternal sunshine of goodness lights on our memories of those who have passed. The reality of their lives, faults and flaws will never change that. As soon as they die, they become as saints and gods to us; incomparable and golden as the setting of the sun on midsummer night."

"You are a wordsmith, Parry," the Queen murmured. "And I know what you say is true. For many reasons, I will never compare to my father as a ruler. But I am determined that the people will remember me for my own sake, and not just for his."

"They will, Majesty," Parry assured her. "But I believe, as ever, that I must advise caution. These are but rumours at the moment, but you well know how fast a man's mind may change from wondering on a problem, to seeking to remove it. A game is played out in the mind, and then the mind thinks that game might be used in real life. De Quadra is happily recounting these rumours to his master in Spain. If our enemies abroad should seek to offer support to those who are voicing discontent, then we might have more of a problem on our hands."

"You think Spain would seek to support my own lords to rebel against me?"

"And they could put her cousin, Katherine Grey, on the throne, married to an English lord or Spanish," I said, leaning against a tapestry of gold and green and silver on the wall. I looked to it, fairly sure it was meant to depict the wedding of Mary Tudor to Louis of France, yet another failed marriage, although that one lasted but months.

"I think it is a possibility, Majesty," agreed Parry. "They are a Catholic country and they like not the religion you have made legal in England. They like not your distance from the Bishop of Rome, and his control. Popes, too, have never been shy when seeking to stamp their authority over distant lands, and even if religion were not an issue, other countries will always look on England with the covetous eyes of a neighbour state, and long to take your lands as their own. My loyalty is always to you, Majesty, and I will support your choices. But I think we should be prepared to move against any who would seek to destabilize your reign before they have a chance to think on it properly. Allow me to keep watch on the members of the Council and nobles who affect dissatisfaction with present affairs. I will report any to you whom I think might cause trouble."

She nodded. "I thank you for those pains. You have ever kept a watchful eye for me, Parry."

"Do you think there was ever, or will be a time she feels safe?" I asked Death.

He shook his head. "Never entirely," he said.

"You are my sovereign, and my master, my lady," Parry said in a firm voice to Elizabeth. "All I have comes from you. In many ways, I owe you my life. I do not forget all that you have done for me."

"I wish all about me were as you, Parry."

"Many are, Majesty," he said. "Do not think yourself alone in this. You have many loyal and loving subjects. And on the matter of your marriage, there are many amongst your nobles and your Council who wish to see you wed, and, to many of them, that consideration ranks higher than the particular choice of man. If those who have doubt in your personal preference could be persuaded that any consort at your side would have their powers limited, and their influence controlled, then they would come around to your way of thinking. It would just take time, that is all."

"Nothing is decided upon in the matter of my marriage, Parry. I have made no promise to any man." She paused and then went on, "but in truth, there is a name which is dear to my heart."

Parry smiled knowingly and leaned in. "The heart is a hard master to us all, Majesty. We think we own our choices, and yet we are ruled by its power. Even the Queen of England must acknowledge two masters; God above her, and her heart within her."

He put his finger to his lips and smiled. "I shall say nothing, Majesty. But I will keep a watchful eye open for any trouble. In the meantime all I caution *is* caution. There is time enough to persuade your people on the matter of a husband, if the need should come, and only if the matter is not rushed. There are ways and means to achieve all things, if they are done correctly."

"Two months later, and the storm came," said Death.

Chapter Thirty-One

Cumnor Place

September 1560

It was the day I died.

Death and I stood outside Cumnor. It was early in the morning, the birds only just starting to sing. Darkness was a cloak over the world, the hazy light of dawn sneaking in, little by little. "It was not a bad place to live," I said and smiled. "Perhaps not such a bad place to die."

I breathed in the air of that morning of shadows and looked up at the last place I had known life. Master Anthony Forster, treasurer of Robert's household, leased the house from a Master Owen, who still occupied part of the generous house with his own family. Cumnor Place was situated on the road betwixt Oxford and Abingdon and was a small manor house, where brick was first laid to solid ground almost three centuries previously. Once a retreat for the Abbot of Abingdon, the grey-bricked mansion by this time boasted two storeys in a quadrangle around a central courtyard. The formal gardens were kept well, as was the house.

"When I came to Cumnor I brought with me a small party of servants, including Mistress Picto, and Mistress Odingsells." I paused. "She was the widowed sister of my kinsman, Master Hyde, I don't think I said we were related before. The house was a full one, for there also lived at Cumnor Master Owens, his elderly mother, and Master Forster and his wife. The Forsters had been supporters of the new Queen during the reign of Mary."

We walked the outside of the house. "We lived in the west wing of the house, above the great hall," I said. "The others who lived here had their own sets of chambers. We went to dances and meetings, sometimes we sang or played cards by night. All the families who lived here were related to the Dudleys by marriage and were prominent in the local society, into which they introduced me. They kept a civilised household where music and singing was much encouraged."

I smiled at Death. "Although I was not a merry maid often, I was happy enough at Cumnor. I was ill and that was not a fine thing to be, but with so many in the house I could fool myself into thinking I had more company than before. Some of them even wrote to court, asking for tonics for me, asking Rob to come home, as my spirits were often low. It was nice that someone noted such about me, and in truth, though that might seem strange it made me feel better."

"It is nice when someone takes an interest in us, and our welfare," said Death.

I nodded, thinking it odd that sometimes Death spoke as if he were human, and sometimes as though he were a creature altogether different. I wondered what he was, human or divine, or demonic? He seemed too polite and wise to be demonic.

He noted I was looking at him, and shook his head. "I am not the enemy," he said.

"Who is, if not you?" I asked. "You end life."

"I come at the end," he agreed. "But all things must end, that is the way of things. But other beings than me, grief, bitterness, resentment, these are the true enemies, for they steal life still there to live. They make people think life, this precious and unlikely gift, is not worth living, and the worst of it is, it is a lie and people are tricked into believing it." Death stood up straight, his cloak billowing out under him in a light breeze. "I am not the enemy, just the end," said Death. "Those who steal away life from those still living, they are the enemy."

I sighed. "I fell for the tricks of the enemy, then."

"Do not feel bad for it. Many people do. The tricks used are various and clever, they come often disguised as other things."

"It does not make me a fool?"

Death shook his head. "It makes you human," he said. "But fear not, this is not the only chance you will ever have to make good your existence."

I smiled. "Thank you."

We entered the house through a side door, and came through the great hall and up the stairs. I nodded to a now not so much younger Amy, only a few hours younger she was, sick in a bed. "Some days I was fine, and others I was so weak and tired," I said. "Members of my new household, as I said, wrote to the Queen's own Professor of Physic at Oxford University, Doctor Bayly, and asked him to prescribe medicines for me to lift my heavy spirits. Bayly, however, refused to do so; rumours of the Queen's affection for Robert had reached him, along with darker tales of a plot on my life, which had circulated at court and beyond. Bayly wrote to the company at Cumnor Place, stating that he believed I had no real need for medication, adding that *'if they poisoned her under the name of his potion, then he might have been hanged to cover their sin.'* And by *they* he meant Rob and the Queen."

"It was not the only place poison cropped up," said Death. "There were many odd goings-on at court. On the Saturday of the Queen's birthday, September the 7th, de Quadra wrote to his master, Phillip, of an entirely fictional conversation he had apparently had with the Queen. He claimed that Elizabeth had relayed to him, upon returning from the hunt, that the wife of Robin Dudley was 'dead, or nearly dead' of a malady of the breast. The Queen then apparently asked this man, in whom she had never confided, nor ever trusted, to keep what she had said a secret."

I thought for a moment. "If it was not the Queen, with whom did he speak?" I asked.

"If not the Queen, perhaps someone deciding to talk on her behalf," said Death. "On the Sunday after the Queen's birthday, Cecil strangely took it upon himself to confess to de Quadra that he was thinking of leaving the Queen's service, due to the manner in which she was conducting herself with Robin."

"It is a bad sailor," we watched Cecil say to de Quadra, "who does not make for port when he sees a storm coming." Cecil went on to say that Elizabeth was ruining herself for love of her favourite, that the realm would never accept her marriage to Robin, and that Cecil wished to retire to the country, but had no doubt his enemies would see him safely to the Tower before that time. "I beg, lord Ambassador, for you to persuade the Queen to see reason and sense, and abandon this match before she is abandoned by her people."

Last of all, Cecil confided to de Quadra that there were rumours afoot that, "the wife of Robin Dudley was to be removed," and this could only join with the Queen's present disgrace should it be linked to her.

I looked at Death. "Why is Cecil confessing any of this to the Spanish ambassador?" I asked, puzzled. "Does he *want* the Queen's reputation darkened? Or perhaps a threat of it to emerge so she sees what peril lies beyond the troubles mere rumours can bring?"

Days flew and hours moved, and we were back at Cumnor.

On that same Sunday, *Our Lady's Fair* opened at Abingdon; a day of revelry, markets and entertainments, all most welcome diversions to the common people. Archery contests, shopping excursions, plays and music would go on through the day and into the night and it was likely to be a merry affair.

"I told the servants to go," I said. "Including Mrs Odingsells. She objected, but I insisted."

We watched me, all but shouting at the woman who had been my personal companion for more than a year. "In truth, I did not like her," I said. "She was always complaining about her lot in life, and I was not of a mood to hear the pains of others, for I was too wrapped up in my own. I also wondered if she was writing to Robin about me, if she was the one spreading rumours I would die soon."

"I do not wish to go to such an event, my lady," Mistress Odingsells was saying. "I might rub shoulders with commoners at such an event, and I would rather go on the day when noble company is to go."

"I want to be alone," the slightly younger me was almost shouting. "I order you to leave me alone today. Go to the fair and leave me be!"

"But you will be left with no one to dine with, my lady!"

"I will dine with old Mother Owen who is happy to have my company."

I breathed in, standing near Death as we watched my companion lady flounce out of the chamber, deeply affronted. "Since Odingsells was not a servant, I could not command her to leave as I did all the other servants, but the row caused my personal companion to leave my company for the day, and retire, hurt, to her own rooms, alone.

The servants went to *Our Lady's Fair*, both bemused at their good fortune in having a whole day off, and confused as to the strange behaviour of their normally temperate mistress."

"Later, all of them would say that your behaviour on that morning was most out of character," Death said. "Some of them wondered later whether their mistress had an appointment to keep that she did not want observed by the eyes of her household, but there was no evidence to support this speculation."

"I had a letter early that morning," I said. "It said it was dictated, and that was why it was in another hand. I thought little of it. Robin did dictate letters from time to time. He said he was coming that afternoon, that he was sorry for all he had done and the Queen had cast him off. He was deeply shamed, so the letter said, and he asked me to send the servants away so he could speak to me in private, for the Queen was to marry another, and had used him for games and negotiations, like a toy. He said it had made him realise that she had played his emotions, and although he could say little more he wanted me to know he never had stopped loving me. He wanted to take care of me." I laughed, bitterly. "I should have known it was not real. There was too much of all I wanted in that letter."

Just past eleven in the morning, we watched as a meal was served to me and old Mother Owen. Mistress Odingsells kept to her chamber, still in high dudgeon, and took her dinner there. Mistress Forster was also at home, in another part of the house, although she, too, took dinner in her own rooms with her own servants. Later that afternoon, Cumnor Place was quiet and peaceful with all its residents keeping to their own chambers.

"I waited, as I was told," I said. "I heard nothing but some soft-stealing steps behind me. Thinking it was Robin, I got up and turned. My heart was alive with hope, just for a moment, and then confusion. Briefly I saw a face, a man I have never seen before, and it was not Robin. There was a pain in my head. Then I remember falling." I looked at Death. We stood at the bottom of the stairs again, looking down at me.

"It was so fast, I never even said a word, not a single word," I said, watching my still body, the open eyes, the damp I knew was under my dress. "I did not even get a moment to say no." I laughed a little. "All that time, praying to God, asking for more life, and then when the moment came when life was to leave me, I had no words."

I looked at Death. "It was so fast. Life was gone before I knew it."

"That often is the way," he said. "Even when there is long illness, when a person and those around them expect death, death always is a shock."

"Something in me never thought it would happen," I said.

"Because all you had known was to be alive, you could not imagine death," he said. "Your kind have been trying since the day you first understood there was an end, trying to imagine what that end was like and what came after."

Late that day, we saw the servants wander into the house chattering, happy and flushed with the excitement of the fair, until they were struck silent and dumb to find the body of their mistress prostrate at the foot of a shallow set of stone steps leading from her rooms to the hall. My body lay where it had been left hours before, small in death, quiet and still, glassy eyes staring at the ceiling above. I lay on a small landing that connected two short flights of stairs. My neck was broken.

Someone touched my throat. I watched them recoil at the coldness of my once-warm flesh.

There was commotion to follow the silence. Shouts, noise, people running hither and thither to tell the tale to those in the house who knew not that one of its members was dead. No one who was in the house when I had died had heard or seen a thing, and the stairs on which my broken body lay seemed entirely too short to have been guilty of causing the fall that had apparently brought about my death. The mysterious circumstances of my death and my odd behaviour before it led people to immediately question whether this was an accident, or if it were, in fact, murder.

"I knew they would think it was odd," I said as we watched people shout to each other and rush about like rats on a sinking plank. I watched as a man was sent to tell Robin I was dead, as servants wept, as Mistress Odingsells sat down, dazed on a stair.

"But I still do not know," I said.

"But you know the suspects," said Death.

I thought a moment. "The Queen, but she was too clever for this, and I do not know if she even wanted to marry Robin. Robin, but then why not poison me? Why throw me down the stairs in such a way? Was the letter even from him? Cecil? But why would he darken the reputation of the Queen? Norfolk, because he hated Robin?" I pondered. "Certainly it seems clumsy enough, but also too subtle in a way. De Quadra, to force the Queen to marry a Hapsburg? Perhaps, but I doubt he would have taken the risk that she would have married Robin, unless that was the plan, to unsettle her throne by getting her to wed a man all suspected of murder? Parry?" I thought a moment more. "Could even the French have done it? Trying to make Elizabeth marry a man in disgrace, and then they could put their Mary of Scots and France on her throne after her people rose in rebellion against her?" I shook my head. "Was this done for simple reasons, for love or for hatred, or for political ones?"

"The world was less confused than you," said Death, smoothing his robes. They shimmered like the wings of ravens under his hand of bone, glinting purple and blue and black so dark. "As the world heard of your sudden, suspicious death, they all had the same thought. When a person dies and murder is suspected, it is always those who have the most to gain who fall under suspicion. People said they knew who had the most to gain. With his wife dead, Robin had a chance to marry the Queen of England and become a king. The Queen had a chance to marry the man she loved. The two people who had the most to gain from the death of Amy Dudley, were Robin and Elizabeth."

"Are you saying it was them?"

"This is not the end of the story," said Death. "It began with love, and so shall it end."

"With love? They will marry?"

"She will never marry. Your death decided that finally for her."

"I am the cause of her never marrying?"

"One of many, but there is always one last part of any puzzle, that shows us clear the picture we know is there." He looked at me. "Does it make you feel better, knowing they did not marry, that she never did?"

I thought a moment. "That was up to them," I said. "After I left this tale, no choice was up to me anymore."

Chapter Thirty-Two

Windsor Castle

9th September 1560

I shivered, though it was not a cold day. There was a chill wind, though, something of winter already stealing into autumn.

The Queen and her Master of Horse were out riding when they heard about me. New crossbows had arrived, a present from France, and they had gone with a small party to test them in the butts in the field near Windsor.

They rode to the range early, where the crossbows were much used and approved of. As Elizabeth made a fine shot, she turned to gain praise from Robin, but for once he was not looking at her. "What is it?" she asked.

"A rider," he said, "coming fast, Your Majesty." Rob looked to the guards a little way off and whistled to St Loe, who glanced up from giving orders to his men and looked in the direction Rob indicated with his hand.

Suddenly, there was a tense air about the party. Guards rose, St Loe ordering them to stand and be ready, but it was soon clear that there was but one rider, and he was seeking the party of the Queen. His horse rode hard across the wet earth of the park, sending clumps of mud flying from its hooves. As the rider pulled up and dismounted, St Loe's guards surrounded him to discover his purpose.

"He says he's here to give an important message to you, my lord," St Loe called to Rob. "His name is Bowes, and he says he's a servant of your house."

"I know him," shouted Robin. "Let him come forward."

The man was filthy; mud-splattered clothes and a red, sweaty face spoke of riding hard and fast on sodden roads.

"What on earth is it, Bowes?" Robin asked, gazing at him with confusion.

"My lord," the man tried to catch his breath even as he spoke, an expression of trepidation and of something darker on his face. "I bring ill news of your wife, the Lady Amy Dudley."

"What of her?"

"She has died, my lord." Bowes looked at his filthy gloves suddenly, as though he could not meet Rob's eyes. "We found her body, my lord, at the bottom of a staircase in Cumnor Place."

Robin stared at the man.

"What do you mean?" Robin demanded, his voice harsh with shock. "*Speak,* man! What do you mean, she was found at the bottom of a staircase?"

Bowes seemed unwilling to answer but he did so, his gaze flitting from Rob to the Queen, his cheeks flushed. "It, it seems as though she may have… fallen, and broken her neck, my lord," he stammered.

"Fallen down the stairs and broken her neck?" repeated Robin slowly, as though he did not believe it. He sounded bewildered. I studied his face, but all I saw was confusion.

"Aye, my lord." Bowes dared to glance up at his master, his eyes wary and uncertain. "But there are whispers already abroad that…" He trailed off, looking at the Queen, then at the muddy ground.

"That, *what*?" Robin grew pale, but of course he knew the answer.

"The court will enter official mourning for the Lady Dudley," Elizabeth announced, "and an investigation into this matter will be conducted, of course. I am sure this was a tragic and most terrible accident, but all measures will be taken to prove that there was no foul play, for my Lord Dudley's sake, as well as that of the Lady Dudley's family."

Robin paled more and looked at Elizabeth. For the first time I saw in her eyes a question; did she know this man as well as she thought?

As they moved to get on their horses Elizabeth grabbed Robin's arm. "For God's sake, Robin," she whispered. "Tell me that you had nothing to do with this awful event." Her voice was tight, taut with a terrible dread.

Robin stared at her; his handsome face was grey and drawn. He looked suddenly aged. He seemed genuinely confused. "My Queen," he whispered, his ashen face growing whiter and his tone urgent as he saw the look of suspicion on her face. "*Elizabeth*, my lady, believe me, I did not kill my wife. I would never do something so wicked, not for all the wide world."

They rode back to Windsor fast, and in silence.

"Even she suspects him," I said, watching them go.

"Everyone will follow her example," said Death.

Chapter Thirty-Three

Windsor Castle

Summer 1560

"Cecil oversees it," said Death as we wandered along the corridors of Windsor Castle. "The mourning, the investigation."

"Where is the Queen?" Spirals of white smoke and silver thread were now twisting all over my gown, up my arms and about my fingers. I could feel them in the tresses of my hair. White, pearly light glowed upon me. Like children the strands of the other world played, tumbling and twisting, curling and bending about me. Every time I looked at them roaming my body, as if in benediction, it made me smile.

At court no one was smiling. Elizabeth stayed in her chambers in the days that followed. I watched her, thinking, wondering what she thought of Robin. Missives and messages from Cecil and Robin were brought to her. She did not sleep, did not eat much. She looked hollow. "Unless this is the finest act, it cannot have been her," I said, watching her.

The whole country was now talking of my death, and the news had been spread by ambassadors' busy quills and ready mouths through every court in Christendom and most likely beyond. The world knew that I was dead, and the world laid its blame on my ambitious husband, and on the Queen.

"I am known now, as I always wished," I said, with a laugh, for I no longer cared about such things.

From Kew, we watched Robin send messengers to instruct his own men to investigate the matter, and to my relatives to inform them of my death. I did not want to see them, bad enough it was to imagine their sorrow. When Death asked me if I wanted to see my family, I shook my head. "It serves no purpose to me now," I said. "I know they loved me. I do not wish to see them suffer."

Cecil worked quietly, diligently taking reports and recollections of those present at the scene of the death, and sending dispatches to inform local law agents that the inquest was going ahead under the direct command of the Queen. He feared the effect that the vicious tongues of rumour would have on people's feelings towards the Queen.

Robin wrote to his cousin, a servant in his household named Thomas Blount, asking him to investigate the matter himself at Cumnor Place, and to find out what was being said of him and the Queen in the country. He sent word of Blount's findings to Cecil and the Queen at court.

We watched as, pretending to be a stranger to the area, Blount stopped at an inn in Abingdon and fell into easy conversation with the innkeeper. Death and I sat on stools nearby, our table oddly remaining empty though the inn was busy. Since all the news was of my death, it was easy for Blount to find those willing to converse on the subject.

"What is the judgement of the people?" asked Blount as the innkeeper relayed to him the details of my death and strange behaviour I had shown on the day I died in sending away all my servants from the house. Everyone seemed to know all of the details of the case.

I sniffed the air, the scent of sweat and old ale, and my nose wrinkled.

"Some are disposed to say well, and some evil," replied the innkeeper cagily. "Although, for myself, I judge it to be an accident, because it chanced to happen at an honest gentleman's house; his great honesty doth much curb the evil thoughts of the people."

The opinion of this one man, however, was not shared by all, it seemed. Blount intercepted wild rumours that the Queen was pregnant with Robin's child, and that I had been killed to allow for a quick marriage so the new heir to the throne would not be a bastard. Robin wrote to Blount, and sent the Queen a copy of the letter. *"So that you, my Queen and lifelong friend, will see that I have nothing to hide in my entire and absolute innocence,"* he wrote.

The letter from Robin to Blount, which I read over the shoulder of the Queen, ran thus:

"Cousin Blount, the greatness and suddenness of the misfortune doth so perplex me that until I hear from you how the matter stands, or how this evil should have come to light on me, considering what the malicious world will believe, that I can take no rest. And, because I have no way to purge myself of the malicious talk that I know the wicked world will use, but one; which is for the plain truth to be known. I do pray you, as you have loved me, and do tender me and my quietness, as now my special trust is in you, that you will use all the devices and means you possibly can for learning the truth."

"If he was guilty, would he go to such lengths in the investigation?" I asked Death.

The letter went on to say that the Queen was sending her men to investigate the matter, but Robin wanted Blount to do so also on his behalf. Robin insisted on a full inquest into my death, and that whosoever should be found accountable, no matter what their station or title, should be brought to answer for my murder. As commanded by his master and kinsman, Blount left for Cumnor and found not only the coroner and jury that Elizabeth had sent, but also my half-brother, John Appleyard, who had travelled to Cumnor to make his own enquiries.

A full house of investigators, indeed. "Of course my family would suspect," I said, walking about my half-brother. It had been a long time since I saw him, and he looked aged. "If I heard the rumours of poison then they did. They said nothing while I was alive, probably because they did not want to believe those rumours, and then I died." I shook my head. "They must have thought, suspected at least, that Robin killed me."

Under the Queen's orders, Cecil issued a proclamation on my death on the 11th of September. It stated that the death of Lady Amy Dudley was attributed to accidental causes, but that a full inquest was being carried out to make sure of this. There were many mutterings throughout the land after the proclamation; few believed that I had died accidentally.

At Cumnor Place, Blount questioned the servants in my household, but seemed to get no further than had any of the previous investigators. I had been sad for days before, they told him. On the day of the Fair, I had ordered them to leave the house and would brook no refusal in the matter. Some seemed to think my death was self-inflicted.

"I did not kill myself," I said.

"Not many will think it possible," said Death.

"Good," I said. I was not sure why it seemed important, other than it was the truth. I did not want to be blamed for my own death when another, this man unknown, had taken my life. "Why would I choose to jump down a flight of stairs to kill myself?" I asked. "If I were to jump, it would be from something much higher! And what a nasty way to die, why would I not take herbs and sleep my way to death?"

Blount talked to my maid, also. "What do you think of the matter, Mistress Picto?"

My maid wrung her hands. "By my faith, I judge it a chance accident," she said, "and neither done by man or by my lady herself. Lady Dudley was a good and virtuous gentlewoman, and daily would pray on her knees. Diverse times, I heard the lady ask God to deliver her from desperation."

Blount paused. "The lady might have had an evil toy in her mind, and lusted for death to release her," he said.

"No, good Master Blount," said my maid, appalled. "Do not judge so of my words. If you should gather from them such a thought, then I am sorry I said so much."

"Poor Mistress Picto," I said. "She was only trying to say I was full of sorrow. She must have thought she had condemned me to be buried outside of the church, out of the faith."

"Blount wrote that he thought suicide was a possibility," said Death. "He ended his letter to Dudley by expressing some concerns about the other investigators. The jurymen seemed *'as wise and able men as ever I saw,'* he wrote, *'and for their true search I have good hope they will conceal no fault, if any be; for as they are wise, so are they, as I hear, enemies to Anthony Forster. God give them, with their wisdom, indifferency in this matter'.*"

"Why had men who were enemies to Master Forster been sent as jurymen to investigate this matter?" I asked.

"The answer to that lies at court," said Death, touching my hand. Soft and silver spun the world as we arrived in the Queen's privy chambers.

The Queen had had the same thought and had called Cecil to her. Cecil sighed. "The local men of the law are chosen *for* their locality, Majesty," he reminded her. "That they might have a grudge against a local landowner is not unheard of, but all men who undertake these roles for the service of the Crown swear to not let private feelings interfere with their task. We cannot replace them with our own men, Majesty; to do so would look as though we were trying to meddle with the outcome of the investigation."

Forster was intimately connected to Robin's household, and if men investigating the case had a grudge against him then they might be tempted to corrupt the evidence in order to implicate Forster, therefore Robin with him. But Cecil was right, replacing them would only serve to implicate Robin and the Queen.

"You look tired, my old friend," the Queen murmured, rubbing at her own sore eyes.

He looked up wearily. "There has been much to do of late." He kneaded his knotted brow hard with his fingers. "Although, I do not think there is a time in Your Majesty's service when I have *not* had a lot to do."

"You have ever been my good friend, *Spirit*. Sometimes I think I have little deserved your friendship. You have worked so diligently here, for me and for Robin."

"Why *does* he work for Robin?" I asked. "Why does he do all this?"

"Perhaps just to save a little of the Queen, along with her Master of Horse," Death observed, leaning on the table to look at the papers before the Queen and her Secretary.

Cecil shrugged. "Majesty, the world is ever a changing platform of unrest, but within my service to you I have found a stable block against which to plant my feet and keep the whirling nature of the world from causing me to fall. I would want you to believe that all I have ever said or done has been to secure you in your rightful place as our Queen. No matter what may come in the future, I will know that I have always worked for the good of the Queen whom God sent to rule over us."

"You have worked hard to carry out this inquest with attentiveness and care, my friend. There are not so many who would work so hard for the good of a man they liked not."

"I do not dislike Lord Dudley, Majesty." Cecil blinked blearily. "In many ways, I admire him. When I spoke against the idea of your marriage with him it was with the head of the politician. It was not personal."

"I know."

"I would in fact like to request permission from Your Majesty to visit with Lord Dudley," Cecil announced, causing the Queen's mouth to drop open.

"You want to visit Robin?" she asked. "Why?"

"The more support he is shown by men of standing at court, the more the people will come to see that these vicious reports are groundless." Cecil gazed at her gravely, and with compassion. "Your Majesty also misses him, horribly. I can see that. I would that there could come a time when Lord Dudley could return to your side, as a friend and advisor."

"But never as a husband."

Cecil gazed sombrely at her. "I would never advise that, Majesty," he agreed, "especially not now."

"Not now," she repeated dully. "Go and see Robert," she spoke wearily. "And send to him my messages of further condolence and support." As Cecil started to gather his papers together on the table the Queen got up to look out on accumulated mounds of hail, now melting away on the paths of her gardens.

"Cecil?" she asked, not turning.

"Majesty?" Cecil paused in his task.

"If Robert did not kill his wife, as I believe he did not, who do you think would do so, and for what purpose?"

Cecil paused. "Perhaps it was, just as was reported, Majesty, an accident. Perhaps the lady's foot slipped on the stair and she fell awkwardly enough to break her neck. Things like that happen all the time to people of no consequence and so we never hear of it. The reason we all know of it now is only because she was married to your favourite."

She turned. "Do you really believe that, Cecil? Robin has enemies who might stand to gain if they set him up for murder. They might profit from the ruination of his standing and reputation. I cannot believe that your mind might not have considered that, as mine has."

Cecil held her gaze steadily, his face impassive. "If any of Lord Dudley's enemies sought to destroy him in this manner, then I would have expected them to move against him by now, to insist on his arrest and removal from his offices. None have moved to do so."

"And what if the motive was not necessarily to destroy Robin? But, rather, to destroy instead the possibility that I might marry him?"

Cecil did not blink. He knew what she was asking. "There are many things, Majesty, that I have been guilty of in this life," he said, his eyes unflinching. "But this is not one of those. Do not let this matter bring you to suspect shadows hiding about you. I had no hand in the death of Lady Dudley, of that, I will swear to you on the word of God, and on the soul that rests in my body."

She nodded. "Go to Robin and show him your support then, *Spirit*, for God knows, he needs friends about him at this time."

As the door closed behind Cecil, Elizabeth looked back at the hail outside the window. "I did not kill you," she said, and I started, for I knew she was talking to me. "I did not kill you, but one way or the other I am the reason you are dead. I am sorry for that, Amy."

I stared into her thoughtful face, and I saw honesty in it. I looked to Death, unable to say a word, and was met only by the darkness of his eyes, a darkness which seemed no more bleak, but welcome.

Chapter Thirty-Four

Windsor Castle

Autumn 1560

Cecil's words of friendship for Robin proved to be true later that week when he left the court to visit with Rob at Kew, where Rob anxiously awaited the verdict of the investigation into my untimely death. Cecil spent the morning with Rob, commiserating with him and telling him of all the dishonourable reports that had come of the event. He made public his visit, and his support of Rob, to the surprise of the court, and to the Queen's satisfaction.

As he left Rob's house, Robin took his arm. "Please, intervene with the Queen on my behalf and have me brought back to court."

"I will do all I can, my lord," said Cecil.

"*Methinks I am here all this while, as it were in a dream,*" Rob wrote later to Cecil, "*and too far, too far from the place where I am bound to be. I pray that you will help him, who sues to be at liberty out of so great a bondage. Forget me not, though you see me not, and I will remember you and fail you not.*"

Cecil gave Elizabeth the letter and she wept. "I cannot recall him to court until the stain is removed from his name. He must know that?"

"My Lord Dudley is assured of his own innocence," said Cecil, "so for him then, the path to his return to court is as clear as daylight."

"But not so for others. There are many at court who talk openly and accuse him of this act. There are many more on the Continent who say the same. My cousin in France, for one. She makes many japes at the expense of me and my servants, so I hear."

Cecil shook his head. "With time," he said, "this too shall pass."

Elizabeth made a noise of disgust and frustration. "And what of the rumours that I carry Robin's child? Reports come from the country, from my own people. I once thought that they would never think ill of me, but they are saying that I carry his child beneath my heart, and that we joined together to murder his wife so that this phantom child might be born not a bastard!"

Cecil's eyes continued to gaze on his Queen with calm resolution. "With time, those reports will be proved to be falsehoods."

"How can you be so calm, Cecil?"

Cecil shrugged. "How else would you have me be, Majesty?" he asked. "With time, this present horror will become a distant memory. We must in the meantime weather the storm as we ever have done, with care and with caution."

The Queen slumped back in her chair.

A few days later, the coroner's verdict was pronounced; I had died an accidental death, it said.

"It was not an accident!" I cried out.

"To clear the name of the Queen's favourite, and because men who investigated feared he was guilty, they found this way," said Death. "That something is written down does not make it truth, nor will people believe it. Even the coroner was disturbed. He thought the wounds on your head too deep to have been made by the stairs."

The Queen ordered that the report be proclaimed about the country and universally, and a copy was sent to Cecil, Parry, and Robin that day. Within an hour of the Queen's letter reaching Robin, she had a note in return from him, scribbled hastily in a scrappy hand.

"*I find that I must press for a second enquiry into the death of my late wife,*" he wrote. "*For I believe that she died a death unnatural, and until the true murderer is revealed, all men will have reason still to question my name.*"

"It cannot have been him," I said, reading over Elizabeth's shoulder again. "Why press for another enquiry?"

"Because he knows men will not believe the first."

"If he was guilty he would not want more investigation, he would want it to drift out of thought, out of mind, so he can be restored."

Elizabeth, not best pleased, called for her writing materials and wrote to him. *"The demands of your letter are wholly against my own way of considering,"* she wrote angrily. *"The inquest has found the death of your late wife to be accidental and with that finding let us bring a close to this tragic affair. I write now to bring you back to your position at court, once the burial of your wife's mortal remains have been laid to rest, where you will find us still in mourning for the death of Lady Amy Dudley. I ask that you resume your position in my house as ever it was, and that the terrible circumstances of the loss of your beloved wife be given time to heal now, in your mind, and the mind of all people. Seek not to trap shadows in your hands for the grief of losing one so close to you."*

On the 22nd of September 1560, we watched as my body, lying in state at Gloucester Hall, was taken from that place and laid to rest in the Chapel of St Mary the Virgin in Oxford. Men carried me on poles to a quiet ceremony where people I never knew cried because I was dead. In accordance with the long-standing tradition of our people, which dictates the chief mourner at a funeral be of the same sex as the deceased, Lady Norris represented the Queen as chief mourner.

Rob did not attend the service, also in accordance with tradition, but, as was expected of him, he waited at his house nearby to hear news of the event. No husband or wife could expect to see their partner in life laid to rest. We watched him that day. He stood in the gardens, and took a pressed gillyflower from his pocket.

"He kept it," I whispered. "I pressed that, it was from the day we were wed. I thought he would have thrown it away, years ago."

"You meant much to him, once." Death stood at my side.

"Once," I said.

Robin held the dry flower up as he stood on a small bridge over a river, and into the wind he released the bloom. "Amy," he whispered, and then he wept.

"He cried little enough for me when we were together," I said. "To cry now, it is more about himself than me." I stood back, watching my husband weep. Oddly, I did not feel pain or horror. I felt disappointed in him. "I wonder if he cries for me, in truth, or if for his ambition, as dead as my body this day." I looked at Death. "I never really accepted that he had stopped loving me," I said. "I think that is why I believed that last letter, from whoever sent it, so easily. I always thought he would come back to me, but he left long ago." I looked around at the world. "I should leave now. There is nothing here for me," I said.

"Nothing but the answer to your question," said Death.

"And you are to answer it? I have wondered."

"There is an answer, and one last part to tell of the tale."

At the end of that month, Robin came riding back to court, and at his heels so followed all of the rumours and all of the scandal that should have been laid to rest along with Lady Amy Dudley.

But I was more alive now I was dead, than when I had been alive.

Chapter Thirty-Five

Windsor Castle

Autumn 1560

"You will relay to me her *exact* words, Cecil," Elizabeth ordered, almost driving her fingernails through the windowsill with irritation. "I know full well that you know what they were."

I could almost hear Cecil's reluctance, trying to scuttle away in the aching silence. In his report on the rumours circulating throughout the courts of Europe and beyond, Cecil had chosen to omit certain choice remarks uttered by various heads of state about Robin's return to court, and about the inquest's verdict regarding my death. That my death had been judged accidental, thus clearing Robin's name, seemed to ring true with *none* of England's allies, nor with any enemies. They were all laughing heartily at the Queen and at England.

"Her words, Cecil!" the Queen demanded through gritted teeth. "My cousin of Scots' *words*."

"This is what she said, Majesty. '*So the Queen of England is to marry her horse-boy, who has killed his wife to make room for her in his bed*'."

"What more do they say?" the Queen asked, her voice tight and strained.

"In France, Throckmorton writes that one lord has asked, '*What religion is this, where a subject shall kill his wife and his prince shall not only bear it but marry with him for it?*'"

"I have not said, nor ever given word that I would marry with him!"

"I know, Majesty," Cecil exhaled. "With time these rumours will be forgotten. The courts of other countries, they like to think that the honour and grace of England can be ruined as easily as a leaf is shredded in the winds of a storm. They will find themselves sadly mistaken in this matter."

"Yes, they will."

"The Princes of the German states and Saxony are distressed by the news of the death of Lady Dudley," he continued. "They write to me asking to know if reports of your intended marriage to Robin Dudley are truth or mere rumour."

"You will tell them that they are rumour put about by ones who would be enemies to both my state and theirs," she hissed. "I will not have allies run from my path as well as enemies."

"I had already started to pen such a missive myself, Majesty. But it would be… helpful if I could say that reports of any talk of marriage between you and Lord Dudley were irrefutably denied by you yourself."

"Do so. I have no plans to marry at all, Cecil. You have long known my thoughts on the matter."

He looked as though he was about to say more, and then he stopped himself. "As you wish, Majesty."

"With *time*," she said sardonically, aping his recent words, "I am sure you will find within you the bravery to approach me on the subject again, *Spirit*." She shrugged. "But you will ever after find my answer the same. I will have but one mistress here, and no master. Bring all the suitors you want to me for reasons political, but expect me to take not one of them."

"With *time*, Majesty," he smiled, "I hope with all my heart and soul that you will reconsider, not only for your country, but for the peace and wholeness it may bring to your own person."

"I need nothing more to add to my own self to complete me, *Spirit*. I have my friends, my advisors, my country and my people. I have as much as any woman or prince ever needed in life."

As Cecil went to leave he paused in the doorway, a messenger speaking to him. He turned. "The Lord Robin Dudley asks that you receive him, Majesty." Cecil looked steadily at her with a calm face. "Should I have him brought to you?"

She nodded to Cecil, and went back to the window.

Robin walked through the door. "Majesty," he said gently, dropping to one knee. Her ladies were in the next room, a door left open for the sake of propriety, but otherwise they were alone.

"We are glad to have you back at court, Robin," she said, still facing the window. Her voice was flat and calm. "You have been much missed."

"I have missed you too, Elizabeth," he whispered.

She turned.

Still kneeling on the floor, he was dressed in a black doublet that masked the beauty of his eyes, making them seem duller. His eyes were rimmed with dark shadows in shades of grey and purple. He looked thinner, paler than before.

"It will be good for me to be able to ride out once more, Robin," she spoke formally, words coming from her as though there was another Elizabeth speaking for her, one without a heart. "I hope that now you are back, you will take time to oversee the stables for me again. Only you are able to pick the horses that most agree to my mood."

"Elizabeth," he whispered fearfully, walking forward and taking her hands. "What is this? What is wrong?"

She laughed, but there was no mirth in it. "What is wrong, my Lord Dudley? Nothing in the world could be wrong, could it? Never mind the strange and sudden death of your wife, or that the tongues of every man, woman and child in this country lay blame for it at our feet! No! Nothing could be wrong with that!" She yanked her hands from his and walked to the window.

"She knows they are set apart now, forever," I said. I could see the sorrow in her, even if Rob could only see anger. But there was resolution too. Love, it was not worth losing her position, her country, her role in life for. No man was worth giving up so much for.

"With time, Elizabeth," Robin spoke earnestly, coming behind her and gently laying his hands on her shoulders. "With time, all of this will be forgotten, but now, now my love, I am a free man, as you always desired me to be! I am free now to court you as I always wished to, and with time, with time when this matter is forgotten, to offer you my hand, my heart, which has always been for you only!"

"With time…" she murmured. "It seems people have said this often to me. With time, they say all things heal and are forgotten, but that is not the way of things, truly. We never forget, we never heal, we just find ways to continue walking on, even when we have lost all those whom we thought we could never do without. Even when we think we have lost our own selves. The only thing that time brings us is truth, and that truth is all we have to cling to for the rest of our lives. All else is dust and shadow."

"Elizabeth." Robin grabbed her shoulders and turned her roughly towards him. "What are you talking of? What is this? Do you not see that this is only the beginning for us? We can be together! Not now, not whilst the scandal still lives, but in the future. We can be *together,* my love!"

"The scandal will never die." Words came from her numbly. "Do you not see? Whether your wife died by accident or by design, she will always be between us now. If she died by accident none will ever believe it was an accident if we marry, and if she died at the hand of another, they have covered themselves too well to be discovered. We can *never* be together, Robin, not as man and wife. Only ever as friends, or as master and servant. To do otherwise, at *any* time, would only secure the suspicions of these rumours in the minds of the people of the world."

"That is why," I said, understanding. "You said they never married. She did it to protect him, and herself. She will not marry him because everyone would suppose them guilty, and they would turn on her and on him." I stared at Death. "Is that why someone killed me, because they knew she would react thus?"

Death's eyes simply stared back.

"It must have been someone who knew her well," I said. "Someone who thought they could judge how she would react."

Elizabeth was moving away from my widower husband. "Do you not see? You and I will never be able to be together, not like that; as soon as I slipped a ring on your finger and you on mine *we would be held guilty* for the murder of your wife. Rumour and accusation would become *truth* in the minds of all people, because we would have been the ones to benefit the most from her death. *We will be guilty then*! It will not matter what the truth is, it will not matter if we are truly innocent. In the eyes of the world we will be censured and disgraced for the murder of your wife. You would be destroyed, and so would I."

She drew herself up and stared at him. "Kings have been brought down for much less. When they lose the love of their people they can be brought down, replaced, removed, with ease."

"That, is what you fear, then," he spat, his voice shaking with anger. "To lose your position. You would rather have that, than to have the love between us?"

"I *am* my position!" she shouted. "I *am* my titles! I *am* the Queen. *I am Elizabeth! I am England*! I will not reduce myself by claiming that I am anything other than what I am. I have fought and struggled and survived to take my rightful place in the halls of my ancestors and I will not lose that. By God's Blood! Not for you, my lord… *not for anyone*!"

"There is no love in your heart," he said coldly. "You are a woman carved of marble and stone, not of flesh and blood."

"*You*!" she cried. "You dare to accuse me of that? When I opened my heart to you as I have done with no other in my life? When I cast off princes and kings who would have offered my country security and wealth, all for the love of Robin Dudley, the son and grandson of traitors and betrayers? When I thought to set aside my own values and beliefs for love of you? I have offered you more of my heart than any man has ever known, and you would dare to accuse me of heartlessness!"

She pushed him backwards. "And would you have come looking for me, my Lord Dudley, if my title did not enhance that beauty you spoke so well of? Would you have danced attendance on my person if I had been but a lord's daughter, or the sister of a town lawyer? Would you have been so keen to take me as your wife *had I not been the Queen*? Do not make me out to be a thing unnatural and strange for considering my title and position to be as much a part of me as yours are to you. They were things you desired much in me. Do not pretend to me, Lord Dudley that you would leave all title and position of your own in order to have me as your bride! I know your heart and your ambition well enough!"

He stepped back and stared at her. "What are you saying?" he asked, his face grey. He looked sick. "That you do not love me?"

She shook her head angrily. "I have never loved another, and will never love any, as well as I love you." She held up a hand as he went to rush towards her. "But it does not matter anymore what my heart wants. It is over."

She walked away from him.

"I am your friend, Robin Dudley, until the end of my days." Elizabeth sank into a chair. "And I will never suffer you to be punished for your place in my heart. But all talk of marriage between us is done now. Do you not see that? Whether by accident, or by the hand of a killer we are separated from each other by the death of your wife. If we take each other in marriage, it would cause the ruination of both our characters in the eyes of my people and they would take my throne for it. We would both fall. We would both be destroyed. I will not suffer my mother's fate. There will always be others who cast their eyes over my throne. I will not give them excuse to take it from me, just as I will not give them excuse to ruin you, either."

He stood, staring at her, his mouth hanging open, wounded amazement on his handsome face. "It is over, Robin," she said.

"In death, I have achieved what I could not in life," I said. "To stop my husband leaving me for another woman."

"Does it feel like a victory?"

I shook my head. "If he had chosen me, it would be, but someone forced this. Yet it is done now. I am gone, and they are separated." I looked at Death. "I think I feel neither happy nor sad for either state. I accept what has happened."

Robin, however, had accepted nothing. "It will *never* be over between us, Elizabeth, and whilst you may not see that now with the shadow of this hanging over us, I do. There will come a time when you and I can be joined together, and the people of this country will not only rejoice to see it, but you will feel safe to do it. You will feel safe to love me, as I love you."

She nodded. "Perhaps," she said feebly, "with time..."

He started towards her again but she jumped from her seat and walked to the door through which her ladies stood waiting. Kat was talking loudly on some matter, concealing the conversation between Robin and the Queen as best she could.

"I shall expect a good mount ready in the morning, Lord Dudley," the Queen said formally as she marched from the room before he could see the tears in her eyes. We followed her.

"Yes… Majesty," he stuttered.

She closed the door. "Leave me," she croaked to the women in the room, her voice breaking. Kat, Lettice, Catherine and the others did not ask for an explanation, they left for the Privy Chamber outside by another door.

As they left, Elizabeth sank down to the floor with her back to the door and quietly, like a child, she started to weep. "With time," she whispered. "With time comes nothing."

Death beckoned me, and I followed. Outside the chamber where Elizabeth wept stood Kat, waiting at the door. She was alone, so it seemed.

Cecil stepped from the shadow. "It worked," he said in a low voice, barely a whisper.

Kat looked up. "I know not what you mean."

But her face was pale at his words. I looked to Death and he nodded.

"Of course," Cecil said. "But all the same, it had the desired effect. You knew she had too much sense to wed him after such a scandal as this. You have kept them apart, and it was a plan well executed."

Kat swallowed, glancing behind her, but the Queen was so lost in grief for losing Robin I doubted she heard anything of the world, let alone of what was happening next door. "I know not what you mean, but even so, if you thought I was the author of this, why not stop it?"

Cecil shrugged. "I considered much the same, but when I found another would do it for me I simply did nothing to stop it."

"Then you would be as guilty as the one who did it."

He inhaled through his nose. "There are many things I would do for this country, for this Queen. Those in power make terrible choices, we can only hope the best of us try to balance those choices. We like to think our morality is stern, solid, but it is not. We protect our own and ourselves first. Is that moral? Others may be more deserving. So it is not morals we live by, but the will to survive. I would kill an innocent to protect those I love, make choices I knew would not be loved by God to save my country from war. I would make choices I know to be wrong, to save what I consider important. Man is not a moral creature, so when we do good it is because we are acting against our first impulses. But sometimes those impulses are the things that save us.

"Men go to war and thousands die, countries plunge into civil war and the same happens. What is the difference here? One woman, one who was already sick has died, but that one death might have saved so many others, and it stopped our

Queen from destroying herself. Spain was ready to set up another Grey as Queen, France is poised too to plant their Dauphine on the throne. All it would take was for the people of England to turn on this Queen and all would be lost. You saw that the Queen would not give him up without reason, so you provided one. You risked much, her own reputation for one thing, but you gambled on all you knew of her that she would see the peril of marrying a man suspected of murder."

"Her reputation has been damaged before, and she survived."

He nodded. "You did this out of love for her, I know well, as I did nothing to stop you for love of England, and what our Queen might become without that man as a weight about her neck, drowning her." He gazed at her. "I never would have suspected," he said.

"It begins so small. It is a toy, a game the mind plays," said Kat, sounding as if she was in a trance. "The mind plays out a game. It starts small and grows, a toy we add to, putting on clothes and a hat, shoes and a wig. There is a problem, and this toy can fix it, says the mind. Little by little, the mind's evil toy comes to life. Then the game ends, and it is done." She was silent a moment, then snapped her head up to stare at Cecil.

"I understand, the thought came and you entertained it, and then it became a compulsion. The game had to be played."

She looked away. "I know not what you mean."

Cecil nodded. "I shall never say anything ever again," he said. "Of the thing you know not."

"Thank you," Kat said.

"Thank you," he said. "It was not a good choice, but it was a choice made for good reasons."

I looked at Death, and shaking my head, I smiled.

Chapter Thirty-Six

Richmond Palace

February 1603

Death seems to smile at me. "You are the end, not the enemy," I say to him. "I understand. The end has come."

"You are satisfied, not sad anymore?" he asks.

"My life was a fettered existence," I say, lifting hands of whirling smoke and shadow out to take his hands of bone. "My death shall not be."

I look about. We are in the Queen's rooms and she is here. Elizabeth is old and she sees Death, and she can see me. It is many years since I died, I know this without noting the Queen's aged face. I have been gone a long time for her, but for me it is but moments.

Elizabeth has been talking, telling this part of the story of her life. She never did marry him, my husband.

"I came so close to losing all that I had held sacred in my life, all that had kept me safe, all that had kept me alive," Elizabeth says, looking at me. "On the day I walked from that room, eyes burning and my heart bleeding like an open wound, I knew that I could no more join with the man I loved than I could catch the wind in a net. I told him there was still a chance, and in that, perhaps, I was cruellest, for there was no chance, and I knew that even then. But I did not want Robin to leave my side, and so, selfish though it was I could not end things with him, as perhaps I should have done."

Elizabeth chuckles. "Time... It is a strange thing. When I looked across that garden at Windsor on that day I spoke to Robin, I thought I could see all the ghosts of my past looking back at me, all telling me not do as they had done, all whispering to me of the perils of giving up all I was, for love. Time... The past... The ghosts of the past... Perhaps they come to us for our own protection, to guide us when we have need of guidance the most."

Death extends a hand to me, and from the shadows I step. I smile at Elizabeth. I cannot seem to speak to her, but I want her to know that whilst she might have been the reason I died, I do not blame her.

"I died for love," I say to Death. He can hear me. "For the love a woman had for another. Perhaps that is not so bad an answer after all."

"Do you wish to see anything more?" he asks.

"No," I say. "I have seen all I want."

"Not even of what happened to him, to Robin?"

I shake my head. "No," I say. "Whatever will come of him is up to him. What I care for now is what will happen to me. It may have taken the end of life for it to come, this understanding, but what I care for now is for in death to have a chainless heart, a bondless soul, as I wish I could have had in life." I curtsey to Death. "This is enough," I say. "It is time."

He bows to me, and leads me out to dance. Death whirls about the floor of the Queen's chamber, dancing with me in his arms. My loose fair hair catches the light from the chamber window. My blue eyes are bright. I smile at Elizabeth as I pass, dancing in the arms of Death. Elizabeth smiles back at me.

"If you are content in death, that is well," Elizabeth says. "For I gave you enough sorrow in life, Amy."

I laugh and throw my head back as Death twirls me in his strong arms. The room spins as I prance before the Queen as never I did in life. In the shadows I see other ghosts, waiting to take to their turn before her, but my time is done and I am glad of it. There is no changing what was done, but I wish to know what comes after the end.

Death stops to bow to me, and then holds out his hand once more, and into one of bone, so white and bleached, I set my own hand. It trembles as flesh touches bone, trembles with happiness as a soft silver light steals across my skin, and into a hushed, unknown darkness, sweet and silk, I dance.

Author's Notes

This book is a work of fiction, although based on research of the events and people of the time period in question. This book, and the events in it were based on my series on Elizabeth I, *The Elizabeth of England Chronicles*, as I wanted Amy's story, as presented in this book, to mirror what happened in my series on Elizabeth. Amy is therefore present, unseen, at many times and events I detailed previously, but giving her own observations on the events.

It should also be noted that I named this book a historical fantasy, and that is because it is more of a departure from my usual brand of historical fiction, and because of the person I named the killer of Amy Dudley at the end. I believe most readers will have noticed that once you have the ghost of Amy Dudley wandering about the past with Death himself, we have strayed from the realm of standard historical fiction into the realms of fantasy.

I would like to note here that, no, I have no proof that Kat Ashely, lady of the bedchamber was the person who sent an assassin to kill Amy Dudley. Scant evidence exists in any case for whether the death of Amy Dudley was an accident or murder, although plenty of people of the time believed it was murder indeed, and Robin Dudley was behind it. For my part, I have always been willing to entertain the notion that it could have been murder, and equally could have been an accident.

For the accident theory, Amy had certainly been ill before her death, most likely with breast cancer which could have weakened her bones so a simple fall down the stairs could have been enough to break her neck. The most dangerous place for accidents is the stairs of any house, even in this day and age.

One trouble is, Cumnor Place no longer exists, and so we do not know what the stairs in question really looked like, aside from the evidence from reports which listed them as "shallow" and as having a landing between two flights. We do not know therefore whether the stairs in question would have been perilous or steep enough to have caused Amy to break her neck, but it has to be said that if she had brittle bones then a short fall could well have been enough to take her life, if she fell awkwardly.

For the murder theory, we have Amy's odd behaviour on the day of her death. Why did she send all her servants away? And why was she so insistent on this? People noted at the time she was behaving in an odd manner, leading some to suspect later either that she was meeting someone in secret, or that she had intended to take her own life. The wounds on her head were also deep, one about as deep as the top of a thumb, and one double that. Those seem like deep wounds to be caused by a stair.

I included a piece of evidence which is likely to be untrue; that her headdress was in place, which would seem unlikely after a tumble down the stairs. This evidence is mentioned later, in *"Leicester's Commonwealth"* which was a slanderous piece of propaganda set out by Robin's enemies, intended to darken his name, and included the accusation that he killed his wife. It is quite likely to be false evidence, but I included it in case it was based on any reports of the time.

The other aspect of the case which always has me leaning towards murder is the timing of her death. Robin and Elizabeth were as close as ever they would be to marriage at this time, and it seems likely that Elizabeth may well have agreed to marry Robin. She certainly loved him and may at this early stage in her reign have toyed with the notion of marriage, if she could wed a man she loved and retain her power. I believe that her sense of self-preservation would have won out in the end, and she was well aware that marriage could restrict her power and position, but I also think she might have considered it. Robin looked set to become free to marry, possibly within months, if his wife died, and so I think the timing of Amy's death is quite suspicious. I doubt very much that Robin himself or Elizabeth would have been behind any attempt on Amy's life. Robin would have thought, no doubt, he was due to be honourably released from marriage by Amy's natural death, and if it was murder, this was too clumsy an attempt for Elizabeth to be involved. But what of other people? What if, as suggested in this book, someone of the court murdered Amy, a woman already known to be dying, so that Robin would be suspected of murder and therefore Elizabeth would be prevented from marrying him?

Certainly, it would have been a risk. If someone gambled on blackening Robin's name enough that Elizabeth knew she could not marry him, they also risked the idea that she might go ahead anyway, either at the time or a later date, and marry this man. But I think certain people in her household knew her well enough to know that she would not risk damaging her reputation in the eyes of her people, and therefore potentially losing her throne, by marrying a man who many thought was a murderer.

Interestingly, we have an example of this later in history. When Henry Stuart, Lord Darnley, the husband of Mary Queen of Scots, died in highly suspicious circumstances and she not much later (and I believe, under duress) married James Hepburn, Earl of Bothwell, the man many suspected of being Darnley's murderer, her people rose against her, and she was forced to abdicate her throne. The same could have happened to Elizabeth.

My prime candidates for murder, if murder it was, have generally been William Cecil and Thomas Parry. Both men were ruthless when they needed to be, and knew the Queen well enough to take an educated guess at what her reaction would be to the mysterious death of Amy Dudley. My theory in this book just came to me as I was writing, and I thought what if another person, someone who had been with Elizabeth all her life, and knew her better than almost anyone, had taken an awful risk, and taken the life of a person, in order to save the Queen and woman they loved from marrying a man they believed would ruin her? The name that came to me was Kat Ashley, the woman who had, to all intents and purposes, become Elizabeth's mother after the death of Anne Boleyn. People go to great lengths for their children, and Kat in many ways considered Elizabeth her daughter.

As I said, I have no evidence to support this, aside from the knowledge that Kat warned Elizabeth about Robin several times, and clearly was distrustful of his intentions. Kat had also gone to great lengths to protect the Queen before, having been arrested with the Queen and by herself several times in Mary's reign. My idea in this book simply came to me, and it also occurred to me that in the lists of suspects, few are women, yet there were women about the Queen who were rich, well connected, and were obviously loyal to Elizabeth, and loved her. Dangerous and brutal things can sometimes be done in the name of love.

But, as I said, this is just a little theory, and one I cannot support, which was another reason I named this a historical fantasy.

The last option as to how Amy died is that she committed suicide. I think this fairly unlikely. For a start, as Amy mentions in the book, if you were to commit suicide why on earth choose to jump down a flight of stairs? It is hardly a full-proof method to kill oneself. Herbs were well known to most Tudor women, and it would not have been hard to find one or a mixture of several that would take life. If one was to leap from a height, why not choose something higher than a flight of shallow stairs? The other thing to take into consideration is that Amy, in committing suicide, would have excluded herself from Heaven, something taken most seriously at the time, and since she spent a great deal of time praying it would seem she was a woman of great religious conviction. I cannot see that she would have killed herself. Both the manner of her death and the act of suicide itself seem unlikely choices to me.

Most historians come down on the side of Amy's death being an accident, and I understand why, and it may well be that the timing of her death was a simple coincidence, but a little niggle remains in my mind whenever I read the story, thinking that there are just too many things that jangle, things that seem suspicious, for me to entirely accept that her death was an accident.

Select Bibliography

Alford, Stephen. *The Watchers*
Borman, Tracy. *The Private Lives of the Tudors.*
Elizabeth's Women
Brears, Peter. *All the King's Cooks*
Breverton, Terry. *The Tudor Cookbook*
Budiansky, Stephen. *Her Majesty's Spymaster*
Castiglione, Baldesar. *The Book of the Courtier*
Champion, Matthew. *Medieval Graffiti*
Childs, Jessie. *God's Traitors*
Cooper, John. *The Queen's Agent*
De Bray, Lys. *Elizabethan Garlands*
De Lisle, Leanda. *The Sisters who Would be Queen*
Doran, Susan. *Elizabeth I and her Circle*
Duffy, Eamon. *The Stripping of the Altars.*
Fires of Faith, Catholic England under Mary Tudor
Erasmus, Desiderius. *A Handbook on Good Manners for Children*
Evans, Victoria Sylvia. *Ladies in Waiting: Women who served at the Tudor Court*
Falls, Cyril. *Elizabeth's Irish Wars*
Fraser, Antonia. *Mary Queen of Scots*
Goodman, Ruth. *How to be a Tudor*
Gristwood, Sarah. *Elizabeth and Leicester.*
Arbella, England's Lost Queen
Grueninger, Natalie. *Discovering Tudor London*
Guy, John. *Elizabeth the Forgotten Years*
My Heart is my Own: The Life of Mary Queen of Scots
Handley, Sasha. *Sleep in Early Modern England*
Haynes, Alan. *The Elizabethan Secret Services.*
Sex in Elizabethan England
Helm, P.J. *Exploring Tudor England*
Herman, Eleanor. *The Royal Art of Poison*
Hilton, Lisa. *Elizabeth, Renaissance Prince*
Hogge, Alice. *God's Secret Agents*
Lacey, R. *Robert, Earl of Essex*

Loades, David. *The Tudor Queens of England*
Lipscomb, Susan. *A Visitor's Companion to Tudor England.*
Luke, Mary. M. *Gloriana, the Years of Elizabeth I*
Markham, Gervase. *The English Housewife*
Matusiak, John. *The Tudors and Europe.*
A History of the Tudors in 100 Objects
McGowan, Margaret. M. *Dance in the Renaissance*
Mortimer, Ian. *The Time Traveller's Guide to Elizabethan England*
Neale, J.E. *Queen Elizabeth*
Norton, Elizabeth. *The Lives of Tudor Women*
Norris, Herbert. *Tudor Costume and Fashion*
Norwich, Edward of. *The Master of Game*
Onyeka, Narrative Eye. *Blackamoores: Africans in Tudor England, their presence, status and origins*
Parry, Glyn. *The Arch-Conjuror or England, John Dee*
Picard, Lisa. *Elizabeth's London*
Plowden, Alison. *Elizabeth Regina.*
Danger to Elizabeth.
Marriage with my Kingdom.
Tudor Women: Queens and Commoners.
The House of Tudor
The Young Elizabeth
Porter, Linda. *Crown of Thistles*
Porter, Stephen. *Everyday Life in Tudor London.*
Shakespeare's London
Ronald, Susan. *The Pirate Queen.*
Heretic Queen
Roud, Steve. *The English Year*
Rowse, A. L. *The England of Elizabeth*
Singh, Simon. *The Code Book*
Sim, Alison. *Food and Feast in Tudor England*
Masters and Servants in Tudor England
Pleasures and Pastimes in Tudor England
Skidmore, Chris. *Death and the Virgin*
Soberton, Sylvia Barbara. *Medical Downfalls of the Tudors.*
The Forgotten Tudor Women
Somerset, Anne. *Ladies in Waiting*
Starkey, David. *Elizabeth*

Stone, Lawrence. *The Family, Sex and Marriage in England, 1500-1800*
Tallis, Nicola. *Elizabeth's Rival*
Tudor, Elizabeth. *Elizabeth I, Collected Works*
Veerapen, Steven. *Elizabeth and Essex*
Weir, Alison. *Elizabeth the Queen.*
Henry VIII, King and Court.
Britain's Royal Families: The Complete Genealogy.
The Lost Tudor Princess.
The Children of Henry VIII
Traitors of the Tower
Mary, Queen of Scots
Weir, Alison and Clarke, Siobhan. *A Tudor Christmas*
Whitelock, Anna. *Elizabeth's Bedfellows.*

Thank You

…to so many people for helping me make this book possible… to my proof reader, Julia Gibbs, who gave me her time, her wonderful guidance and also her encouragement. To my family for their ongoing love and support. To my friend Petra. To my friend Nessa for her support and affection, and to another friend, Anne, who has done so much for me. To Sue and Annette, more friends who read my books and cheer me on. To Terry for getting me into writing and indie publishing in the first place. To Katie and Jooles, Macer and Heather, often there in times of trial. And to all my wonderful readers, who took a chance on an unknown author, and have followed my career and books since.

To those who have left reviews or contacted me by email or on social media, I give great thanks, as you have shown support for my career as an author, and enabled me to continue writing. Thank you for allowing me to live my dream.

Thank you to all of you; you'll never know how much you've helped me, but I know what I owe to you.

Gemma Lawrence
Wales
2023

About The Author

I find people talking about themselves in the third person to be entirely unsettling, so, since this section is written by me, I will use my own voice rather than try to make you believe that another person is writing about me to make me sound terribly important.

I am an independent author, publishing my books by myself, with the help of my lovely proof reader. I left my day job in 2016 and am now a fully-fledged, full-time author, and proud to be so.

My passion for history began early in life. As a child I lived in Croydon, near London, and my schools were lucky enough to be close to such glorious places as Hampton Court and the Tower of London, allowing field trips to take us to those castles. I write historical fiction for the main part, but I also have a fascination with ghost stories and fantasy, and I hope this book was one you enjoyed. I want to divert you as readers, to please you with my writing and to have you join me on these adventures.

A book is nothing without a reader.

As to the rest of me; I am in my forties and live in Wales with a rescued cat (who often sits on my lap when I write, which can make typing more of a challenge). I studied Literature at University after I fell in love with books as a small child. When I was little I could often be found nestled halfway up the stairs with a pile of books in my lap and my head lost in another world. There is nothing more satisfying to me than finding a new book I adore, to place next to the multitudes I own and love… and nothing more disappointing to me to find a book I am willing to never open again. I do hope that this book was not a disappointment to you. I loved writing it and I hope that showed through the pages.

If you would like to contact me, please do so.

On Twitter, I am @TudorTweep and am more than happy to follow back and reply to any and all messages. I may avoid you if you decide to say anything worrying or anything abusive, but I figure that's acceptable.

You can also find me on Instagram as tudorgram1500. I am new to Mastodon as G. Lawrence Tudor Tooter, @TudorTweep@mastodonapp.uk, and Counter Social as TudorSocial1500.

On Facebook my page is just simply G. Lawrence, and on TikTok and Threads I am tudorgram1500, the same as Instagram. Often, I have a picture of the young Elizabeth I as my avatar, or there's me leaning up against a wall in Pembroke Castle.

Via email, I am tudortweep@gmail.com a dedicated email account for my readers to reach me on. I'll try and reply within a few days.

Thank you for taking a risk with an unknown author and reading my book. I do hope now that you've read one, you'll want to read more. If you'd like to leave me a review, that would be very much appreciated also!

Gemma Lawrence
Wales
2023

Printed in Poland
by Amazon Fulfillment
Poland Sp. z o.o., Wrocław
24 September 2023

d5b9d836-f4a2-4b2f-af64-9a8d4b41d816R01